STERN WALK

2016 W.G Graham. All rights reserved.

Other titles by W.G Graham
Available on Kindle and Paperback
At
Amazon

Scottish Historical Fiction

The Cateran
Glen Arnoch
Sgian Dhu

Historical Fiction

Evil and the Child
Walter
Incres Island

Adventure

Oor Bit
Stern Walk
Yesterday's Soldier

West Barns Mysteries

Charlie's Gold
The Deep
Double Deal
Persona non Grata

Crime Fiction

3rd Key
4th Key
Cannon

Dead Men Don't Talk
Any Street Any Town
Anguish

Stern Walk

Tom could scarcely keep his eyes open in the stifling heat of the bus. Wearily he leaned against the window. The hot glass burned his cheek and he drew back, rubbing his jaw. Suddenly, the bus lurched forward with an ear splitting screech of brakes and he hit the seat in front, the impact knocking him to the floor, amid the sound of exploding glass.

For a moment, he lay there, winded, thankful that the seat had prevented him from arriving at the bus stop before the bus. But what had they hit? Then, he heard it, the staccato sound of gunfire.

As if by magic, a hole the size of a shilling appeared inches away from Tom's upturned face, then another, and another. In an instant, he was backpedalling into the isle, his feet hitting something soft like a quivering jelly, and he jiggled around to look at the huge mound of flesh of a woman staring up at him with uncomprehending eyes. The way one does when one is 'dead'.

That was it, he was oot o here!

Heedless of the screams of panic, or the bodies he was stamping on, Tom launched himself at the exit and into the street, rebounding off the hard metalled dusty road, with the natural reflexes born out of countless Saturday night dances in Sauchiehall Street. Without a second thought, or glance, he headed across the road as fast as his legs would carry his five and a half foot frame. The hail of bullets zipping above his head only accentuated his departure, until he had put the corner of a building between him and his former transport. Only then, gasping for breath he chanced a quick glance back at the smoked filled bus and the soldiers bounding across the road in his direction. The sight of which convinced him that he should be on his way.

He knew this South American city well enough to know that he was running in the opposite direction from his hotel. And, right now, that was where he most wanted to be, with his A1 American courier telling those hot blooded Latins that he, Tom Bell of Glasgow was a citizen of the UK and did not much like the way they had of collecting bus fares in this year of 1935.

"Whit a gemme o' sodgers this has turned oot tae be," he gasped, dodging in and out of a group of startled shoppers, at the same time reaching down to steady Big Dougie's camera from its continual bouncing off his chest. The Kodak was his best pal's pride and joy, with its wee lever that opened it up like a concertina all ready for action. It had cost his best china an arm and a leg…his as well if he was to lose it!

It took him all of ten minutes of intermittent running and resting in a warren of empty alleyways and side streets to realise he was lost, and that he could no longer sustain the pace he had set himself in his blind panic to keep the soldiers at bay.

"I'm knackered" he wheezed, leaning against the boarding of a deserted shop window. "I shouldnae have run. It was stupid. After all, what could they have done to me? Well, it's too late now."

Tom closed his eyes, contemplating his next move, snapping them open at the sound of nailed boots ringing on the cobbled alleyway a little way behind.

"Ch…They've found me already!" he howled, shooting out a hand at the shop door, and swearing louder when the handle failed to turn.

Panic stricken, Tom searched for a means of escape and in three quick strides was across the narrow street and twisting savagely at the door of another empty shop. Suddenly the handle gave, and he fell headlong into its darkened interior, and had barely hit the floor before he was on his feet again and slamming the door shut.

Tom scurried behind a pile of discarded shelving and quickly drew his knees up to his chin, like a child awaiting his parent's wrath at having done something wrong.

A few seconds later, he heard the sound of his pursuers halting outside the door.

"They are outside," he moaned to himself. "They know I'm here." The fugitive was convinced that at any moment the door would fly open.

Still, the door remained closed. All was silent outside.

"They've gone!"

Tom jerked round, startled by the close proximity of the voice, searching for the speaker in the almost total darkness of the tiny shop. Finally, his eyes came to rest on a faintly lighter spot which gradually grew in shape, to encompass first the face, then the upper body of a middle aged woman, sitting on a metal frame that slowly floated towards him.

"I think we are safe for the present," the woman in the wheelchair offered in a clipped English accent.

"Whit's goin on?" Tom croaked. Then, remembering the woman's accent attempted to correct himself. "I mean what's happening out there?"

"I believe it may be the beginnings of a long awaited revolution," the woman replied prosaically.

"A revolution!" Tom exclaimed hauling himself to his feet. "It can't be, I'm due to leave on Thursday! If I'm late back at work, Mr MacKendrick will kill me."

"He may have to stand in line, young man."

Tom narrowed his eyes, attempting to see if this strange crippled lady was serious or not. "Why should anyone want to see me dead? Don't they know I'm here on holiday? A return holiday, if you don't mind me saying," he emphasised firmly.

"That accent, it's Scotch is it not?"

"Scottish, if you please," Tom replied indignantly. "And, yours is English, if I'm not mistaken."

"Correct. So we are both in the same boat so to speak. And, as we come from the same country, it is our duty to help one another. Is it not?"

"Suddenly, I'm British," Tom muttered, leaning back against what once had been the shop counter.

He was still unsure what all this was about. His voice rose sharply, as he asked. "But you still have not answered my question. Why should anyone want to kill me? I'm not part of any revolution!"

"You are, now, Mister...eh?"

"Bell...Tom Bell."

"So pleased to meet you, Mr Bell. Perhaps, I should also introduce myself. I am Miriam Plesher, wife of the late Wilfred Plesher, who until his untimely demise was Ambassador to this country." The woman held up a hand to allay the Scot's fears. "Oh no, Mr Bell, my husband died of natural causes."

"Well that's a relief...I mean that he wasn't killed," Tom hastened to correct himself. "So tell me, how did you get here?"

The woman pointed into the gloom. "That unfortunate man helped me."

Tom followed the pointing finger, letting out a strange choking sound at the sight of a man reclining in a broken chair, his sightless eyes staring heavenwards. "Is he…is he?"

"Yes, I'm afraid he is," Miriam Plesher answered Tom's unfinished question with a sigh.

Tom rolled up his eyes. "Govan, here I come. Next year, definitely Troon."

"You've lost me, Mr Bell."

"I wish tae hell I hadnae found you," Tom uttered under his breath. "Sorry lady," he said aloud. "But all I want right now is get back to my hotel and stay there until my steamer leaves on Thursday."

"You would leave me here?" the woman asked softly.

"Look lady, me they might shoot up the bum, but surely they'd draw the line at harming you. Especially a …"

"A cripple, Mr Bell?"

"No. I was going to say, a British lady, and the wife of a big wig…I mean diplomat."

"In most cases, you'd be right. However, in this case you are decidedly wrong."

"I was afraid of that."

"Perhaps I should tell you why."

Tom held up his hands in a gesture of surrender. "Please don't."

Undeterred, Miriam Plesher went on. "I do not know how familiar you are with the politics of this country Mr Bell? However, let me try and briefly explain some of them to you. President Bieztos was elected just under two years ago on the mandate of nationalising all railways and oil companies owned by foreign investors. This he did, thus making himself a national hero overnight. However, as almost all were exclusively American or British owned, he was far from popular in either of those countries as you can very well imagine."

"I can imagine," Tom chuckled. "And bang went Mr Roosevelt's Good Neighbour Policy."

Miriam drew the man a look of incredulity.

"It's darkest Govan I come from hen, no darkest Africa," Tom replied in response to the look.

Miriam gave a brief apologetic smile. "Sorry… as I was saying…."

Tom listened while the woman explained how her husband had been sent by his Majesty's Government to negotiate with President

Bieztos, and in company with the American Ambassador had finally convinced the President that it would be in everyone's interest to leave at least a percentage of the oil and rail companies in foreign hands. A compromise reached only after both Ambassadors had agreed to discuss with their respective governments the possibility of increasing the present level of aid to the country.

"So, if this was all hunky-dory, why the need for a revolution?" Tom asked trying to forget that there was a dead body only a few feet away, besides being unable to believe that this was still the same holiday, in the same country that he had been enjoying until only a short while ago.

"All should have been," Miriam explained, "had the good President not decided to fill his own pockets with the aid so desperately needed by his fellow countrymen.

"It all started for me about a year ago…just a little after my husband had retired as Ambassador, and we had decided to live out our remaining years here. Wilfred, my husband, loved this country you see," Miriam offered by way of explanation. "We had long since admired Fernando Castilia, Leader of the Official Opposition Party, and were fortunate to count ourselves amongst his many friends.

"One night, as we three sat alone together, Fernando confided his suspicions regarding the President, and the misappropriation of much of the country's foreign aid. What, with Bieztos power increasing each day…thanks to the backing of the army, it was becoming almost impossible for Fernando to acquire the proof necessary to bring any allegations against him to the Senate. Not to say...dangerous.

"Then a breakthrough. Thanks to the help from within the President's own party, Fernando obtained his proof. That is where I was a short time ago. Since my good friend is well aware of his imminent arrest, he has entrusted this information to me, in the hope I may get it out of the country, which is why I am confiding this most vital information to you."

"Stop right there, wee wumman." Tom held up his hand. "I'm only a simple traveller, with the emphasis on simple. I don't want to know this vital information. The only vital information I want to know, is how do I get out of here without having my bum shot off?"

Miriam gestured impatiently. "I do not mean to burden you with the exact information that Fernando Castilia entrusted to me. On the contrary, all I ask is that you help me to my friend's house, which I was doing earlier before that unfortunate man and I fell foul of the roadblock."

"Why not your own home, or the British Embassy?"

"I am quite certain both will be under keen observation by this time."

"So what do you want me to do?" Tom asked feeling more annoyed and frustrated by the whole affair.

"First, I think we should wait until dark before venturing to the other side of the city."

"Why not my hotel?" Tom asked, feeling a creeping constriction in his chest at the prospect of pushing a wheelchair all over town. "They will be expecting me back you know. Perhaps the army will take us for tourists and let us pass. Surely they will not interfere with foreign nationals."

"You may get passed, young man. I very much doubt if I should, for I do not believe there are many women of European origin in a wheelchair, visiting the country at the present moment. Besides, even if I were to reach your hotel, the staff are duty bound to report me to the authorities."

"But Alan, the courier, is an American with A1 Tours, he'd not let them take you. If they did I'd get my bum in gear and notify the British Embassy straight away," Tom exploded indignantly.

"How very gallant of you Mr Bell," Miriam chuckled. "However, I think it best that the sooner you are quit of me the better. We shall stick to our original plan." She gave him amused smile. "Should you succeed in your mission on seeing me safe, you may even get your name in the newspapers back home."

"Aye, in the obituaries," Tom moaned.

Now that his eyes were growing accustomed to the darkened interior, the little counter to his right, rows of broken shelves above the lady calmly reposing in the wheelchair all slowly began to come into focus.

She was older than the voice suggested, fifty at the very least, as old as Mr MacKendrick, and to Tom that was old, primly dressed in a green jacket and skirt and white blouse. Tom studied the face and the auburn hair slightly streaked with gray, deciding she would have been a wee smasher in her time.

For a moment, Tom felt afraid of the woman, not physically of course, but rather for what she stood for. Here he was, a young twenty three year old from Govan in the year 1935 AD, who had never previously travelled further than Wembley. "God," he whispered as the thought struck him, "they'll never believe this in the office when I get home! If I get home! Mr MacKendrick will believe I made up the whole story of the revolution and this hoity-toity dame as an excuse for not having made it back on time."

Tom slid to the floor and rested his back against the counter, his thoughts on the supercilious Chief Clerk who's entire world revolved around the drawing office of Johnston and Son, and who, since his elevation from a wally close to a semi-detached in Douglas Street, had become even more contemptible of the working class, such as himself and Big Dougie, his best 'china'.

He could hear MacKendrick now, saying in his pan load self-cultivated upper-crust voice as he rocked back and forth on his heels. "Come, be honest Bell, you were most likely inebriated out of your tiny mind, or mixed up with some floosie or other. Your type are all the same. I told Mr Johnston up at the 'Big Office' (the name given to where the heads of the departments worked), "that it was a mistake to let you go."

To let him go! That was a laugh. How had it all started? Tom made himself more comfortable. Oh yes. It had all began the night of the office Hogmanay party, when Mr Johnston the younger, slightly the worse for wear – slightly, that was putting it mildly – had beckoned him over to the table after his dance with Sonya the delectable typist from the 'Big Office' who was seeing him in a different light if not double.

Tom smiled at the recollection and the usual patter as he took her up to dance.

"You've had a skinful Sonya have ye no?"

"Only wan or two."

"Aye, in a bucket maist likely"

Sonya giggled. "Well in that case when I hae another wan ye can haud on tae ma heels when I reach the bottom. She peered up into his eyes feigning seriousness. "Anyhow I only took them fur medi…medic… I had an upset stomach, nothing would lie on it."

"Ye didnae try me pet," Tom winked.

"Cheeky sod!"

The dance ended and they edged past the 'heid bummers' table. Mr Johnston caught Tom's eye and beckoned him over. "I hope you are enjoying yourself and not leading this young lady astray, Bell!" he inquired, lifting his whisky glass and staring at Tom unsteadily.

"Yes Sir. I mean I am, and we are enjoying ourselves, and I'm not leading Miss Henderson astray."

Sonya giggled.

"Good. Very good, Bell. We must have you with a steady hand and eye the day after tomorrow. Make the most of your holiday Bell, it will be the last until The Fair." Mr Johnston took a sip of his drink. "When probably it will be down the water again eh? As you people most quaintly put it."

Tom's eyes swept the table, at the appropriate chuckles emanating from the 'yes' men, letting his eyes fall momentarily on the Chief Clerk before travelling back to face the speaker.

Whether he had resented all that booze on the head table, enough to feed half the folk in his close for a week, or the condescending way his snob of a boss had spoken of the 'Fair', their annual holiday, he was never quite sure why he had said what he did say.

He remembered standing there thinking. How would this snob know what their annual holiday meant to the ordinary folk on Clydeside, or their struggle to make ends meet, week after week? Then if there was that bit overtime, they might…just might put enough by to get that precious summer holiday this stuff shirt was so contemptuous of.

So, looking his employer straight in the eye and fighting to keep his voice steady replied, "I'm sure you are well aware of the expression We people so quaintly use is… doon the watter fur the Fair."

"How dare you speak to Mr Johnston in that manner you impertinent boy!" the Chief Clerk hurled across the table at him, leaping to his feet, the appropriate look of indignation on his face at this affront to his god. "You will apologise immediately, Bell!"

Tom's heart raced, conscious of Sonya squeezing his hand tight, and of Mr Johnston holding up a hand to halt his Chief Clerk's tirade. Slowly, Tom's employer drew on his cigar and calmly watched the smoke curl towards the ceiling. "Then tell me, Bell," he asked without shifting his gaze, "should these people who you so righteously champion did have the means to go elsewhere, where do you think they would spend the ' Fair'?"

Tom glanced around the table at the knowing nods of approval, at those sitting there who believed that a hard day's work was to carry their pay cheques to the bank. This he could tolerate from the idle rich who knew no better, it was the others he despised, the Chief Clerk and his like, working class like himself, sitting there kow-towing and looking down their noses at him as if they had been weaned on this luxury all of their lives.

"Come on Bell, Mr Johnston has asked you a question," the Chief Clerk commanded. "You are a single man. You must be able to save a bit. You get paid weekly do you not?"

"Aye, very weakly," Tom replied sarcastically.

And to Tom's surprise Mr Johnston's face broke into a grin. "You're all there for guile, Bell." A little of the Scots accent permeating into his voice. "So tell me if you had the money where would you go for the Fair?"

"South America," Tom replied without hesitation.

"For the night life, no doubt," Mr MacKendrick jeered. "You have been watching too many American movie films, boy."

"Wrong, Mr MacKendrick." Tom swung to face his senior. "There happens to be a South American country whose history interests me very much. However, it would take more than a year's wages and a lot longer than the Fair Holidays to get there…and back."

"This is all very interesting young man, but I am sure we are boring Miss…." Mr Johnston struggled to remember the name. He made a dismissive wave of his hand. "Away and enjoy yourself laddie. Let's put away what has been said with the auld year and let us look to the new. Suffice to say Bell," he drew on his cigar, "should you ever find the money to get yourself to that country of yours, I'll see to it personally that you get the time you need off work." Chuckling, he threw his Chief Clerk a look that only his class were capable off, "without pay of course."

"Naturally, Sir," Tom replied. And, with a slight bow, lead Sonya back on to the dance floor, leaving those at the table to make out of it what they might.

"Whit was that aw aboot? You and some Amer-ikan country?" Sonya asked perplexed. "You sure wisnae half feart aboot loosin yer job the way you spoke tae ra boss, Tam."

Still seething, Tom shrugged. "He knows damned well I'm as close to South America as I am to my first sh...t...dinner," he corrected himself. "Any road let's forget aboot auld shiny Bum", as the lower office of which he was a part called those in the higher ranking desk jobs, "and enjoy what's left o' the auld year." With which he swung his partner off her feet, much to her consternation as the band was playing a waltz at the time.

"Ye big gowk, aw the folk are starin at us!" Sonya admonished, attempting a head butt.

Tom jerked his head away, laughing. "What's the matter pet?"

"The way ye swung me aff ma feet, folk wid see ma knickers!"

"I wish I could." Tom threw back laughing at Sonya's shocked expression. "Don't look like that Sonya hen, that was meant as a compliment, I didn't know you were wearing any."

"Tom Bell!" Sonya hurled back, her indignation lost as the band broke into a Rumba.

Seizing his partner and the opportunity, Tom swung her round in time to the music.

"Oh Tam, I think I'm goin' tae spew!" Sonya cried, clutching her stomach.

"Quick hen, lets get oot o' here before you do your aqua impression of Joseph and his coat of many colours!" Quickly taking hold of his partner, Tom guided her expertly though the dancing couples, while trying to ignore the ribald remarks from his fellow workmates. Eventually they reached the safety of the top landing, where, throwing on their coats they ran down the flight of steps and out into the cold night air, where, Sonya, moaning curled herself round a lamp post.

"They say you feel better if ye pit yer heid between yer legs," Sonya wheezed, staring up at Tom from her centurions position.

"Even better if you pit yer heid between my legs!" Tom guffawed. And was immediately ashamed of what he had just said, as the keen night air hit him. Though not enough to prevent him from extricating Sonya from her beloved lamp post and guiding her up the nearest close mouth to its far end, where, a little beyond a row of dustbins he leaned her against the wall.

"Whit are you up tae, Tam Bell!" Sonya queried feeling much recovered.

"Only wan wee cheeper on the cheek, Sonya hen."

"Then try kissing ma arse, Tam, it's made o' the same stuff," Sonya hiccupped.

"Ye're pure dead romantic so ye are, Sonya," Tom chided unbuttoning her coat and engulfing them both inside his own.

"I've never did this afore Tam…well jist the wance, and I didn't mean tae dae it."

"Wis it against yer will, pet?"

"Naw. It wis against ma Granny's coal shed actually."

At that precise moment, there was a shuffle of feet in the direction of the stairs and a woman in her mid thirties, her hair in curlers swung hurriedly around the corner towards them carrying a pail of ashes. Momentarily taken aback by the sight of Tom and Sonya so intimately wrapped up in themselves, she quickly emptied her smouldering ashes into the bin and, without a glance or a word spoken, headed back for the stairs, throwing over her shoulder as she reached the first step amid a guffaw of laughter, "Aw' the best whit it comes, son!" the echo of her laughter filling the close long after she had disappeared out of sight.

Blushing crimson, Tom extricated himself from the folds of garments. Then bending forward kissed Sonya on the cheek as the bells rang in the New Year. So had ended his first 'close' encounter of the intimate kind.

That had only been the beginning. Tom stole a glance at Miriam Plesher, blushing that by his expression she might read his thoughts. He had been drunk that night, but after all it had been Hogmanay.

Even if he had not been, what would this memsab know about such crass thoughts of the lower class? No. He found it impossible to imagine the likes of Miriam Plesher doing it up a close. In fact he found it impossible to think of her doing it…period...or periodically.

Anyhow, that had been in another world and in another lifetime. How was he to know what was to happen in the weeks following that night in the close?

Sam Dalgleish, a neighbour, had come to the office to tell him his Granny had passed away. He could still remember Granny leaning out of the third floor window that morning throwing down his 'piece' and shouting to him he'd starve to death if she didn't keep an eye on him. Sadly, he reflected those had been her very last words to him.

Of course, if he'd not been busy leading his own life, he could have read the signs. Such as finding his fish supper in the coal bunker, or tripping over a saucer full of milk for the cat which had left six months previously to live in sin with a feline Tom from Cathcart Road.

Perhaps, it had started the day Granny had thrown down the carpets from the front window of the tenement instead of the back, engulfing a passing elderly cyclist who had thought he'd gone suddenly blind, and run into Luigi, the ice cream man, peddling his barrow from the opposite direction.

In the resulting fall, Big Dougie, his best pal, watching Luigi take a heider from his machine, and skidding along the road, had guffawed at him, "Tam, if Luigi could sell sliders like that he'd make a fortune." Sliders being slang for ice cream wafers.

To which he had replied, "Shut up Dougie. Come on and help these two afore they send for the polis." He had then thrown a swift look up at Granny's window, and was relieved to see that the old lady had disappeared from sight.

"Look at ma good new barra!" Luigi wailed. "The wheel she is fuckled!"

"Buckled is the word, Luigi." Then, taking a closer look at the wheel, Tom corrected himself. "Aye, maybe ye were right the first time."

Luigi banged the top of his terminally ill ice cream barrow. "I must sue your Granny for constipation, Tom Bell, if you cannae keep her under control."

Dougie laughed. "Aye, ye right Luigi. I don't know whit her generation is coming tae. Then again pal, if ye don't mind the pun, you vendors are .aye screamin' at somethin'."

It had been enough for Tom, who had pulled his friend away by the jacket. "Come on Dougie, we're in enough trouble withoot yer daft jokes."

"We're in trouble, Ding? You and the auldest delinquent in the business is in trouble, no me."

And before he could find a suitable retort, the second victim had butted in. "And whit aboot ma bike? That's the third puncture this week!"

"Aye they say punctures come in cycles," Dougie bellowed, obviously enjoying it all.

"Will ye no' shut up, Dougie! Can ye no see I'm tryin tae straighten things oot here."

"Well, ye better start wi Luigi's fuckled wheel!" Dougie said, with as much chance of keeping his face straight as he had of straightening Luigi's wheel.

Suddenly, Tom found himself laughing at the memory and a strange voice cutting in.

"You find something amusing in our dilemma, Mr Bell?"

Tom returned to the darkened room. "Passing thoughts Mrs Plesher, just passing thoughts."

Three weeks after Granny's funeral, Tom received his greatest surprise. Uncle Don and his wife arrived from America.

"You must be Tom." Granny's eldest, his uncle, surmised thrusting out his hand. A trace of the Scot's accent percolating through that of his adopted country. "Ma told me you lived with her. The old girl practically brought you up single handed since your own ma and pa passed away, so I hear."

At a loss as to what to say, Tom nodded and shook the outstretched hand. "Please to meet you. Will you both come in? But how?"

"Your Aunt Betty," his uncle answered, sitting down in the proffered chair, his wife the other. "We came as soon as we got the cable. I always meant to show the little lady something of the old country and meet ma. Well, it is too late for one, but not the other."

Tom nodded his understanding and crossed between them to put the kettle on the hob.

"Sorry nephew, excuse my manners. This is Connie, my wife. Sugar, meet ma's only real son, seeing as the rest of us lit out as soon as we were tall enough to toast bread," he chuckled.

"Pleased to make your acquaintance, I'm sure, Thomas." Connie flickered her eye lasses at him, limply holding out the back of her hand.

Tom hesitated, not knowing whether to kiss or shake the tiny hand extended to him, finally deciding on the latter.

Uncle Don's eyes swept the room, which Tom wished he had done before his visitors had arrived. "We were all born here, Tom," he said, a touch of sadness in his voice. "Besides myself, there was your own father James, and your Uncle Willie. Now the only ones left are your Auntie Betty and myself."

By the end of the evening, Tom had warmed to his long lost uncle, though holding some reservations as regards his wife. At length, they had risen to leave.

"Have you somewhere to bide? I never thought to ask. There is some room here, or at Aunt Betty's," Tom spluttered, not wishing to appear unsociable, but hoping they would choose Aunt Betty's as he had not kept the house as neat and tidy as had his Granny. Then again who could have? Even though she'd be dying on her feet, the daily ritual had to be adhered to. Blackening the grate, polishing the brasswork of the cooker, water tap, the doorbell knocker. For nobody would ever say I kept the hoose like a midden, she would say with an indignant toss of her old white head.

"We have reservations at the central. No don't ask which platform," his uncle wagged a finger. "I have not lost all my Glasgow humour."

Tom tugged at his ear smiling, while Connie, mystified by this strange parochial sense of humour, glided towards the door, happy to be leaving.

Outside on the landing, his uncle touched his forehead in farewell. "We shall look you up in a few days time nephew, when I have done showing the little lady something of this country of ours."

Then, they were gone. Only the heavy smell of Connie's perfume lingered in Granny's 'hoose'.

Tom's Uncle Don and his wife Connie returned three weeks later. It was a Saturday, so in company with Big Dougie, the men set off to watch Rangers play at Ibrox, much to the chargin of Tom who wanted to make for Firhill and his beloved Partick Thistle. After the game, they all met up with Connie in town and had tea in a posh restaurant in Argyll Street. On the following Monday, Tom's American kin came to take their last farewell of him, before leaving for home.

"Well, boy we had ourselves a swell time visiting the old place. And seeing you and my sister Betty again who, I must say has not changed a bit…in her ways that is," he grinned. "Connie enjoyed seeing the sights. Did you not, sugar?"

"Yes Don," his wife replied dutifully, sitting herself down in Granny's chair by the fire, the smell of her perfume even more overpowering than on the first occasion.

Inwardly, Tom smiled at what Big Dougie had said about her at work that morning in the conversation that had followed.

"You're no tryin' tae tell me Ding, that yon things married tae yer uncle?" She's got that much lipstick on you wid think she'd been hit in the gub wi an axe!"

"Come on Dougie, she's no that bad."

"Yer right, she's worse. And that mooth o' hers, it's like Plymooth."

"Why are ye sae nasty Dougie? Her mooth's no that big."

"No big!" Dougie exclaimed in horror. "It's that big you've tae stand ahint her arse tae read her lips!"

Now, searching in Granny's sideboard, listening to the lady in question extolling Scotia's wonders, Tom was apt to agree with his china (his pal). How, she was saying she had found everything here so small and cute. How she just loved 'Lock' Lomond and would love to take it back home to show off in the States if she could have found something big enough to hold it in.

Leaving Tom to mutter to himself, ye hivnae tried yer mooth hen. At the same time as he came across the note on the shelf from his Aunt Betty.

"Would you credit this?" Tom exclaimed to his uncle. "It's from Aunt Betty. Dear Tom, it reads. Yer Granny always promised me her best china when her time came, which I have taken before you break it, together with the silver cutlery set. So don't go thinking you have been burgled. Also, I have given old Mrs Irvine, Granny's best coat and hat. They are of no use to anyone else. I'm sure the old soul will appreciate them. With love, Aunt Betty."

"As I said before nephew, our Betty had not changed." Don let out a loud laugh, his eyes twinkling with amusement. "You better nail down the table and chairs before you come home some night to a house stripped bare."

"She takes a lot of believing that Auntie o' mine." Tom shook his head. "At least," he sighed, "Granny had the foresight to put the house in my name. She told the factor, Uncle, that as I was paying the rent it should be mine by rights."

"Good for ma. At least, you will still have a home."

Prompted by an impatient look from his wife, Uncle Don rose. "I guess we best be on our way, nephew. We have a lot of packing to do before tomorrow."

Outside in the street, while Connie was buying some 'cute' little knickknacks from the corner shop, his uncle put a hand on Tom's shoulder. "I guess I won't be back, Tom. There's not much point. My home is in the States now. Though seeing this again…" the man turned to gaze up the street a far away look in his eyes, as if seeing all those childhood scenes once more. "We had some real good times here son, though I never have regretted leaving. You see Tom, I never could have achieved here what I managed to make for myself over there. If I were you, I'd get myself out of here before it's too late. Time flies you know son, you don't stay young for ever you know."

Just then, Connie emerged from the shop clutching her bag of 'goodies'. Don held out his hand to his nephew. "Well this is it Tom. Look after yourself. Who knows you might look me up in the States some day." Tom nodded and said his goodbyes, and Connie came and kissed him on the cheek, more cheerful now that she was leaving. "You take care now. You hear?"

It was three weeks before The Glasgow Fair Holidays when he heard from his uncle again. His letter was brief and to the point. He was sending him a little 'something', in the hope it might help in his career, or give him that 'certain' holiday in South America he'd told him so much about.

Next day, Tom asked Mr MacKendrick to take him up to the Big Office to see Mr Johnston.

Recovering from a state of near apoplexy at the thought, the Chief Clerk fixed Tom a stare that would have frozen a fish supper just newly out the pan.

"You, Bell? What in heaven's name for?" he exclaimed, adding with a sly smile, "of course if it is to tender your resignation, you must first give it to me."

His face expressionless, Tom stared back. "No, Mr MacKendrick, you're not that lucky…yet. It's a personal matter. I have been having an affair with Mrs Johnston, and I think Mr Johnston should be the first to know."

Dougie grinned at the two men standing in the middle of the floor, like schoolmaster and pupil, everyone in the office having stopped work to listen to Tom's disclosure. "You too Ding? And here was I thinking I was the only one in her life. Can ye keep her in the manor, or big hoose that she is accustomed to pal?"

"Will you two cease!" the Chief Clerk exploded. "Must I remind you that you are speaking of the wife of your employer. I shall report this to him immediately."

A hush spread around the room as the clerk moved towards the door.

Tom sucked his bottom lip. Perhaps he and Dougie had gone too far this time.

"I hope you will still find it amusing when you are both standing in the unemployment line," the Chief Clerk said stiffly. "However, firstly I shall find out if Mr Johnston is free."

Refusing to be intimidated, Big Dougie took his parting shot. "I know his wife was, she never charged me once."

"How many times did she charge you?" a fellow worker asked.

"Oh, I bet she gave him quite a charge!" another wit added.

The clerk,defeated by this united front of defiant humour, by his staff his cheeks bright red and fighting a bad bout of hyperventilation, stormed. "That is quite sufficient. You are all on report. Now, get on with your work. You too Bell, there is no need for you to stand there until I return."

Relieved by this timely show of support, Tom winked his thanks across the room.

Ten minutes later, standing in the open doorway, the Chief Clerk drew himself up to his full five feet two inches. "Bell." He pointed a finger at Tom. "Mr Johnston will see you now. Although, personally I think he is making a grave mistake," he added indignantly. "What is more, count yourself fortunate I decided not to mention to your employer your recent gross insubordination." He swept an indignant eye across the room. "That applies to you all."

Apprehensive, now that the time had come to meet the great man, Tom followed his elder up the stairs and through the 'Big Office' where senior staff and personnel worked. The Chief Clerk,clearly embarrassed at having to disturb the elite by bringing a 'downstairs person' through their midst.

Once through the office, Mr MacKendrick knocked timidly on the inner sanctum door, waiting to enter and prostrate himself and offer his humble apologies once again for this unnecessary inconvenience.

Momentarily left in the anteroom, Tom made his way to one of the many high backed chairs that stood against the wall, passing glass cases of ships designed by the company; his feet sinking in the deep-pile carpet, and sniffing the smell of leather and varnish…and money…mostly money.

Folding his arms, he leaned back and ran an eye over the line of Johnston's past, glowering down at him in icy silence, each clearly angered by the intrusion of a plebeian such as this from as low as the drawing office.

Eventually, Mr Johnston's door opened and the Chief Clerk, with an impatient gesture, summoned him to his audience with his god.

Unable to resist the opportunity to taunt the wee man, Tom rose slowly, and taking his time crossed the anteroom while suppressing a grin as his senior clerk's face changed from carrot to tomato to beetroot.

"Well, Bell?" Mr Johnston asked, without looking up at Tom, standing on the carpet's edge just inside the door.

"Yes, Mr Johnston, thank you, Sir," Tom answered in his best English.

"I was not inquiring after your health Bell. I should merely like to know what is so important that you cannot follow procedure, by first informing my Chief Clerk as to the nature of your business…is it in connection with your late grandmother?" Mr Johnston asked, setting down his pen and glaring at this jaunty young man standing at the far end of his Private office.

"Not exactly Mr Johnston…Sir. But you may recall saying the night of the Hogmanay dance that should I find enough money to go to South America, you would give me time off work." Tom halted as the simultaneous gasps of astonishment reached him across the room.

"You have not come here to take up Mr Johnston's most valuable time with all this nonsense Bell!" the Chief Clerk exploded, his face now a deep purple.

"I beg your pardon, Mr MacKendrick, but it is not nonsense as you put it. I do have the money, and Mr Johnston did promise. Or were Sonya…Miss Henderson and I both mistaken? Perhaps Mr Johnston cannot recollect the occasion? After all, we all had a bit too much to drink."

Unable to believe his ears, and searching for a suitable retort, Mr Johnston's mouth opened. Finding none, he leaned forward in his chair asking huskily, "How long do you need?"

"I can't do it in less than three months. My Uncle Don in America will arrange everything for me, once you say it is all right with you."

"Is this a game you are playing Bell, this obsession with South America? Why South America?" Mr Johnston stormed.

"I have always been fascinated by the Inca and Mayan culture of South America, Mr Johnston. There is more to life than just drink and football for some of us, you know."

Tom's employer glowered at him. The Chief Clerk's sharp intake of breath audible across the room.

"I take your point, Bell. It is also refreshing to know that one of my employees has such an interest, albeit a most unusual one."

Mr Johnston's face stopped short of a smile. "Have a good holiday young man. Work out the details with Mr MacKendrick here, so that he can inform personnel, and deduct your wages accordingly." The lifting of his pen off his desk signalled the end of the interview.

Tom had just reached the door, his hand out to turn the handle when he heard his lord and master call out. "Have you a camera, Bell? If not get one, as we shall be all very interested to see what is taking you so far from home."

And that was how he came to be sitting here, terrified out of his tiny mind, instead as he should be doing, enjoying the 'Fair' with Big Dougie and his mates.

"I think it sufficiently dark now, Mr Bell. Shall we make a start?"

The voice jerked Tom back to his present circumstances.

Now that the time had come to leave, he would have much preferred to have remained here until found, and plead insanity. Perhaps, if he was to mention that he was a Partick Thistle supporter, it might just swing his case.

Tom rose stiffly and, with a self-conscious smile at the lady in the wheelchair, cautiously opened the door.

"Can you see anyone? Is it all quiet?"

"Except for ma knees knocking missus, yes."

"Excellent. Then let us make a start. We shall turn right. Go up the street. At least, it is in the direction of your hotel. It is the Astora, I believe? Should all still be quiet you can make a dash for it."

"Aye it is. But, what about you? If you can't come with me to the hotel, as you said, then I'll take you to your friend's place," Tom grunted, tilting the chair over the doorstep.

Tom had scarcely finished speaking when he heard the firing, coming as he feared from the tourist section of the city.

The lady indicated to her right. "We best detour this way, I think."

Tom swung the wheelchair, his hands firmly clasped on its back, and swiftly guided it through a warren of unlit cobbled streets.

After a time, his passenger held up a cautionary hand. "Slow down young man, we are almost out of this section of the city. We must now cross the boulevard and head uptown."

Grateful for the break, Tom ran his finger round the inside of his dank shirt collar and with his other hand pushed the chair towards the kerb, unaware of the black sedan hurtling around the corner towards him, hotly pursued by a military truck which, when almost level with the chair, raked the back of the sedan in a sudden burst of gunfire, shattering the rear window, and hurtling a terrified Tom and his charge back onto the pavement. And before he and his passenger had time to recover, both squealing vehicles had disappeared over the crest of the hill and into the night.

Tom's heart thumped at their narrow escape. "No way can we cross that road, hen." He shook his head and stared up the road at a line of burning cars. "If the Keystone Cops decide to come back when we're crossing the road, we're mincemeat."

Unperturbed, Miriam pointed in the opposite direction from the burning cars. "Go that way. If I remember correctly, the street narrows at the corner. Then we'll have to make a dash for it."

"We'll?" Tom broke off embarrassed, as he looked down at the lady in the chair. "Okay, if you say so. You're the boss."

"You have a nice turn of phrase, Mr Bell," the lady chuckled. "You do make me laugh."

"Aye, that's what all the lassies say," Tom grunted.

Reaching the junction, Tom cast a quick look left and right, then, gripping the chair tighter, bolted across the boulevard, bumping the chair up on to the pavement and around the corner, into what appeared at first in the dim street lighting to be a fashionable shopping area.

"Stop here, until I get my bearings," Miriam commanded with a gesture of her hand. "Yes. Oh yes. Down that way if you please." She pointed to a furniture store a little distance away.

Tom did as he was asked and, several blocks later, guided by the woman in the wheelchair turned another corner.

"It won't be long now until you are quit of me, my Scottish friend," Miriam said cheerfully, clearly relieved that their hazardous journey was almost over. "Marion, my friend's house, is the third house on the left just over this hill."

Behind the lady, Tom made a face, too happy at the prospect of being rid of this domineering old woman. He was about to let this upper crust little English lady know that to him their journey had been nothing more than a doddle. No more fraught with danger than the aftermath of an 'Old Firm' game between Rangers and Celtic, when at that precise moment the first of three trucks screeched around the bend at the foot of hill, spilling out their cargo, and instantly turning this rich tranquil community into one of terror.

"Oh no! I'm almost certain Marion is one of those!" Miriam wailed, as the first of the stunned residents were already being pushed, dragged, and prodded at bayonet point over their well-manicured lawns to the line of waiting trucks.

Somewhere to their right at the foot of the hill amid the screams of hysterical women and children, one man broke free of his captors and ran up the hill towards them, reaching almost half way before a rifle shot rang out hurtling him to the ground where he lay clawing at the smooth bitumen road, writhing in agony until a second shot found him and he lay still.

"This cannot be happening!" Miriam hid her face in her hands.

Quickly, Tom swung round the chair. "It is. So let's get oot o' here before it happens to us!"

Some holiday this, Tom muttered to himself, feeling that his back was the size of the South Stand at Hampden Park, with Big Dougie's camera threatening to choke him at every stride as he bolted for the protection of the nearest corner.

"Do you think they have seen us?" Miriam's voice was scarcely audible to Tom above his own wheezing.

"I don't think so. But with my luck, we'll probably lose the soldiers, and get stopped by the polis for speeding!" he gasped.

Despite the situation, Miriam let out a laugh. "You'll do young Mr Bell. We'll be out of this in no time."

"And into what?" Tom shot back.

It was at times like this that Tom knew his sense of humour was his only means of protection. He never did say things with the express purpose of making people laugh when he was scared, only that it made him feel better. It was his own express mechanism to make him feel safer when he was at his most venerable, such as right now. So thinking, he kept on running.

An hour later, the fugitives found themselves on the fringe of parkland which eventually gave way to a less prosperous part of the city. Here, all was quiet, except for the few curious inhabitants standing on their darkened verandas, staring out across the city in the direction of the gunfire and burning buildings.

Suddenly, Miriam threw up her hand. "Do you see them? There," she whispered, pointing a finger in the direction of a dowdy block of four storey flats, where a row of silent soldiers, bayonets fixed stood facing the shanty town. "Quick, before they see us, down there between those buildings. Quietly now."

Silently, Tom did as he was told and headed for a backyard, away from the line of soldiers, hearing the lady add. "Over there, Mr Bell. Behind that shed will do."

Too tired to argue, Tom obeyed.

"Well done. This will do 'till morning." Miriam straightened her skirt. "Then we can be on our way. I have friends in Corona who will help us."

"Is this the next town?" Tom asked, slumping down against the shed, and apprehensive now that each stride was taking him further away from his hotel.

"Not quite dear boy. I should say about three hundred miles."

"Oh! Is that all? For a minute there, I thought you were going to say it was quite far. You must be joking! I'm in no way going to try and get you to this Coronary place."

om scraped at the hard ground with his heel. "And what about those Zulus back there? Why are they just standing there? Shouldn't they be ransacking the place as their pals are doing on the other side of town? After all, they are the same army. And it's rifles they're carrying, not tambourines."

"I can well understand your frustration. One day you are enjoying a carefree holiday...the next." Miriam waved a hand in the dark. "It would be difficult for me to explain it all to you, when I really do not understand all of it myself." The woman shivered.

Tom rose and, taking off his jacked, draped it around the woman's shoulders.

The woman went on as not having noticed the gesture. "I have tried to piece it all together, to make some sort of sense out of it, and have deduced that although President Bieztos still commands the loyalty of the army, or at least most of it, he still believes the main threat to his authority will most probably come from what we will be pleased to call the 'upper class', as it is they who hold the wealth and power."

"So that is why the soldiers attacked your friend's suburb?"

"Quite. The President needs the backing of the common people who are no threat to him at present as they have no leader, no spokesman so to speak. As these people have seen dictators come and go, why should they risk their lives in what they see as a rich man's struggle?"

"What about your friend, what's his name? Does he not speak for the common people?"

"Yes, in a way. But Fernando himself comes from a middle class background, and traditionally the peasants mistrust them. Time only will tell whether they will accept him or not. You see, they might just see him as just another 'hacendados' ranch owner out to fill his pockets at their expense."

Miriam pulled Tom's jacket more closely about her as if aware of it for the first time. "Oh, I am sorry young man you must be feeling rather chilly yourself."

Tom slid back down again against the shed door and drew his knees up to his chin. "I'll survive."

"Yes, I think you will Mr Bell. I think you will."

"But for not much longer if you keep calling me Mister every time you speak," Tom suggested as politely as his circumstances would allow, and suppressed a sudden urge to shiver now that the sweat was drying under his thin cotton shirt. "Tom is the name. Mister was my daddy's."

Miriam chuckled. "Very well then…Tom."

Chapter 2

Bereft of the cover darkness, and now in the full glow of the morning sun, the road seemed much wider to the fugitives, leaving them more exposed, more vulnerable to any vehicle which might suddenly appear around the next bend.

Since crossing a narrow derelict bridge, on the outer fringes of the city, a few hours earlier, Tom's nerves were now almost at breaking point, listening out for any sound of pursuit, which he was certain would surely follow his run in with the soldier.

He sighed. Had they started out a few minutes earlier, they would probably have missed the solitary soldier making his rounds. As it was, they had come upon one another in tangle of brightly coloured washing strung across the narrow alleyway. For the hundredth time since leaving the bridge, Tom visualised what had happened as the soldier challenged them, his bayoneted rifle only a few feet away from where he had hastily drawn up the wheelchair.

"What do we do now, Oh guardian of the Empire?" he growled down at Miriam.

As if in response to his question, the soldier pointed to Tom's camera, commanding that he should give it to him.

"Not on yer life, Jimmy! It's no mine for starters. It's Big Dougie's. If I go back without it, he'll kill me!"

"So will he, Tom, if you don't hand it over," Miriam's sibilant voice floated up to him.

Growling, Tom unslung the camera and the soldier stepped forward in the same instant that the Guardian of the Empire launched her wheelchair, catching the unsuspecting warrior in the knees.

"Now Tom!" Miriam cried over the sprawling body that had almost capsized her chair.

"What do you mean now?" Tom shouted, his mind racing at the options open to him. Such as running like the clappers and leaving this particular little lady to sort things out for herself. Or perhaps instead, showing this uniformed moron the inside workings of Big Dougie's camera. Instead, much to his surprise. he found himself substituting the soldier's helmet for that of a handy dustbin lid, bringing it down with all his might on the unprotected head of the soldier, who, with a grunt of resignation, folded in a heap on the dusty alleyway.

"Quick Tom! Let us be off!" Miriam howled, propelling her chair forward.

"B….off is the word, lady," Tom shot back, helping with the acceleration, too scared to try and retrieve his best friend's precious camera in the event that the soldier may have regained his feet.

Frantically, Tom pushed until they were out of the maze of back alleyways and into the bush beyond, only slowing down when the derelict bridge came in sight some time later.

"If my memory serves me correctly, there should be a small kiosk a few kilometres up this road Tom," the woman informed him, cutting into his reverie.

"Mm? You don't expect anything to be open after last night do you?" Tom asked incredulously.

"And why not? These people are used to such things. Life and business must go on if one is to survive. How far have we come, do you think?"

Tom rolled his eyes heavenwards, unable to fathom the logic of this whole affair. "That last mile…kilometre stone," he corrected himself, "said twelve kilometres from the city."

"Twelve! That is good going Tom!"

"Oh yes, only another thousand to go to Coronary. I wonder what will pack in first, me or my Bayne and Duckett shoes. I got these to see the sights, and boy am I seeing the sights!"

"I hate to dampen your spirits, for this is not the road to Coronary, as you quaintly call Corona, at least not the direct road."

"Oh it's not, isn't it? Just a wee detour via Cape Horn or something," Tom spat out sarcastically.

"Of course not, silly boy," Miriam chuckled. "However, it is the safest road. Or it should be, once we veer off in another twenty kilometres or so. Still, I am most pleased with our progress young man. Twelve kilometres this morning already."

"Not really." Tom straightened to ease his aching back. "Don't forget we did about seven last night before we reached yon shanty town," he reminded her.

"True. I had almost forgotten that. However, push on Tom." She chuckled happily.

"Push being the operative word," came the caustic reply.

It was almost an hour later, rounding a bend that they came upon the kiosk, which in truth turned out to be no more than a shack, where at that precise moment its yawning owner, dressed in faded blue overalls was lazily, pushing up a shutter. Who, after only the briefest of glances in their direction, turned to prop up his second shutter, as if the sight of a man pushing a middle-aged European lady was an every day occurrence.

"We must be the last in the parade," Tom wisecracked. "He's never turned a hair."

"It never pays to be too inquisitive," Miriam responded softly.

Leaving the road, Tom pushed the chair over the hard baked uneven ground towards the shack.

"We best sit there, Tom, where we can have an unobstructed view of the road," Miriam suggested, nodding to where a table and chair stood by the side of the building. "Then if need be we can make a dash for the bush."

"What do we use for money?" Tom asked, backing the wheelchair to the table. "I have only a few Pesos. The rest of my money is in the hotel safe."

Miriam made herself comfortable at the table. "Not to worry, I have some."

The proprietor came and Miriam greeted him cheerfully, though by the end of the conversation she was somewhat less than happy.

"What's wrong, wee wumman, is his prices too high?" Tom joked at Miriam's downcast expression.

Miriam ignored the comment. "He says he can manage coffee and a few rolls. Will that do? I know you must be simply ravenous after all that exertion."

"Simply," Tom mimicked in his best English accent.

Miriam Plesher encompassed her companion with an icy stare. "Do I detect a hint of sarcasm, Mr Bell?"

"Not at all your Majesty," Tom yawned. "Not at all." Then looking through his brows ventured at this woman he still did not know much about. "You didn't just ask Pedro there what was on the menu did you?"

Closing her eyes, the lady sat back in her chair. "The radio news bulletin from the capital states all is quiet for the moment. Also, that last night's riot was the work of right wing agitators backed by a few rich hacendados who sought to use these poor innocent misguided people as a means of overthrowing their rightful government.

However, aided by the army and the paisanajes, the riots are quashed and everything is now back to normal," Miriam concluded, stroking her closed eyelids.

"Great! So now we can go back!" Tom smiled up at the proprietor, who had now arrived with his tray of coffee and rolls.

"You are naïve, Tom." The lady opened her eyes to study the young man sitting across the table. "What else do you expect a government owned wireless station to announce? The truth?

Tom hesitated from biting into his roll. "You mean…"

"Propaganda, dear boy, simply propaganda."

Tom shook his head. The effect of what Miriam had just said rolling around in his head.

"But what if it is true? Could we not at least phone my hotel, speak to Alan the courier and ask him to contact the British Embassy? Or have him contact my uncle and tell him what is happening down here? Besides, I don't want to be late returning home and losing my job. After all…" Tom's voice rose dramatically, "I am a tourist. Surely they would not want anything to happen to a foreigner visiting their country? I didn't come here to get involved in someone else's politics, you know. It wasn't included in the travel brochure," Tom sputtered, rising to look inside the kiosk.

"Oh they have one young man," Miriam smiled up at him. "A telephone, that is, what you are looking for?"

Annoyed, Tom sat back down studying his coffee cup.

"You must understand what you have got yourself into Tom. Had you met anyone other than myself, doubtless you would now be safely back in your hotel impatiently waiting to get back home to tell your friends how you found yourself in the middle of a revolution. No doubt adding a few gory details to impress…Big Dougie? Or that clerk you loathe so much."

Tom rolled his eyes regretting ever having told this woman something of himself last night in order to while away the time.

"However," Miriam Plesher went on, "you did meet me and now that you have, even if you wanted to, you cannot go back to your hotel or your embassy, as they will be watching both by this time. You see," Miriam splayed out her hands, "they cannot afford to let you leave. I am certain they will have found out that you are in my company, and this being the case, will be anxious to know what information I may have imparted to you."

Tom, his heart sinking ever lower, sat staring over the speaker's shoulder at a small animal sitting hunched by the side of the road, contemplating it would seem whether it was safe or not to cross, and he felt a certain affinity towards the wee thing.

Should he, he wondered, go on with this stuck up Sassenach of a woman, or call her bluff and simply get up and walk back to the city?

"How would they who ever they are, know who I am, and that we have ever met?" he threw at her caustically.

"Until this morning, they didn't. Unfortunately for you, young man, you lost your camera."

Tom watched the wee creature disappear back into the undergrowth, having obviously weighed up the odds against crossing, although the road was completely deserted. Perhaps, Tom thought, it had a sixth sense, six more than he had at present, and cursed himself for printing his name and hotel in the inside of Big Dougie's camera case.

"Well that's it now. No going back," he sighed as the wee creature reappeared, the recesses of his mind trying to establish if this was the same wee animal or not. It seemed to be he decided: four legs, two ears, twitching nose.

Smiling at his own humour, Tom turned to the woman and held up his coffee cup in salutation, treating her to his best Humphrey Bogart impersonation. "Here's looking at you sister," he said with a grin.

"Really, Tom," Miriam Plesher tittered, "you are a one."

At the same time as the two fugitives sat sipping coffee, a few kilometres outside of the city, Colonel Roberto Segovia strode down the concrete corridor leading to what was humorously known as 'the reception room', his eyes firmly focused on the corridor's far wall, oblivious to the pitiful cries emanating from behind the numerous iron studded doors lining either side, and without breaking stride threw open the last of the heavy doors.

Unemotionally, Segovia took in the macabre scene of the naked middle aged man suspended from a beam a few feet above the tank of molten lead, before riveting his gaze on the Sergeant and Private soldier springing quickly to attention at his unexpected entrance, their hands raised in a nervous salute.

"Has he spoken?" Segovia barked at the Sergeant.

"Not yet, my Colonel!" the man replied, swallowing hard.

Segovia swung his attention to the man dangling above his head. "Come Ricardo, you must save yourself further pain," he addressed the Minister of Finance in a falsely pleading voice. "See what a little persuasion has already cost you." He tapped the man's burned and swollen feet with his swagger stick. "We know you have already transferred large sums of our country's wealth from the capital. What we must know is to where?" Segovia's tone changed to one of anger. "Also to whom it was that gave you such an order without the express permission from our beloved President!"

Ricardo Menanaze stared down and through his tormentor to the chamber wall beyond, his mind and body racked in pain. For him, it was only a matter of time before he died, this he knew. Now it was of little consequence, for he did not fear death, only that he should die before the pain became too great and he betrayed his friends, even in the smallest way.

As if from afar he heard the harsh voice of the Chief of State Security. "I believe I smell the work of that fascist Castilia somewhere behind this, Minister."

Ricardo moaned. It was almost uncanny, unnerving, how Segovia came by his information.

Castilia, as a member of the opposition, had no authority over a government minister such as himself. No, it had been his own idea to move some of the country's assets to a safer place before they found their way via their 'beloved' President to a Swiss bank. True, he had come to respect Fernando Castilia and, having put country before politics, had confided to him his President's corrupt intentions.

One clandestine meeting had lead to another and through the intermediately of the crippled Inglesa had set about ensuring the safety of their country's wealth. More importantly he had engineered microfilm of President Bieztos's illegal transactions. This more than anything if made public was sufficient evidence to have him deposed. If not by his own people, at least in the eyes of the world, and, with it, would go the international financial credit upon which his country was so heavily dependent.

With a moan of despair, Ricardo felt the beam move. Closing his eyes, the minister once more called upon his patron saint to give him strength.

"Come, Menanaze, do not be a fool. Do you wish to leave here a cripple?" Segovia hurled up at him. Briefly, the eyes of the two men met, until with a shrug of indifference Segovia stood back.

Slowly the beam descended, halting momentarily over the bubbling molten liquid.

His eyes riveted on his commanding officer, the Sergeant awaited the order. At a flick of the swagger stick, the beam continued on its way. The feet then the legs, up as far as the knees disappearing into the tank.

The scream that followed startled even the complacent Chief of State Security, as the dangling man twisted and turned to escape the pain. The sweet nauseating smell of burning flesh turned to one of repugnance as the beam lifted, molten lead already solidifying on the lower limbs of the tortured man.

Sweating profusely, the Sergeant's nails bit deeply into the palm of his clenched fists. Silently, he cursed this old man and his silence. Did he not realise he was going to die? Even if he were to talk now, they would never let him go, to tell what they had done to him here in 'the reception room'. Knowing his Colonel only too well, if he did not make this stubborn old fool talk soon, it could easily be him up there in his place.

Staring up at the writhing mass of pain, Segovia slowly extracted a cheroot from its case, his eyes firmly fixed on his victim's face. "We already know Castilia is behind your action. To which he will, no doubt, readily confess to when we find him, and he replaces you from where you now hang."

Through the mists of pain, Ricardo's heart lifted at the news that his friend was still free, to be instantly dashed by his tormentor continuing remorselessly. "As for your crippled Inglesa friend, it will not be so very long before she too is found." The Colonel blew smoke up at his victim. "Oh yes, my friend, it will be a simple matter to find her. How inconspicuous can a crippled foreign lady be in our country, do you think? It was most ingenious of her having a fellow country man come here in the guise of a tourist to help her leave the country, armed with false information…lies… about our beloved President, in order to discredit him in the eyes of the world."

Segovia stood back to let the hanging man see his look of triumph. "You see, we know everything, my old friend. Therefore, your suffering is merely a minor irritation to me. However..." Segovia let out an exaggerated sigh, "our President insists that you declare all."

Finished, Segovia calmly drew on his cheroot, knowing what he had said was not strictly true, as at present they had no idea of Castilia's whereabouts. So, instead he had utilized his resources on finding the English lady and her accomplice. Find them and he would make them tell where Castilia was.

"I cannot afford to waste anymore of my precious time on you," Segovia rapped at his captive, his voice rising in annoyance. "Your next little dip will be a trifle deeper. Do you wish to be left half a man?" At the other's continued silence, Segovia signalled with a quick movement of his hand to the portly Sergeant. The last long inhuman shriek following him back through the long corridor, ending when he had at last reached the steps, leading up to the plaza and the sunshine of the outside world.

"I should like to halt here Tom," Miriam Plesher requested, indicating a clump of bushes.

Tom bumped the wheelchair off the metalled road and on to the hard red earth, expertly manoeuvring round fallen branches and small stones littering the undergrowth. "Over there, if you please, Tom, behind that tree."

Tom's face, already red from the heat and exertion, deepened ever further, it never having occurred to him that Miriam Plesher would ever 'have to go'. She was one of those people whom you thought would never be in need of any bodily function. Whether it be sitting or lying down. Such actions were strictly for peasants.

As if having read his thoughts, and to allay his fears, Miriam looked up at him. "It's all right my boy, I can manage perfectly well. You go and have a well earned rest," her voice gently sympathetic.

Embarrassed, as much by the tone of her voice as by the situation, Tom forced a smile. "Okay. But don't pee long," he joked, and heard the reprimanding 'tut tut' as he moved off.   Tom wandered almost to the end of the bush and sat down with his back against a tree, grateful for the shade and the rest.

His watch read three thirty. He closed his eyes trying to calculate what he had been doing at this time yesterday. Was it only yesterday? So much for being the innocent tourist, and innocent was the word.

Why was it so much different from the American pictures he always saw with Bogey rescuing the beautiful damsel in distress from the deepest Hollywood studio swamp, and she looking as though she had just stepped out of a beauty parlour? The only flaw in her make-up was the usual minute speck of dirt on her cheek for Bogey to delicately wipe off. Then, there was the hero himself, a bit worse for wear, but never short of a bob or two. Down to his last smoke maybe, but still able to throw it away almost whole, and with bullets whistling all around, hurl the heroine into his arms and break into a monologue of how she was the only one for him lasting half the picture. He'd always wondered what the 'baddies' did in the meantime while this was going on. Probably they were sitting in the next studio smoking Bogey's throw away cigarettes. Or having a pie and a pint.

For a moment, Tom had been back home in the Odeon on a Saturday night. Now with his present surroundings coming back into focus, his heart sank. It was all right for Bogey, he'd never had to worry about losing his job in the middle of a depression. Or being afraid of how it would all end. He had read the script.

"Tom. I think we should make a start now," he heard Miriam Plesher call out.

"OK sweetheart," he quietly mimicked his hero. "Here's lookin' at you sweetheart!"

Wiping the sweat from his brow, Tom pushed the chair on in the mid day heat, having long since given up on how far they had travelled that day. At least it was giving him a suntan, if nothing else. So, if one followed the popular principle that the better the tan, the better the holiday, he should be in for a sensational time.

It was these same thoughts which failed him hearing the car drawing up behind. With a start he swung round, jerking the sleeping woman awake, as the car with a squeal of brakes shuddered to a halt.

Tom was ecstatic. At last, a lift! Perhaps his nightmare was at an end. He would get to Corona, then phone his uncle Don to get him out of here.

Doubling his recent efforts on the chair, Tom rushed to the driver's side of the car and thrust his head through the open window.

"Good day. I was wondering if you would be so kind as to give 'mater' and I a lift?" he requested of the portly driver in his best Oxford accent.

Taken aback, it took the American some time to catch his breath. "What in the name of Sam Hill are you doing away out here?" he asked in a southern drawl.

Tom threw a glance at the back seat where two small children sat huddled against their mother in silent apprehension of this slovenly young man framed in their car window. "We are merely taking our constitutional before tiffin," he smiled with a slight bow of his head.

Angrily, Miriam hauled at his sleeve. "If you please Tom, enough is enough. This is no time for jest. I must apologise for my young companion," Miriam was saying. "Too much sun. Scots, you understand."

The driver and his wife nodded in sympathy as if this explained everything.

"Allow me to introduce myself," Miriam went on. "I am Nancy Stevens of the Suffolk Stevens. No doubt you will have heard of us?" Both Americans nodded simultaneously determined not to show their ignorance.

"I was...that is, my man servant and I, were on holiday when this frightful...affair broke out. Tell me, what is happening in the capital now? Our car was commandeered by heaven knows what type of ruffians." Miriam cast her eyes to the sky in horror. "We must get to Corona as quickly as possible as you can appreciate."

"Sorry lady, no can do, not with that wheelchair of yours." The driver splayed his hands on the steering wheel in a gesture of finality. "Maybe we could just about squeeze you in. And, if this servant guy of yours was to stand on the running board, you might ...and I say might, just make it, although we do not plan on going as far as this town you are headed for. But, as I said, lady, not with that goddamned chair of yours and all. Me and the little lady are hightailin' it out of here just as fast as this old jalopy will take us. All that goddamn capital needs right now is for that Nero guy to turn up with his fiddle."

"It cannot possibly be that bad. You are not seriously asking me to believe that the capital is actually burning?" Miriam asked, visibly shaken.

Running a hand through his hair, the driver lowered his eyes away from the questioner. "Well," he drawled. "I guess that is a might strong. But I tell you this: I do not know who the hell is fighting who! Is that not right, honey?" he asked of his wife, looking at her through the rear mirror and daring this upper class Limey to contradict him. "I saw peasant fighting peasant and soldier fighting soldier. So all I know is, that we are not sticking around to have our asses shot off by any son of a bitch wop who happens by with a gun. Do I make myself clear? Now do want to hitch a ride or not? If so dump that chair and hop aboard."

Tom did not know whether to laugh or cry at this last remark. "If madam will allow me?" he winked at Miriam, and bent to lift her out of the chair.

"No Tom! Not without my chair!" Miriam declared emphatically, gently removing his hand from hers. "You go. There's room. You deserve to. Perhaps, Mr Johnston, or is it Mr MacKendrick will keep your job until your return."

Tom could not believe his ears. Exasperated, he stared into her upturned face. "Why? What does a silly old chair matter when your life depends on it? And don't tell me you are attached to it," Tom spat out the pun in an attempt to hide his surprise and disappointment.

"Something like that, Tom. Now go. I have no right to hold you back."

For the first time, Tom saw Miriam Plesher for what she was: a determined, resilient woman. A cripple, maybe, but in physical terms only; here the handicap ended, who, for reasons best known to herself was willing to sacrifice her life for something in which she dearly believed. And, what was more, she was sufficiently astute to know he would not leave her here stranded in the middle of nowhere by herself.

Still in a daze that their chance of a lift had gone, Tom turned to the driver. "I believe it is time for tiffin. Please be good enough to drive on." He bowed stiffly.

"Goddammed Limeys. Nobody, but nobody can ever figure them out!" the driver exploded, spinning the white walled tyres into motion, the car disappearing up the shimmering road in a cloud of dust and blasphemy, the trunks on the roof bouncing and shaking with the speed of its departure.

Still affecting his accent, his eyes still on the speeding car, Tom asked, "What now ma'am…eh Mistress Stevens…what?"

Miriam's slight frame shook with relief. "As I said before Tom, you are a one."

"Aye. That's what all the lassies say." Tom sighed pushing the wheelchair forward. But somehow he did not feel like asking why she would not depart from her beloved chair.

"I think I will have a bit of a rest here," Tom announced guiding the wheelchair into the undergrowth on a straight stretch of road about a half hour after the Americans had made their hasty departure. He gave a wee secret grin. I bet yon driver will be talking about it in his swimming pool and boring the pants of his neighbours for yonks.

"I should think so too Tom. You have excelled yourself." Miriam smiled up at him turning her chair round to face the deserted road, a genuine note of admiration in her voice.

"Jings, I could murder a pint," Tom grumbled, the vision of his local pub flashing before his eyes. "And I wouldnae say no tae a fish supper either, even in this heat," he reflected morosely, sliding down against a tree.

"Will this suffice for the present?" Miriam asked, holding out an apple.

"Where in the name o' the wee man did you get that, you wee smasher?" Tom exploded in delight, taking the proffered fruit. "Do you do conjuring tricks as well?"

Miriam laughed. "I purchased them at the kiosk when you were attending to your toilet."

Tom bit greedily into the apple as she extracted an orange from the side of her chair, thinking what a refined phrase to use, and how only a woman of Miriam Plesher's breeding could have described what he had been doing in the shunkie in such a delicate fashion.

Perhaps, this is why he had never been able to bring himself to address her by her Christian name, though she had insisted that he do so.

No, he had never been quite at ease with this type of person. Perhaps it was his upbringing, he did not know. Only, he felt it improper, failing to show respect, especially to his elders, if he did not address them by their correct title. Not that he thought that they were any better…better off may be; still, it was best if you knew when to keep to your place.

"What are you thinking of, Tom, that you'd be packing your suitcase and all ready for the off, if you had not had the misfortune of stumbling upon me?"

"What?" Tom grunted nibbling his apple to its core, unaware at first of the woman having spoken. "Oh yes. No."

"Perhaps when this is all over and democracy is again restored, this country will give you a medal."

"Aye as long as it's not posthumously." Tom made a face.

" Or they might even name a street after you," Miriam went on.

"Aye, Ding Street," Tom laughed mockingly. "Sounds about the right place to put a dole office. Jings, I might have a job after all, behind the counter. Then, maybe, Hollywood will make a film about me fighting in the revolution, and call it, Mr Ding of Dole Street. Or, Whose for Bell's Dole?" Tom scratched the hard red earth with his heel.

"Why put yourself down, Tom Bell? Even should you lose your job, surely there must be other companies willing to take on a resourceful young man such as yourself."

"In the middle of a depression? Sure, I can just see the interview now," he said bitterly. "'Now Mister Bell.'" Tom affected an upper class accent. "'At present, we are working on the plans of laying down the keel of a new Cunarder. Your last employer states you were given absence of leave to visit South America, but you buggered off for three years. Furthering your experience in your profession, no doubt?'

"'Well not exactly, Sir,'" Tom answered in his own voice. "'I was running a clapper business if you must know. They fired the bullets, and I ran like the clappers!'" Bitterly, Tom stood up and savagely threw away his apple core.

"I seemed to have messed up your life," Miriam replied dejectedly. "You should have taken the American's offer of a lift."

Tom wiped the seat of his trousers. "This is all I have to my name, that I stand up in. All the money I have is back in the hotel safe, except for a few Pesos in my pocket. He looked down at the woman in the chair. "What worries me, besides getting out of this alive, is what will happen to Granny's hoose, if I don't get back for awhile? Who pays the rent? They don't discuss these wee details in the Bogey pictures, do they?"

Miriam stared up at her young companion. "I cannot divulge all the information I was privy to, Tom. Even if I could, I wouldn't…for your own sake. Suffice to say, you are rendering this country a great service. When, and I do mean when, you return home you shall not go unrewarded. Of this, I can assure you."

To hide his embarrassment at the lady's sincerity, Tom wiped the seat of his trousers again, and asked, "What have you got hidden in your kitchen for supper lady?"

Miriam curled a lip in a conspirator smile. "Domestics should not ask such questions."

Tom bowed in mock servility. "I am sorry m'lady. Would you like me to shut up and give your chair a shove?"

Suddenly, the sound of a heavy motor cut short their laughter. Tom threw Miriam a worried look and ran to the edge of the undergrowth, where a truck filled with green clad uniformed men sped past in the direction of the capital.

"Soldiers heading towards the capital, some of the President's mob no doubt," Tom explained, running back to the woman.

"Wrong young man, there is every doubt. Not all men who are in uniform support the President. This you must understand. Some day, your life may depend upon it," Miriam lectured sternly. "However, if you have rested sufficiently, we had better be off."

Back on to the road, the lady continued her lecture. "And be on your guard, we cannot afford to be apprehended; not on any account." She gave a sigh. "It is a long dangerous road to Corona, and if you still intend getting me there, young man, I believe it could be rather a stern walk, for want of a better description."

"I could think of one," Tom muttered to himself. "Aye, and no' sae polite either."

They had carried on for the best part of an hour before they saw the smoke rising in the distance, about a kilometre or so away on this particular stretch of road.

Tom stopped the chair and put a hand up to shade his eyes. "I can't make it out. It could well be a building of sorts. Maybe a kiosk like the one we stopped at."

"I've been on this road once or twice, Tom and I don't remember seeing anything around here," Miriam reflected through her knit brows. "Be careful Tom."

"That's me lady. 'B' for Bell, 'C' for coward," and pushed the chair forward.

he reason for the smoke was explained some time later, when they came upon the partially burned out American's car lying on its side some distance off a bend. The spoked-wheels and white-walled tyres almost intact, lending a bizarre touch to the scene.

Tom stared down at the burned out wreck, hoping that none of the family were still inside. "I think I better go and take a look see," he said, jamming a stone in front of one of the wheels of the chair. "Probably been going too fast and run out of road," recalling how anxious the man had been to be on his way and the speed he had taken off at when leaving them.

For once, Miriam Plesher held her counsel.

Scrambling down the embankment, fearful of what he might find, Tom slowed down as he neared the vehicle. There was a smell of burned flesh, and he looked up to where the woman sat in the wheelchair, then back again at the car. Whether he liked it or not, he would have to find out what had happened.

Tentatively, he put a foot on the rear axle and hauled himself up. For a moment or two the side windows were obscured by a wisp of smoke, but not enough to hide the charred bodies inside. Feeling the bile rise in his throat, he jerked his head away, gulping in fresh air, concentrating on the high mountains across the valley, as if by doing so it would erase what lay beneath him. "You poor, stupid fool, why could you not have taken your time?" he choked, angry at the man, and what he had done to his family.

This was too much for a man to take. Before coming to this accursed country. he'd never seen a dead body, at least not anyone who had died of unnatural causes. First, there had been the man gunned down back in the suburbs, now this.

It was as Tom jumped down from the still hot wreck, blowing on his hands, and again damming the driver, that his eyes caught the long line of neatly spaced bullet holes along the bodywork, as in plates of steel awaiting the riveter.

Horrified, Tom scrambled back up the banking. "Mrs Plesher! Mrs Plesher!" he yelled. "They've been murdered!"

Miriam Plesher wiped an imaginary speck of dust from her lap as if she had not heard.

"l said they have been murdered…killed! Yon American family

who stopped to offer us a lift." Tom halted in mid sentence at the sudden realisation of how narrow an escape they themselves had had.

"I was afraid that would be the case," Miriam replied slowly, a faraway look in her eyes.

"But why?" Tom howled. "What had they…especially those poor wee weans got to do with this damned revolution?"

Miriam answered with a helpless shrug of her shoulders. "Having power sometimes affects peoples reasoning. Such as those soldiers, for example, who passed while we were resting back there. Perhaps, they commanded the American to stop and he was too afraid to do so, so they fired on him."

Tom shook his head. "Those poor wee weans," he said again, not bothered whether the woman understood him or not, his eyes fixed on the road ahead. "Where do we go from here?"

"Where we were going before…before this happened." Miriam threw a hand at the burned out car. "Now, there is even more reason for us doing so, so that we can prevent this type of thing happening again."

A glance at his watch told Tom they had been travelling for the best part of twelve hours. Perhaps, this was why he felt tired and hungry, his legs and arms ached, his heels were chaffed and he was in a foul mood.

It was three hours since they had left the burned out car behind, and over half an hour since they had turned off the main road on to this rutted pot holed track which passed in this god forsaken part of the country for a secondary road.

In order to bolster his flagging spirits he enquired of the woman: "I hope you've had this vehicle serviced lately." He swung the chair round another minor chasm and saw its occupant grimace as it hit a bump. Perhaps he should spare a thought for the old lady, he thought, it couldn't be much fun, spending the entire day bumping up and down in a wheelchair dependant on a complete stranger for survival. Or not knowing when he was likely to say, bugger this for a geme o' sodiers, and leave you high and dry in the middle of know where. Would he do that? For bloody sure, if his feet did not stop aching soon.

Tom tried again. "Have you any idea where the next place is?

Perhaps, get a decent meal and a good night's sleep."

"A few…more…kilometres, Tom."

"This road getting to you, missus?" he asked sympathetically. "I'm doing the best I can to avoid the holes."

"You could have fooled me, Tom Bell, I thought it was the road you were trying to avoid."

Tom stooped over the back of the chair, unsure whether she had been joking or not. If so, it was the first attempt at humour he had heard from her.

"Are you criticising my driving?" he asked, still bent over, Miriam's answer lost amid screeching brakes.

Fearfully, Tom spun round. A few yards behind them a run-down truck had slithered to a halt with more explosions than on a Guy Fawkes night. Behind its grimy windscreen a startled elderly driver sat mopping his brow in disbelief that he had not taken this strange apparition for a ride on his bonnet.

"What do we do now? Any ideas, missus?" Tom asked, turning Miriam round to face the truck.

"On no account tell this person our intended destination, understand? Let me do the talking," the lady commanded.

"I intend to, unless you want to die of starvation while I learn the language," Tom replied, his eyes fixed on the old driver hobbling towards them with all the grace of an arthritic duck.

He drew back, resting his hands on the back of the chair as Miriam greeted the old man with a wave, the intonation in her voice designed to put him at his ease. The old man in return, mopping his brow with a red chequered handkerchief, who drew closer with a few indiscernible mutterings,

After a few minutes of meaningless dialogue to Tom, Miriam turned her head slightly to him. "He says his village lies about thirty kilometres from here, if you turn right at the crossroads," she explained.

"What do you mean if we turn right at the crossroads? Is the old bugger not going to offer us a lift?" Tom exploded, already feeling his feet aching with the thought of further torture.

"I informed him we were heading for Meda, as we have friends there who can help us, as our car was stolen. Meda is in the east, Tom, and Corona lies west of here. So his village is well out of the way of either."

"Beggars can't be choosers as they say in China. If the old bug…boy will give us a lift, and whether this place is off the beaten track or not, what more can we ask for?" Fearing an objection he went on hurriedly. "Besides, it will be dark soon, and I don't think I can take much more of this. Anyway, my dogs are barking. Any longer, and it could turn in to a nasty case of rabbies."

"I take your point young man. Now, a word of caution, no names, no pack drill. Refer to me if you must, as Mrs Stevens.

"Of the Suffolk Stevens would that be ma'am?" Tom mimicked.

"Not that again, Tom, if you please. This is serious."

"So is my condition," Tom growled back.

"We simply cannot afford to trust anyone," Miriam went on firmly. "On no account must anyone learn, who, or what I am, a courier for…" Miriam smiled at the patiently waiting bewildered driver. "Let's omit that name for the present shall we."

Later, much later, due to the speed of the truck, they came in sight of their driver's village. Having listened to his continual babbling for the entire journey, Miriam, jammed in the bench seat between both men, was now near to exhaustion, while Tom, having felt the effects of the day's unaccustomed toil, and unable to understand a word that passed between them, had fallen asleep almost instantly.

"We are here, Tom." Miriam nudged her travelling companion in the ribs.

Tom forced open his uncomprehending eyes on rows of corrugated shacks bordering either side of the rutted road. "Airdrie already," he yawned, as the old man rattled off the road heading towards a two-storied hotel also sporting a corrugated roof, enhanced solely by a wooden veranda surrounding it at first floor level.

Wearily, Tom clambered down off the truck which had jolted to a halt in front of the hotel's dilapidated entrance and reached up to help his companion, while their still gabbing host dropped the wheelchair down beside them.

"He says the hotel is reasonably cheap, and he will speak to the owner," Miriam translated.

"You mean they might not let us in? Perhaps we are not suitably attired." Tom yawned, his eyes on a brood of hens holding a meeting in the middle of the road. Or was it a hen party? Suddenly, he found his humour was not helping. Why had he allowed himself to get mixed up in this? He should have taken a chance and returned to his hotel. After all, he had only the word of this stuck up old woman to go by.

At last, the old driver returned with a younger man, who addressing himself to Miriam gestured excitedly to the hotel entrance. With an effort, Tom levered himself off the side of truck as it screeched in to life, taking off down the road, scattering a wildly protesting hen party in all directions.

"What a fowl thing to do," Tom muttered, angry that his brain would not switch off these senile puns. Perhaps, he too, like the departing truck, was heading round the bend.

Their entrance into the long high-ceilinged room was met by a silent clientele, turning to stare in ill disguised curiosity at a tired dishevelled young man pushing an equally tired but dignified middle aged lady towards the bar counter.

"Shouldn't there be someone playing the piano as we come through the bat wing doors?" Tom commented in a stage whisper, whilst taking in the sawdust floor and metal tables, all of which seemed to make Govan that wee bit closer.

As Tom fought a losing battle with his brainless puns, Miriam apprised the young proprietor of their needs, who, with an apologetic shrug, pointed to the stairs.

"What's wrong are his rates too high?" Tom asked tongue in cheek, his spirits rising at the thought of a pint.

"No," Miriam countered, "but his stairs are. Although he is endeavouring to find a suitable ground floor room for me. You are on the first floor."

"Oh! I am glad." Tom yawned

A few minutes later, both settled down to their first real meal in twenty-four hours, the eyes of the entire establishment firmly fixed on them.

Tom greedily filled his mouth with food, and quickly reached out for his much sought after pint of beer, sucking in air. "Jings, Mrs Plesher, this is hot. What in the name o' the wee man is it?"

Miriam chuckled at her companion's expression. "I don't expect you experienced this type of food back at your hotel?"

"No. It was against fire regulations," Tom spluttered, fanning himself.

"It's chilli peppers and red beans."

Tom took another gulp of his beer. "If I eat anymore of this stuff,

I'll be backfiring more than that old truck we came here in. Still, it has its compensations it will help self propel that wheelchair of yours, should God forbid I have to push it another day."

Tom felt a slight touch on his arm and looked up into the smiling face of a young woman of about his own age. "Much wine?" she asked, filling a glass out of a carafe and giving Tom time to savour the ready smile, dark flashing eyes and olive skin. The white off-the-shoulder blouse accentuated the curvature of her full bosom.

"I was really going to stick to beer, hen, seeing as I'm drivin' the morrow," he smiled up at her. "But if you insist," he grinned, taking the glass of wine from her.

"I see you have recovered somewhat from your tiredness," Miriam chuckled, her eyes sparkling with amusement.

A cry of delight from across the room spared Tom an answer as the old truck driver hobbled towards them, happy at seeing his foreign friends again.

"Much wine," Tom signalled to the young waitress to fill up a glass for their deliverer, already relishing the sight of a repeat performance. This she did, giving him her most scintillating smile. Then, setting the carafe down, she left them to their meal, Tom's eyes following her to the kitchen, oblivious to the conversation between the other two at the table.

"Monola has agreed to take us as far as the next village, but no further, even though I have promised to make it worth his while." Miriam informed him.

"Mm?" Tom murmured absently, his eyes on the kitchen door in the hope of the waitress reappearing.

Impatiently, Miriam repeated herself.

"That's nice. Will save my feet a bit then."

The old man raised his glass in salute to his new friends and with his free hand, lifted the carafe from the table. Then, with a few departing words to Miriam, left to join his friends in the far corner of the room.

"What business have you been up to Monola?" one asked of the old truck driver, pushing forward his empty glass in the direction of his friend's newly acquired wine carafe.

"The Inglesa wishes that I, Monola Montan, take her and her young friend to Meda. This I said I could not do, but said I would take them as far Rieux."

"Why did you not agree Monola? Have you not the gasoline?" A younger man inquired.

"Do you take me for an old fool, Faustine? I would not have a shirt on my back if I took everyone who promised to pay me at their word. These people are not rich. They tell an untruth about the automobile, when they say the soldiers took it. Though, I think they have enough Pesos that I may take them as far as Rieux without burning a hole in my pocket."

"I wish I could hear what they are saying, Tom." Miriam took a sip of her wine, looking to where Monola and his friends sat. "No doubt that old scoundrel is boasting on how much he intends making out of us." She stifled a yawn. "I have the only downstairs room, through that doorway, Tom." She pointed a finger. "Should anything be amiss during the night, you will know where to find me."

Tom held his tongue, hoping the young miss would be that raven-haired waitress.

"I think I will retire now, young man. No Tom! Before you say another word, not to the old age pension."

Laughing, Tom drew his chair back. "Good night m'lady," he added, watching her expertly propel herself towards the door.

"Goodnight, Mister Bell. Don't over imbibe. I hope to see you fresh in the morning," she threw over her shoulder.

One more beer and Tom himself headed for bed, though much to his exasperation he found sleep to be elusive. Thoughts of home, and the events of his extraordinary day, flashed before him without sequence or semblance of order. One time, he was seeing the Americans burned out car. Next, Aunt Betty stripping Granny's house bare at the news he was missing, believed 'deid'.

'A victim of yon Sooth Amerikan rev ul ushun.'

Then, he was back pushing that damned wheelchair again.

Studying the progress of a spider on the opposite wall, he reflected on his journey from home. More than ever he missed Big Dougie and his pals. Funny part was that until yesterday the time had flown by, but now it seemed a lifetime since he had last seen them.

He was still unsure what he had got himself into. Was that sweet resolute English lady taking him for a ride instead of the other way round?

He was also having trouble establishing what was real and what was not. The killing was real enough. But what had it to do with him? Could he not just stand up and say, "I'm with A1 Travel and have seen enough of your wonderful country (tongue in cheek) so please may I go home now?

At last, drifting into welcome slumber, the smiling face of the young waitress floated towards him, although from far away he was well aware that it was only the beginning of a wishful dream.

Tired though he was, he'd been ever hopeful of a knock at the door and the young Senorita slinking into the room as they did in the Bogey pictures. But, knowing his luck, the knock would be from the old truck driver or the barman. Yawning, Tom turned on his side.

A few hundred yards down the road from the restless wheelchair pusher, Faustino also lay awake. Propped up on his pillow, he pondered over what old Monola had said about the Inglesa earlier in the saloon that evening. If Monola thought there was no profit in taking them to Meda then this must be so, for the old man was seldom wrong. This is why Monola had a truck, and he a bicycle.

Faustino drew greedily on the last remnants of his cheroot. Perhaps there would be no harm in informing his contact in the capital of the presence of the Ingles, and their intention of travelling to Meda. Perhaps, too, it would earn him a few Pesos, as it had on numerous other occasions.

Faustino flicked the butt of his cheroot out of the open window of his shack. He would have to wait until morning, as he would have to journey to Rieux to make the necessary telephone call. In Rieux, the instrument was in a Private room, and the operator, unlike here, not cousin to almost everyone in the village.

He would leave while it was still dark, take a short cut by wheeling his cycle up the mountain path, and with any luck reach the road on the other side by first light. Then pedal the rest of the way into the town. Should he leave early enough, he could be there before Monola was out of bed. Perhaps, someday, he also would own a truck like old Monola. Yawning, he too turned on his side.

It was the sun filtering through the narrow windows of his room that awakened Tom next morning. Yawning, he levered himself to a sitting position and stiffly swung his legs over the side of the bed. It was then he realised his limbs had gone out on strike and that the remainder of his anatomy had also come out in sympathy.

Through his splayed legs, he studied his blooded broken toe nails, his chaffed heels, and bit back a gasp of pain when his arms refused to help to lift his leg to scrutinise his heel.

That was it, no more wheel chair pushing for him. His whole body ached from the back of his neck where he'd continually crouched over the chair, to the balls of his feet back up to his balls again.

Displaying the agility of an arthritic septuagenarian, Tom rose to his feet to begin the momentous task of struggling into his clothes, and turning up his nose at the smell of stale sweat from his one and only shirt.

A good twenty minutes later, Tom had managed to drag himself to the top of the stairs, where in the saloon below the good lady was already ensconced in breaking her fast.

Miriam saw him and gave him a wave of good morning with her coffee cup. Tom waved stiffly back, cursing her exuberance and immaculate appearance and reluctantly let go of a helpful pot plant to set about descending the stairs.

"Just in time for breakfast Tom," Miriam enthused. "Monola will be some time yet I fear. Or so I am told."

Across the table, Tom eased himself into a chair, plucking at his shirt. "Pongs a bit, needs a good wash," he said wrinkling up his nose. "Perhaps I should have my man attend to it."

"You have time if you want. It will dry in no time in this heat. I noticed from my bedroom window that there is a trough at the rear of the hotel you can use." She held up the coffee pot. "Coffee?"

Tom nodded and stared at the food on the table while she poured. "What in the name of the wee man is that?" he gasped, pointing in disgust at the yellow green slivers on a central plate.

"Cheese," Miriam informed him with an amused chuckle at his expression, of disbelief. "I will admit to it being a bit strong."

"Strong! I'd give odds it could go all the distance with Joe Louis!"

Miriam skewered a slice with her fork and dropped it on to his plate. "It doesn't taste too bad with bread. No bacon and eggs, I'm afraid. Nevertheless, needs must suffice. It is mature though," she added, watching him chew.

"Did I hear you correctly? You did say mature?" Tom made a face as he took his first bite, gulping down his coffee to drown the taste.

"Well, as they say in China, if that's breakfast, I've had it." Tom pushed back his chair. "I think I'll do something about this shirt, I'd hate the cheese to get all the credit for the smell."

Tom found the trough that Miriam had spoken about and taking off the offending garment plunged it into the cold water, scrubbing at it with all the pent up frustration and anger he could muster at ever having found this woman, and the fact that each hour was taking him away from what little safety he had known since arriving in this country.

So engrossed was he in his determination to get his only shirt clean, that he did not hear the giggle, until turning to wring it out, saw the young waitress standing there, a hand to her mouth to cover her amusement. Blushing, she moved to him to run a finger over his naked chest.

"My lucks in at last, unless, of course, she's after my shirt." Tom let out a slow breath and rolled his eyes to the heavens, as the giggling girl traced a finger down his back.

"Don't flatter yourself, Tom, it is the whiteness of your skin that amuses her." A little way up the path, Miriam wheeled her chair towards him, the mockery in her voice deflating him. "I think you had better put this on. Don't you? Just in case you get burned. With the sun, that is," she winked, holding out his jerkin to him.

Tom slipped in to it, now disappointed that the girl had only been interested in his peely-wally skin.

It was in that instant that the first burst of gunfire shattered the morning stillness.

"Quick Tom, turn me round! The gunfire came from the hotel! Into the bush as fast as you can!" Miriam shrieked her commands at him.

Cursing that things were going from bad to worse, Tom threw his jerkin into Miriam's lap, and spun the chair around, pushing and bumping it up the narrow path, spurred on by the closeness of the continuing gunfire, until he had reached the top of a slight incline and into the cover of a clump of trees, where gasping for breath he halted to take stock of what was happening below.

Suddenly, from around the corner of the hotel, came a panic stricken figure, who Tom instantly recognised as the one who had greeted them when they first arrived, running and gesticulating wildly, almost reaching the water trough before a volley of shots rang out, hurtling him to the ground.

"Look!" Miriam cried, pointing to her left where the small figure of Consquala was being hotly pursued by four or five laughing soldiers.

Tom stared in horror. Now he knew he could not do what Bogey would have done in his place. Frightened and ashamed, he knelt down beside the woman.

"Nothing. You can do nothing, Tom. Do not even think to try." Miriam knew what her young friend was thinking. "Except to get us out of here and in double quick time, if you will pardon the presumption."

It was not long until it was evident to Tom that the path of sorts he was running on was far too narrow for the chair, and that he could not possibly avoid or manoeuvre over or around all that lay in their way. Already, the vibration off hidden stones and tree roots, besides hampering their progress was taking its toll on his already aching muscles. What it was doing for the chair's occupant, he shuddered to think.

"I'm going to turn your chair round, that way I can pull you, and kick at anything I see blocking the way," Tom gasped.

For a time, Tom's plan worked until the chair came to a sudden stop, almost wrenching his arms from his body. Cursing aloud, he grasped the arms of the chair and lifted it over the offending pothole.

"Tom, they are following us!" Miriam flung into his ear as he bent to lift the chair again.

"Ye almost deafened me there hen!" Tom returned angrily. "It's bad enough not to see them comin' withoot not hearin' them in to the bargain."

Tom grabbed the back of the chair and drew it behind him regardless of the pain he might be inflicting on its occupant, knowing that if they had been seen there was no way he could outrun them. Their only chance was to hide. But where?

A little way further on, Tom hauled the chair a little distance into the high grass which bordered each side of the path, which to his relief sprang back into place as they passed.

Miriam held up her hand. "I think I hear them coming now, Tom." Both man and woman looked at one another and held their breath.

Tom let out his breath in a sigh of relief. "I think the buggers have gone past. But we'll have to wait to make sure, unless that is, they come back, if they do the ball burst as they say in China."

"They seem to have a lot of sayings in China. Have you been there Tom?"

Tom lay down, the tall grass almost hiding him from his questioner, as he answered. "Nearly, I knew one who ran a shop, near Cathcart Road."

"Do you think we should just lie here Tom? Shouldn't we be on our way?"

"Maybe," Tom shrugged. "But I'm a bit scared they might see the grass move if we do, and I don't know what's in front of us." In more ways than one, he thought.

"Oh, all right, General, you know best," Miriam answered, clearly impressed by the Scots quick thinking.

Pleased that a hoity-toity dame should think that someone as lowly as himself was capable of working out such a ploy, Tom clasped his hands behind his head and stared up though the narrow funnel of light to the deep blue sky beyond.

Despite his heart beating as fast as when the 'Jags' had almost scored, he found himself beginning to doze. Somewhere through the thickening clouds, Big Dougie was shaking his head in disbelief at the 'Miriam Plesher Story'. "Yer tryin' tae make me believe ye pushed an auld English wumman, auld enough tae be yer Granny, half across some heathen country because she telt ye she wis workin' fur the goodies'? Come aff it Ding ye were shacked up wi' some doll, that's why yer late back for work."

Suddenly, the 'doll' was speaking to him. "I think it will now be safe to go. What do you think, Tom?"

Not another surprise, Tom thought, she's actually asking for my opinion; must be too much sun. Tom rose swiping at the flies and other insects that had come all the way from Mexico for a bite of prime Scotch beef. "I better take a wee look see. Then if the coast is clear wherever the hell that might be, we can be on our way."

Some time later, turning a corner on an unfamiliar road, Tom brought the chair to an abrupt halt, totally unprepared for what lay before them.

For a moment, Tom stood there frozen, unaware how tightly he was grasping the back of the chair, then, as if having awoken from a nightmare moved round the chair to the scene of carnage.

The bus had once been green. Now rust showed through the

bodywork: the tyres almost threadbare. Slowly, reluctant to see more, he moved along its length, aware of dead staring eyes looking out at him through the shattered windows.

The stench was almost unbearable as Tom reached the door, and he put one hand over his nose and mouth, and with the other swiped at the incessant flies, swarming around the mutilated body of the driver lying on the steps.

Drunkenly, Tom reeled against the handrail and wrenched up, his vomit running down the rusted door. Trembling with shock, he wiped his mouth with the back of his hand, and stumbled back to where he had left the woman in the chair, angry at the seemingly senseless barbarity of it all.

"Why?" he croaked at her. After all, was not this all her fault? Her game? It had nothing to do with him.

Miriam understood the young Scot's look and the accusation in his voice. Poor Tom, how she wished it had not been he who had come to her aid. This rough, sometimes course Scot with his weird sense of humour.

"This is why I am trying to reach my friends, Tom, so that in my own small way, I can play a part in preventing such horrors happening again."

Tom heard the words but did not look at the speaker, for now he was staring at the green clad soldiers silently emerging from the trees behind the lady in the wheelchair.

Chapter 3

Entering the military compound, the open topped car swung in a wide arc and drew to a halt in front of a squat whitewashed building, and before Tom knew what was happening rough hands had dragged him from the vehicle and up the steps into a tiny office, where behind a desk, much too large for the room, and its occupant, an elderly soldier, sat flicking at a fly with a swatter.

At the sight of this pusillanimous newcomer's interruption to his aerial attack on the insect, an amused smile spread over the officer's face.

Admitting to an instant fear of this evil looking man who was signalling to the guards to stand him up against the wall, Tom sought safety by focusing on the patched wooden ceiling, and wanting more than ever to cry out that he was simply a tourist in the country and knew nothing, and cared even less about their internal and infernal politics, except that for once he could not get his tongue to work. Or he would also have told them he knew even less about this woman in the wheelchair the two soldiers had planked down beside him.

"What kind of outrage do you call this?" Miriam exploded in English, swinging her wrath from the elderly Captain to the one remaining guard and back again.

"Que?" the Captain asked taken aback by the crippled woman's fortuitous outburst.

"Get yourself ready Tom," Miriam gave her would be interrogator a saccharin smile, pretending to have mellowed. "This old fool hasn't understood a word I've said."

"Get myself ready?" Tom choked studying the ceiling again, and wishing he'd stuck to the west coast of home for his holiday, even Saltcoats on a bad night was miles better than this. At least there, you had a chance of survival.

When he looked again, Miriam was in the process of handing her handbag to the guard, while at the same time bringing her free hand up from the inside of her chair, her finger wrapped round the trigger of a pistol.

"Now Tom, relieve both these kind gentlemen of their weapons, if you please," she asked of him prosaically.

Glued to the spot, Tom was unable to believe his eyes at the expert way Miriam Plesher was holding the small Beretta and if this lady made a habit of this sort of thing.

Gradually his senses returned, and he moved shakily forward, gingerly extracting the weapons from each of his would be captors, and clutching them to him as if they were red hot, and trying not to pass wind, or something similar.

"Not quite the Bogey type, are you Tom?"

Tom glared down at her, as she explained.

"I mean Bogey would be pointing one of those at the baddies by this time and not leaving it all to a mere woman."

"Bogey didnae come here on a A1 Tour either," was all he could say in defence of his masculinity. "But, as another of my hero's would say, another nice mess you have gotten me into. If somebody comes, we're history."

Miriam pointed to a door to her left. "What's through there?"

Jerking the door open, Tom stole a quick look inside. "It's a toilet of sorts, washbasin and things."

"Good. Shove them in there and lock the door."

Obeying orders, Bogey Junior pushed their prisoners inside, still afraid of the noxious little Captain and the hostile way he was looking at him, and vehemently hoping that they would never meet again…not after this.

"Find out if there is a guard outside." Miriam rapped out.

Tom crossed to the slightly open door, and nervously snapped a look outside. "It's all clear, the guards are on the other side of the compound."

"Good. This is what we have to do."

Miriam 's instructions were that Tom should carry her down to the car parked by the step where their captors had left it, ignoring her protests that something was wrong when he returned to retrieve her precious wheelchair.

"I'm on the wrong side! That's what I was trying to tell you. Did you forget this is a left hand drive, Tom?"

"No, I didn't forget. It's all the same to me, I can't drive." Tom blurted out darting a look across the compound and dreading the moment the guards would look in their direction.

"Don't you have cars in Scotland?"

"Aye, tramcars, and I wish I was on one now."

"Quick! Round the other side and I will tell you what to do."

"What a bloody time for a driving lesson!" Tom burst out, running round to the driver's seat, surprised to find Miriam had somehow managed to pull herself over to the passenger's side.

Miriam shot a quick glance past her pupil to the guards. "Listen carefully, Tom. The guards are certain to look across here as soon as the car starts up. So, when I say now, push your foot up and down on that pedal." She pointed to the accelerator. "And, when I give you a second instruction, press your left foot down on this pedal, that's the clutch. I'll do the rest."

"I'll do it all wrong!" Tom wailed, his despondency compounded by this imperturbable creature by his side. "I'm sure to cross my legs. And when those soldiers look up and see me, I'll keep them crossed."

"Press your foot down now," Miriam continued, unperturbed, as if she was at home instructing her favourite nephew on his first driving lesson.

As Tom gripped the wheel tight with both hands, Miriam turned on the ignition and the engine leaped into life.

"Not so hard!" his female instructed shouted in his ear above the roar of the engine.

"Sorry."

"Now you've taken your foot off too quickly!" she berated him, as the engine died. "Now press down again!" Miriam's voice rose. "They've seen us! Down with your left foot...No! No! Keep your right foot on the pedal as well!" she yelled as the vehicle leaped forward.

"I'm running out of feet, wee wumman!" Tom yelled at her over the din of the racing engine and the gunshots now levelled in their direction.

"Lift your left foot...very...very slowly," Miriam coaxed, her hand on the gear stick. "Keep your right foot on the other pedal."

With a bang, the car backfired and shot forward in first gear towards the gate, then the wall, then the gate again, soldiers running after them, shots pinging all around.

"Take your left foot off the pedal now, Tom. Keep your right foot on the accelerator and concentrate on steering," Miriam snapped, clutching his jerkin in her lap.

The wheel bouncing and jerking in his hands, Tom aimed for the gate, as a shot, closer than some, ricocheted off the side of the car.

"See, you've made them angry. They know I don't have a licence," he yelled, as another shot thudded into the panel between them. Then, they were through with inches to spare on the driver's side.

Miriam reached over, and helped him slide the steering wheel through his hands. "What's up wee wumman? You'd think I'd never driven a car before!" Tom hurled at her, believing the danger to be over.

His passenger threw him a cautionary look. "Put your left foot on the pedal again. It might help if we get into second gear. Good boy. A little more...push with your right."

And, in this way, the woman coaxed him through the gear changes until they were travelling at a respectable speed in top gear.

A mile or so from the gate, Tom's instructor threw a quick glance behind her. "A little faster, Tom, I believe we are being followed, though they are still some distance away."

"Oh! A car chase as well, and on my very first day! Eat your heart out Bogey!" Tom faked.

Inwardly, he felt sick. There was no way in the world he could outrun experienced drivers or even inexperienced ones. The very fact he'd got the thing to move at all was in itself an achievement.

"Put your foot down, boy. Don't bother with the rest of the pedals. Oh! By the way the other one down there is the brake. We do not use that one in conjunction with the accelerator."

"What's all this 'we' stuff, I'm doing the driving," Tom reminded her out of the corner of his mouth.

"Sorry, I thought we were in this thing together." The woman commanding at a bend looming before them, "Ease your foot off the accelerator, Tom. Now push your left foot down and hold it there. I want to change down a gear or two. If you don't mind, that is?" she asked sarcastically, and received a grunt as a reply.

Once round the bend, the woman pointed to a dirt road climbing off to their right. "Keep it at this speed until I tell you to slow down. Now a bit slower...that's about right. Turn now! Keep it steady...good. Take it nice and slow up here, we don't want to kick up too much dust and give away our position," she cautioned, casting an anxious eye down the hill behind them. Then satisfied that they were not being followed, turned her attention to the road ahead.

For a time, they travelled on in silence, the passenger deep in thought, the driver concentrating on keeping the car on the rutted road. Eventually, Miriam nodded at the road ahead. "Halt on the crest of this hill, Tom, it's pretty open country around here, so we shall have an unobstructed view of anyone following us. Also, I think we should find out where we are, and where this road leads to…if anywhere."

With a jerk and a shudder, Tom brought his vehicle to a halt. "Sorry about that lady." He gave her an apologetic grin.

"You did remarkably well for your first lesson," Miriam praised, leaning over to switch off the ignition.

"Did I pass? Do I get my licence now?" Tom stretched himself, proud of his achievement. "Or do I have to do it all in reverse?"

Ignoring his banter, Miriam rummaged around in the glove box, extracting what looked like a map. "This might tell us something," she said hopefully.

While the woman studied the map, Tom got out of the opened topped car, and surveyed the barren landscape, a landscape which contrasted sharply to the bush country around the hotel they'd left earlier, reminding him of the soldiers chasing after Consquala. "I wonder if she is all right?" he said aloud as if Miriam had been privy to his thoughts.

"Who is all right?" Miriam asked absently, while concentrating on the outspread map on her lap.

"Consquala and the rest, back at yon hotel," Tom explained, scanning around for a place to relieve himself.

"You know it was us they were after."

Tom spun round from skimming a stone into a pile of rocks. "What makes you think that?"

Miriam peered through her brows at him. "Simple. The soldiers did not bother to surround the village. They made directly for our hotel."

"You mean someone informed on us?"

The greying head swung back to the map. "Something like that. Now they know where we are."

"Which is more than we do," Tom added contemptuously.

Once again, he had an overwhelming desire to be out of this unreal evil world he had involuntarily got himself into. Also, he found it difficult to reconcile these happy friendly people with those who had attacked the hotel earlier that day. Nor could he get it out of his head that it was their unsolicited presence there that had led to the death of at least two innocent people. Then, there had been their own capture, however brief…well so far at least that was, by those who had attacked the bus. Tom shuddered at the vision and at the thought of that wee shit and his fly swatter.

"This road will not lead us anywhere near Meda or Corona, at best we shall come out about sixty kilometres east of Meda," Tom heard his patriarchal guardian say from where he had strayed to the edge of the road.

"Oh well, it cannot be helped." Tom climbed back into the car. "Where to now ma'am?" He touched his forelock in a fair imitation of a chauffeur.

"Only one way, my good man," Miriam responded in the same vein, "that way." She pointed to the road ahead.

Tom was beginning to enjoy this new driving experience, now he'd got the hang of it. At least, if he got nothing else out of this holiday, excluding a bullet up the bum, he had learned to drive. And, much to his surprise, the lady had left him to it, only intervening when necessary. Or to offer up a prayer when he looked like he was running out of road.

The wide expanse of desert that they were now passing through reached as far as the distant mountains shimmering in the hot afternoon sun. He was thirsty and hungry. One piece of toffee and a tepid drink of water he'd managed to scoop up in a cabbage like leaf was all they had had since morning. Even a slice or two of the hotel's revolting cheese would not have gone amiss.

"The place looks a bit stoorie." Tom nodded at the lunar like landscape. "It could do with a good dusting," he explained.

Miriam screwed up her face. "I'd hate to be the housemaid to have to do it." She consulted her map. "Shouldn't be too long 'till we're off this road. I'd say about thirty kilometres on we should come to a junction, meeting a road running east, which with any luck should take us north, and nearer to Corona then Meda." Her appraisal done, the lady folded the map and sat back.

An hour or so later, the map reader proved correct, when, with a screech of brakes and a crash of gears, they swung on to a metalled road.

"That town we saw from up there on the mountain road should not be too far from here, Tom." Miriam pinned a finger on the map.

"Good. I'm starving. And with this heat, I could murder a pint." Tom eased himself in his seat, the car slowing as his foot came off the accelerator. He pushed down again but the car continued to slow.

Miriam caught a glimpse of sunlight reflecting on a stream a little way beneath them. "Do you think it safe to stop here? We're sitting ducks for anyone coming round the bend ahead?"

"I'm not stopping, but this damned thing is! What am I doing wrong?" Tom pushed harder on the pedal.

Miriam leaned towards him. "You're not doing anything wrong my boy, we are simply out of fuel."

"Back to Shank's pony, then. I thought it was too good to be true." Tom heaved a sigh, swearing under his breath at the prospect of having to push that contraption he'd thrown in the back once more, and wishing he'd left it in wee Mussolini's office.

"'Fraid so."

The car crashed down the embankment, disappearing into the trees with a crack of snapping branches and a shriek of tortured metal.

When all was still again, Tom slung his jerkin over the back of the wheelchair and began to push. Already the sun was hot on his back and the heat off the road burned through the soles of his shoes. He pushed harder, damning the soldier who had only half filled the petrol tank. "How far did you say this town was?"

"I didn't, but at a rough guess, I'd say about ten kilometres."

"In the name o' the wee man, I'll be burned tae a frazzle by that time." The shock of the distance momentarily slackened Tom's pace.

"We better be on the lookout for oncoming traffic." Miriam fanned herself with the borrowed map. "We must be very careful. After all, they know we are in the vicinity."

Tom did not much care for this 'they' business. Who were the 'they' she kept going on about, he'd like to know, but then again, perhaps not.

"We must keep our eyes peeled, Tom."

"If I see anything peeled around here, I'll eat it!"

Later, rounding a bend, they almost run into a road-block some distance ahead, saved only by their silence from being seen. Too afraid to turn the chair round for fear of the movement catching the eye of one of the guards, Tom retraced his steps, until he was round the bend once more and out of sight.

"What do we do now, wee wumman?" Tom asked, his voice barely audible, as he retreated even further from the bend.

"Obviously, we shall have to find an alternative way around this obstruction."

Tom damned her coolness, when he himself was shaking with fear. "How do we do that? Not with your gun again, I hope?"

"Not we, Tom. You."

Tom kicked angrily at a stone. "Serves me right for asking. I should have known better."

The Chief of State Security stood looking down at the trembling girl, sitting hunched in the chair, her glazed eyes fixed solidly on the table, now and again pulling at the blanket draped around her shoulders in an attempt to hide her nakedness.

Segovia moved slowly and deliberately towards the terrified girl, his smile devoid of any warmth as he asked. "Senorita, I shall ask you one more time. Why was the hotel owner whom I believe is also your cousin, helping people who are enemies of our country?"

Consquala bowed her head, her voice barely audible. "I told you before Colonel, he was not."

"So you say." Segovia blew cheroot smoke at the ceiling. "Perhaps this will help you change your mind." Savagely he grasped the girl's hair, thrusting back her head to point out of the window at the two figures tied to wooden stakes.

Through the open window, Consquala heard the old truck driver, his face streaked with blood, cry out his innocence. Beside him, her cousin Sergio, his face contorted with the pain of a bullet wound sagged against his bonds.

"It is not too late to save them. Now will you tell me why the old man brought the two foreigners here…to this hotel, when they told him they were journeying to Meda!"

Segovia thrust his face close to the girl's ear. "You must see there is no logic to it," he whispered. "Your village is nowhere near where these Inglesa say they were going. So why did that old fool bring them here?"

At her silence, Segovia straightened, deliberately dropping ash from his cheroot upon her bare arm.

Clenching her teeth to fight back the pain, Consquala focused on the rows of silent villagers constrained by a line of stern faced soldiers.

"You do not want to see either of them executed, do you Senorita?" the Colonel asked, following her gaze. "We know Monola does not believe the reason given by the Ingles for being on the road without transport."

Segovia turned his attention away from the window to the shaking girl, offering her time to digest this information. Suddenly, with one quick movement he wrenched away the blanket, leaving her to cover her nakedness as best she could, and crossing the hotel's tiny kitchen threw himself into a chair in the corner of the room, smiling crookedly at the girl sitting with her arms crossed to hide her breasts.

He was only too well aware of the facts of the situation. The old man had told the truth, but it did no harm to instil a little fear into villagers such as these, and perhaps in doing so, prevent the outrages against his President from spreading.

The Colonel let his eyes and imagination wander over the naked girl, feeling a sudden excitement for her, as well as a deep enjoyment at the power he had over these stubborn peasants; and, should they fear him personally, so much the better.

Rising, Segovia smoothed down his already immaculate uniform. "Perhaps if you are a good girl and do as I say, you may yet save yourself and your friends." Segovia threw away the last of his cheroot and crossed to stand over the terrified girl.

Staring at the floor, Consquala's lips moved in a silent prayer, as the Chief of State Security bent to stroke her cheek.

"In other words, you are telling me there is no way round." Miriam Plesher faced her young associate across the space of the tiny adobie hut.

"There was barely cover for myself on this side of the roadblock, and none on the far side."

"Did you see the town?"

Tom sank wearily down against the wall. "It doesn't seem large enough for a town, more a village, I'd say."

"So we're trapped in this valley. All we have to do is wait until we are picked up. Damn these useless legs of mine!" Miriam clawed at Tom's jerkin in her lap in frustration. "So, we cannot bypass the roadblock and continue up the valley." Miriam stared at the wall, her mind searching for a solution. "Then we must leave it by another way."

"Do you mean go back the way we came?" Tom scratched the back of his hand. "Won't it be a bit risky? They must know we are headed in this direction, hence the roadblock."

"Who said anything about going back? Since we cannot go up the valley, then we must cross it…or should I say over it?"

Tom leapt to his feet, glaring down at the woman, all sympathy instantly dissipating. "What do you mean over it? Have you seen the height of those mountains? I couldn't get over them in an aeroplane," he exploded, having decided he had enough.

"Do you want to be caught and tortured for what you know? Or should I say for what you do not know?" she asked icily, intending to shock. "And it will avail you nothing to protest you are simply a tourist from an obscure place called Scotland."

Tom choked back an impulse to say, they play football too in this country so they will have heard of Scotland. Then, thinking of his own team, the Jags quickly changed his mind.

He found her, looking at him intently. "It's our only chance Tom. Besides, if Hannibal could do it, why not us?"

Defeated, Tom murmured under his breath, "aye maybe so, but Hannibal didnae have tae carry his bloody elephants."

Later, in the growing darkness, the Scot stood by the door of the hut looking at the woman sitting there, hands clasped in her lap, never before having felt so conscious of her vulnerability.

To all appearances, she was nothing other than a helpless old woman, yet inwardly he had never met so resilient a personage. If he was as quick at pushing her chair as she was with her brain, they would already be in Corona.

Aware of Tom's consternation, Miriam gave him a reassuring smile. "I'll be all right. You mind and look after yourself. You do remember all we shall require for the journey?"

Tom's answer was something between a grunt and a sigh as he pulled on his jerkin. His thoughts of what would become of this stubborn old Sassenach should anything happen to him, for there was no way in the world she could negotiate that path by herself. If so, to where and what?

As if Miriam had read his thoughts, she wagged a finger

reassuringly. "I've been in worse situations than this, Tom."

"Aye," Tom thought, "that's what Big Dougie said before they half kicked his heid in at Parkheid." Aloud, he said, "What should I do if I get caught? I mean, should I tell them to come here for you? I can't very well leave you...."

"No!" the venom in the woman's voice startled him. "No Tom, on no account tell anyone where, or who I am. Is that clear?"

Recovering from the ferocity of the woman's unexpected outburst, Tom held out his hands in surrender. "Okay, okay, keep the head then woman," he fumed, as if things were not bad enough. "I best be on my way then," he managed to say a little calmer.

Only when he was in the act of closing the door did he hear Miriam call out, in a tone more in keeping with her old self, "please be careful, Tom. After all, I am responsible for you, you know. Whatever shall I say to Mr MacKendrick if you fail to appear for work?"

"Bugger Mr MacKendrick," he said through the closed door and heard her laughing as he turned away. Then, there was only the silence of the night.

Chapter 4

Hauling the wheelchair behind him, Tom pushed the door open, shuddering in the early morning's chill.

All things considered they had both spent a reasonably comfortable night, thanks to the blankets he'd acquired from the shop, and despite the lack of light in the hut when he had returned from his shop breaking, had made a fair job of packing his newly acquired knapsack with tinned food whilst relating his earlier adventures to the lady.

Much to his surprise, Miriam had not chastised him for returning minus a few important articles, but on the contrary praised him for his cool head in the face of such odds. He remembered the conversation. "After all," she had said wistfully, "it has been your first attempt at breaking and entering."

Feeling better for this, though angry at having his jacket torn whilst attempting to squeeze through the back shop window of a small store, Tom attempted to equal his companion's trick with the apple, by producing his piece de resistance, six blocks of some sort of Latin American chocolate, guaranteed not to melt due to the lack of the main ingredient…chocolate.

"Well done, Tom," Miriam stifled a giggle. "For this, I shall happily carry that monstrosity of a primus you acquired, it could make all the difference where we are going."

Tom frowned. "As long as it's not to jail, for now I'm wanted by both sides, the polis and the peasants."

"Cheer up," Miriam encouraged him. "You'll be a hero when you get back home. You may even impress Mr MacKendrick, and tell him where to put his job."

Tom stared at her through the darkness unable to believe what he had heard, and unable to resist a laugh at her earnest expression. "I would gladly, wee wumman, except I think he's got a few o' Big Dougie's blueprints there already!"

"I'm glad we're not going up there." Tom nodded at the wall of mountains, shrouded in the early morning mist.

"No, Tom, we will have to go round them."

Soon, Tom was confronted by the first rise of ground, a molehill in other circumstances, but right now a major obstacle to someone pushing a wheelchair. Leaving the chair, he scrambled to the top of the grassy slope where, shedding his pack, he studied the surrounding terrain to work out an easier ascent. At last, satisfied at finding one, he returned to the foot of the 'molehill'.

"Jings, you're heavier that I thought wee wumman," Tom rasped, setting down the uncomplaining woman by a rock halfway to the top of his molehill.

"I'm afraid I will get heavier as the day wears on," Miriam said ruefully, rearranging her skirt. "I know this sounds perfectly beastly from one who is causing you all this unnecessary toil, but we must push on, for fear your theft has come to the attention of those soldiers at the roadblock, should they at all guess the purpose of the rope, extra clothing etc."

Although Tom knew the woman meant no offence, he felt angry. They had hardly made any progress and already he was knackered. Instead he said, "point taken," and started back down the hill for her chair.

Having toiled unceasingly all morning, and now in to the late afternoon, Tom collapsed exhausted in the lee of a hillock. Leaning his back against a boulder, sweat streaming down his bare chest, he blinked through salt-filled eyes at the woman sitting so imperturbably in her wheelchair.

"I need a wee rest...just a minute or two to catch my breath," he pleaded.

"I know, Tom, but we are not so very far from the roadblock and the village." Miriam's voice shifted from the sympathy she felt for this likeable young man to one of firmness. "We must keep going. Leave me here for a while and take yourself off to where you can see what is happening at the roadblock. Perhaps then it will give us some room to manoeuvre. And, put your shirt back on, you'll burn if you don't." She held the garment out to him

Tom struggled to his feet and took the shirt from her. "I won't be long and, if I think we are safe enough here, we can have something to eat."

"Did you see anything, Tom?" Miriam asked as he returned.

"No, there was too much heat haze. But, there was no one on the lower slopes or coming this way, as far as I could make out."

He settled down beside her. Miriam handed him an open tin of fruit, her tone derisory as she said. "Pears Tom. You picked tin pears!"

"At least, you will not have to cook them. Besides, it was dark in that shop," he mumbled between mouthfuls. "And, I shouldn't grumble if I were you, they sold tins of fertilizer there as well."

A little later, he left her dozing in her chair and went off to climb the next hillock. An hour later, they were on its top.

"We can use them to hold water," the perspiring woman held out the two empty pear tins for his inspection. Tom turned them over in his hands. Both lids had been squeezed back into place. "I also unravelled a few strands of rope and tied them around the cans, it will make them easier to carry when we fill them with water."

"So, there is still hope for the Empire yet, you English can actually think for yourself," he teased and was greeted by a suitable retort.

The redoubling of his efforts to ensure they'd not been seen had now left him completely drained. Involuntarily, Tom shivered in the approaching chill of the evening, finding it difficult to comprehend how the intense heat of the day gave way so suddenly and easily to the bitter cold of night.

It was so different from home. At home, when it was cold, it stayed cold. If it was hot…it was a miracle. If it was wet, it was the 'Glasgow Fair', their annual summer holiday. Jings, he must stop thinking about home, or he would find himself goin' roon the bend.

Gathering the last of the wood together, he made his way down the hill to the tiny figure almost completely hidden in the shadow of the surrounding rocks.

Frustrating as it may be for him climbing and re-climbing these foothills, what must it be like for someone with the mental astuteness of Mrs Plesher, almost unable to help herself physically, and believing herself to be more a hindrance than a contributor. Sadly, he shook his head. He had a lot to be thankful for.

"This is all I could find. If we run out of wood during the night, please leave my head alone, wee wumman."

"You flatter yourself…you'll be safe enough, some things don't burn." She answered without lifting her head from her task. "There! You may put this on the fire to heat." She handed him the can. "At least, it's not pears this time!"

"You should think yourself lucky, lady. You know I can't read the labels." Tom pushed the can into the centre of the fire with a stick.

Their frugal meal over, Tom threw the last of the twigs on to the fire.

"Would you mind lifting me out of this chair, Tom?" Miriam asked suddenly above the noise of crackling twigs. "I should very much like to lie beside the fire tonight."

Tom crossed to where she sat and lifted her out of the chair. Miriam put an arm around his neck. "But first, before you tuck me in, a little detour…behind a boulder."

Tom rounded the boulder and sat her down. "I think I'll take a walk up the hill a wee bit," he got out awkwardly and knew he was blushing. "See if our fire can be spotted…maybe a wee bit more firewood into the bargain. Though lord knows where, seeing as there are no trees around." Embarrassed, he turned away.

At the top of the slope, Tom stared into the darkness of the night, relieving himself. Nothing but emptiness. For all he knew, they could be the last folk on earth. Done, he started back down the slope.

"Could it be seen?" The question came at him from the figure wrapped in a blanket by the fireside.

"What? How did you get there?"

"Have you never crawled, Tom?"

"Aye, every day at Johnston's." Tom's voice shifted to one annoyance. "You should have let me carry you back. It's no bother."

"You have done quite sufficiently for one day, young man. Besides, you will need all your strength for tomorrow."

"How far do you think we have to go?" Tom settled down, drawing the blanket up to his chin.

"I really can't say. All I have to go on is this scanty road map I found back in the car. But, at a guess, I'd say three days."

"Three days!" Tom choked, the blanket dropping from him. "We cannot bide up here for three days!"

"We can if we must." That was said determinedly. "So get your rest, you have another big day ahead of you tomorrow."

Miriam was right. The next day was much a repetition of the first. Except, coming upon a stretch of water, not much larger than a pond, they took the opportunity to wash and dry their clothes.

Hidden by the rocks, Tom lay floating on his back, basking in the sun. At last! This was the life! He closed his eyes and splashed water on his face to help him recover from the sight of his own reflection in the water.

There was stubble on his chin and his face was a bright red. His nose too, was the right colour for halting traffic. As for his chest? At the moment, it was in several different stages of decay from sunburn. And how his back itched. Had not the lady warned him?

Tom stole a glance in the direction of the main pond, glimpsing the white body of his advisor and source of all his troubles bathing some distance away. Self consciously, he averted his eyes. How different all this could have been if, instead of the body floating over there, it had been a Jean Harlow type. Tom bit his lip, loathing himself at the thought.

Again, he was unsure what was happening to him, and who this strange English lady really was. He'd taken all she'd told him at face value but for all he knew she could be the head of an international smuggling ring. Being a cripple was no criteria for honesty, just as one did not suspect a woman dressed in a religious habit of being a bank robber. Tom bolted upright in the water. What if he had been pushing and carrying a woman who was not in fact a cripple at all? He slid back down splashing water with his toes. No, there were too many things against that. Her invalidity had almost cost them their freedom back at the hotel. And even if the soldiers were trying to catch Mrs Plesher in her capacity as a criminal, and not as a stalwart of democracy, she'd still stuck to her original role. And, with those soldiers breathing up his…Tom pushed his feet against a rock. Boy, if that were true…it took guts! And, come to think of it, when it came to guts the old dear had those in plenty.

The early evening chill found them much higher in the surrounding hills than the previous day. Sitting at her feet, Tom glanced at the road map, then up at the range of mountains Miriam had called a serria on the first day of their mountaineering.

"They dods of stone are getting a bit close for ma liking." Tom nodded at the mountains.

"I'm not quite sure that I understood all of that, Tom. However if you mean those mountains, well I didn't expect the distance to be so great between the valley and our destination."

Tom held up the map for her to read. "Where exactly is our

destination, if not over those Cairngorms there?"

Miriam stabbed a finger at a point on the map. "There...Izeda."

"That's miles away! It will take us days to get there." He held the map up to his eyes as if by doing so it would help bring the town closer. "Even if I don't keel over with exhaustion, we don't' have enough food."

"I know, Tom. It's my fault. A bad decision. We should have lain low instead. Perhaps, back in the foothills, we could have watched the roadblock from there."

"It's too late for that." He saw her dejection and rushed to console her. "No. You were right. Had we stayed, sooner or later we'd have been seen. What's for supper?"

Happier at his deduction, the woman searched inside the knapsack.

"Pears!" she said, holding up the can.

The British Attaché slid the passports across the polished desk. "We are rather concerned over the disappearance of two of our Nationals, Colonel. We hoped...that is..." the young diplomat hesitated, pulling at his ear lobe. "I was hoping, despite," he hesitated again, "shall we say the unrest your country is at present unfortunately experiencing, that you might somehow spare some of your most valuable time to render His Majesty's Government a very great service by assisting us in our inquiries as regards their whereabouts." The young man wriggled in his chair, conscious of his shortcoming in diplomatic phraseology.

Colonel Roberto Segovia picked up the documents and carefully examined each in turn. "They are missing, Mr Attaché? You British do not know where you have put them?"

Ignoring the laugh and obvious sarcasm, the Attaché continued. "The lady, I believe, you already know. Wife of the late Ambassador Harry Plesher?"

"Yes...yes...I know all about this Mrs Plesher," the Colonel broke in impatiently. "Presumably you have first called at her home?"

Recalling his training, the young man strove to project an air of decorum befitting his position. "Of course, Colonel, we have also contacted her friends, no one has seen her for several days. We fear with all the disturbances in the city, she may..."

"Disturbances! Phew! The work of a few fanatics whose sole

purpose is to defame our beloved President and all that he stands for in this great country of ours. Be assured they will be dealt with, and most severely, and very shortly."

Segovia reached for his box of cheroots, thought better of it and drew back his hand.

"Have you tried the hospitals?"

The young man nodded.

"If I remember correctly, the lady does not have the use of her legs. Si? Should this be so she cannot be so very far away. And this man?" Segovia held up the second passport. "Does he know this lady?"

"There is no evidence to substantiate that he has ever made her acquaintance. I am satisfied that each disappearance is completely unconnected."

Segovia shrugged, a small smile flickering at the corner of his mouth.

The young Englishman continued. "Mr Bell is a tourist from Britain, Glasgow to be exact."

"Glasgow?"

"Glasgow in Scotland."

"Ah Scotland! Where the Scotch comes from." Segovia raised an imaginary glass to his lips. "Whisky! Yes!"

"Quite, Colonel," the young Attaché conceded, becoming more exasperated by the turn of conversation. "Mr Bell came here on an arranged holiday by the American tourist company A1 Tours. He was residing at the Hotel Capital until five days ago, and according to his courier he has not been seen since. And, as Mr Bell's entire belongings, including his passport you now hold in your hand, were left in the hotel, we can only assume the worse. Mr Bell's steamer left yesterday. We are now in the process of contacting his next of kin…an uncle, whom I believe, was instrumental in making this holiday possible."

The young man hesitated to let the man sitting so smugly opposite him digest the international ramifications of the situation.

Suddenly, and without warning, Segovia stood up, indicating that the interview was at an end. "I shall see what can be done to assist His Majesty's Government. Meantime, I suggest while you wait to hear from me, you enjoy the product of the place you call Scotland. Myself, I prefer it …how do you say…neat?"

As the door closed behind His Majesty's junior diplomat, Segovia pulled a file from his desk drawer. Why had they sent that young oaf to confer with one such as Roberto Segovia, he wondered, opening up the file? Did the British take him for a fool? He ran his eyes over the report, tapping the file when the significance of a particular passage arrested his attention.

With the file spread out before him, the Chief of State Security stared without seeing the portrait of the man he had sworn to protect stare back at him from the opposite wall.

According to this report, after the escape of the two foreigners from the hotel, they were eventually apprehended and taken to the garrison at Tordessa, where that imbecile of a Commander had let them escape. Not only that, but in a vehicle of the armed forces! Segovia shook his head in exasperation.

How could this be so? Unless, of course, his deductions were correct concerning the young man, that dolt of an Attache would have him believe was a simple tourist, which would explain how that young man had engineered an escape from the compound of an army garrison, burdened with an ageing woman confined to a wheelchair! Also, how he had locked up the Commanding Officer in his own toilet! Controlling his anger, Segovia turned his attention once more to the file on his desk.

The stolen vehicle had eventually been found a few kilometres south of a roadblock, near the village of San Roa. To him, this was the most interesting part.

Besides, taking into account the ingenuity of the young British agent, he was certain they could not have succeeded in getting around the roadblock unseen. Therefore…Segovia studied the map of the area enclosed with the file. As the roadblock was set up at the entrance to the valley, and there were mountains on either side, it stood to reason they must still be somewhere in that vicinity.

This, he concluded, was substantiated by a villager who had reported the looting of his store to the soldiers at the roadblock. An incident which, at first, appeared to be completely unconnected, until the itemised list was included in the report and forwarded to him later here at headquarters.

Lighting a cheroot, Segovia tapped the list with his pen. "Food? A necessity to remain hidden for any length of time," he deduced. "Stove for cooking, blankets for warmth at night. Rope?" Here, the security chief halted, his cheroot hovering over the last item. "Rope," he said aloud, addressing the martially attired President on the wall. "Rope to pull the wheelchair, perhaps? At a loss, Segovia sat back and closed his eyes. When next he opened them, it was to stare in astonishment at the portrait on the wall, his lips working soundlessly.

"It could not possibly be...rope for climbing? Yet it makes sense. Would not the British agent be expected to do the unexpected?"

Eagerly, almost triumphantly, Segovia poured over the map. "Meda! Yes! Meda could be reached from the valley. How, he should not like to guess. Yet these were two desperate people both of whom were well aware of the importance of the information they possessed. And, should it fall into the hands of the enemies of the President? Segovia dropped his eyes to the desk, away from the portrait. Bug...the President. Should Roberto Segovia hang, then he would not hang alone. Therefore, it was in both their interests that these two meddlers be caught...and soon.

There were now no more green foothills sporting brown woolly Marino sheep; dirty looking beasts in comparison to the white-fleeced black-faced sheep of home. In their stead, rose stark desolation of glaring cliffs. Hoisting the woman back into his arms, Tom struggled on across the high valley, his eyes aching from the glare off the glittering stones, his sole consolation that he had only one more trip to make to retrieve the wheelchair.

Littered with almost pure white stones, the valley floor lay like some dried up riverbed to the cliffs beyond. Now that there was no other way forward, it was not necessary to leave the woman and her chair to pick out the best route. How he had come to loathe that chair, probably as much as the woman did herself.

Stumbling for the hundredth time, Tom sat Miriam down against a rock, laying the knapsack down beside her. The woman's voice was little more than a whisper as she implored him to have a rest before he returned for the chair. Having no need for a second invitation, he settled down beside her.

"What a place. A man could go blind with the glare off those chuckies," he said dejectedly, taking a blanket out of the knapsack and draping it over the woman's head and shoulders. "I think this will help a wee bit while I return for your transport. There you go,

Mrs Lawrence of Arabia," he chuckled, adjusting her new headdress. "That should give you a wee bit shade."

"You're a good boy Tom." Miriam gave him a worn tired smile. "It is a singularly peculiar country this. So hot by day, freezing by night."

"Aye, it reminds me of a lassie I once knew," Tom grimaced.

The woman carefully lifted a can of water from the sack and offered it to him. Gratefully, Tome took it, painfully aware that only three cans remained.

"What about you, wee wumman? Don't try and tell me yer no' thirsty?" His eyes travelled over her pain riddle face.

"I'll save mine for later, if you don't mind."

"See that you do." Tom rose, and handed her the half empty can. "Put that in the fridge 'till I get back, will you please?"

"You shan't be asking that tonight," she called after him, watching him stumble back across the glittering quartz for the chair.

They had spent most of the afternoon struggling across the valley to reach its northern wall, and with it a modicum of shade. Now, they lay exhausted, thankful for the rest and the luxury of closing their eyes against the painful glare off the shimmering stones.

Tom knew his strength was waning. Wearily, he reached into the sack for a can of water. "I'd hate to think after all this, they baddies are waiting for us in that town of yours," he croaked. "Jings!" Tom's voice rose a few decibels as he blew on his hands. "If only we had a way of preserving this heat 'till the night, we wouldnae need to humph that muckle great Primus around."

"You've lost me, Tom. Would you mind awfully repeating that in English please?" Miriam requested, screwing up her brows in puzzlement.

Tom changed the burning hot can from one hand to the other. "Skip it. As I was saying, in my best English, as was learned me at the public school I went to." Tom stared at the woman in mock severity. "What if the baddies are waiting for us in yon place…?"

"Izeda." Miriam apprised. "I should hope not. However, should your 'baddies' deduce we have out manoeuvred them by leaving the valley and crossing the mountains, it is my earnest hope they will think we have gone east to Meda, having given the old truck driver this impression back at our hotel, instead of westward to Izeda, and eventually Corona."

Tom drew up his feet from where he lay against the cliff wall. "Well, if you are right, all we have to do is get ourselves there." He levered himself up, dusting off his trousers. "I think I'll go roamin' in the gloamin' as they say in Outer Mongolia, and try and find the best way out of here. It's beginning to give me the creeps." He shivered, "I'll no' be long. Have a wee snooze while I'm away." And, with this, he set off across the valley floor.

After a while, he turned to look back at the tiny figure, sitting so peacefully in her chair in the lee of the cliff wall, surrounded by a sea of sparkling quartz, shuddering at how much depended on him for their survival. For, should anything happen to him away out here? He shivered again.

From the cliffs above, a flock of birds suddenly took to the air, screeching their protest at this gratuitous intrusion to their privacy. Tom followed their flight with a jealous eye. From the height in which they flew, he must look like an ant, struggling amongst grains of sugar.

A mile or so from where he'd left his charge, the cliffs finally relenting, allowed the climber a gradual access to the summit. Clutching at a rock, Tom hauled himself over the top where he lay for a time gasping for breath, his eyes on the mountain he'd first seen from the valley floor and which now looked even more foreboding at close quarters.

Rising, Tom held his face up to the cool breeze and began to walk away from the cliff edge his mind still on the mountain, when his foot hit a stone and he stumbled slightly. Cursing himself for not looking where he was going, Tom looked to where his next step would have taken him: there was nothing there. Shaking with fear, he slowly raised his eyes to the sky above, away from what lay beneath him. He tried to swallow but there was not enough saliva. He could not move. With an effort of will, he steeled himself to starc straight ahead, and sank to his knees, then slowly, ever so slowly crawled back. Then, as if drawn by some unfathomable curiosity – the way a person does when having suddenly seen something grotesque but unable to restrain themselves from looking again – Tom brought himself to stare into the midst of a black bottomless pit, well over a hundred yards in diameter.

Was he awake? Or was this his worse kind of nightmare? One, where no matter what you did you found yourself helplessly drawn towards the void, and without warning slipping over the edge twisting and turning, falling until you woke up screaming and drenched in sweat, and your heart was pounding with relief that it had all been a dream.

Summoning up his reserves of strength, Tom closed his eyes and backed away on all fours, oblivious to everything but the pounding of his heart. A few feet away, his groping hand found a stone and he hurled it angrily into the gaping black cavern. "Ten, eleven, twelve, thirteen." He counted off the seconds, waiting for the sound of it hitting the bottom. "There's no' bottom to the thing!" he cried in alarm. "Just like Big Dougie's stomach on a Saturday night's bevvy!"

Cautiously, Tom got to his feet and even more cautiously backed away, as if afraid the ground would open up around him. "That hole must go right doon tae China," he said aloud. "I wouldnae like tae be a quarry worker there when that chukkie I threw comes beltin' through. If it catches him in the wrong place, it could put a different slant on things, so to speak."

Now, feeling a little safer, Tom turned away from his nightmare, watching carefully where he stepped, and contemplating on how it had not seemed so long ago since he'd complained about everything under the sun, but now after his recent fright, he was only too grateful to be alive.

"One more tin of meat left after this one, Tom." Miriam stirred the contents of their second last can of meat on the primus.

Hunched against the cold of the evening Tom stared across the darkening terrain he'd struggled and stumbled over all of that long hot day. To reach this ridge they were now on had drained him of what little strength he had left, especially that last mile which had seemed longer than all the others put together that day. Finally, he had collapsed at Miriam's feet, angry and frustrated that no matter how hard he toiled this damned ridge had refused to come closer.

The woman had encouraged him, of course, coaxing him on to one final effort, forcing him to snap back at her that it was no use, as he had thought his braces had caught in the rocks a mile or so back. Then, it had been the woman's turn to collapse in a heap at the thought of his braces stretching and stretching, until he too was laughing and rolling on the hot hard baked ground at the very same thought. It was good they could still laugh, but for how much longer?

Tom crossed to the opposite side of the tiny ridge. Somewhere out there lay the town they were headed for. But how long would it take? And had he the strength to do it?

"Tom, your stew is ready," he heard Miriam call out, and he came back to sit beside her, warming his hands at the stove.

"Perhaps we should keep the stove on a little longer, Tom?"

He shrugged, past caring, too tired to argue. "We are no' goin' tae make it wee wumman on one wee tin of meat."

"Nonsense!" Miriam retorted angrily, though afraid to think that the boy might be right. But she had to keep him going somehow, for his own sake…for both their sakes, for so much depended on them reaching Corona. "Where is this famous fighting spirit you Scots always boast about?"

"For me, it's usually in a bottle, lady." He heaved a long shuddering sigh. "According to my reckoning, it will take another two days to reach a road, any road. I don't think I can carry you that far." He waved the can with his share of stew Miriam had given him. "The country on the other side of this ridge is as barren as the Rocks of Aden." He rubbed his hands together coaxing some warmth into them. "Now tell me something. When did you last see another living thing up here? An animal for instance…any animal. That's a sure sign our four legged friends, not to mention the slithering slidey ones, know better than we do that there is no water up here."

Miriam gave her own can a gentle stir. She must not let him give up now, not when she believed they were so close to Izeda, though Corona still seemed an insurmountable distance further on. "Then, you must proceed alone. Leave me in a safe place. I'll give you some money to purchase food. You can return and fetch me. Or just keep on going as you please."

Tom sprang to his feet his tiredness momentarily forgotten. "No way! What do you take me for? Do you think I could leave you here?" He waved a hand angrily. "There might not be many four-legged friends around to harm you, but I cannot speak for the two legged ones. At least, not the ones I've encountered since making your delightful acquaintance."

Miriam waved her spoon at him, the unexpected action halting him abruptly. "Oh, you are the one, Tom Bell, with that look of righteous indignation on your face," she scolded him. "Now eat your supper before it gets cold," she pointed to Tom's discarded can. "I apologise for even thinking you'd go on without me. We shall make it somehow, you wait and see, now that you have shown me some of that fighting Scot's spirit you say you apparently lack." She bent her head to scoop the last of her stew out of the can, hiding a smile at the boy's obvious pleasure.

Tom licked his spoon. "I wouldnae leave ye away up here." He examined his spoon to make sure he had licked it clean. "You see, ma sense o' direction is that bad, I might no' be able tae find ye again."

Miriam shot the speaker a quizzical look, unable to decide whether he was serious or not, then thinking better of it decided not to ask.

They left the ridge behind at first light, descending into a never-ending series of foothills. Tom struggled on, carrying the crippled woman for most of the day, the terrain in which they now travelled too rugged to wheel her chair.

Now, growing more despondent with every step, Tom cursed the ever increasing necessity to rest more often. Without fear of contradiction, his strength and spirits were at their lowest ebb, and unless he found some sustenance soon, he could not go on.

"Rest a while Tom, you look all in, my boy." Wearily, Miriam put out a hand to steady herself against a rock, biting back a cry at the pain in her back as the exhausted man dropped her more roughly than intended.

"Sorry," Tom said. After all, it was not his idea to climb over the Alps. Oh, how he wished he had just let them arrest him on the bus, then there would be no need for all of this.

Tom saw the state the woman was in and relented. "Never mind, wee wumman, we'll soon be there. In fact, I might write a postcard or two while I'm resting," he joked, holding his hand out and pretending to write. "To Mr Johnston and Mr MacKendrick, Dear both, wish you were here."

"You dislike them that much, Tom? You do make me laugh at the most inappropriate times."

Tom gave her one of his most mischievous smiles, and she answered for him. "Aye, that's what all the lassies say!"

The rain came without warning, drenching them within seconds, churning the dust-covered landscape to mud. Sliding on the banking, Tom felt his burden slip from his grasp, the woman's lifeless legs swinging like a rag doll. "I will have to put you down, it's impossible to carry you up yon slope," he bellowed in her ear above the wind and rain, and nodded to the cliff above.

Tom laid the saturated body down against an outcrop of rock and began to scramble up the slope, climbing steadily head bent against the wind until reaching the top, where he halted to draw breath and run a hand through his matted hair. It was then he saw the huge rock barring his way.

Tom screwed his eyes up against the blinding rain, sizing up the situation, it was either retrace his steps and search for an alternative way up, or with the aid of the rope manhandle both woman and chair over the obstacle. As the rain seeped through his good Co-op jacket, he contemplated on finding another way up. If, in fact, one did exist.

"It will be hard going," he shouted in Miriam's ear when he got back. "The only way I know of getting you up there," he nodded to the cliffs above, "is to carry you piggie back as they say down your way. Do you think you are up to it?"

Shivering in the torrential rain, Miriam pushed back a strand of sodden hair.

"If you get fed up for conversation, you can always listen to my teeth chattering," Tom tried to joke, putting his arm around the woman, and bellowing through the mounting storm, "just like Glasgow Fair holidays this, you know, except here, it's warmer."

Miriam gave no sign of understanding. Coughing, she buried her face in her hands.

"Come on Mrs Plesher, no time to give up now," he coaxed, drawing her closer to him. "Where's that English fighting spirit? The guards and all that…what?"

The man looked down at the woman's matted hair, feeling more pity for her than he had ever done before. If ever he doubted her genuineness, at least of one thing he was certain, she was indeed unable to use her legs. And, whatever else she may pertain to be, it was of no significance at this particular moment in time. Right now, all that really mattered was getting himself and this pitiful bundle of humanity to the top of this accursed chunk of rock.

Tom knelt down with his back to the woman, and tried to sing,

"Put your arms around me honey, hold me tight."

"Oh Tom," the woman moaned. "I wish I could appreciate your humour at this time."

Still kneeling, Tom waited until she wrapped her legs around his waist, then realising she could not, put his hands behind him, and grasping them, he hauled himself to his feet.

By the time he was back on the path again, the incessant rain had turned the path to mud, with the added danger of the wind blowing him and his burden against the rocks. Turning his head to the side, he sucked in great lungfulls of air, as with each slippery step his burden grew heavier. Then, without warning, he was down, clutching at a rock with one hand, while trying at the same time to prevent the woman from slipping off his back.

Miriam clung to him in fright, unaware she was choking and strangling the breath out of his struggling body. A final slide brought Tom to a halt, he, face down in the mud, the woman lying by his side.

"Leave me, Tom! Go on by yourself! You will never get me over that rock," she cried at him angrily, beating her fists in to the cement coloured mud in frustration.

Tom scraped mud from his hands. How long had they been trudging around these 'molehills'? How much sign of life had they seen? Even when he'd come across the odd snake, he'd been far too exhausted to feel afraid. At a guess, he'd say they were no more than thirty miles as the crow flies from the roadblock, and around the valley by road to that town he kept forgetting the name of, would be no more than two hours by car.

If the lady was wrong about their pursuers hunting for them on the opposite side of the valley from the roadblock, those same guys would be sitting cosily in a hotel awaiting their arrival. And, all his backbreaking climbing would have been for nothing. Well, maybe they could fool them by dying up here instead. It would serve the bad buggers right if they had to pay the hotel bill out of their own pockets.

Tom wiped mud off his face and put his hand out to help the woman.

Miriam recoiled, her face contorted with pain. "Leave me! You will never make it with me hanging around your neck like an Albatross," she screamed at him.

The sight of Miriam Plesher losing control for the first time made Tom feel afraid, a fear that quickly changed to anger. "No way! You got me into this, so you can bloody well get me out of it!" he hurled at her with all the anger he could muster. Even now, amidst his anger, he could not help feel pity for this poor wee soul, lying there so helpless in the mud, all semblance of dignity gone. The matted hair over her face, the once immaculate blouse and skirt caked with mud, her useless spindly legs showing through the rips in her stockings.

"Will you take a telling, Tom Bell? Go!"

All at once, the rapport over the last few days was gone. Roughly, and without mercy, Tom hauled her to her feet, and despite her protestations precariously made his way back to the foot of the slope where, still protesting, he dumped her without apology into the wheelchair.

Nursing his anger, Tom swung on his heel, and through the stinging rain searched the base of the cliff for an alternative route to the top. Suddenly, a small animal crashed out of a clump of bushes taking him by surprise, bolting away towards the foot of the cliff.

Fleetingly, Tom lost sight of it through the sheets of rain, before spying it again high on the cliff top. For a moment, he stood there blessing the unknown creature, and relishing their change of fortune, now he knew he had found their alternative route to the top.

It was almost dark when he returned to the top of the ridge with the wheelchair. Sweeping an arm under the woman, he sat her as gently as he dared in the chair, she avoiding his eyes as she had done during each and every rest.

Exhausted, he sank to the ground a few feet away from her. All at once, it was too much for him. Were they not miserable enough without this unnecessary self-infliction? He dragged himself across to the chair. "Can you see any shelter at all?" he asked as a means of reconciliation. "It's almost dark and we cannot bide here all night."

To his relief, Miriam responded to his overture, her tone intimating that nothing untoward had happened between them.

"No, Tom I cannot see very much at all through this rain. I think the best we can hope for is a little shelter down there." She pointed to a spot a little way down the slope.

"We'll try there, then," he answered, anxious to appease.

Their refuge was a clump of bushes, growing out of an outcrop of isolated rock, the illusion of shelter more mental than physical. Tom turned the wheelchair upside down to act as a roof and jammed it hard against the side of the outcrop, laying Miriam down inside it and wrapping an almost dry blanket from the knapsack around her.

Breathing some warmth into his cupped hands, Tom then set about gathering some stones which he piled in to a rough makeshift wall. Inside this, he made a shelter and as close to the rock as possible, he set up the Primus, spreading the remaining blankets around him as a windshield. Three matches and several Govan swear words later, he had the stove lit.

"Have you opened that last tin of meat yet?" Tom had to shout above the wind and rain, though Miriam lay close to his shoulder.

"Just." Miriam swiped at her wet hair and handed him the can. "No need to add water this time, Tom."

Tom moved the flaming stove closer to the woman wedged on her side under the chair, which he had managed to raise on a few stones.

"Shouldn't be long now 'till it's hot," he said hopefully, moving aside to let the shivering woman hold out her hands to the Primus flame. "Can't be too far now to that road you were on about," he said, with as much cheer as he could muster.

It did not take long to devour the contents of the tiny can. Now, there was nothing left to do except sit out the remainder of the night as best they could.

At first, in order to while away the time, and take their minds off the incessant rain, they spoke of everything and anything. Tom was tempted to ask how the woman had come by her incapacity, but as she had not touched on the subject he had thought best not to ask. Finally, as if mutual agreement, they both withdrew into their own silent world.

It was the woman who finally broke the silence, her voice trembling with cold. "I think now is the time for the last of our emergency rations young man." In the light of the glowing stove, Miriam held out two bars of chocolate to him. "If you take my advice, I think we should melt one in a can of hot water: hot chocolate of a sort. What do you say, Tom?"

"Say," Tom exploded. "Besides Eureka! I've never been so ecstatic since we scored at Wembley!"

"We Tom?"

"Scotland."

"At what for goodness sake?"

"At football of course! Your education had been sadly neglected…What?"

"Oh that." Miriam's edification of the sport destined to continue until the last of the hot chocolate had been drunk.

"Pity there wasn't any more," Tom complained, swallowing the last of the bitter sweet drink. "You wouldnae happen to have another bar or two tucked away for an emergency…like the noo?"

"Sorry, Tom, there is only one left. Melt it down now, or keep it for breakfast? Her question instantly answered, as with a final 'swoosh' followed by a spiral of black smoke the stove gave out.

"Well, that's it. No need for decisions now," Tom sighed, holding out his hands to the hissing stove.

Suddenly, without the comfort of the stove, the night seemed colder, larger. Miriam shivered and pulled the blankets more closely about her against the rivulets of water seeping through where she lay propped up on an elbow. "What time do you think it is, Tom," she coughed. "I saw it was about eleven o'clock on my watch before the stove went out."

"I can't read mine in the dark. A few hours 'till dawn I'd say."

Miriam coughed, as another icy gust of wind shook the bushes above their heads, the spray adding to their misery. Tom huddled closer to the woman, praying for daylight and the sun.

Chapter 5

"I'm sure that's the town I was telling you about, Tom." Miriam thumped the arm of her chair with delight.

Tom shaded his eyes against the sun, the nightmare of the previous night all but forgotten now that they had survived and were nearing the end of their journey...or, at least a phase of one.

Already his mind was on a hot bath, soft bed, and food...lots of food...and a pint. Oh, how he deserved a pint! And, with any luck, a change of socks which the present ones over the last few days had alternated from hard lumps of corrugated iron to a soggy mess of stringy spaghetti. A shave would not go amiss either, he thought, rubbing a hand over his chin. As for his clothes, he sighed, shaking the empty tin cans they had used as cups from his knapsack, well, that was another story.

Tom threw the rope into a clump of bushes and inspected his trousers and the tear in his jerkin, wincing at how much they had cost him.

"Come on, Tom, the sooner we get started, the faster we will get there. Are you hungry?"

"Silly bloody question," he mumbled to himself, and once more took hold of the wheelchair.

It was much later in the day before the young Scot and his charge entered the outskirts of Izeda in the first stage of their prearranged plan. As yet, he had not come across the much sought after taxi he was sure a town of this size could produce, which when found was to return to pick up the 'suddenly ill' lady, left sitting on a public bench some distance away from the empty cattle pens, where for the present he had hidden the wheelchair.

Four blocks on, his steps had taken him into a busy shopping centre. He hurried on, his feet aching on the hard pavement, his grumbling stomach changing to one of outright rebellion at the tantalising sight of a bakers shop. Turning a blind eye, as well as a corner, he increased his pace, the aroma wafting after him, with only the shock of his own bedraggled reflection in a shop window preventing him from doing a quick about turn. Now, all he needed was a 'bunit', a cap, and he'd not be out of place squatting on a street corner. The smell from the bakers still with him, he found his waiting taxi.

The taxi driver squinted up at him suspiciously, discreetly holding a hand over his nose. Magically, his passengers' repugnance was instantly nullified by the sweet smell of the Pesos that same passenger held under that same offended nose

A little later, Tom's charge was seated beside him, issuing out her instructions to the befuddled driver.

"What did you say to him?" Tom asked staring out of the window at the crowded street, a lot happier now that he was back in civilization.

"I told him I had been taken ill and now wished to find a hotel where I might convalesce for a time, a quiet one preferably. Hopefully, it will ensure us avoiding a large or expensive one."

"You think of everything, wee wumman," Tom replied admiringly. "Why not ask him how the revolution is going?" he suggested, impressed by Izeda's appearance of normality and the fact that it seemed to be riding out the world depression quite well.

"No. I do not think so. The least said, at this juncture, the better. Any attempt to further the conversation will only invite our friend here to start asking questions which may prove to be a little difficult to explain. The last thing we want is for him to report us to the authorities, after all we've been through."

Tom was about to reply when their taxi drew to an abrupt halt, the driver gesturing despairingly, amid a torrent of abuse at this gratuitous delay.

"What seems to be the trouble, a pipe band coming is it?" Tom leaned forward to ask the irate driver.

From around the corner, three troop filled trucks suddenly appeared, snaking in and out of both mechanised and horse drawn traffic to disappear as suddenly as they had come.

"Now is a good time to ask Fred here what it is all about," Tom suggested, sitting back in his seat.

Miriam dramatically threw a hand to her throat and spoke to the driver in short nervous bursts.

"Well?" Tom inquired anxiously. The trucks having reminded him they were still in the midst of a revolution. "What's the score?"

"Really, Tom!" Miriam replied irritably. "It's not one of your mundane football matches we are talking about." Then, as if contemplating whether or not to tell this unpredictable young man, took her time in answering. "It appears now there is some sort of pattern emerging to this revolution. Most of the ordinary citizens, whilst not actually taking up arms against Biezots, are opposed to him. The army too, according to our friend here, appear to be split, and who thinks it is mainly the officers who are firmly behind their President.

"The fighting around the capital has spread to some other cities nearby. As for the north of the country, he only knows what he hears in the street."

Guessing that his information was being translated, the driver turned round, beaming and nodding his head vigorously.

Eventually, they were on the move again, winding through the traffic to city centre, and leaving the main square with its palm trees and neatly cut lawns, its rows of covered walkways to eventually slide to a halt at the entrance of a three storied hotel of modest appearance.

"Follow the driver inside, Tom. I have told him I am unwell and need only to rest. He will reserve two rooms for us." Miriam explained.

Tom looked up at the building. "I hope it's luckier than the last one," he said to himself, remembering poor Consquala again.

He got out of the car and touched his forehead in mock servility. "Yes m'lady, and are we Mrs Stevens of the Suffolk Stevens?"

"Yes, we are young man," Miriam Plesher replied tersely, her tone reminding Tom of their first encounter.

"Snobby bitch," Tom muttered under his breath in exasperation, and followed the driver to the hotel.

By late afternoon, both sat scoffing coffee and sandwiches in Miriam's room.

"These must be the world's greatest pieces," Tom announced, his mouth full, and pouring out another two cups of coffee.

"Your 'pieces' are quite wholesome, Tom." She eyed him despairingly. "The cucumber gives it a little something, don't you think?"

"Cucumber? So, that's what it is." Tom studied his sandwich. "Just goes to show, you'll eat anything when you're hungry." He gave the woman a smile, who turned her eyes up to the ceiling in exasperation at this uncouth youth.

Tom was glad to see the old lady returning to normal. Well, as normal as anyone of her class could ever be. Even now, as she sat on the bed, looking as if she'd been dragged though a hedge backwards, she still exuded breeding.

Miriam had told the manager they were tourists who had the misfortune of having their car break down a kilometres out of town, and had been walking for most of the night in that 'simply beastly storm', hence their dishevelled appearance. Then, to cap it all she had taken one of her 'turns.' It had taken a rare gift of imagination to come up with that one, Tom thought. Almost as much imagination as it took to get a rise out of auld shiney bum Johnston back home.

Tom gulped down the dregs of his coffee and got to his feet. "I think I will have a bath and a good lie down," he yawned. "What about yourself?"

"I think I can manage thank you. It will be a luxury to steep in a hot bath. Quite some time since I enjoyed such pleasure."

Tom gave a mischievous smile. "Aye. It's quite some time since I enjoyed such pleasure too. Come to think of it, it's quite some time since I had a bath as well."

"Mind your manners, young man!"

"Only joking, missus wumman. I've got painful memories of bath night at home."

"Why was that, Tom?" Miriam asked concerned.

"Oh, I think it was the lumps o' coal up my bum."

"You kept coal in the bath?" Miriam cried in horror as he opened the door.

"Hi! I am Dane McAndrews from New York State," the tall broad shouldered American blocking the doorway said cheerfully. "And this is Gillian More and Bev Lucas from down under," he added, stepping aside in way of introduction.

Taken aback by this unexpected intrusion, Tom stood opened mouthed, staring past the tall ginger-haired American whom he already disliked for his twin good fortune, to the two daughters of kangaroo land, puzzled as to why neither were called Sheila or Matilda.

"G'day," the raven haired Gillian greeted him. "We heard there were two foreigners here, so we came to say hello."

"Who are you speaking to, Tom?" Miriam called out authoritatively from behind.

"Sorry…excuse my manners, please come in, my mammy doesnae like me speakin' to strangers," Tom said aloud for Miriam's benefit, ushering his unexpected guests into the room, his tiredness forgotten but not his rumpled appearance.

Miriam sat on the bed, her back resting against the headboard, the top cover spread over her legs, exchanging introductions in a manner reserved solely for persons of her class, as the newcomers arranged themselves around the room.

"Gee, how come you two are away out here?" Gillian perched herself on the side of the bed, her sing song voice a mixture of sympathy and surprise at finding two fellow members of the Empire in such an unlikely place.

Still impressed by the way Miriam had greeted her visitors, Tom retreated to a far corner of the room and let his eyes wander to the blonde drawing up the remaining chair by the bedside.

"Oh, it is a long story and quite boring, though it accounts for our most unsightly appearance." Miriam had spoken in her best Stevens of Suffolk accent.

"Are you ill, ma'am? I think I saw your son here carry you in earlier," the man asked, casually throwing one leg over the other at the bottom of the lady's bed.

One more reason for not liking you Yank! It was bad enough having to act the manservant, without being taken for her son. Tom rolled his eyes towards the ceiling, where a spider, disturbed by such an unusual array of people, was busy scurrying for a crack in the wall. That was two cracks he did much care for, the third already coming from his 'mother'.

"Yes that would be Tom helping me upstairs. I took one of my turns earlier. He's a good boy…at times." Miriam flashed a smile at her 'son', her eyes twinkling at the humour of it all.

Tom smiled back through clenched teeth. He saw the blonde watching him and looked away, his heart throbbing at the sight of this trim girl a couple of years younger than himself.

"Gee, that's a bit crook lady," Gillian sympathised. "Anything we can do?"

"Not at present, thank you kindly, perhaps a little later. There are one or two tiny things you could do for me. However, tell me how did you all come to be here? Are you all travelling together?"

The American dashed Tom's hopes. "Yeah, we all attend the

same university in the capital. We each have a grant from our respective countries to study Inca and Mayan culture."

"You what!" Tom exclaimed. "And I had to…" he stopped, suddenly aware of Miriam glowering at him. "I mean…I always wished I had received a grant from mine."

"Are you interested in Inca culture too?" Bev spoke for the first time, the undulations in her voice fascinating the Scot.

"It is a hobby of his," Miriam broke in quickly, shooting her companion a look of castigation. "But, please go on young man…you were saying."

The American uncrossed his legs. "We were up north a spell, when this here trouble broke out, so we decided to get ourselves back down to the capital. That's when it happened."

"What happened? Tom asked, thinking this eejit doesnae speak like Bogey.

Gillian answered for him. "We were hitch-hiking down this country road when we were halted by the military. They drove us to a town…God knows where. It was horrible, wasn't it Bev?" Gillian gave a shiver and looked across at her friend for confirmation. Bev nodded back. "They took us to their jailhouse," Gillian went on.

Tom propped himself against the window ledge, enjoying the way these Aussies had of making each sentence sound like a question.

"They took Dane's watch and all his money, Bev's wallet and wristwatch, and my necklace. The Latin bastards! It was me mums!"

Tom turned away to prevent himself from bursting out laughing at Miriam's look of horror at such unladylike language, unaware of the common usage of the great Australian adjective.

"It was the next day that had me shaking," Bev trembled.

"You mean when they made to take us to the cells to search us?" Gillian asked angrily.

Suddenly, Tom was all ears at the thought of these two being stripped and searched, especially the blonde. Wish I had had that job, he thought, unashamed at his crudity.

"When I tried to stop them, they rifle butted me," Dane countered, as if having to justify his masculinity. "It was only the appearance of a young officer that prevented them from doing just that."

"Apologies or not, it did not prevent them from keeping all our possessions, including our passports," Gillian spat out.

"So, that is how we came to be here, lady." Dane sighed, giving his legs a shake and sitting more upright in his chair. "Now, all we have to do is wait for our embassy car in the morning, and hope they will also pay the hotel bill. It is also lucky you arrived when you did, for when our return call came through advising us to stay put until we were picked up, we mentioned that there were another two foreigners who had just arrived, though not having met you we could not give them any details. However, they did suggest that we advise you both to wait here for safety's sake, and return with us to the capital."

"What embassy was that, young man?" Miriam asked nonplussed, only her eyes betraying to Tom her concern at this unexpected turn of events.

"Well…it was kinda both U.S.of A. and the British one," Dane drawled.

"We don't have one here as yet," Bev explained almost apologetically. Her tone changed at the sight of Miriam unsuccessful attempt to stifle a yawn. "Don't you think we should let the lady rest a bit?" she suggested to her two companions.

"That is most considerate of you, dear." The elder woman gave her most disarming smile. "But, do you mind if I impose on you a little further?" She halted, feigning embarrassment. "Perhaps you two men would like to go for a drink before dinner?"

"We can take the hint, can't we, Dane?" Tom levered himself off the windowsill, pretending to be offended.

Dane rose and joined Tom at the door, the sound of female laughter following them into the corridor.

"I hope you will not take offence, pal if I don't have that drink until after dinner, I'm a bit tired right now. Plus, the fact I feel like a dod o' manure."

"Excuse me?" Dane furrowed his brows.

"I mean." Tom held his fingers to his nose.

"Yeah, I get you man. Okay, I will see you at dinner may be?"

Although dead on his feet, Tom afforded himself the luxury of a bath and a shave. After which, he did his best to scrub his shirt and trousers clean, before settling down for a few minutes sleep.

Through the mists of sleep, he was vaguely aware of the pounding on the door, someone with an American accent calling out something about dinner, and he would see him downstairs.

Somnolent, Tom rose and staggered to the balcony, where he had hung his clothes, and was surprised to find his clothes had dried after only a few minutes of sleep. A bleary eyed glance at his watch told him that he had been asleep for over two hours.

Tom was still struggling to keep his eyes open when he poked his head around Miriam's door, and found her crumpled figure laying stretched out on the bed fast asleep. Gently closing the door, Tom yawned his way down to the dining room where his new friends were already gathered around a table.

"Is your ma not joining us?" Dane asked, acknowledging Tom appearance with a wave.

"No, the old girl's fast asleep." As I should be, Tom thought, smothering another yawn with his hand. "I'll have something sent up to her later."

Surreptitiously, he put his hand into his trouser pocket and adjusted the still wet lining into a more comfortable position. At least, he was not out dressed, he thought at the sight of Dane in jeans, the women in neat fitting slacks and chequered shirts, though they were all a bit cleaner and less wrinkled than his own 'Burtons' wear.

Gillian took a sip of water. "If you don't mind me asking, Tom, why does your mother talk different from you?"

"Oh, that's because my voice broke sooner than hers."

Gillian's glass hit the table with a thud at this unexpected answer, her laughter mingling with that of the two others, reinforced by the added sight of Tom's dead pan expression.

"No, you know what I mean, she is a real Pom…you know…English! But your accent is not as…"

"Stuck up?" Tom volunteered.

"Yeah that's what I mean."

"Well, that's easily explained, mother spent most of her time in England, and when my father died, we returned home." Tom buried himself in his menu, believing Miriam and Big Dougie would have been proud of his impromptu answer.

"Oh, so your'e not a Pom?" Bev cut in.

"Pom!" Tom lowered the menu glowering from one to the other. "If by Pom, you mean English? No, and I will kindly thank you not to swear, remember there are gentlemen present." Tom flicked a hand in Dane's direction.

Gillian took another sip of water, her eyes searching Tom's.
"What are you then? I mean what nationality?"

"Scottish. Can't you guess?"

"From Scotland!" Bev cried. "Which part?"

"All of me, hen, all of me."

The girls laughed again, the American distinctly relieved when the first course was placed before them.

"And what brings you and your ma to this neck of the woods?" Dane sprinkled pepper on his meat while waiting an answer.

It was inevitable that the American's question should eventually lead to Tom's obsession for Inca culture, a subject each warmed to enthusiastically, and pursued well after the meal was over.

Suddenly, Dane was on his feet. "Well, I would love to sit around and jaw all night, but if you all have no objections I'd like to turn in."

Tom's eyes darted to the girls hoping they would elect to remain, considering this was the first opportunity he'd had since coming to this country of discussing his pet subject...next to football that was.

"Yeah, I think you're right Dane." Gillian pushed back her chair. "Could be our chauffeur will be here early in the morning. Are you also for retiring, lady Bev?" she asked in her best English accent, and striking a ladylike pose.

"'Suppose. How about you Tom?"

Tom took a chance. "No, I think I'll stay on a bit. Try some more of this local brew." He held up his glass. "You're welcome to join me if you like?"

"No. Thanks all the same, I'm bushed. See you at breakfast, then sport."

Tom raised his glass in a farewell salute. "See you all in the morning."

All at once, he was tired again, and also strangely disturbed by the thought of the tall good looking American sharing a room with one of the girls...especially the blonde. A little later, he followed suit.

Tom saw the light under Miriam's door when he stepped out of the elevator. He crossed the hall and knocked on her door.

"Tom! I thought you'd never return. Or worse still...retire without calling in," she admonished as he flopped down wearily in a chair.

"Sorry, wee wumman I meant to have them bring something up."

Miriam sat fully dress on the bed. She pointed to the remains of a meal on a tray. "Never mind that now. We must leave here as soon as possible. I had not realised I'd been so long asleep."

"What! Now! At this time of night?" Tom wondered if he was hearing correctly. "Why the sudden rush? I've only just eaten my first real meal in days. Besides, I'm still knackered after all that mountaineering we've been through."

Miriam pushed herself forward on the bed, the urgency filling her voice. "I'll tell you why, young man, those Antipodal friends of yours, on alerting their respective embassies of our presence here, have also inadvertently broadcast this same fact to those whom we wish to avoid.

"Let us hope Segovia is sending his people straight from the capital to apprehend us, and not soliciting the help of his local thugs, for if he has, we have even less time to make ourselves scarce."

"Segovia?" Tom screwed up his brows. "Who, or what, in the name of the wee man, is Segovia? It sounds like some kind of disease."

"He is Tom, I can assure you," Miriam shuddered.

"And, what other wee charmers have you in store for me, Lady Stevens? Doesn't you son not have a right to know?"

Ignoring the sarcasm, Miriam levered her legs over the side of the bed. "We don't have much time."

Tom stared despondently at the floor, shoulders hunched.

"Are you thinking of staying, Tom?" the woman's voice was strangely subdued. "I know I should have let you go your own way that first night in the shop. I really am sorry I have got you involved in all of this."

Tom lifted his head and stared hard at the woman. "Let me tell you something," he wagged a finger at her. "This is the very last holiday I will ever spend with you. What do we do now?"

Miriam beamed her appreciation, her relief only too transparent. "Point taken. Now, let me explain my plan. It is possible Segovia's men will be here tonight, so we must leave right away. Spend the rest of the night in a church. I got those two girls to acquire a few necessities for us. They were quite curious as to how we came to be in such a mess."

"What did you tell them?" Tom brushed at a stubborn stain on his trouser leg.

"That we had a brush with the authorities."

"Wish I had one now, then maybe I could get rid of this stain."

"Will you be serious?"

Tom saw she was coming more agitated by the minute. "I had the girls bring me back a pair of stockings…and these." She threw him a pair of socks. "Not quite Bond Street any of it. Nonetheless."

"Jings, just what I wanted for Christmas. I know, put a sock in it eh." He grew serious for he knew his humour was adding to her anxiety. She must be really scared of this Segovia bloke, he thought. "Pity you could not have got those lassies to bring a shirt as well."

"I did not envisage such a hasty departure, or I would have. I had hoped you would wash yours overnight."

"I did." Tom sniffed at his shirtsleeve. "Well, not quite overnight."

"I also got these." Miriam handed him a half dozen bars of chocolate.

"Here we go again," Tom sighed.

"Also some needle and thread. I mended that tear in your jerkin." She threw the garment at him. Then, quickly drawing a map out from beneath her pillow, she pointed at a spot. "There is a church no more than a quarter of a mile away. You can leave me there and sometime during the night you can leave and retrieve my chair from the cattle pens. When you have done so, order a taxi and we'll take it to here." She pointed to another spot on the map.

"But that's south, almost back where we started! They'll pick us up for sure. Anyway, I thought we were headed in the opposite direction for Corona?"

"We are," Miriam chuckled, "that's the beauty of my plan."

Tom shook his head in despair. "If only I'd listened to my Granny about not talking to strange women!"

They found the church and settled down as best they could in one of the empty pews, and before the first streaks of light had broken through the false dawn, Tom was on his way to retrieve the wheelchair, happy to be on his way own for a time. In less than an hour, he was back and, resisting the temptation, as he carried Miriam down the steps, of crying out to the first of the curious early morning worshippers that it had been the longest christening he'd ever been at: she had been only a child when he'd brought her in. Then, thinking better of it, held his peace.

"Do you really think this is going to work?" Tom looked out of the taxi window at the sleeping city coming to life. His thoughts, that working class people were much the same the world over, and they were not really any bad people or nations, just bad leaders, like the 'heidbanger' this one seemed to have. Or, so he was led to believe by such sweet spirited souls such as Miriam Plesher.

"Let's hope so. If my plan succeeds, we'll pretend to take the first train to Alloux which is next big town south of here and in the opposite direction to which we are headed. I'm sure either our driver or the ticket vendor will remember us should they be questioned."

"Then what do we do?"

A young girl was brushing the pavement at the front of her shop, Tom gave her a friendly wave as the cab slid into a lane of morning traffic.

"We…or should I say, you will purchase two tickets while I wait in the taxi. I'll teach you what to say. After that, you'll wheel me across to the station. If all goes well, the station staff will remember you and your appalling Spanish. I think our driver will also swear that he saw us go into the station. Both parties, by way of deduction should believe we departed on the train leaving for Alloux." Miriam adjusted her skirt slightly, and sat back in her seat, quite confident that her plan would work.

"What will we really be doing?"

"I'd rather not say or mention any names right now if you don't mind." Miriam nodded to the driver's back. "As they say in the army, no names, no pack drill."

By mid morning, the Scot stood waiting in the ticket queue of Rieux railway station, quietly repeating his well rehearsed line to himself. At length, it was his turn at the window.

"Que?" asked the man behind the grill.

Tom slowly repeated his request for two single tickets to the town Miriam had decided was to be their bogus destination, above the rising protests at his back.

"Que?" asked the official again.

"Is that the only word you can say in your own language, Jimmy?" Tom asked the agitated clerk, looking around helplessly for assistance. Then, he saw it, the train destination board.

"There!" Tom pointed to the board triumphantly.

"Si! Hombres."

"No! No! Not the toilet," he cried in exasperation, his head hitting the iron grill as the queue behind him surged forward fearful of missing their train because of some eejit from Glasgow. He tried again, one eye on the woman behind him with a crate full of chickens.

"Ah!" Suddenly two tickets and his change were thrust at him from under the grill.

"Si! Si!" cried the happy line, edging Tom out of the way.

"Oh, all right, I'm going. A bloke could get sa sick with all that shouting and shoving," he hurled angrily at them.

Tom ran out of the entrance to where Miriam was already waiting in her wheelchair. She put a few notes in the driver's hand and swung on Tom. "Quick Tom we must not miss our train or our plan is all for naught!"

Tom gave the driver a quick nod of thanks and swung the chair round. "Where to now, oh genius of the hump?" he puffed.

"Out of a side entrance and wait for our taxi to depart."

A few minutes later, Tom was outside and pushing the chair up a grimy side street in the outskirts of this large strange town, and hoping their planned had worked.

Little did Tom realise, the conclusion of Miriam's plan was to head for Corona by a secondary road running parallel to the one they'd driven down that same morning.

"You really kept this wee bit of the plan to yourself," Tom gasped, collapsing by the empty roadside a few kilometres out of Izeda, and not a little angry at the woman. Although he accepted that what she had said about the consequences of being caught, he still resented the feeling of being used. He dabbed at his brow with a hankie. "You didn't say anything either about me having to push this chair again."

Ignoring the comment, Miriam bent over the arm of the chair, tilting the map towards him. "Look Tom, we are here on the other side of the hills from Izeda, this quiet country road leads to Hijar, where there is a railway branch line running to Corona."

Tom lifted his head from the map and stared up the shimmering road ahead. Where, he thought, have I seen all of this before. "How far is this new town?" he asked, afraid of what the answer might be.

"About fifteen miles."

"Miles…not kilometres? Just my luck."

The Scot stood up sliding the rucksack over his shoulders, now filled with a water bottle, bread cheese and the bars of chocolate Miriam had supplied him with the previous evening. "Well, I better get started. Do we stay the night in…what's its name?" He handed her his jerkin with its neatly stitched tear.

"Hijar. It all depends on the time we arrive. If we catch a train tonight, we might just keep a head of a certain Roberto Segovia, Chief of State Security."

"That is it. I'm for resting. When I get back home, they'll think I'm a black pudding with this heat. What I'd give to be up Loch Lomond now in the rain." Tom hauled the chair behind him and threw himself down in the shade of a tree.

"A little bread and cheese will help." Miriam delved into her rucksack.

"And a pint," Tom added, licking his lips.

Suddenly, Miriam jerked her head up in alarm. "Do you hear a noise?"

"My belly rumbling," Tom answered caustically. He got up and stared down the road at three figures trudging towards them.

"'Struth, would you look whose there, Bev?" Gillian cried, loud enough for them to hear and pointing a finger in his direction.

Tom moved out on to the road, a broad smile on his face, the heat temporarily forgotten, as the American stepped in front of his companions, bringing them to an abrupt halt. Dane drew closer.

"How about you two Limeys telling us who you really are?" he asked contentiously, his chin thrust forward.

Tom's heart missed a beat, the feeling reminiscent of many a prelude to a Saturday night pub brawl in darkest Govan. Gone were the happy smiling faces and sparkling conversation of the previous night, and in their stead looks of suspicion, and if he was not mistaken, hostility.

"We're bank robbers." Tom made a face, attempting to defuse the situation. "And that's our getaway vehicle," he jerked a thumb in the direction of the wheelchair.

Only Gillian's face showed any sign of changing, a faint smile playing on her lips.

The girls walked to Dane's side, while Miriam edged her chair closer to the road.

"You are quite right in demanding an explanation for our unseemly conduct, Mr MacAndrews." Miriam swung her chair to face the girls. "What you must think of us, my dears, after you were both so kind as to get those few essentials we so desperately needed?" She humbly tilted her head to the side. "However, our leaving so abruptly was purely for your own safety as well as our own."

"How come, lady?" Gillian walked into the shade out of the blazing sun, her female companion doing likewise.

"We are being sought after by the so called 'authorities', depending on what side of the revolution you happen to support, that is suffice to say, those who would wish to apprehend us are no friend of our respective countries. You have my word on that.

"When you alerted your embassies of our presence in the hotel, I'm afraid you also alerted those we would much rather avoid. This is all I can say at present…for your own safety."

"So those guys banging on your doors last night were the authorities?" Dane, now beside his travelling companions, raised his eyebrows in disbelief, having already decided these two oddities were more likely to be a danger to themselves than any revolution, and also guessing the girls were thinking likewise.

Tom and Miriam exchanged glances, the same thought passing through their minds. So, they had been right to get out of the hotel when they did.

"So, Segovia now knows we are not at Meda." Miriam spoke softly as if to herself.

"Who's this Segovia, lady?" Gillian asked with a frown

"He's the leader of the baddies," Tom hastened to enlighten them, now more than willing to appease, especially the silent blonde.

"So where are you headed now?" Dane asked, the tension ebbing from his voice.

"I might ask the same of you, Mr MacAndrews. When last we met you had already arranged transportation back to the capital."

Dane shook his head and sat down facing the wheelchair. The girls followed suit, and a feeling of normality returned to the little group.

Miriam held out a piece of bread and the American thanked her, explaining as he took a bite. "The Embassy car arrived as planned all right, getting us as far down as…"

"Allotz," Bev spoke up.

"Allotz," Dane confirmed with a nod. "It must have been about…say five…six miles further on when we came upon a roadblock held by rebels…anti government troops, or so our driver said.

"Although he showed them his credentials, they would not let him pass, so we backtracked to Allotz where he phoned his Embassy, who advised us to return to our hotel in Izeda until the situation cleared, so we headed back, except this time the darned road was blocked as well." Dane's voice faded.

"Perhaps, he was going too fast, Dane," Bev consoled the man. "Anyhow, the poor fella had no way of knowing what was round that bend." The girl squeezed the man's shoulder. She turned to Tom and Miriam, her eyes glistening. "They opened fire, whoever they were, killing Bert…our driver." She trembled. "Dane succeeded in steering the car from the passenger side, and somehow prevented it from going out of control. Dane got us out of there as fast as he could, for we didn't want to go through what had happened to us before. We had to leave poor Bert by the side of the road." Her look asking Tom and Miriam for some understanding or absolution, as she brushed away a tear.

Gillian handed her friend a handkerchief and took up the story. "Eventually, we made our way back towards Allotz, where we intended to contact the American Embassy who had sent the car and explain what had happened, especially about Bert being killed, except Allotz was also out of bounds by this time. Lucky for us, Bev spotted this road on the map, so we took it hoping it would lead us in a round about way back to Izeda."

"Unfortunately, no one checked the gas." Dane made a face as if somehow he was to blame.

"So here we are!" Gillian threw out her arms feigning cheerfulness.

"There is no short way round the mountains to Izeda from here." Miriam divided up the bread and cheese, ignoring Tom's scowl at this misdistribution of what after all was his hard-earned food. Clearly, this company had a penchant for arriving at the wrong time.

"Though, if you accompany us as far as Hijar, there might be some transport from there to Izeda." Miriam went on, handing Dane a drink.

The American studied the drink as well as the proposal. "Seems reasonable thinking to me. What about you two gals?" They nodded.

"Well, that's nicely settled then," Miriam said cheerfully, adding with a chuckle. "Now you won't have to do all the pushing, Tom. Neither will I have to listen to your warped Scotch humour by myself."

"Gees you came all this way from Izeda pushing that!" Dane cried incredulously.

"I did the pushing," Tom pointed to Miriam, "she did the puffing. Anyway, I think I should sit on her knee, and let the lassies do all the pushing seeing as my daddy was a Laplander."

"See what I mean girls?" Miriam puffed out her cheeks throwing her hands in the air in a gesture of resignation. "Please, whatever you do, don't encourage him."

"Oh, I don't know, I think that was quite clever," Gillian laughed.

Grinning with pleasure at this unexpected compliment, Tom gave his best Bogey impression to date. "Here's looking at you sweetheart."

Even the reluctant Dane had to laugh at this, as they rose to continue on their way.

Chapter 6

Sergeant Marco Casova pulled on his tunic, yawning down at the figure of the sleeping woman on the bed. It was not that Theresa was an oil painting, for if so, the paint had run, and in several different places and directions; not that he had any reason to complain, for he, himself, was no Don Juan. Therefore, how could he, a forty three year old militiaman, stationed in a remote village in the back of beyond, with very little chance of promotion, pass judgement on the woman who fulfilled his every desire.

Marco studied his bulging midriff with despair, then at the partially covered body of his mistress. He leaned forward, gently covering up the woman's nakedness and what remained of her beauty, which seemed to evaporate even more with each approaching dawn, and tip toed silently to the door.

Ten minutes later, the Sergeant headed through the sleeping village to the militia station, groaning at the prospect of another dreary day and how nothing ever happened up here, even the revolution seemed a million light years away. Perhaps, it was already over. No, this could not be so, for the newspapers from the Capital still reported isolated incidents of resistance from traitors vowing to over throw their President.

Should this uprising, or revolution, or whatever the hell you wanted to call it, not end soon, it was only a matter of time before its effects did reach the village. Marco spat angrily at a beetle on the hard dirt road. What was he supposed to do then, with one Corporal and three Privates, all weaned in this very place, and unless he was very much mistaken, none in sympathy with their President? Marco climbed the four steps to his office that was never locked. What was there to steal? Cockroaches? He leaned against the door until it yielded against his bulk.

Still yawning, he lit the stove, and put the coffee pot on to boil. "Where are those lazy bastards of mine?" he belched, flopping into the chair behind his desk.

Lazily, Marco stretched out his hand and lifted the brown envelope lying on his desk that he'd decided to leave unopened until this morning, slitting it open with a nicotine stained finger.

A moment later, the fat Sergeant sat back in his chair, exploding oaths at the ceiling.

What was he to do now? His orders clearly stated that he was to place himself and his little company in readiness for the arrival of a full company of regular troops from the Capital. He also had to prepare a list of all inhabitants whose sympathies might lie with the revolutionaries.

Marco rose and waddled his bulk across the tiny office to the window where he stood there, blind to the sleepy village slowly coming to life, with sweat running down his jowls like water over a washboard.

Angrily, he turned to throw the calamitous missive upon his desk. Clearly, he was between the proverbial rock and a hard place, for should he follow orders and name one, even one villager, then his days here were over. When the Goverment soldiers -the Regulars- left, so must he. But to where? Bang would go his easy, if somewhat mundane, life he had only just stopped moaning about. More importantly, no more woman, no more Theresa. "By all the saints, me! Why me?" Marco moaned aloud.

Pouring out a few more obscenities with his coffee, Marco reminded himself that he'd only joined the militia because the pay was better than that of the police, whom they had replaced in the mountains, and which until now he had always believed had been the right decision. But now this!

Marco threw himself back into his chair staring hard at the peeling whitewashed walls. He knew there was no way he could comply with his orders, to do so was paramount to signing his own death warrant, but not to do so would probably have the same result. How he wished he'd never opened those accursed orders.

Suddenly, the seeds of a plan began to germinate in the portly Sergeant's mind, after all, who was to know what day he had opened them, considering the inconsistencies of the mail deliveries. Should he and his men not be here when the Regulars arrived, so much the better.

Marco downed the last of his coffee and drew open his desk drawer, and fumbled through the untidy bunch of posters lying there until he found the right one. Then, with a grunt of satisfaction, rose stiffly and made for the door.

It needed no stretch of the imagination to deduce where his entire brave little company would be at this time of the morning: sipping coffee in the bar of the uncle of Corporal Pablo Enrico, and discussing the latest news of the 'disturbances' as the official government newspapers were wont to describe the revolution. So, this would be as good a time as any for him to break the good news, which was that they were once more headed into the mountains in pursuit of their 'favourite' local bandit. Marco chuckled. Perhaps, with a little good fortune, by the time they had returned from their usually fruitless search, the village would be under occupation by the Regulars without any help from them, or with any luck having failed to find any so called traitors would have departed. Now, all he need do was to reseal that accursed envelope. Marco closed the door behind him, whistling in the already humid air and marvelling at his own ingenuity.

Tom rested his hands on the back of the wheelchair and steadied himself against the swaying train. From where he stood in the corridor, he had an unobstructed view down the central aisle of the compartment to where his friends sat facing one another deep in conversation. Suddenly, as if she had been aware of his eyes on her, Bev glanced up, giving him a shy smile and a tiny wave. Tom waved back, his grin freezing at having his gestured reciprocated by a rather large woman sitting in the seat immediately in front of the girl.

"Jings, yon wan thinks I'm waving at her," Tom mumbled half aloud. "Just my luck to attract something that's built like the Bailliston roundabout, and that smile she gave me is like a row o' condemned houses."

"You were saying something, Tom?" Miriam asked, staring out of the corridor window at the changing landscape. The rugged mountain land they were now passing through replaced the rolling pasture land of Hijar a few miles back.

With a squeak, the corridor door slid back. A line of soldiers, each wearing blue sashes diagonally across their chest squeezed past them into the next compartment.

"Looks as if the Orange Walk's a wee bit lost this year," Tom quipped.

Completely oblivious to Tom's joke, Miriam studied the backs of the disappearing soldiers. "It would appear, 'El Presidenti' has not all the army under his control, as he would have us believe." She glanced up at Tom as she spoke.

"For a moment, I thought the game was up, until I saw the sashes." Tom gulped down at her. "It's a good job we first saw them in Hijar or I'd have chucked a fit. Come to think of it, I've had more fits, than your average chiropodist."

Miriam shook her head despairingly. "Your English, Tom, Your English," she scolded.

"No I'm not, I'm Scottish, I'm Scottish," he countered, laughing.

"Come on fella, let me talk to the little lady for awhile."

Tom swung round at the sound of Bev's voice, grateful for this timely reprieve from Miriam's predictable reprimand.

"Go on," Bev urged, nodding to where their two friends were seated. "You two men must have something to talk about."

Reluctantly, Tom squeezed past the young Aussie, only too well aware of their bodies touching, and how much more he would have preferred talking to her, rather than the big he-man. "Okay, sweetheart. Don't go away, I'll be back," said Bogey.

"Off!" Bev pretended to scowl, pointing down the corridor.

Tom did as he was told and slid into the seat opposite Gillian, who with a lopsided grin, suggested, "changing of the guard is it okker?"

"Seems that way. My feet are killing me."

"Has your mother always been in a wheelchair?" Dane interrupted, glancing away from the window.

"As long as I've known her," Tom said solemnly.

"You could have knocked me down with a feather when I saw you two way out there on your own." Gillian screwed up her face in disbelief.

The big American studied the Scot through knit brows. "Just what are you two up to, if you do not mind me asking? Okay." He made a buffer with his hands. "We agreed to tag along cause we are stoney broke, and your ma has friends in Corona, and right now the road back to the Capital is blocked. But hell, man, no one in their right mind goes trailing through country like this in a wheelchair. To hear that dame talk, you would think she was taking a stroll in some goddamn Limey estate. As for pushing that contraption all the way to the station, how in the name of Sam Hill you managed on your own beats the hell out of me, pal."

Tom was still thinking, and me pal, if only you knew the half of it pal, when he found himself propelled through the air towards the luggage rack, and swiftly passing a sign on the wall which he was sure either read 'please give blood' or 'mind your head when leaving the train' as the side of the train opened up like a tin of sardines, and he was hurtling twisting and turning down the side of the embankment, while all around him, as if in a separate world the sounds of screams and explosions penetrated his torpid brain a millionth part of a second before his head hit the rock, and he knew no more.

Obscure signals to a nebulous brain told him he could not have been long unconscious, for the sound of hysterical screams still filled the air to be joined by the sporadic chatter of gunfire. Groggily, he staggered to his feet and, shaking with shock, stared at the wreckage in disbelief, momentarily stunned into immobility by the extent of the carnage and his own miraculous escape. Unconsciously, he rubbed his arm, dabbed at the cut above his right eye and moved further away from the hissing engine lying on its side like some dying monster, its life blood flowing down the embankment from its open belly, and setting both scrub and debris alight.

Tom's eyes travelled to their former carriage lying slewed at an awkward angle, its side ripped open, to the rear of the train which had escaped the worse damage, from where blue-sashed soldiers were emerging to engage an otherwise unseen enemy.

"Tom! Tom! Over here!"

His head aching, Tom searched for the source of the sound. Through the smoke Bev waved frantically up to him from further down the slope. He felt a sudden stab of pain at the back of his head, and moved unsteadily through the wreckage taking care not to look too closely at the dead and the dying, and dabbing now and again at the cut on his head, besides trying his best to ignore the all too many plaintive cries for help.

"Down here!" Bev cried again, waving.

Tom began to fight a way through a pile of broken crates, mumbling a half forgotten prayer that this little old lady he'd come to hate and love would be all right, and angrily threw the last of the crates aside that stood between him and the inert figure of Miriam Plesher, and dropped to his knees beside her.

"Is she…is she?" he stammered, unable to know what to do if she was.

"Your mother will be all right, Tom," Bev assured him brushing back a strand of her golden hair.

There was a bruise on the girl's forehead and despite his concern for 'wee wumman', he asked anxiously: "Are you all right yourself lassie?" After all, it was their fault, or precisely Miriam Plesher's fault, that she had her friends were here at all.

"Yes sport, I'll be all right."

Tom's was surprised by the resilience in the Aussie girl's voice, having until now looked upon her friend Gillian as the stronger willed of the two, now she had shown him that same attribute.

"I think she is just concussed." Bev knelt back down beside Tom, and cradled the unconscious woman in her arms. "Lucky for us, we were in the corridor when it happened. The door flew open and next thing I knew, your ma and me were flying through the air and down this embankment. I think her chair has landed somewhere down there." She pointed to further down the slope.

Tom gave the old lady another look of concern as a stab of pain shot through his head and he got shakily to his feet. "Never mind her chair for now. Do you think she is going to be O.K? We've been through a lot together, Mrs P…mother and me," he quickly corrected himself. The least he could do for the old lady was play out the part. Bev nodded.

Relieved by the girl's assurance, Tom swept the scene of devastation. "I wonder where Dane and Gillian are?"

"Oh no!" Bev cried. "I had forgotten all about them!" She made to rise. "Look after your mother, Tom, I must go and find them."

"You stay where you are. I'll go."

Tom left the girl cradling Miriam in her arms and clambered up the banking, threading through the mangled wreckage to the gaping hole in the side of their carriage.

"Dane! Gillian!" he shouted above the screams of the trapped, and squeezed through a hole of jagged metal.

A sudden burst of gunfire punched holes into the carriage a few inches above his head, and he ducked down behind an upturned seat. "No again!" he cried, thinking again of the bus in the Capital, and cringed even further behind the seat. Cautiously, he crawled into what had been the corridor. A piece of chequered cloth protruded from under a pile of twisted metal. He gulped at thought of having recognised it as a shirt worn by Gillian, the Aussie girl, and tore at the wreckage, with his heart pounding at what he might find.

For a moment, Tom's whole body shook at the sight of the sliver of wood transfixing Gillian's neck. He looked away as if trying to make believe this had not happened, then back again at the dead girl and around him for some sort of assistance.

"Is that you fella?" came the shout from above the chatter of machine gun fire. "I am searching my tail off for Gilly? Is she with you, or outside with the others?"

"She's with me," Tom croaked at the bloodstained face fighting through the wreckage towards him. Then, louder. "She's here, Yank."

"Jesus H Christ! What a shit hole to be in!" Dane swore, pushing a twisted luggage rack aside and pretending not to have noticed the sightless eyes of an old woman staring up at him.

He saw Gillian at the same time as he reached Tom's side. "Is she…is she…" He put out a hand to the lifeless girl, aware of the sliver of wood for the first time. Tom nodded slowly.

"Oh shit! What am I to tell Bev?" Dane bowed his head. "How will we get Gilly out of here? And…"

The full weight of a falling body hit Tom in the small of the back catapulting him forward. "Christ! Here I go again!" he shouted hysterically at Dane.

The American grabbed at the dead body that had hit Tom and pushed it roughly off the Scot. Then, turning his attention again to Gillian, gently eased his hand under her head, his action in direct contrast to that in which he'd handled the dead soldier.

The firing which had ceased momentarily started again, both men looked at one another, each hoping the other would find the solution to their problem. Dane was the first to speak, coughing in the black smoke that had began to engulf the carriage. "How are we going to get her out of here?" he asked in desperation, cradling the dead girl protectively in his arms.

"We don't have time for that Yank! We've got to leave her here! That sound of gunfire is getting closer, and this place is going to go up any minute!" Tom shouted in Dane's ear, now close to panic himself.

"We cannot leave her to burn!" Dane coughed, his eyes although watering with the smoke glared menacingly at the Scot as if what he had suggested had been an obscenity.

"What else can we do?" Tom's angry reply was almost drowned in another hail of gunfire.

For a moment, Tom thought the American was going to offer some sort of a protest to his suggestion, when without another word, laying the girl gently down, turned for the gap in the carriage. Tom followed, landing awkwardly on his side knocking the breath out of himself and, for a moment, lay there with his eyes closed, and when he opened them again it was to stare into the sightless eyes of a plump woman displaying a frozen grin of rotten teeth.

"You're alive!" Tom shouted, stumbling through the human chaos and burning wreckage to the foot of the embankment where Miriam sat reunited in her wheelchair.

"You actually sound relieved, Tom." Miriam gave a wan smile, secretly pleased by the Scot's concern, and swatting delicately at the flies swarming around the cut on her forehead.

"Only being a dutiful son."

"It's fortunate for us the Government troops set their ambush on this uphill gradient," Miriam deliberated, now coming more to life. "Also, that these local trains are not renowned for their speed. No Flying Scot here, Tom."

"You didn't see me taking a header out the window," Tom grunted, making light of what they had just been through, and hoping Dane would come to his assistance for he knew what the women's next question was going to be.

"Didn't you find, Gilly?" Bev interjected, staring passed them to the train beyond.

"Yeah, we did gal."

Tom moved behind Miriam's chair thankful that the Yank was taking on the task of breaking the sad news.

"She's gone gal," Dane whispered softly, putting his arm around Bev.

"No! Not Gilly…not her!" Bev extricated herself from Dane's hold and attempted to run towards the rain as if by doing so she could negate her friend's fate.

Dane's hand shot out, spinning the distraught girl around. "Gilly's dead, Bev" he cried angrily, " and if we do not get the hell out of here so too will we! So come on!"

Tom heaved at the chair, jerked into action by the sudden

realisation of what the big man had said, while above them the blue sashed rebel soldiers returned the Government fire from behind the cover of the derailed engine.

"Why can't we stay here, like those folk?" Bev howled at Dane, referring to a disconsolate group of passengers sitting by some rocks.

Dane pulled her roughly along. "If you want to live, you better keep going, honey." He let her go to help Tom lift the wheelchair's buckled wheels over a rut.

It took all of twenty minutes to get themselves behind the first screen of rocks and away from the train, their progress hindered by the uneven terrain and the stream of panic stricken passengers.

"We must keep going," Miriam urged, holding a bloodstained handkerchief to her forehead.

"Give us a minute to get our breath back, wee wumman...mother," Tom pleaded, leaning on the chair.

"I will take it from here." Dane took hold of the chair and began to push, as fellow passengers tramped by their side, or wordlessly hurried past, each searching for the elusive portal that would free them from this nightmare.

After a time, Dane pushed the chair to the edge of a shallow pool. "Let's rest here for a time," he suggested, his voice tired.

"Only for a little while," Miriam countered.

"Listen lady," Dane spun round on her angrily, all tiredness momentarily forgotten. "It may be 'A' okay with you acting Queen of England, but it's us guys who have to push and carry this goddamned contraption." He walked a little way up the pool, and Bev who with a shrug of resignation followed.

"Touchy." Miriam made a face.

Tom rested himself beside the chair, wondering if the water in the pool was fit to drink. Suddenly, a cloud of apprehension and dread enveloped him at the thought of having to go through all this again. Perhaps, the woman had forgotten he'd pushed, trailed and carried this same goddamned contraption for over five days, and that it had only been last night that he had had his first real meal in all of that time. Then, when he was just beginning to get used to the idea, he was up and at it again.

He threw a stone at the water. A little distance away, Bev gestured to him to join them. He rose, and Miriam gave a grunt as he walked to join the other two.

"Your ma is a bit bossy," Dane commented, scooping up some water.

Tom kneeled between them and cupped his hands in the water. He drank deeply and sat back and shook his hands dry. "I think we had better get one thing straight, big man, yon lady over there is not my ma, I met her in much the same way as you three…two did. I think she should tell you what it's all about, then you can decide for yourselves what you want to do."

Dane stared into the pool, suddenly he jerked himself to his feet and started back to the chair, while Bev shook her blonde head in bewilderment at Tom as if it this was his doing, and had they not had the misfortune of meeting them both, and had not needed the money to see them on their way, her friend would still be alive.

"Well ma'am," Dane drawled at Miriam, "suppose you tell us what the hell is going on. Your son here has filled us in a mite, so maybe we can come to some sort of agreement as to what we should do next."

"Certainly, Mr MacAndrews. However, not at this precise moment, if you please." Her tone urgent as she darted a look back the way they had come, then back up at the tall athletic figure standing arms akimbo.

"Okay." Dane rapped out, in no mood to compromise. "We'll head up there." He nodded at the hill in front of them, "But, come the first breathing space, I want to know what the hell is going on."

"Jings, I just love the way you Yanks talk," Tom smirked, offering Miriam some water he'd collected in a leaf. "Do all New Yorkers talk like you?"

"Who said anything about me being a New Yorker?" Dane spat out at Tom, clearly still angry and not a little afraid of the situation he and Bev now found themselves in, and silently cursing the soldiers who had stolen all their money. "I said I was from New York State, I did not say I was born there."

"Excuse me for breathing, Mr Crocket!"

"Stop it! Stop it, both of you!" Bev shrieked glaring at both men in turn. "It's bad enough as it is, without you two having a go at one another."

"You are right, my dear," Miriam sided. "As I said before, we can settle our…misunderstanding when it is safer to do so."

"Right," Dane said firmly. "As I was saying, let's head up there, and fast."

It was almost dark by the time they found the adobe hut and, though derelict and dilapidated, it afforded some protection against the encroaching chill of the night.

Tom knelt beside the crippled woman's damaged chair and undid the clip which had held her handbag secure during the train's derailment and the long journey through the hills. Though he was aware of Bev sitting forlornly in a corner, staring at a spot on the floor, he kept his mind on his work.

It's a good greet that lassie needs after all she's been through, Tom thought, it will do no good keeping it all bottled up, and I should know. The wheel she is…he was about to say out loud remembering the scene back home a few months ago, which in turn lead him to think of home and if the news of his disappearance had reached there.

He could visualise the ascetic Mr MacKendrick rocking back and forth on his heels, pocket watch in hand, announcing to Big Dougie and the office gang with ill concealed delight at his non appearance. "Late as usual, I told them up at the big office it was wrong…completely wrong to let one of his breeding go off to…."

Tom stared through the wheel of the chair to his home. Would his Aunt Betty know he was not home? Probably word would not yet have reached her through his Uncle Don in America. Boy when it did, his aunt would be round at Granny's like a shot, Eric Liddel would not be able to pass her on the way. If he did not get home soon, allowing he still had a home, they'd be nothing left but the floorboards, should his Aunt Betty have had anything to do with it.

For a few minutes, Tom had been back home, away from all of today's tragedies and all that had gone wrong before. If only he could get away from this holiday turned nightmare, Aunt Betty was welcome to all he had.

Tom looked up, Dane stood over him breathing heat into his cupped hands. "If we had some matches, we could start a fire. I think I saw some timber a little higher up."

Tom fumbled in his jerkin pocket. "Will these do?" he asked nonchalantly, holding up a box he had 'acquired' from his robbed haberdashery.

"Sure will!" Dane tried to hide his delight. "Let's go before it gets too dark to see what we are doing." He crossed to the broken door and hauled it open. "You staying with the little lady, Bev?"

"No. Let the girl go with you, it will give her something to occupy her mind." Miriam's austere voice came out of the semi-darkness.

Bev shrugged her shoulders as if not caring whether she went or not. Then, as if having decided anything was better than sitting here freezing and thinking about poor Gilly, trancelike she got to her feet and silently followed the two men out of the door.

Now alone, Miriam closed her eyes, contemplating on what Dane and Bev would do now that they knew the truth about her, though certain she already knew the answer.

They were no different from the Scot, decent law abiding people, who were not very likely to leave her stranded here, or any other place, and unless she was very much mistaken, would also see her through to Corona.

It was a pity to involve them, and should Segovia find out, he was unlikely to treat them any differently than he would her. So, knowing this, why did her conscience not trouble her more?

Of course, she was sorry for the girl, who understandably had taken the death of her friend quite badly. At her age, death came only to the old or infirm. Her mind too must be in turmoil on how best to explain to Gillian's parents the manner in which their daughter had died.

No, she did not hold herself responsible for the unfortunate incident of the ambush of the train, life was too full of 'ifs and buts': if only the chauffeur had not been shot…if only they'd not met on the road etc. Just like her own personal tragedy…If only she'd obeyed her mother and gone shopping with her instead of slinking off to the stables. If only she'd taken time to saddle Brown Boy, and not Flo…if only she'd not attempted the high gate…Miriam sighed. Regrettably, sometimes there were far too many 'ifs and buts' in life.

She had been told every cloud had a silver lining, which for a newly crippled teenager was hard to contemplate. Every day she had grown more bitter at her unjust fate, resenting the way people complained; as she herself had undoubtedly done, about being on their feet all day…or having to run to the shops again…or climb the stairs for the hundredth time.

Then, as predicted, her silver lining came along in the shape of

Wilfred Plesher, an aspiring young man who looked right through her infirmity to her real self. One year later, they were married.

Wilfred's posting as a Junior Diplomat to Durban separated them for the first time. There was trouble with the Boars and she did not see him for almost two years. Two years of going through the turmoil of not knowing, whether the same things that had brought them together, would still hold. She need not have feared, if their love had been strong before his leaving it was even stronger upon his return. There and then, she vowed never to be parted from him again, even should he be posted to the farthest corner of the Empire.

Taking an active part in Wilfred's work made her disability more tolerable. Calmly and unobtrusively, she would assist him in a few difficult situations where a woman's wiles came to the fore. Soon, she had become indispensable in furthering his career.

Posting after posting followed, from Hong Kong, Singapore to India, the last where they spent most of the Great War, then finally here to South America.

"Look what we've found!"

Startled, Miriam swung her head to the door where Dane stood with an armful of wood. Had she fallen asleep? Or had she been awake when reflecting on her accident? It must have been the former, for it was now quite dark.

Bev threw her pile of wood down beside Dane's. "At least, we can keep ourselves warm," she shivered.

"Don't forget who made all of this possible," Tom teased, adding to the pile.

"Okay, man, let's have your indispensable contribution now." Dane winked at the girl, whose brief smile did not reach her eyes. Gloomily, Bev turned away from the company slumping down in a corner and drawing her knees up to her chin.

Miriam caught Dane's worried expression. "And I'll lend my contribution to the effort," she offered as cheerfully as possible.

"You wee smasher!" Tom cried out, his eyes on the four bars of chocolate in Miriam's hand. "Ever had the feeling you've been through this sort of thing before?"

"The French have a word for it," Miriam chuckled.

"So have I," Tom shot back, taking a bite of chocolate. "So have I."

Dane looked up from the map he was studying to his three companions huddled around their modest fire. "Were we to follow the railroad tracks, we would eventually come to Corona. And…" He glanced at the map again, "I'd say we'd hit a rail town before that."

"Can we afford to take the risk?" Bev asked. She was feeling a bit better now, perhaps it had been the chocolate, though she'd not felt any hunger for it. Could it be that she was coming to terms with Gilly's death? No, that was absurd; it was far too soon.

Relieved that the girl was taking an interest in the conversation, Dane asked of the elder woman, his eyes still on the girl. "What do you say, ma'am, should we take the risk? We cannot hope to get you to Corona through those hills. Besides, we have no money or food."

Miriam seemed to mull over the questions before answering. "First," she began, weighing her words, "I should advise you both now that you know who I really am, not to mention my real name or destination to anyone." She studied them through her brows. "I say this in your own interest."

Miriam spread her hands in a gesture of indecision. "As to your question, I really do not know, except to say, we know very little of the general situation, and until we do, the fewer people we encounter the better. We have all witnessed for ourselves the atrocities the soldiers are capable of."

"We surely cannot haul you over these here hills," Dane spoke more to himself than the company, weighing up the odds. "So, how in the name of Sam Hill are we going to avoid the towns, especially when we need food?"

Tom scratched his head. "Are you suggesting that we keep as close as possible to the railway, and steal…sorry acquire, food from the towns without being seen?"

"Got it in one, partner." Dane fired an imaginary pistol at the Scot.

Digging into her handbag, Miriam extracted a few peso banknotes. "I still have a little money left after buying the rail tickets, so it should be possible to buy food from little towns en route without arousing too much suspicion."

"Well, that's settled then, we head down hill tomorrow," Dane concluded. "Now for some shut eye."

"Jings, I still love the way you guys talk," Tom proclaimed, tongue in cheek, curling up beside the wheelchair and pulling his jerkin over his head. "Good night all."

They had risen early that morning, as much to escape the cold as to steal a march on the heat of the day, and as yet were no closer to a town, or the elusive railway line. Now, two hours later, they were lost, which was not surprising considering the number of times they had altered direction in order to find a way round a hill or similar obstacle.

Bev had gone on ahead to pick out the easiest way for the wheelchair, glad to be doing something that kept her from thinking about poor Gilly. She could still not believe it. She had asked Dane what would happen to Gilly's body, and he had consoled her by saying he was sure she would be taken to the British Embassy. How much of this was true she did not know, though she would like to believe her friend would have a Christian burial. She shuddered, forcing her mind away from yesterday's tragedy.

Bev turned at the top of the hillock, shading her eyes against the sun she watched the two men below, making a slow painful progress towards her. How had the Scot stood it for so long? Why had he not just up and left the old Pom? She would have, though she knew she was lying.

Tom was the strangest person she had ever met. Perhaps all Scots were the same. No, old MacPherson back in Manly did not talk like that. His sense of humour was different too. Bev forgot her grief for a moment, smiling at some of the things Tom had said, though she did not always understand him.

A twig snapped and she spun around, freezing at the sight of five armed men who stood there. Bev ran a wet palm down the side of her slacks, and nervously addressed them in her best Spanish. "My friends were hurt in a rail crash," she pointed down the slope, her hand shaking. It was all she could think to say.

"A train crash? Where Senorita?" the one who appeared to be in command asked, stepping forward.

Bev stifled a shiver, hoping Tom and Dane would leave the old woman and hurry up here. She studied the dark unshaven face and protruding belly of the speaker, resisting the urge to turn and run. "Somewhere over there," she flicked her hand.

"Is this the right road for Govan?"

Bev was never so glad as to hear a friendly voice in all her life, even though it was the insufferable Scot running up the slope towards them.

"Que?" asked the leader.

"Pay no attention to him, soldier," Miriam Plesher cried up from further down the slope where both men had left her to hurry to the girl's assistance. "What have you told him, Bev?" Miriam asked in English.

"The Senorita has kindly informed me there has been a train crash," the portly Sergeant called down in answer.

On the crest a little later, Miriam offered the dishevelled Sergeant a disarming smile. "Ah! Then you must know how the train crash came about, Sergeant?"

"Marco Casova...at your service Senora," the Sergeant replied, plainly relieved to find himself addressed once more in his native tongue. Perhaps he had made a mistake by answering this ageing Senora in English, something he should have kept to himself. "No, unfortunately not. We are..." Marco turned to his troops as way of introduction. "My men and I are in the process of chasing a notorious bandit. One you should not wish to encounter, I assure you. So, we know nothing of what has transpired these past few days."

"Did you follow any of that any of you?" Miriam asked of her friends.

"Dribs and drabs," Dane confessed, a little uncertain.

"I'm still at the dribs bit," Tom commented.

"May I please ask how you all come to be here?" Marco tried out his English again.

"'Cause we are lost." Tom made a gesture of hopelessness.

Marco drew him a look of annoyance. "I mean why are you here in these hills, and not by the railway where you had your crash and await help from the authorities?"

"Your move, O wise one." Tom gave Miriam a nudge.

"Our train was attacked by rebel troops who were firing their guns indiscriminately...I mean," at Marco's puzzled expression at the word, Miriam reverted to his native tongue, "that they were firing their guns at everyone, killing many innocent women and children, so it was safer to take our chances here amongst the hills than remain where we were."

"It is not possible! Rebels do not kill women and children!"

Taken aback by this sudden outburst from one of the soldiers, all eyes swept to the speaker.

"My English…she is not good," the speaker apologised, drawing closer as if to emphasis what he was trying to say. "It is not true what you say."

There was a moment's silence while the foreigners digested the implication of this announcement, not least of all their leader.

So, Pablo was not one of the President's men, this he should have guessed, and he would not be at all surprised if the other three were also like minded, as he was sure were most of the villagers that these men came from. But what if they were not? Personally, he did not care a donkey's shit who came out of this revolution on top, as long as he was one of them, for he intended always to side with the majority, or the side he thought was most likely to win.

Marco took a chance. "Not all who wear the uniform of the army or the militia are devoted to the President," he countered. "It is as the Corporal says, we do not make war on women and children," he addressed Miriam in his own tongue, feeling a surge of triumph when his three militiamen nodded in agreement.

"I apologise Sergeant Casova, what I told you was not strictly true. In fact, it was the Government soldiers who attacked our train. One of our number…a girl was killed."

"This is, as I thought, Senora." Pablo nodded to his comrades.

Marco shrugged helplessly. "What are going to do now? And where are you headed?"

"To Novas," Miriam flashed before any could reply.

Marco scratched his unshaven chin. "It is many kilometres away, and much trouble by way of the mountains."

"Not if your men were to help us," Miriam ventured, smiling.

Startled by the suggestion, the Sergeant scratched at his beard again. It could be to his advantage to string along with these strange foreigners for a time. The longer he and his men were away from the village and its imminent occupation, the better. Also, he was curious as to why a party accompanied by a cripple woman, should be so high up the hillside, unless as they say they were in fact lost, or endeavouring to avoid someone or something.

"Si," Marco said at last. "We must help the friends of our people."

"Who said anything about friends, Sergeant Casova?" Miriam challenged mischievously. "We are simply tourists caught up in the midst of your revolution, who are merely trying to keep alive, and out of the way of either side. Do you understand me? Or shall I repeat myself in your own language?"

Marco nodded, expelling heavily. "Si Senora, I understand good enough."

Marco's proclamation had its desired effect, for in one stroke he had lulled his own men into believing he was wholeheartedly for the rebel cause. Whilst the foreigners stared at one another in relief at having come across rebel soldiers who had no intention of harming them but on the contrary who now meant to assist them.

"How far is this village you have mentioned from here Sergeant Casova?" Dane asked in English.

The portly Sergeant hunched his shoulders. "Five, maybe six kilometres." The remainder of his sentence cut short by a burst of gunfire from further down the mountainside.

Quickly, the men ran to where they could look at the fight below. Where blue sashed soldiers attacked a convoy held up by a roadblock of felled trees.

"Shouldn't you guys be down there helping out?" Dane asked excitedly, his eyes riveted on the melee below.

Shaken by the American's suggestion, Marco tugged at his holster, playing for time. To show his true colours, by joining in the fight, would prove fatal one way or another.

"No, we shall go back up the hill," he said with as much authority as he could muster. "Whoever loses will be coming this way, no?"

"The man has a point," Dane agreed tearing his eyes away from the conflict.

"So what are we waiting for?" Tom yelled, swinging around on the soldiers. "Unless you guys want to be the Jimmy Cagney of the outfit?"

Marco answered quickly for his men. "We are militia…mountain police, not regular army you understand."

"Come on let's go!" Dane started off impatiently. "If they get a glimpse of us we are gonners."

Chapter 7

"You are now headed back to your village?" Sergeant Basilo spooned the chilli into his mouth. "Your men have all the supplies they require from here in Rosa?"

"Yes Sergeant, I have signed the necessary requisition forms," Marco answered, following every mouthful.

Basilo wiped his mouth with the back of his hand. "Tomorrow, a mounted patrol will head for Casado. Should you wish, I can have them call at your village with any message you may care to send."

"No!" Marco answered faster than he intended. "My entire command is here, there is no one left at the station!"

"Strange you did not leave one Private behind, there is always trouble of one sort or another in these villages. Already, there is a detachment of Regulars here in Rosa," the speaker belched. "We must keep our peasants in their place. Eh?"

"Yes Sergeant," Marco mumbled, flicking Pablo a furtive glance. His thoughts were that this pig of a Sergeant did not have the good grace to offer them a seat, less a glass of the wine that he was gulping down his fat hairy throat.

"Are there no Regulars in your village, Sergeant?" the pig asked, picking his teeth with a match.

"Not when we left."

"Do you not think it best that you return to your village immediately? I do not think the Regulars would wish to find a village station completely deserted, not under the present circumstances. Do you not think?"

Marco felt the sweat gather under his armpits. This glutton was going to ask him the name of his village, and this was the last thing he wanted him to know, at least at present. Aware of two pairs of eyes on him, he struggled to remain calm. He did not wish to return to his village, at least not for a little longer. Should the villagers have come out against the Regulars, there would have been much bloodshed, and of this he wished no part, as his presence there would have forced him to have taken sides, which he had no wish to do so at this juncture. "There is time enough. I should like to return with the bandit we have chased all over the mountainside for the past five days."

"Bandit! At a time like this? Phew! Sergeant Casavo, there are many better things to do with your time." Basilo belched again. "I have a bulletin somewhere from Colonel Segovia." The Sergeant gave a lazy sweep of the desk with his eyes, "which says that all Regulars and militia are ordered to assist in the repatriation to the Capital of all foreign nationals."

Now that he had caught the attention of these two perspiring morons before him, Basilo sat back in his chair, his tone condescending. "Our Chief of State Security has given his personal assurance to all Ambassadors, that he will do all in his power to ensure that these nationals have safe passage to their respective embassies," Basilo went on, enjoying imparting this information to his fellow Sergeant who, had he remained at home, would now be in possession of this very order. "He specially requests the safe return or information of a crippled Inglesa . It appears that the Ingles Ambassador has paid a call to our President expressing his concern over her safety. She is the wife of the late Ingles Ambassador. There is also a reward." Basilo gave a lazy shrug.

Though he ate, and in some ways looked like a pig, here the resemblance ended. Sergeant Basilo was no slouch which was substantiated by his having committed Segovia's orders to memory. This was a man, Marco thought, with whom he uld do business, but not with Corporal Pablo Enrico standing at his elbow. Therefore, he must devise some way of relaying his precious information to the Sergeant, without arousing Enrico's suspicion.

"So, there is a reward for escorting foreign nationals to the capital? Though I find it unlikely that we shall stumble upon any crossing the mountains while hunting our bandit," Marco cogitated, turning to acknowledge a shout from Tino that they had now acquired all their supplies.

"How am I not to know you are not renegade militia obtaining supplies for your own ends?" Basilo belched at their backs, pushing away his empty plate.

"Rebels wear blue sashes as they did at the roadblock, Sergeant, unless you think we have sashes stuffed in our pockets?" Pablo laughed over his shoulder at the door.

Sergeant Basilo sat quickly forward in his chair, but Marco's look deterred him from inquiring further.

"As I said before, Sergeant," Marco countered, overjoyed by the enormity of his Corporal's mistake. "It is scarcely likely we shall encounter foreigners in our mountains, especially a crippled one."

A flash of understanding passed between the two Sergeants as with a final wave of his hand, Marco followed his Corporal out of the door.

"Got the supplies OK? Any trouble, you guys?" Dane asked of the returning militia men.

"No, it is a simple matter when one is wearing the uniform," Pablo smiled guiltily, plucking at his tunic to emphasis his point.

"What have you got to offer, wee man?" Tom pointed at Tino's pack.

"Que?"

"Oh I forgot no one has learned you how for to speak English as is spoke in Govan," Tom chided the man good humouredly.

"I don't think I got all that myself," Bev frowned.

"Never mind," Tom grinned cheekily. "I will learn you some day myself. Now, joking and English lessons aside, what's for eating?"

Though at a loss to understand the Scot's conversation, the soldier had at least understood Tom's gestures, and handed him a long roll of bread.

"Would you look at the length o that thing, as the actress said to the bishop!" Tom proclaimed, ignoring Miriam's cry of disgust.

"Not everyone appreciates your sense, or should I say, non sense of humour," Miriam scowled up at him.

He should have left her in that shop where they had first met, he seethed. "Och well, not everyone has had the good fortune to have been born in Scotland." He pretended to sigh. "Which reminds me of another saying we have there, blessed are the 'piecemakers'," he pointed to the loaf, "for they shall never go hungry."

Sitting a little bit away, chewing on his own food, Marco hid his delight at this little episode between the foreigners.

Should everything go according to plan, that great mountain of blubber Basilo should even now be struggling and sweating up the hillside with, he hoped sufficient men at his back.

Even a moron, which the fat Sergeant decidedly was not, could not fail to understand the implications of Pablo's remarks. Having intentionally admitted to having not known anything as regards the attack on government forces at the roadblock, when Basilo had asked by explaining they had been on the opposite side of the mountain, they would have been ignorant to rebel soldiers wearing blue sashes, unless they in fact had been there. This, and his own subtle hints as regards the Inglesa surely could not fail to arouse the soldier's suspicions. Therefore, the longer these cretins delayed in their eating and squabbling, the easier should be their capture.

"Hi you guys!" Dane yelled, running down from the skyline. "There are a bunch of goddamn soldiers climbing up the hillside, and they're headed in this direction!"

As one, everyone grabbed for something or other, translations unnecessary: the militia shouldering their packs and rifles; the civilians running for the wheelchair. Within seconds, all were on their way.

"What did you stupid Dagos say down there to have half their goddamned army after us?" Dane fumed at both English-speaking soldiers.

"Say Senor? We say nothing," Pablo pleaded, running at the side of the wheelchair.

"So those wee men are chasing us for nothing?" Tom panted, deftly guiding the chair around a rock. "I'd hate them to be chasing us for something. Maybe they just want to tell us the score at Parkhead?"

Ignoring the wild ranting of the Scot, Pablo pointed. "Go this way, we can make better time going down hill."

At a shout from one of his comrades, Pablo dropped behind. Soon, he was back by their sides. He heaved at the chair, his breath coming in snatches. " I do not see…where…the Regulars go."

"As long as its no' this way" Tom drifted aside to let one of the soldiers take over pushing.

Someway ahead, Bev ran beside a soldier, whilst the rest took turns at pushing the chair and, in this way, they continued for well over an hour, until, at length, Dane called a halt.

"It appears we have a new leader." Miriam passed the water bottle to Tom

"Perhaps he thinks he's Clark Gable," Tom said, taking the bottle.

"If he does, it's the first film I've seen starring both him and Bogart," Miriam said pointedly.

Tom wiped his mouth with the back of his hand, and nodded to where Dane had sat down. "Him, Gable…me buggart." He flopped down on the grass and closed his eyes.

"Come on, let's go!"

Tom sat up blinking into the hot midday sun, scarcely able to believe his ears. "Ch'…I've only just sat doon," he muttered to himself. "Hills, hills and more hills, the only hill I ever want tae see again is Maryhill."

"Come on Mac, take an end," Dane gestured impatiently at the chair. "Tino says those guys are not so far behind."

Tom pushed heartedly at the chair, Dane at his side. "Where do we go from here?" he found himself asking.

"Search me?"

"No thanks, you're not my type."

Dane glared across the chair at the Scot. "You are so full of shit, man"

"That's why some of its running down my legs, Yank. That's not suntan you're looking at."

"We are all scared, Mac," Dane puffed, his tone softening in understanding.

In the chair, Miriam gave a smile, perhaps, despite their pride, they would pull together after all.

"This way Senore!" Pablo waved to the two men to follow the goat track.

Unfortunately, as the track that Pablo had indicated was too narrow for the chair, they had to compromise by letting one of the wheels run on the path whilst lifting the other one.

"A bit bumpy, wee wumman," Tom asked, bending over the back of the chair.

"I'm all right boys," she said, her hands tightly gripping the chair arms.

At the other side of the chair, Dane gestured to where Tino and Pablo stood arguing and gesturing to one another at the convergence of two paths. "We seem to be coming to a halt."

"Which from here must we take, Senor Dane?" Pablo shouted, running towards him.

"How the hell should I know, if you don't!" Dane shouted at him. "They're your bloody mountains, not mine!"

"Perhaps if we knew where it led, it would help," Bev suggested, arriving in time to hear the American's outburst.

"A very sensible idea," Miriam calmly agreed. "Pablo, what do you think?"

The soldier pointed to the path on their right. "That way leads towards, how do you say, many trees?"

"Forest," Tom assisted.

"Then to higher hills."

"And the other way," Dane's question was rushed as he took a hasty look behind him.

"To the road, Senor."

At the sound of Marco and Tino joining them, the American swung round, his tone growing more desperate. "I think we should head for the forest Sergeant Casova, as I do believe those soldier guys following us may think we'll go the easier way. That sit all right with you?"

Prudently, Marco agreed, for this was no time to disagree and fly in the face of logic. "A good choice Senor," he nodded. "I will send Chico and Calos one way and we can go the other. But we must hurry, the Regulars are not so far behind."

"Let's go. What have we got to lose?" Dane agreed and grabbed a handle of the chair.

"Besides our lives," Tom muttered and pushed the chair as hard as their new leader.

The path they had chosen twisted and turned through the low foothills, gradually rising until meeting what Pablo had described as a forest.

"We cannot take the chair through there," Dane panted, drawing up, aghast at the formidable barrier before them. "Pablo! That's a bloody jungle!"

"Forest, my arse!" Tom agreed, swatting at an insect.

Pablo rushed up behind them. "The soldiers, they do not split up as you hoped, Senor Dane. They all come this way," he wheezed.

"Damn. How did they know to do that? Was our trail so easy to follow?"

"Maybe their scout's a Red Indian, for this is becoming more like a cowboy picture all the time," Tom commented sarcastically, and a little jealous at the way everyone was beginning to treat the American as their leader.

"Can it Mac! I'm trying to think," Dane snapped.

"Bit late to start now," Tom muttered.

As they spoke, Pablo and Tino emerged from the forest each

carrying a length of wood which they pushed under the arms of Miriam's chair.

"There you go lady," Bev cried in delight, though a little shakily, "your own personal rickshaw. Or should it be sedan chair?"

The density of the undergrowth soon brought the party to a halt and, despite the soldiers unstinting efforts to hack a way through with their machetes, they still found themselves having to back track on numerous occasions.

Tom dearly would have liked to have left the others to their own devices so that he could have been out of there at the first sign of the slimy crawling insects that lovingly clung to him. Or the knee deep swamps he seemed irresistibly drawn to, but knew he had to help carry the chair and get out of there as quickly as possible.

Neither could he stop a shiver at the thought of what the two-legged species of reptile who followed them would do to him, if they should catch up; not to mention the fate of the ladies, especially one lady in particular, which was why he had carried the rickshaw longer than anyone, whilst urging on every new partner whose turn it was to take an end, until at last they emerged from the jungle in to the broiling sun once more.

Tom blew out his cheeks. "At least, it was a wee bit cooler in there." He swiped an insect off his arm.

"Sure was old buddy." Dane rested a hand on the Scot's shoulder, grudgingly admiring the way he had worked at carrying the improvised rickshaw. "I sure hope we've lost those sons of bitches this time."

"They come again, Senors!" Pablo plunged through the undergrowth behind them, wildly waving his arms. "Very close this time."

"You spoke too soon, Yank." Tom drew a hand across his eyes.

"Okay let's go up that way, and run parallel to the trees. Then, duck back in and double back on ourselves."

Having made the suggestion, Dane did not wait to ask Marco's advice before he was urging on the pole bearers, Tom grabbing an end and wincing at his blistered hand as he stumbled after the American.

After what had seemed an eternity of intermittent painstaking slogging and resting, they at last broke free of their green labyrinth onto a high barren plateau.

Wearily, Dane threw himself at the brown withered grass. "Let's rest a spell."

Bev threw herself down beside him. "Is there any water?" she croaked at the soldiers, making the necessary signs

Tom sat with his back against the wheelchair. The desperate sight of Marco's puffed out cheeks gave him an added strength. "Would you take a look at Louis Armstrong over there," he chuckled at Miriam. "I think he would have a heart attack if he had the energy."

Miriam looked across at the exhausted soldier, as the jerkin she was holding up to her chin for protection against the ravages of the so called forest slid down exposing the enormous insect bites on both her arms.

Tom's smile froze. They had met everything in there: creepy crawlies, insects nodding down at them as they went past. He was sure the word had gone out amongst the insect world, 'dinner is being served, it's Ding Bell today.' He pulled up his trouser leg and scratched at a bite on his ankle. What a mess to be in, and he wasn't alone either, judging by the state of the others. How they'd managed to get through that infernal undergrowth he would never know. Twice he had fallen into something knee deep.

Gingerly, he took off his right shoe. Shaking it, he emptied out a long yellow and green insect and angrily brought down his shoe with all his force on the squirming interloper before it had time to scurry for the safety of the nearest rock. "Try and get a free ride at ma' expense wid ye!" Tom hit the already crushed creature again.

"They blend into the foliage very well don't you think, Tom?" Miriam declared, scratching at her arm.

"This one does now!" Tom hit it again.

While Tom was fossilizing his insect, Dane on the other side of the clearing was asking the gasping Sergeant, "What about Chico and carlos,Sergeant Casova, do you think they will find us again?"

Marco waved a hand, his face beetroot red, signalling Dane to wait while he caught his breath.

"Please, Senor Dane," he rasped, "we must rest…perhaps if we do, it will give them time to find us."

"More likely those Regulars you talk about will find us first."

Marco held his head in his hands. "Perhaps, Senor Dane, but how long you think we go without food and rest?"

"Just long enough Sergeant Casova, my friend, I'm sure you'll get us out of here." Dane looked up at the sky. "Even Regulars cannot travel in the dark in this terrain."

Dane kicked Tom awake. "Come on Mac, the Sergeant says we should be on our way. Shake a leg."

Yawning, Tom stretched himself. "If I do it will probably fall off, just like a loose woman I once knew in Govan." He got to his knees and shook the chair. "Anyone at home?" He lifted up a corner of the poncho one of the soldiers had given Miriam.

"Good morning, Tom. Did you sleep well?" Miriam extricated herself from the folds of the garment.

"No. I was freezing. I'm glad we've decided to make an early start." He yawned again, his attention drawn to the fat soldier trimming his moustache, as a sudden burst of sunlight burst through the mist catching his hand held mirror and sending a million rays in as many different directions, the same break in the mist, revealing the snow covered mountains in the distance.

Now, more than ever, Tom wished he was away from it all. This country could keep its burning sun and freezing nights, if he must tramp over hills then let it be those of home. Absently, he saw Bev fold up her poncho, aware of never having felt so much passion towards his homeland. Despite the depression in the yards, there was always someone, one of your ain folk to hae a crack with.

Tino handed him some food and he came back to his present surroundings. At least if these soldiers, or militia, or whatever you choose to call them, were not exactly home themselves, they were damned sight closer than he was to his.

"Did you sleep well, sport?" Bev called across to him cheerfully.

Evidently, sharing a poncho with the American had contributed to her present demeanour.

She was a peculiar lassie, Tom thought, not unlike a younger version of wee wumman, resourceful, uncomplaining, each day toiling out in front to pick out the best route for them to follow with the wheelchair. "Not very," he replied scratching his ear.

"Gee. I thought coming from Scotland, you'd not feel the cold."

"Do you think we all live in semi-detached igloos or something?" he snapped, a little harsher than intended.

"Sorry. I suppose it is a bit cold here." She walked towards him. "The Pommie lady told me something of how you carried her over the mountains to Izeda." Her smile said she wanted to be friends.

Tom put his ill temper down to getting out the wrong side of the bedrock this morning. This, and how this pretty blonde had snuggled into the big Yank under the poncho. He kicked savagely at a stone. "It wasnae over mountains. You can't push a chair over mountains," he said sullenly.

"How did you both manage to keep warm at nights?" The girl's interest was aroused.

"We just kept getting into heated arguments." The spiteful Scot left the bewildered girl to work it out for herself.

Tom reached the circle of conspirators in time to hear Marco apologise to the American. "My men say they now wish to go back to their village."

"You know we cannot make the next town without your help! You just do not get up and leave an old crippled lady who is trying to help your cause!" Dane threw his hands in the air in exasperation.

"The Senora did not inform us she is the wife of the late Ingles Ambassador!" Pablo challenged.

"You are all quite right in questioning my decision not to disclose who or what I really am." Miriam Plesher's voice invaded the coterie, which sheepishly opened to let her speak.

"I refrained from informing you who I really was until I knew each of you better. Surely this you can understand?" Miriam's voice softened, and she continued in their own tongue. "But now that I do, I can tell you categorically, it is absolutely vital that I reach my destination and Fenando Castilia."

Tino shook his head. "Our first concern must be to return to our village."

"Perhaps the Regulars are already there. We do not know what they will do to our people should they think they are not for the President." Pablo voiced what his comrades also feared.

Marco could not have wished for more at this unexpected turn of events. Although he did not want to return directly to the village, he did want to abandon these foreigners as quickly as possible, which, by so doing, should make that fat Sergeant Basilo's task of finding them the easier.

"We must go Senors," he said, a note of sadness in his voice. "All my men have families to think of. Whereas I..." he pretended to make light of it, "have only my Theresa, and if I know her, she will already be the commanding officer's woman."

Laughing, the soldiers nodded their heads knowingly.

"Then, you must do your duty to your village and your families, and I shall do mine for your country," Miriam surrendered. "Though how long we may elude our pursuers, without your help, I myself do not know. I can assure you if we are apprehended we shall do our best not to divulge any of your names."

"You would tell them who we are?" Pablo exclaimed, suddenly frightened by the implications of these foreigners falling into the wrong hands.

"As the lady says," Dane lent his support to the game he now knew the woman was playing. "We may have to, for I as sure as hell do not relish the idea of being tortured for someone else's country."

Marco did not like the way the conversation had suddenly turned. Shifting the weight of his holster a little, he mopped his brow with his free hand. Having practically told Basilo he knew the Inglesa whereabouts, he himself may be safe enough, but he could not vouch for that of his men. And, should anything happen to them, and it got back to the village…this he did not care to think upon.

"But that Sergeant who pursues us already knows who and where we come from, Sergeant Casova," Pablo stared at his senior dejectedly.

"I did not tell him which village. Also, there are many who bear the same names as ourselves in our country." Marco said, with the intention of further convincing his men of his support for the rebel cause.

"You are a very wise man, Sergeant Marco Casova." Tino bowed his head, tracing a line in the dirt with his boot. "I am ashamed I have not trusted you better."

Marco smiled at the embarrassed man. "I understand, Tino, my friend, it matters a great deal that you have told me this."

"Let's cut out the holy confessions," Dane snapped, having understood a little of what they had said in their own tongue. "Now that we know this guy whose on our tail does not really know any of your names and where you are from Adam…"

"Or Manolo or Miguel," Tom added tongue in cheek.

Dane glowered at him, and turned again to the soldiers. "It still leaves you with the decision, do you help us or not?"

Marco was stunned. Had he fallen into his own trap? The Inglesa was the only one known to Basilo by name. Now that his men were aware of this, would they now elect to help these foreigners instead of returning to the village where there was every possibility of their landing slap bang into what he had taken all this trouble to avoid?

Tino drew away from the company a little, beckoning the rest to do so. "We must talk."

The fugitives waited in silence, all eyes on the militiamen huddled together. After a few minutes of animated talk, they broke up and returned to face them.

"My men have come to a decision, we will, as you ask, help you reach Novas," Marco informed them with a trace or resignation.

Bev bent to whisper in Miriam's ear, "But we are not going to Novas."

"No but our comrades in arms do not know this," she replied softly.

"You are a wily wee wumman," Tom chuckled, having overheard. "So I take it they are willing to push that contraption of yours over hill and dale, to save their very lives?"

"Something like that Tom," Miriam acknowledged with a nod, "Something like that."

Happy that they had now left the torturous part of the hillside behind, Tom suppressed the urge to whistle. The path, a drove road back home, on which they travelled, was sufficiently wide to push the wheelchair instead of carrying it. At least, for a time, their worries of overbalancing or slipping were gone, which also had the added benefit of giving his tortured muscles a temporary respite.

Sadly, he took in his torn and stained trousers. That wee woman has a lot to answer for, he thought, walking on behind the column. Then he saw it, down through the trees a, metalled ribbon of road. Without thinking, he slid down the banking to investigate. Now, he was sure of what he had seen. "You beauty MacAdam!" he exclaimed aloud, already anticipating the feel of the smooth tarmac under his feet. So Casova and his boys knew this part of their country after all!

As he turned to re-climb the embankment, Tom thought he had caught the slightest glint of sunlight on glass in the bush land opposite. Still uncertain as to what he thought he'd seen, he stopped and waited. There it was again, so his eyes had not deceived him.

Seconds later, he was chasing after the column.

"Dane! Fellas! Halt a minute!" Tom caught up with them, gasping for breath.

"You do not want to halt for a rest already do you?" Dane rounded on him angrily. "We shall soon be down off these damned hills. And, for good, I hope."

"That's just the point!" Tom grabbed the man's arm, but spoke directly to Marco. "I think there are soldiers waiting for us on the other side of the road. I'm sure I saw a reflection from their binoculars!"

"Goddamn it!" Dane exploded. "How in the name of Sam Hill did they get here in front of us?"

"I don't think they did, Dane. This could be another mob!"

"Are you trying to say we are trapped, young man?" Miriam asked exactingly.

Bev hurried round the chair and slipped her hand in to the American's, her eyes pleading. "Dane?"

"How the hell should I know what to do? I'm not a bloody soldier!" Dane's voice rose in exasperation. "I am only a student, after all. What would I know about tactics? This, I leave to the professionals like Sergeant Casova here!"

"I should say you have done jolly well so far," Miriam voiced auspiciously. "So do not let ourselves be fooled into thinking we are beaten now."

Suddenly, realising the American's panic, Marco seized his opportunity of taking command once more. "I shall take a look and see what is happening down there," he referred to road below. "You will all be pleased to remain here."

"Tom! Go with him. Find out how many there are lying in wait if you can," Miriam commanded, gesturing that he should follow Marco who had already started on his way.

"Yes, general wumman." Tom threw Miriam a salute, much to the bewilderment of the militia.

"The guy's a fool," Dane mocked, watching the Scot disappear in to the trees, screening them from the road.

"Do not let his sense of humour fool you," Miriam smiled coyly, "it has got us through some p...r...e...t...t...y tight spots before now."

A few minutes later, the two were back.

"I'd say there must be about a hundred or so down there," Tom gasped, scrambling back up the banking, as Marco informed his own soldiers of the situation.

"What shall we do, Sergeant Casova?" After all, Bev thought, he is a soldier.

Marco turned at the sound of the girl's voice. "We must not go near the road. Not go near the village as we planned. Go round it. Cross the road other side of the village eh?"

It was the only sensible action to take at this juncture, Marco thought, for to do anything else would only arouse suspicion, especially by his own men. There would be other times with much better opportunities to lead them into a trap. But who were these men down there? And where was that fat Basilo?

"Sounds all right to me. What about you Tino?" Tom asked the soldier who had not understood a word that had been spoken. "See! Tino agrees," Tom cried at the soldier's nod.

Despite the seriousness of the situation, Bev managed a grin. The big American, however, refused to alter his opinion of the Scot.

The path on which the soldiers had decided, took them well beyond the village.

"Senor Dane, I must leave one of my men on top of the hill behind us. Perhaps we are still chased by Sergeant Basilo." Marco clutched at a tree to prevent himself from sliding.

Drawn to a halt by Marco's suggestion, all looked back up the slope. "You could be right," Dane called from further down the slope.

"As Sergeant I will go," Marco called back, secretly excited by the opportunity having presented itself, whereby he could signal their position to the Regulars without being seen by his own men.

Dane steadied himself against a tree. "Why don't you let Tino go, he's a mite lighter on his feet than you are, Sergeant…if you don't mind me saying so?"

"Yes, Sergeant, we must make the very best of our time," Miriam urged.

Determined to overrule this added opposition, Marco opened his mouth to speak when Pablo broke in. "It is best Tino goes Sergeant, I told him to do so," he said sheepishly, pointing to the departing figure. "He is very much younger than you," adding, "You or I," to soften the unintended insult.

Hiding his anger at this lost opportunity, Marco pushed past the wheelchair. "Come, we will cross the road here," he said pointedly.

Twenty minutes later, all were safely across the road. Tom, who had elected to remain behind and await Tino's return, lay hidden in the undergrowth a little from the edge of the road, and was on the point of giving up waiting when he heard the shots.

Cautiously drawing back the branch of a bush, Tom saw Tino head bent, running towards where he lay hidden. Then, when almost at the point where he lay, Tino looked up, a look of anger and surprise crossing his tortured face as he saw Tom, and suddenly veered away plunging into the undergrowth on the opposite side of the road, to be followed a few second later by the first of the Regulars bursting in to view, and fanning out almost opposite from where Tom still lay hidden.

Suddenly, there was a shout. Across the road, a soldier stood pointing to the cliffs above.

There, clawing his away over a rock at the top of the crest, his progress painfully slow, Tino hauled himself inch by inch over the barrier of rock that would protect him from the soldiers below.

It was then Tom heard the first fusillade of shots, and looking up, saw Tino fall and bounce off the rocks as he fell.

Sickened, Tom dropped back down behind the bush, unable to believe that this was happening, and thinking of the joke he had made only a short time ago at the dead man's expense.

Closing his eyes, Tom lay there cursing himself for ever having heard of this accursed country. "Why did you do it, wee man? Why did you draw them away from me?"

Once out of the undergrowth, Tom followed a hard packed dirt road bordering on open farmland, beyond which lay the village they had been at so much pain to avoid. In the distance, a figure led a horse and cart, the peaceful scene in direct contrast to that which he had so recently witnessed.

According to his limited knowledge, this relatively flatland ran all the way up the west coast, unlike the central and western part of the country with its wild jungle and even wilder men and beasts. His own country in reverse, he thought.

A little way further on, the path took a sudden turn to the right and Tom caught sight of his friends for the first time, with the rotund figure of Sergeant Casova a little behind, acting as rearguard. Tom ran to catch up.

"Where is Tino?" Pablo shouted as Tom drew to a halt, the soldier's eyes on the empty road behind.

Tom fixed his eyes on a wheel of Miriam's chair, unable to look the soldier in the eye. "He drew them off in the opposite direction. He almost made it…"

"Tino, my cousin, is dead?" Pablo leaped forward as if to challenge the authenticity of Tom's statement. Then, realising it must be so, but still willing his cousin to appear, stared back down the long brown road.

Dane quickly moved between the two men.

"We best keep moving." Miriam cleared her throat. "No use us giving up what Tino has paid so dearly for."

At the crippled woman's words, the company silently moved off, each alone with their own thoughts.

"Sergeant Casova! Corporal Enrico!" Heads jerked up at the sound of the voice.

"It is Chico, Senor. I wonder how he came to find us? But Carlos is not with him!" Pablo exclaimed pushing the chair faster to meet the figure running and waving towards them.

"There he is!" Bev pointed to the figure running down the hillock a little way off.

Later, grouped in the middle of the dusty road, all endeavouring to make themselves heard, and none succeeding, Dane at a gesture from Miriam, bawled out, "Hold it! Hold it! Let's have some order here before all the Regulars in the country hear us! Will someone ask this guy how he came to find us?"

Marco did so and, after much gesturing and shrugging, turned to inform the civilians. "Chico say he was lucky enough to see us from the top of a hill back there. He almost headed in the wrong direction. But does not know where Carlos is. He was skirting the village when he heard gunshots and came to investigate. The rest you know."

"Does he know about, Tino?" Miriam asked quietly.

"He does, Senora," Marco nodded. "He also says he was infused by you going back on yourselves at the forest."

Dane grinned, not by the soldier's misuse of the word, but by the success of his own tactics.

"Maybe I will make General some day?" He made a face.

"General confusion, most likely," Tom tittered.

"Jealousy is a terrible thing, Mac," Dane said, good-humouredly.

Tom winked at him. "Never mind, you'll get over it some day."

"You're impossible, Tom Bell!" Miriam scolded.

"Aye, that's what all the lassies say! Come on. I'm starving."

The road was taking them to where they did not want to go…the village. Aware of this, Chico led them up a hillside and away from it, and out of sight of the open pastureland.

"Where do you think this road goes, Dane?" Bev hopped on one leg emptying a stone form her shoe as she asked the question.

"Nowhere it just lies here." Tom said quietly.

"S'ppose you think you're a real smart Pommie…" She halted before the adjective. "You Poms are all the same, think you own the world."

"Poms?" Tom wrinkled his brows, pretending not to have understood.

"That's Aussie for us English," Miriam ventured to explain.

"English!" Tom shrieked. "Dane!" he cried in mock outrage. "Did you hear what your girlfriend just called me?" Tom rounded on the girl. "I warned you about your language before, didn't I?"

"She's a cheeky Sheila," Dane answered, keeping up the pretence.

Exasperated, Bev clenched her fist. "Sheila! I'll give you Sheila, you good for nothing sons of…"

"Now, now, children," Miriam scolded them, "what are our hosts to think of us foreigners if we keep on so?" She halted at the sudden sight of an old man leading a donkey down the road towards them.

"One of you soldiers better speak to him," Miriam suggested, her eyes on the approaching figure.

Unhurriedly, the old man drew to a halt a little way from them, calmly stroking the animal as his eyes travelled from the woman in the wheelchair to the uniformed soldier moving out of the group and up the road towards him.

Pablo returned, drawing up a few feet away from where they stood. "The old man he says there are many Regulars in his village." He jerked a thumb at the village perched on the cliffs some distance above. "But says if we take shelter down there," he pointed to a path veering off to the right, "And wait until after dark, he may be able to slip us into the village and arrange to have us fed."

"Ask him if there are any vehicles we could commandeer...borrow?" Dane asked with an apologetic look at Marco, as if he had overstepped himself and the soldier should have first reported to his Sergeant instead.

Marco gestured that Pablo should continue, and that somehow he might still be able to reach the Regulars, and if he kept out of these discussions no suspicions would fallen on him.

Pablo faced the old man again, and when done, turned to inform the company. "He says...how do you say?" he scratched his head. "There is an enamoured car."

"Dear, dear," Tom quipped, and Bev flicked her foot at his ankle.

"It's no use our climbing this road to the village if we cannot obtain transport, for all we might hope for is some food from the villagers," Miriam sadly reflected, looking up at Dane.

"Point taken. Let's rest in the shade of that orange grove down there as this old guy suggests, and get off this road before any of those Regulars guys see us from up there. Do you think we can trust him, lady?"

"I don't think we're going to find out, or get that rest folks!" Tom groaned.

Dane followed Tom's pointing finger to the valley below, where a column of troops were trotting up the hill in their direction.

"How in the name of Sam Hill did they get to know we are here?" Dane exploded.

"Never mind that now. Where do we go from here?"

As if having understood Tom's question, the old man pointed to the orange grove, barking a few words to Pablo.

"He says to go that way, follow the valley in amongst the hills. We should be safe there until dark."

"Not more bloody hills," Tom moaned, taking hold of the wheelchair and staring in that direction.

"We are safe here." Pablo's eyes shone in the inky darkness of the hollow.

"Then perhaps they do not know for sure whether we came this way or not," Dane muttered more to himself than the company.

"They got pretty damned close, just when we thought we had given them the slip." Bev handed Miriam a water bottle, dabbing at her own face with a dampened handkerchief.

Taking a sip or two, Miriam handed it back to the girl. "When you have a minute, and are not too tired, could you give me a little help?" Miriam sounded all in and the girl sensed she must be in pain.

"Sure. I'd say this is as good a time as any."

Tom watched them move off into the darkness. "We'll soon be out of food Yank. How rough it's going to get from here is anybody's guess."

"We need transport and quick," Dane said with conviction. "How much more can the girls take do you think?"

Never mind the girls, Tom thought, watching something slimy crawling in the grass. "The old lady's game enough, and she has a purpose to keep going, where as the rest of us are mainly concerned with our own survival."

Contemptuously Dane swung on the Scot. "Are you saying man, you do not give a hill of beans whether the old girl gets through or not? Or what it will mean to the people of this country? I mean you English pride yourselves in democracy and being a peace loving nation do you not?" His question met by a sharp intake of breath from Tom.

"Firstly, I'm not English. Secondly, the English are the most peace loving people in the world, haven't they fought everyone in the world to prove it, including your own? As to my not giving a hill of beans, and if you don't mind one of my 'simply awful puns,'" Tom mimicked Miriam, "those beans backfired for me a long time ago. Nor could I give a hill of beans about this country's politics, though I am sorry for what is happening to some of its people. All I want, and I think you do too, is to get to where we are going…safely. And in my case that means Bonnie Scotland via your own fair land, and the sooner the better." Savagely, Tom turned up the collar of his jerkin, and drew his knees up to his chin. "So if you will excuse me, I will bid you a very good night, you Canadian."

They had only just set out next morning when Pablo came running to tell them that once again the soldiers were not so very far behind.

"Again!" Dane roared. "They seem to know every move we make!"

How did they come to find us so easily amongst these hills?" Miriam voiced what was on all of their minds.

"How close are they, Pablo?" Dane hurled at the soldier.

"Perhaps half an hour behind."

"I think we need to dissuade them…if that is the right word?" Marco tapped his rifle.

"It is good you should say that Sergeant Casova." Pablo unslung his own weapon. "It is a duty Chico and I will gladly do."

"I am the senior here, Corporal Pablo Enrico, I shall make the decisions." The resonance in Marco's voice had suddenly changed. "Chico and I will go. Should anything happen to me, you at least can speak the foreigners language. Come, Private we shall position ourselves up there."

"Well, there's authority for you," Tom whistled, watching the two trot for the hillside.

"Yip." Dane agreed following Tom's stare. "Except, how will those guys know which way we go when we do not know ourselves?"

"I could stay behind," Bev volunteered, waving back a storm of protests from all three. "It makes sense. You fellas are needed to push the chair, which leaves me free."

Reluctantly, they agreed and set off.

Ten minutes later, they heard the first of the rifle shots echoing around the hillside. Pablo cast a worried glance behind him. "I think they get close."

"I hope those two do not overstay their welcome," Miriam called out, clutching the arms of the chair as it was suddenly hoisted over a boulder on the narrow path.

"I'm worried about Bev," Tom panted guiding the chair around a depression, and handing over to Pablo.

"She can look after herself, man, as I should know," Dane muttered through his clenched teeth, the chair having caught itself on a rock.

After another exhausting half hour of pushing, Dane called a halt, crumpling over the back of the chair.

Tom straightened up stiffly, rubbing his aching back. He tapped Dane lightly on the arm, drawing his attention to the back of Miriam's neck where the chair's constant vibrations had blistered her white skin around the collar of her blouse, and to the bruises on her bare arms. The American saw it and gave a shudder.

Aware of the men standing silently behind her, Miriam tilted her head back a little. "Too exhausted for wisecracks, Tom?" she asked, laying his neatly folded jerkin on top of her jacket across her knee.

"No, wee wumman, just having a quick shifty at your chair just in case your solid tyres need pumped up," he lied. The remainder of his wisecrack lost in the sound of gunfire.

Pablo let out an oath in his own tongue, his eyes wide at the closeness of the guns.

"Let's go you guys. All hands to the wheel!" Dane cried, throwing Tom the half empty water bottle and pushing the chair.

With his turn at pushing over, Chico ran ahead to scout out the best route to eventually lead them round the side of a hillock, the others running and pushing the bouncing chair in turns, while its occupant held on for dear life, until they broke out into open ground once more.

"We can make good time from here," Dane panted, swivelling round at Tom running behind. "Pablo and I will keep pushing. You go back…" he choked for breath and started again. "Find Bev…tell her…which way we've gone, and remind her not to stay too far behind and to be careful."

"Got you pal!" Tom shouted as he turned away, happy to be away from the backbreaking pushing of the chair, and the chances of being alone with the girl for however brief, despite the circumstances.

It was in fact the girl who found Tom. "Psst!" she cried from amongst the tall grass at the top of a slope.

"How dare you! I've never touched a drop in weeks!" Tom shouted, bounding up the slope and throwing himself down on the grass beside her.

"Shut up, moron." Bev regaled him. "Danger, I can handle, your jokes, no. It makes me want to stand up with my hands in the air and surrender."

"To me or the enemy? No need to answer that." Tom tugged at a blade of grass, his apparent nonchalance interrupted by a thunderous sound of gunfire.

"Down there." Bev gestured to the valley below, over which close on fifty soldiers were advancing in line.

"In the name o' the wee man are we no' the popular ones! There's too many down there, even for Bogey to handle!" Tom whistled, burying himself deeper into the grass.

"It's all right, hero, Marco and his mate are the targets, not you,"

Bev mocked.

"You never know, maybe some o them have heard my jokes. Even worse, maybe some are Rangers supporters!"

"There you go again Tom Bell, how am I supposed to understand your parochial humour?"

Ignoring the jibe, Tom swung his attention to the events in the valley, then to a hillock a little to his left where two soldiers lay partially hidden.

Now close to the 'front line', he was amazed by the noise of fifty rifles going off intermittently, and the puny response of his comrades as the uneven battle continued.

"I hope those two know when to quit." Tom nodded towards his allies.

"They sure do okker, they've been doing it for the last two hillocks."

A Regular threw his hands in the air and fell to the ground. Tom shuddered. Some holiday.

Tom did not know what to make of the girl's attitude. He'd have thought she would have been affected by all of this killing. God knew, he was! Perhaps, it was a kind of revenge for her friend's death.

He rose and for a few seconds believed his legs had other ideas. "Oh aye...I must be off now as your average Pom would say." He hoped she would not notice the tremor in his voice. "Follow the hollow 'till you come to a clump of bushes, take to your left round the shoulder of the embankment, we're following the open ground. Don't ask me where it leads, it's the only way to go. We can't take the chair up hills, we're merely going round them and up and down the valleys. Whether it will take us closer to our destination, beats me."

As he spoke, the sound of gunfire had increased. Another soldier fell. Tom gave Bev a look of propensity. "Don't wait here too long, Bev, and please be careful."

"I sure will sport." The girl gave him a quiet smile, and called out after his departing figure, "And thanks." And to herself: well I'll be damned, I think MacTavish really means it.

It was Pablo who found the hiding place for them. Whilst climbing along a ledge, to gain a better lie of the land, his foot slipped and he had fallen into the bushes below, landing almost unscathed in a small rocky amphitheatre totally hidden from the outside world. Finding a way out, he quickly summoned his friends to inspect this unexpected hiding place.

Once Bev and the two soldiers had rejoined them, they diligently set about covering up their tracks, and huddle together in the fading light to await the arrival of their pursuers, all acutely aware that should they be discovered there was no escape.

"I think they might have missed us, gone a different way," Tom whispered.

Bev shook her head. "No, they were pretty damned close when we took to our heels."

The sound of running footsteps confirmed Bev's deductions.

"Leave that rifle alone Sergeant," Chico hissed at Marco. "Do you want them to hear?"

Marco glared at his subordinate. Other eyes swung on him. Feeling their hostility, he slid his hand off the bolt.

Outside, the sound grew louder. "Now we'll know," Dane mumbled, his eyes glued on the entrance.

To each encased in their own private thoughts, it seemed an eternity before the sound of tramping, running feet finally receded.

"Phew! I think they've gone," Bev trembled, laying her head on Dane's shoulder.

Setting aside his rifle, Marco started to crawl to the entrance.

"Not yet Sergeant," the American cautioned, touching him lightly on the leg. "They may have left a few of their pals behind."

Rebuked yet again, this time by a civilian, Marco halted, the look of hatred for the American hidden in the semi-darkness of the hollow. There would be another time, and for this little incident the foreigners would suffer.

"Well, I believe there is nothing for us to do but wait 'till morning," Miriam said calmly.

"We could eat," Tom suggested, looking expectantly at the soldiers, hungry now that the tension was leaving him.

"You are hungry at a time like this?" Bev was scarcely able to believe the Scot.

Tom made himself comfortable against a rock. "Can you think of anything better to do?"

Chico held out what little supplies he had gathered from his comrades. "We have very little left, Senor Tom."

"We must reach a village." Dane squashed an insect crawling up his leg. "Find us some transport. Different if we could climb higher, as it is…"

"You have a crippled woman to push," Miriam finished the sentence for him.

"You are correct, lady. Then again, we would not be here if it was not for you in the first place."

"Chicken and the egg, would you not say, Mr MacAndrews?"

"Yeah something like that."

"Right now I'd settle for the chicken," Tom grumbled. No one laughed.

After a less than a fitful night's sleep in their new hiding place, Tom stretched himself to his full height, yawning in the early morning sun. He stepped into the glade, where Pablo and Chico stood a little distance away deep in earnest conversation, while on the ridge above Marco sat staring intently into a small mirror, clipping delicately at his moustache.

Tom rubbed the stubble on his chin. It was again time to ask one of the soldiers for a loan of a razor.

"'Morning, Tom, looks like another hot day," Bev greeted him warmly, shading her eyes.

"A good day for drying, so my auld Granny would say."

"Beg yours?"

"Ach, I don't suppose you Aussies don't have to bother about the cold and the rain."

"Depends where you live in Aus, I reckon," Bev reflected, lowering her hand. "Gee, I wish I was back there now. Bondi or Cronulla would do me, sport."

Tom caught her by the sleeve of her stained checked shirt as she was about to turn.

"You miss it Bev? You'd rather be out of all this and at home the same as me?" he commiserated.

She stared over his shoulder a far away look in her eyes, a slight tremor in her voice as she said, "Too right, sport."

Tom squeezed her arm. "Never mind, sport, I'll see you all right."

"No worries, MacTavish, I'll be right." Then, she was gone greeting the tall Yank with a friendly good morning.

"Bugger you Sheila," Tom said half aloud. Then, smiled at the new language he'd picked up from a girl who had never given him a second glance.

"They're here! Over there!" Pablo came plunging down the hillside above their glade.

"I thought they were all gone!" Dane cried unbelievingly. "Quick. Tell the old girl in there, what's happening and to stay put!" Dane threw an arm in the direction of their hideout.

"Let's go! This way!" Bev yelled up at Marco still sitting on the ridge, the other soldiers already on her heels.

A half hour later, exhausted from their narrow escape, the party halted.

"Well, at least they won't find the old lady," Tom panted.

"If she'd been with us, we'd be done for." Bev drew a hand across her brow.

"Well, that's it for me!" Tom barked, "I've had enough! I say we leave her where she is." He made a buffer of his hands against the looks cast his way. "We can travel faster without her. Maybe have the chance of getting out of this alive." Tom spread his hands in a gesture of desperation. "Then, in the chance that things might go all right, we can always go back for her. Perhaps with some food."

"You miserable little Scotch bastard!" Bev howled. "You know you have no intention of going back once you're out of here. You said as much to me this morning…You and all that so called Scotch pride…Gee, you make me sick!" Bev swung round, her face contorted with rage. "Well, we Aussies are a different breed sport, we do not run out on our mates."

Dane swung the outraged girl round to face him. "As much as I hate to admit it, Tom's right, we stand a better chance without her. Anyhow, it is really her these guys are after not us. Maybe they will leave us alone when…" Dane hesitated. "If they find her."

Bev stared hard at the American, unwilling to believe this could be coming from the man she was beginning to fall in love with. "You too, Dane?" she cried, breaking free from his hold, and leaping back to regale him and the company. "Are you all forgetting what this lady has sacrificed to do what she is doing? Okay," she stormed, "you all pushed and shoved, but it was no picnic for her either! You do not know what she has been through…physically and mentally, and for what, for God's sake? For doing what she believes in! For these people!" She waved a hand at the militia. "For trying to help…and when the going gets tough you all up and leave her! Well, not me folks…not me."

Self consciously, Tom studied his feet, while Dane stared anxiously back the way they had come. The soldiers who understood what had been said stood shuffling from one foot to another. Then, just as suddenly, Dane grabbed the girl again and called to Tom for his assistance.

"Sorry, hen," Tom apologised, bending one arm behind her back, and simultaneously side-stepped a kick aimed at his shin and pushed her into a run. Four mystified militia following in their wake.

It was only when the danger of being seen by the Regulars that Bev agreed to run with the company. Running, dodging, now at liberty to climb higher without the encumbrance of the chair, they finally came to a halt.

"We might just do it," Dane stared across the valley they'd just crossed. "Perhaps if we were to split up, and head for the village we saw earlier when we were higher up, we might be able to get some supplies and return for the old lady. She'll be pretty safe where she is, if she keeps herself hidden."

"You mean if she has not yet found out the rats have deserted her," Bev mocked.

"If you put it that way," Dane replied caustically. "You for one are coming with me, I do not want you ballsing it up, for the old lady or anyone else. Okay?"

Sullenly, Bev agreed with a nod. "Okay, let's split up. See you all in the village, I hope."

When each had gone their separate ways, Sergeant Marco Casova smiled to himself, while retracing his steps to where Miriam Plesher hid. Twice now, he had failed to gain the attention of the Regulars, but now when he most wanted them they were nowhere to be seen.

Eventually, the portly Sergeant recognised the glade where they had left the old Inglesa a few hours earlier, gloating at his prospective wealth, and the thought of fat Sergeant Basilo's face when he discovered who had found the Tullido-Inglesa.

Scrambling up the same ridge where he had prepared his toilet that morning, Marco unslung his rifle. Reaching into his kit bag, he extricated the small hand mirror and held it up to the sun's rays, its reflection travelling to the opposite side of the valley. His face glowing with satisfaction, Marco flicked the mirror, then again. This time he was rewarded by an answering signal from the hillside opposite, then another from farther away. Puzzled, Marco swung to his right where another flash answered his signal, he cursed and swung to his left. There it was again, another glint in the afternoon sun.

"Perplexed are we, Sergeant?"

Startled by the sound of the voice, Marco spun round to face the American, who gun in hand climbed the ridge to confront him. "I think you're good buddies will be a mite puzzled as to where we actually are, eh?"

Unwilling to trust himself to speak, Marco sank to the grass, his mouth working, saliva trickling down his chin, then with something akin to a wail held his head in his hands.

"You big Yanky...B..." Bev howled up at Dane from below.

"Sorry about that Sheila," Dane grinned down at her. "All will be revealed in good time."

However, it was upwards of two hours before they were all assembled in the glade, the soldiers having arrived last, their looks changing from one of utter disbelief at Miriam Plesher sitting dozing in her chair as if in an English country garden, to one of hatred at the man who had so treacherously betrayed them.

"I shall kill him!" Pablo snarled, advancing on the cringing Sergeant, bayonet in hand.

"No Pablo, not yet awhile." Dane grabbed him by the shoulder.

"Would someone mind telling me what this is all about?" Bev stamped her feet in angry frustration.

"It was Mac here, who first cottoned on to Marco's little game," Dane began, waving the pistol at the Scot.

"Aye. It was seeing how the light fell on Marco's mirror while he was trimming his moustache one day that first set me thinking," Tom explained. "I mind seeing something similar in a Bogey picture. Besides, it seemed a wee bit too suspicious to me how our hero here always volunteered to act as rear-guard, seeing as he is no Jesse Owens."

"This, and the fact those Regular guys always seemed to know when we doubled back on our tracks or changed direction, without them ever dividing their forces." Dane continued.

Not to be outdone, Miriam took up the story, swinging her chair round to face the girl. "Tom mentioned his suspicious to me, though at first we were unsure which, if indeed any of our militia were the traitors, then, when we discovered that Marco's fellow Sergeant had reinforcements awaiting us, we knew that somehow he was aware of the importance of whom he was chasing. We came to the conclusion it was likely to be one or both of the militia who had the greatest opportunity of speaking to Sergeant Basilo in the village that day when they went for supplies.

"Sorry, Pablo," Miriam apologised to the man who was translating what she had said about their Sergeant. "But, since your cousin Tino was killed by the Regulars, we thought it unlikely that it would be you."

"Si! Senora, Tino was my blood cousin." Pablo rose. "Chico also say our Sergeant found it…how you say, not so easy to hit any Regulars when he was back in the valley with him. This makes him also suspicious, so we set a trap for the rat…this rat!" He shook his fist angrily at Marco.

"But the mirrors? How did you manage that? And how?" Bev turned to each in turn for an explanation.

It was Tom who obliged. "We knew Mrs Plesher was safe enough where she was, so we told her what was intended, she agreed, giving Dane her gun, just in case, and our friends set out to flash their shaving mirrors all around the hillsides, hoping of course that Basilo would dismiss Casova's signal as a fake, having already passed this way. Our little charade worked in making Casova believe we were in fact leaving wee wumman here, thanks to you, Bev. We knew you'd never stand for leaving her behind, hence the reason for us not including you in our plot. Also, our splitting up gave Casova the best chance he ever had. Besides, he had to be here to show the Regulars where she was hidden."

Still bewildered by it all, Bev sat down on a rock near the wheelchair taking Miriam's hand in her own. "What now?" she asked, staring straight ahead, her question directed at no one in particular.

"I think we can safely leave that to the militia," Miriam said softly. "Although I think it is about time we were on the move again, there is no way of being sure our friends will not come this way again."

They did not head for the intended village. After catching up with them, Pablo expressed his preference of bypassing the place for a village higher up the mountainside which he was sure would prove to be of greater safety. After the events of the day, no one was inclined to disagree.

Chapter 8

"This is the life!" Tom sang out cheerfully, scrubbing under his arms with a cake of black soap, only his head and shoulders showed above the rim of the tall barrel of hot water.

"You can say that again, Mac." Dane stood wringing out his one and only shirt, his back to the wide-open landscape of the valley below, now growing faint in the evening light.

They had reached the village late in the day, their welcome warmer than previously given to the militia, who had gone on ahead to ensure that it was friendly, and not in enemy hands. Now that they realised which side Pablo and his men were on, things were now different.

After a meal, Tom was enjoying his first real wash since he did not know when. He was wiping soap from his eyes when the wheelchair edged around the corner of their hosts house's tiny balcony.

"Hello there!" he called out, perhaps a little too cheerfully, in an attempt to eradicate the memory of the day's events. "Your turn for the barrel Bev!"

"Go bite your bum, MacTavish," Bev replied stonily.

"Such a lady," Tom chuckled. "You'd be next wee wumman, except I think it would rust your wheels."

"You are in no position to get smart, Tom Bell," Miriam scowled.

"Say you guys, how about calling a truce, at least for tonight, okay?" Dane asked hopefully, hanging his shirt over the low-whitewashed wall bordering the small garden.

"Suits me, especially that bit about tonight," Tom grinned at the girl.

"You've got a one track mind MacTavish...and a dirt track at that," Bev answered back "It's going to be a beautiful evening," she said, turning to Miriam to get away from the annoying Scot and hoping her insult would shut him up, at least for a time.

"Promises! Promises!" Tom threw his eyes to the heavens and ducked beneath the water.

That night Tom fought off the desire to sleep, choosing to relish the satisfaction of a full stomach and the comfort of the big bed for a little while longer.

Should everything go according to plan, they could well be on their way to Corona by this time tomorrow. Now that it was almost over, it did not appear as bad as it had a seemed. Who are you kidding Ding, he thought. You wouldn't go through all that again for all the tea in China, or all the Tennants in Govan.

What a tale he would have to tell when he got home though; worth a few free pints, if he was not mistaken. Then, he fell asleep.

"What the hell's going on!" Tom growled, attempting to cover his head with the pillow, only to find himself grabbed by several pairs of hands and dragged out of bed and dumped unceremoniously on to the floor, his bleary eyes travelling up the leg of a highly polished riding boot.

"I wish you a very good morning, Mister Escoces," the owner of the boot was saying in English. "Allow me to introduce myself, I am Colonel Roberto Segovia, Chief of State Security. And you, my young friend, are my prisoner."

"You have all their names, Sergeant?" Segovia asked, holding out his hand for the clipboard.

"Yes, my Colonel. The young Escoces was most willing to co-operate."

Segovia ran his eyes down the list, his face slowly contorting with rage. "The young Escoces you say? Come, let us meet this man."

By the time he had entered the adjoining room, Segovia had once again regained his composure. Slowly, he let his eyes wander passed the crippled lady calmly sitting in her wheelchair with the young girl perched on its arm, to the tall American leaning against the far wall, the Scot by his side.

Smiling, Segovia eyes lingered on the latter. Stepping slowly, deliberately towards the Scot, his smile broadened. "So, it is you we must thank for this excellent contribution?" Segovia scanned the names on the board.

"It was nothing," Tom shrugged, returning the smile.

"In this, you are correct my young friend. Let me see... Who do we have here?" Segovia spun round jauntily to face the old woman, beginning to enjoy the situation, and what was about to follow. "You, it would appear are none other than Mistress Rosie Houses." Next, he pointed to the girl. "You are...?" the interrogated consulted his list, "Leeza Lane."

"Too right sport, that's me," Bev sniggered, Tom having explained the pun to her. Segovia nodded.

With slow deliberation, he turned to face the men, wagging a finger at Dane. "Am I correct in addressing you as Mister Percy Vere?"

"Right on man," Dane hung his head in miserable defeat.

Suddenly the inflection in the Colonel's voice changed as he swung menacingly on the Scot. "And, now we come to the master spy, himself, Mister Tom Foolery!"

Segovia examined the list, his eyes cold. "You may well believe these names fool such people as my Sergeant here, who is not so conversant with your language," Segovia hissed, "but me, they do not! Allow me to introduce you to my language."

Lashing out, Segovia caught Tom on the side of the head with the clipboard, savagely repeating the blow as the Scot staggered forward.

"So that's why they call it a clipboard!" Tom wheezed, and had his comment rewarded by a further blow to the head that brought him to his knees.

Satisfied he had demonstrated his power adequately, Segovia turned to address the women only to find himself catapulted across the room, his guards reaction slower than Tom's knee which had caught the angry Colonel squarely in the groin. Wheezing Segovia clutched at a chair to retain his balance as well as his dignity, while the guards fell upon the Scot, pounding him to the ground with their rifle butts.

Once again, Tom was up on that high ridge and falling into that bottomless cavern he had been so scared of that long hot day, falling and falling, ever falling until at last there was nothing but blackness.

Somewhere, there was the sound of someone speaking. Close to his blurred vision, bright red patches danced to the brass band playing in his head, each instrumentalist blaring out a different theme, and all out of tune. His eyes focused slightly, and the patches became a pattern, the pattern a shirt, a warm shirt on which he rested his head.

"I think he's coming round, Bev," Tom heard Dane say from afar.

Cradled in her lap, Bev stared down at him anxiously.

"That was a bloody stupid thing to do sport, if you don't mind my French." She spoke directly into his upturned face, her voice a mixture of concern and anger.

Under different circumstances, Tom would have welcomed his present position. Had he not dreamt of being so close to the girl? But, right now, with his head playing three different Pibrochs, it lacked that certain something. He saw the fear in her eyes and knew it was not reserved for him.

Despite the fact that all he wanted right now was to close his eyes, and wish away the pain, he knew he had to reassure her that all was not lost, and that they could all get out of it somehow.

"A natural reflex reaction," he grumbled, sitting up shakily and gingerly feeling the back of his head. "For a wee while there, I thought I was back in the Band of Hope in Cathcart Road and getting the back o' my head clouted with the back o' a tambourine for singing out of tune as usual."

Giving the impression she had ignored the remark, Bev examined the bruises above Tom's eye. "That beating you took 'sworse than I thought: it's affected your humour." She poked at the bruises none too gently.

Tom bit back a yell and sat up.

"Right on, baby." Dane was amused by the girl's action. "Now, he knows what it feels like to be on the receiving end for once."

If they were relieved to see that he was not badly hurt, they had a funny way of showing it. Then again, perhaps he had got what he deserved, Tom thought, having subjected them to his 'patter' long enough.

Tom's heart jumped as he looked around him. "Where is the wee wumman?" He freed himself from the girl and rested his back against the wall.

"Mrs Plesher? Big ma mountain came while you were out. "They carted her away," Bev told him bitterly.

Tom grabbed at the edge of the bench on which he sat, not wanting them to see how worried, or how much he was shaking over the disappearance of the old lady. "And you let them?" A pain stabbed at his eyes, and he closed them for a second. He heard Dane gurgle, "it was bigger than both of us."

"He tried, Tom. See the cut on his face."

"Okay," Tom conceded, "but what really happened?"

"Segovia, or whatever he's called, came back with a guard and this enormous woman and took her away. As you know, your friend is the one he is really after...." Bev was about to go on when the door crashed open and the most colossal figure of a woman Tom had ever seen burst into the room, wheeling Miriam Plesher before her in her chair.

"Well I've heard about Suma wrestlers, but this is the first one I've ever seen," Tom breathed to Bev, more than a little relieved to see 'wee wumman' again.

"What have you done to her, you big..." Bev seethed, a lump coming to her throat as she crossed to the disconsolate figure slumped in the chair.

Tom winced at the girl's outburst. There goes that Aussie diplomacy, he thought, afraid to think of the repercussions.

"You would not be addressing yourself to me, Senorita?" Segovia asked, emerging from behind the mountain of flesh.

"And I never saw her lips move once," Tom gasped in fake astonishment. "Boy would she no' make some goalie for the Jags, that's if she did not get stuck between the posts."

"You find something amusing, Mr Tom Foolery? Perhaps you do, but I can assure you your English colleague does not." In order to accentuate his words, Segovia held up a narrow strip of celluloid.

"Not cunning enough I am afraid, my dear," Segovia laughed, dangling the microfilm tantalizingly in front of Miriam's eyes. "Did you think you could outwit such a one as Roberto Segovia? You may be wondering how we came to find you? Well, here is the reason." Segovia snapped his fingers. There was a sound outside and Pablo stood in the doorway. "It is he you must thank for your capture."

"Not you!" Dane cried, while the others also stared at him in disbelief. "How could you, after your own cousin was killed by this mob?"

"I have many cousins, Senor, but only one father." The man drew himself up to his full height. "My beloved President, the father of my country, Rafael Biezoto."

"But you killed Marco! And we know for a fact it was he who betrayed our every move."

"Did you actually see me do this thing Senor? It was a good trick, eh? Sergeant Casova is at this time heading back to our village to help the Regulars there."

"How much did they pay you?" Tom asked scathingly. "Thirty

pesos of silver?"

Pablo took a quick step forward but Segovia restrained him with a slight touch on his arm. For a moment, both militiamen and the Scot stood glaring at one another across the tiny room until with a sudden movement, Pablo swung on his heel.

"Do you still find this amusing, my friend?" Segovia asked of Tom. "Now that I have achieved what I was seeking, it leaves me with nothing more to do than have you shot as a spy Mister Tom Foolery." Segovia smirked. "Perhaps both your friends as well. After all, did they not help the treacherous Inglesa reach this far?"

At Segovia words, Tom felt he had been hit on the head again, and wished he had not just kicked this sneering Colonel where it had hurt. Through the mist that was clouding his vision, he heard the lady's voice, soft, low. "You have what you want Segovia, now let them…all of them go."

Tom could have cried the way wee wumman had said it. She had sounded so dejected, beaten, as if now past caring and wishing it was all over. She…they had come so far. Suddenly weak, he leaned against the wall for support.

"You know damned well none of these people are spies," Miriam was saying, staring straight ahead, all fight knocked out of her frail body. "I merely used them for my own ends." Miriam moved her head to look the leering soldier straight in the eye. "Perhaps you would care to think again Colonel Segovia? You are dealing with three distinctly different nationalities here. Should you make a mistake, create a diplomatic incident, resulting in an investigation, your beloved President may not reward you as you may think."

If Miriam thought to dissuade Roberto Segovia, he showed no sign. Instead, calmly lighting a cheroot, he blew smoke into the air studying the ceiling. What the old lady said was true, this he already knew. However, he was not so certain of the Escoces innocence in all of this. Also, he would like his revenge. His groin still ached.

Segovia pointed accusingly at Tom. "Do you expect me to believe that this man helped you all this way without knowing the reason why?"

He was angry now, the pompous old woman's words had disturbed him and he shook with rage. "No, my dear, even this charade he has concocted for my benefit, has more than convinced me that he is not as stupid as he would have me believe him to be.

Are you Mister Tom Bell?"

At the mention of his own name, Tom's head shot up as his antagonist went on.

"Ah yes, Mr Bell, I am aware of who you are, and how you connived to enter my country, through the disguise of an American tourist organisation. However, this did not fool me for one minute."

"How many minutes did it fool you for?" Tom countered, anger replacing fear.

"Always the court jester, eh my friend?" the Colonel sneered. "Well prepare yourself for your final performance."

Segovia swung back to the lady in the chair. "You were correct in bringing to my attention the nationalities of your three…acc…friends." He smiled at his deliberate faux pas, "also of the repercussions that their execution may have brought to my country. However," he paused for effect, "should they meet with an unfortunate accident in these…unsettled times." His face lit up triumphantly at the gasps of disbelief. "You must understand my dear friends, I cannot possibly afford to leave any witnesses to this little eh…episode."

"Do you think this Segovia guy will go through with it?" Dane's voice came at Tom through the darkness of their fetid cell.

Tom found a less damp patch and squatted down against the wall. "I don't think he's got much choice now he's gone this far," he replied, gingerly massaging his jaw. "You heard the man…no witnesses."

Suddenly to Tom, Glasgow was so very far away. If only his uncle had not come home for Granny's funeral. If only Granny hadn't died. All the past events leading up to where he was now flashed in no particular sequence through his brain. Now it was no longer funny, he was all out of jokes, these eejits here were actually going to do him in!

Now, he was no longer a bystander in a revolution that did not concern him, this was the stark realization of it all. Nor was he a cinemagoer watching a picture, who, because he didn't like what he saw on the screen, could just as easily get up and walk out. The cold fact was he was in the picture.

So, now that it was inevitable, how was he going to react? Go out fighting and kicking, just like any Saturday night back home after a few bevvies, or casually ask for a cigarette, though he didn't smoke. Or on the other hand just pass out with fright.

"I suppose it will be a firing squad." Dane interrupted his thoughts.

"As long as they stand in a circle," Tom answered wearily. His mind was still somewhere back home and he didn't want to let go.

Dane's laughter echoed eerily. "I will pay that one Mac."

Tom's eyes searched the cell, found a darker shape in the opposite corner. "We should get shot more often Yank, that's the first joke of mine you've laughed at," he said addressing the shape.

"Captive audience, Tom."

Tom stretched out his left leg to relieve the pain in his hip. "Don't expect me to return the compliment, all I want is to be alive to do encores, although with my type of jokes I'm used to dying as they say in show biz."

There was silence for a time until Dane voiced what was on both their minds. "Where do you think they have taken the women, Mac?"

"Beats me. That bastard's got the film wee wumman worked so hard to keep from him, and to think it was to end like this after all she has gone through."

"You did not do so badly yourself, Scottie. The little lady told me something of how you practically carried her clear over the mountains before we met."

Despite himself, Tom felt pleased. "She exaggerated, no man can carry a chair over mountains, you saw that for yourself. It may have felt like mountains, but it was just wee foothills. Anyway, that's all by the way now."

To hide his embarrassment, Tom changed the subject. "What about Bev? She doesn't deserve any of this. First, her pal Gillian, then…" he trailed off, leaving the rest unsaid.

"She's a strong minded gal, Tom. Once she had got over the shock of Gilly, you saw how she came round; hid her feelings real swell I'd' say."

"I know," Tom agreed. "You're a lucky man Yank."

"How come, Mac? What makes you say that?"

"Bev and you, I mean," suddenly surprised by his own candidness.

"Gee fella," Dane chuckled in the darkness, "that I should be so lucky! No, Bev and me are just good buddies."

"That's what they say in the papers," Tom sighed wiggling his toes to bring back some warmth into them. "I've seen the way she looks at you, she thinks the sun shines out of your ar…Arizona. You can do no wrong."

"Gee I never noticed! Seems I shall have to make it up to her when we get out of here."

"When?" Tom emphasised.

"Sure man. Where there's a will, there's a way."

"Pity my names Tom."

"Well, you are good at making up names, how about Will Power?"

"I don't think I'm ready for this," Tom answered tersely, for he was now thinking of Segovia and the way he had of looking at Bev.

As the hollow sound of footsteps in the corridor drew nearer, Bev instinctively retreated into the far corner of her tiny cell, her mouth dry. It had to happen sooner or later, she told herself. Segovia was not the kind of man to leave a defenceless Sheila like her alone. Had she not seen it in his eyes when he'd issued instructions to have Mrs Plesher taken to a cell further down the corridor? Now he was here.

She bit her lip hard. Surely not here on the floor? No, she decided, the Colonel, she was sure was a man who enjoyed his comfort and his pleasures. He would not take her here.

Tears sprang to her eyes as she damned her own weakness. Was she not of good Aussie outback stock? Well fella, she whispered resolutely, let's see how far you get. What MacTavish did to you is nothing compared to what you'll get from me. See if you can stand having your bells rung twice in one day!

There was a click, the key turned in the lock. She dug her nails into the cold stonewall at her back and waited.

"Quickly Senorita, before Colonel Segovia finds out I am here." Framed against the dim light, Pablo stood beckoning to her in the doorway.

Afraid and suspicious, Bev did not move. Was this another of Segovia's tricks?

"You must come," Pablo said urgently, beckoning her again. He opened the door wider and took a step towards her. Bev froze against the wall certain that it was a trap. "We have very little time before they discover I have fooled them."

This time there was no mistaking the fear in the man's voice. Bev took a hesitant step forward, wanting to believe him. She made up her mind. If it was a trap, well what was the difference. Abstractly, her feet followed the man down the dimly lit corridor.

"We meet again, my dear." Miriam Plesher suddenly appeared from a cell doorway, Chico at her back. She grasped the girl's hand. "Not all is always as it seems," she said, hoping to keep the strain out of her voice.

"You can say that again, lady," Bev croaked and, for a brief moment, thought that her knees were about to fold.

Pablo put a finger to his lips. Silently, they followed him further along the corridor. Bev clutched Miriam's hand tighter. The older woman would have liked to have whispered something reassuring to the girl but was afraid how it might sound in the hollow confines of the corridor. Finally, they came to a flight of stairs, and Pablo signalled them to stop.

"You must stay here. Si?"

"We understand perfectly," Miriam whispered.

Pablo was on the third step, handing Chico a rifle when the first shots rang out, the sound propelling both militiamen up the stairs and out of the door at the top.

"What do you reckon is happening up there, Mrs Plesher?" Bev's voice shook, her eyes on the top of the stairs.

Miriam shifted uncomfortably in her chair, not wishing unduly to alarm the girl, resilient though she may be. "At a guess I'd say, either Pablo and Chico are in deep trouble or they are getting a little outside assistance from some friends."

A few anxious minutes later, Chico burst back through the door, closely followed by Tom and Dane.

"What are two nice girls like you doing in a place like this?" Tom called out cheerfully hobbling down the stairs to meet them, the relief on his face at seeing them both safe, only too plain.

Bev thought she would have been pleased to see the Scot: happy to hear one of his jibes again but somehow it was all too much for her. "Trying to escape from your tiresome jokes, Tom Bell," she retorted giving him the full glare of her anger. It was much too much by far to have the good fortune to have escaped or, partly so from the clutches of a monster like Segovia due to the bravery of the two militia men only to be confronted by the imbecility of this insufferable Scot!

Miriam flashed Tom a sympathetic look. Didn't the girl realise the boy was just as every bit as worried and afraid as she was? "Bad timing, Tom," was all she could find to say.

"We'll soon have you out of here." Dane lifted up one side of the chair, Tom the other and began carrying her up the steps. "You all right, Bev?" Dane panted at her over his shoulder.

"'Suppose," Bev answered, bending to help lift the chair from behind.

"Please to wait here," Pablo commanded them to halt on the midway landing. Then turned to run to the top of the stairs where he cautiously poked his head out of the half open door.

Miriam motioned to where Pablo crouched by the door, her tone a mixture of curiosity as well as anxiety. "What's happening up there Tom? Do you know?"

"I don't know wee wumman, Dane and me were not held this far up."

Pablo returned, descending the steps two at a time. "Those who do not like our President are here…my people! They are trying to hold…how do you say…ah the courtyard." He slid down beside them. "The Regulars are firing at them from the upper windows as they enter through the gate. I think it is too dangerous for us to move from here at present, or at least until we are sure that it is all our people out there."

"Perhaps Corporal Enrico…Pablo," Miriam smiled at her first use of his Christian name. "You could tell us how you came to outwit the infamous Colonel Segovia, if you are not too busy?" Miriam suggested clutching at the arms of her chair and hoping no one would notice, for should this firing continue to intensify, this waiting was sure to get to them sooner or later. Sooner, she guessed, after all they had recently been through.

Pablo shot a hasty look up and down the stairs. He was not quite sure this was the right time. He shot another look beneath them and cradled his rifle in his arms. The Inglesa woman gave him a quick wink and he guessed there must be a good reason for her asking at a time like this.

"It was not difficult Senora." He threw another quick anxious look upwards. "When I saw the Regulars crossing the valley to the village that morning, I knew we had no chance of escape…not…"

"Pushing a wheelchair," Miriam aided him.

"Si, Senora. So I say to Manuel who's hospitality you enjoy, go tell the Regulars the Inglesa lady and her friends are here. Tell them it is Corporal Enrico, of the militia who has sent you." Pablo spread his hands in way of explanation. "This way I hope to stay free to help you and also save the village from…I do not know the word Senora," Pablo shrugged helplessly.

"Reprisal…burned, people hurt." Miriam suggested, clutching the chair slightly harder as the gunfire intensified from above.

"Si, Senora. I did not choose to tell my comrades of this. You must all look surprised and afraid when the soldiers come."

"Well, you succeeded where I was concerned, pal," Tom conceded, letting out a deep breath.

"Pablo! Pablo!" Chico called in alarm from the top of the stairs. "Regulars, they are coming this way!"

Miriam quickly translated his message to the others.

"I do not have a blue sash, Senora," Pablo apologised, quickly wrapping a blue handkerchief round his arm. "Now, perhaps my friends will not make the mistake and shoot me! Eh?" he laughed.

"Let's hope they are all Rangers supporters there, Pablo," Tom suggested helping to tie the hankie tighter, and aiding him on his way with a friendly slap on the back.

A few seconds later, the first of the Regulars attacking the half open door were met by an accurate fire from both militiamen. Hardly had this ceased before a second attack was mounted, and a dead attacker tumbled down the stairs to land a few steps above them.

"Just like the movies, is it Tom, Bogie and all that?" Miriam asked sarcastically, glancing across at the Scot's ashen face.

"Worse…Parkhead."

As if the corpse lying a few steps above would suddenly rise and attack her, Bev crossed quickly to sit by Dane.

"We'll be all right, gal," he soothed in a voice that was far from convincing, wrapping an arm around her.

"Got an arm for me, Yank?" Tom called across from where he sat in the stairwell above. A body tumbled past and he drew himself against the wall, knees drawn up to his chin, wishing he could completely disappear.

"Chico has been hit!" The panic in Pablo's voice reached down to them. "Here come the Regulars again. Segovia must have given orders to have us all killed!"

Seizing one of fallen rifles, Dane scrambled up stairs, and threw himself down beside the two militiamen, firing into the courtyard.

"A regular Errol Flynn if you ask me," Tom muttered.

"What about you MacTavish? Aren't you going to help?" Bev stared at him, accusingly.

Avoiding the question, Tom's eyes met those of the lady in the chair. Perhaps this girl did not realise all he had gone through since meeting this little old lady. From first becoming a fugitive from justice, to burglar, thief, cheat and, despite all this, they now expected him to kill people into the bargain. Well, somewhere the line had to be drawn.

Holding Tom's look, and despite the seriousness of the situation, Miriam could not bring herself to condemn his action, or rather lack of it. Still looking at him, Miriam addressed herself to the girl. "I am sure Tom has his reasons."

"Not religious?" Bev moaned.

"'Fraid so, Bev. I am a practicing coward. I practice it religiously," Tom apologised. "I'm afraid cowards run in our family."

It was no use, he thought, he couldn't sit here, not the way she was looking at him. Then with a shrug as if it would be all the same in a hundred years from now, he snatched up a rifle and vaulted up the stairs to offer Dane the weapon.

"Can you not shoot?" The American spat at him, throwing aside his own empty rifle.

"Shoot through!" came the Aussie reply from below.

Ignoring the comment, Tom knelt to help bind Chico's wounded arm. "I couldnae hit a coo in the arse wi' a shovel, Yank." His explanation terminated by having his head thrust to the floor by Pablo, as a murderous fire poured over them, the fusillade ricocheting off the walls and pinging a lethal way down the narrow stairway.

He was going to wet his breeks. He just knew it. Tom buried his head on the cold stone floor. Then, after a few seconds mustering up courage, took a quick look at the line of Regulars crumbling under the rapid fire of Pablo and Dane as they charged towards them, while to his right, rebels were exacting a heavy toll on the vastly outnumbered government troops, who were in the act of fighting a do or die rearguard action, bayonets against machetes. Everywhere maimed and dying staggered away with wounds that made Tom want to vomit, empty his stomach on the steps, to turn and run, run as far as his cowardly legs would take him, instead he rose to help Chico reload the rifles.

"Dane, Chico! They've got behind us!" Bev's shrill voice echoed up from the stairwell. Without thinking, Tom hurled himself down the stairs, snatching up a bayonet on the way.

In a few short seconds, he was past the two women, reaching the bend in the corridor at the same time as Carlos appeared from the opposite direction. "Don't shoot, Carlos! It's me, the Escoces!" he yelled out in terror, throwing up his weapon.

"Que tal Senor Tom?" the soldier's face broke into a wide grin of recognition.

"He is asking how you are going?" Miriam called down from the landing.

"By rocket oot o' here, if I can!" Tom answered shakily.

"What's going on down there?" Dane shouted, his voice bearing the strain.

"It's all right Yank, the cavalry have arrived and Carlos is with them!" Tom shouted back.

In the next few minutes, the new arrivals had completely taken over, with some running to reinforce the stair-head whilst others shepherded the two women and Tom out by the back passageway and into the clear night air, with Carlos explaining how he had lost Chico but had found their rescuers' and had brought them to free them. An hour later, the two men accompanied by their militia friends sat in the back of a truck with the women travelling in more elegant style in a motor car in front.

Tom sat back in Miriam's wheelchair, the look on his face, akin to a cat who had stolen the milk, and let out a yell of triumph. "Well, we did it. With any luck, it's next stop Corona."

"We did it?" Dane cried in disbelief.

"With a little help from our friends," Tom amended.

Exasperated, the American rolled his eyes heavenwards. "If you ever get to the States, fella, do not bother looking me up. OK?"

"Don't worry pal, I won't. I don't know where you live. I don't have your Gettysburg address for starters."

Chapter 9

By the fountain of a finely sculptured figure of Pan, within the walled confines of the garden and its profusion of colour, Mrs Plesher sat deep in conversation with the dapper little man in the neatly tailored white suit, while almost directly above them, Tom threw open his bedroom window and stretched himself to his full height in the early morning sun.

Resting his elbows on the window-sill, Tom thought how good it was to have had nothing to do these last few days except recuperate, which he had done to the extreme. Now there were not so many bars in Corona that he did not know about or vice versa.

By the time he had dressed in his newly-acquired shirt and trousers, and reached the garden, the dapper little man had gone.

"Mornin' wee wumman," he greeted her cheerfully, resting his hand on the statue. "I thought I saw you talking to Senor Castilia, the one you introduced me to a couple of days ago?"

"Good morning Tom. Happy to see you up and about. Yes, that was the gentleman in question," she responded happily. "However, he had much more important business to attend to than to sit chit-chatting with the likes of me, you know."

"What can be more important than us getting out of here?" Tom could not understand the woman's reasoning.

"Patience, Tom. It's not a game you know," the lady scolded him.

"It is where I come from. I used to play it with my Granny. Cheated a lot too."

Tom screwed up his eyes at the cloudless sky, and his manner changed abruptly. "I only want to go home, wee wumman," he said sadly. "Back to the pleasures of the dole queues and fish and chips. All the wee things that make life simple and safe, if you take my meaning…hen?"

Miriam knew she was back to her old self again. All she really had needed was a few days rest, a new, well a nearly new, skirt and blouse, and now she was ready to take on anybody and anything.

She looked up into Tom's bruised face. "I think I understand you quite well, young man," her tone was sympathetic, almost patronising. "Senor Castilia told me this morning that he is in the process of trying to arrange our departure within the next few days.

By plane no less. Which should also give me time to acquire a new wheelchair." She patted the tattered armrests.

"By plane! Or bi-plane?" Tom could not resist the joke.

Ignoring the obvious pun, Miriam continued. "Yes. He said he should like us to be on our way as quickly as possible. It appears that government troops are already advancing on Corona. Castilia hopes their own forces may be able to halt their advance until reinforcements arrive from further north of the country."

"So, we are not so safe here as it appear to be?" Tom frowned, slightly disillusioned by the news.

"Not to worry, young man, no need to panic just yet."

Tom let go of the statue and came round to stand in front of her. "What happened to your handbag…and your pistol? Has yon big wumman got them? I believe she and Segovia managed to escape."

"Yes, they and a few others did. It is not so much the pistol I miss, as the few personal items I had," she said ruefully.

"And yon wee film?" Tom scratched his head. "I've never seen anything like yon before."

"Not even in the pictures, Tom?" Miriam teased. "It's quite a new invention," she explained. "It's called micro-film."

"Are you not worried you've lost it, after all you've gone through?" he asked, puzzled by the woman's apparent lack of concern.

"Not to worry, dear boy, these things happen. Segovia did not get all he was after. I still have a few secrets locked away," Miriam chortled, tapping her temple.

The woman's expression changed. "Your face Tom, does it hurt? All that bruising, I mean."

"A bit. Bev says it improves my looks, so maybe there's a chance for me yet."

Miriam looked away, her voice full of remorse. "I'm sure you've cursed the day you ever met Miriam Plesher. I really have made your holiday a misery."

A holiday, Tom thought. He'd almost forgotten how it had all started. At least, he had seen more of the country that he'd ever intended. However, it was too nice a day to argue the point. Also, he liked the way he was feeling right now. Besides, it was almost all over, they were as good as home. Well, at least America, so he could afford to be magnanimous. "Och, it wasnae that bad wee wumman," he soothed. "You didn't do too badly yourself."

Miriam scanned his face. "It was easier for me, Tom, I had a cause to fight for."

Tom shrugged. "Maybe we all had. Maybe it took someone like you to make us see it." He laughed to hide his embarrassment. "Listen to me, the great philosopher. Come on, how about breakfast? Then, afterwards, I'll try out my new razor."

"Not on the local citizens, I hope. I have heard all about you Glasgow types." She was suddenly relieved by the nonchalant way the young man had swept aside her self-reproach and her attempt at an apology.

"Of course, wee wumman!" Tom guided her through the door of the house. "That's why I'm known as the comedian. I have everybody in stitches. But first, breakfast!"

It was strange how the news of their imminent departure and the ensuing parting of the ways affected each of them differently. Bev, in particular, had distanced herself from him, Tom thought, regarding him as a first rate coward, due no doubt to his having refused to take an active part back at the prison.

This aside, he decided to take up his holiday where he had left off. Therefore, when he learned of some interesting cave dwellings on the outskirts of the town, he'd been certain that his two fellow enthusiasts would also be so inclined, only to be informed in a rather elusive manner that they had both made other arrangements. Bitterly disappointed, and not a little hurt, Tom made his way there alone.

Later, to compound his misery, he'd spotted them strolling hand in hand down one of the quaint alleyways peculiar to the town, arousing in him a feeling of overwhelming jealousy of Dane and a unfathomable anger at the girl.

That same evening in order to avoid them, he had purposely missed supper and had gone off in search of a good bar. After a skinful, and a few well chosen choruses of some auld Scots songs, which he had unsuccessfully tried to teach to a small but rather appreciative, though equally inebriated audience, he'd staggered home.

Four days later, they left for the North and their transport to America.

Tom had decided to ride in the back of the supply truck in the middle of the convoy instead of with the others in the motorcar cruising a little way behind. Now sitting in Mrs Plesher's shiny new transport, Tom nursed his bruises and the same foul mood that he had adopted these three days back in Corona.

To take his mind of the two lovers in the back seat of the car behind, Tom examined his chair more closely. He really would have something to moan about if he was confined to this, he decided, slapping one of the chair's padded arms. The poor soul would have to get used to this new contraption; no innovation on this model, such as the little hooks to hang her handbag, tiny knicknacks, or...Tom gave a little chuckle, his black mood lifting a little, or her berretta on.

It must be like getting used to riding a new bike. He shook his head, leaning back against the truck's canvas sides. No one would ever know what the wee lady had endured, both physically and mentally at having reached this far. Soon, he hoped, it would be safe for her to hand over the information she'd worked so hard to keep. What that information was, he did not know, or had any desire to know. He remembered, too, the look of utter dejection on her face when that pig Segovia had dangled the microfilm in front of her eyes.

Obviously what information she had was still in her head. Therefore, if all this was to be worthwhile, the resolute lady must get through. A fact substantiated by the size of this convoy escorting her to an improvised airfield in the middle of nowhere.

Tom closed his eyes, letting the swaying truck lull him into a trance which in turn conjured up visions of Pablo, Carlos and Chico taking their emotional farewell back in Corona earlier that morning.

Pablo had seized him by the shoulders firmly planting a kiss on each cheek. He had never experienced anything like this before, and vowed this would be one part of his adventure that Big Dougie and his pals would never know about. He had been taken so much aback he could only stammer to the man 'does this mean we're going steady?' And, when Bev showed her usual disapproval, he had added to her annoyance by exclaiming, "If it is, what do you think he will do when it's your turn."

Then, their convoy was on its way, their three allies standing in the middle of the road, waving goodbye.

Some time later, Tom was still wondering if the three would make it home, when the first of the explosions rocked the truck, catapulting him into the back of the cabin. Shooting out a hand, he grabbed vainly at the green canvas sides for support as the truck slewed sideways, and shuddered to a halt with an expiring roar from the engine.

Thrown to the floor by the impact, Tom picked himself up and blindly clawed his way to the tailgate, dropping down on to the road just as Miriam's vehicle reversed and pulled up beside his stricken truck, with Dane leaping from the car and shouting to him to get the wheelchair.

"Their guns or ours?" Tom panted amid a chatter of machine gun fire as he and Dane carried Miriam's chair to the car.

"Theirs. They have them sighted up on the hillside. We were lucky our car was partially hidden by your truck." Dane hauled at the chair. "Quick! Help me lift this thing up!"

Together, they hoisted the chair on to the next truck and vaulted up on to it.

"Shit, there is only one truck left besides ours!" their driver exploded in English as he took off amid another burst of gunfire accelerating after Miriam's car which was headed for a village precariously perched on an outcrop of rock at the top. The sole access to which lay across a narrow stone bridge spanning a bottomless gorge.

Halfway across, the leading truck slid to a halt, the alighting soldiery hot footing it after Miriam's disappearing car.

"Grab the chair, man, and let's get the hell out of here!" Dane yelled, as their driver and guard were already halfway across the bridge.

By the time both men had reached the inside of the village, soldiers were already dispersing to left and right, crashing into houses of the startled inhabitants, to take up firing positions flanking the bridge.

The wheelchair between them, Tom and Dane headed for Miriam's car now halted in the tiny cobbled square.

"We meet again, wee wumman!" Tom cried out, much more light-heartedly than he felt. "We brought you your alternative transport." He pushed the chair at her.

"Thank you gentleman." Miriam swung her legs out of the car, and the two men lifted her into the chair.

"That was a narrow escape we had back there." Bev smoothed down Miriam's collar, thrusting her shaking hands quickly out of sight behind the chair.

"Some escape if you ask me." Tom pretended not to have seen the girl's action. He run an eye passed the whitewashed church with its square bell tower dominating the cobbled square to a wall beyond, then back towards the covered archway through which they had just entered.

"Will the Senora, Senorita and Senors, be pleased to follow me? I am Sergeant Alix Rodrigo. " Behind them stood a tall lean faced man, dressed in grey striped trousers and a white open-necked shirt, with the now familiar blue sash draped across his chest. "Please, for your own safety," he pleaded, gesturing that they should follow him.

They quickly followed their new acquaintance round the corner of the square into a narrow alleyway where two youngish women ran forward to greet them.

"Please if the ladies will be so kind as to follow them." Again, the man gestured with a hand. "They will give you some refreshment. You will be safe there." Then, asked politely of the men when the women had gone, "You will be pleased to follow me."

Wordlessly, they followed the man to the corner of a house where he pointed down through the garden to a low whitewashed wall at its foot. "For your safety you must understand the situation. Captain Velor insists. My orders are to hold this village so that you may be on your way without delay. We expect the Regulars to attack very shortly. Fortunately for us, their only means of entry to the village from here is the bridge you have just crossed."

Tom and Dane craned their necks round the corner of the house at the bridge spanning what appeared to be an interminable drop to the turbulent waters below.

"If the Regulars cannot force their way across the bridge, the only other way in to the village is to follow that ridge for sixty kilometres." The man indicated to the ridge opposite. "Then they will come to another bridge which they must cross to come at us from the rear."

The speaker touched Tom on the shoulder. "Come, I will show you what must be done."

They retraced their steps, crossing the cobbled square passing the church to the wall Tom had noticed earlier at the opposite end of the tiny village. Here, the lean man threw a hand at the open plain below, dotted with orange groves and ploughed fields. "Now you will understand what I mean: should the Regulars come at us from this side..." The man shrugged his narrow shoulders. "However, by that time, it is hoped it will be of little concern to you."

Tom shaded his eyes against the blazing sun, scanning the open landscape from the steep rocks below to the distant fields beyond, where in the distance, ant-like figures who presumably until a short time ago had been toiling in their fields were now running back towards the village, panicked no doubt by the sound of gunfire.

Tom turned to the tall soldier. "How are we to get out of here? Not down that way surely? We could, but the crippled lady could not."

"Risky perhaps. However, Captain Velor has already solved the problem," their guide announced proudly. "Look! It is already happening." He nodded to where a dozen or so soldiers armed with pickaxes, hammers and shovels were running to a small gate in the wall.

"Demolition squad, Mac," Dane muttered.

"But for what?" The unexpected sound of gunfire interrupted any further conversation.

With a yell of trepidation, the lean man spun on his heel and headed across the square with Tom and Dane at his heels, back to where they had entered the village by the bridge.

"Profesionista soldado!" the lean man gasped at the uniformed men edging past the two trucks blocking the bridge. "They are the best. How do you say it? The elite? We cannot hope to stop them for long."

As he spoke, a sudden burst of gunfire sent the advancing soldiers scuttling back for cover behind the trucks.

Tom tingled with excitement. "Oh, I don't know. Your lot's doing none too badly."

The attack over for the moment, the men whom Dane had christened the 'demolition squad' were now returning to their work on the far wall, their numbers having been necessary to reinforce the position on either side of the arched entrance.

"Come!" their guide gestured, "we must seek out Captain Velor. It is essential that the wall continues to be demolished."

"I wonder if there is any chance o' something to eat?" Tom said in a stage whisper to Dane.

"You want to eat at a time like this man?"

"What time is it, man?" Tom's sarcasm brought negative responses from both his companions. "Oh well," he moaned, "I suppose I had a good breakfast a couple of days ago."

Half way along the low wall, overlooking the orange groves, they found the lean man's much praised Captain Velor rapping out orders to his tiny command, who halted only briefly to return the lean man's salute and listen impassively while he explained the situation to him.

Tom eyed the swarthy well-built man of medium height who swung to face him, and even before the man had spoken, somehow felt assured that if anyone could save the situation, it was he.

Without introduction, Velor pointed across the square in the direction of the ridge. "The elite of the Regulars are over there on the other side of the bridge; not all of them unfortunately." The weather beaten face broke into a broad grin, showing a row of even white teeth. "But enough, yes?"

He looked past the foreigners to his Sergeant, whom Tom had secretly christened the Lean Man. "You must enlist the aid of the villagers to help knock down part of the rear wall for our friends, Sergeant Rodrigo," he commanded vigorously. "It is for us to ensure our friends escape, especially the English lady."

"Si, my Captain." The Sergeant snapped to attention. "Immediately, my Captain." And, with a final hurried salute, set off across the square to carry out his Captain's orders.

When he had gone, Velor turned back to the two men, barely suppressing a smile. "Sergeant Rodrigo believes that I, as a former Regular, can perform miracles. Nevertheless, he is a good soldier...for a civilian," he added conspiratorially. "Now, I must see if the rest of his civilians can fight."

"You mean to say you do not know?" Dane asked incredulously. "I thought our...or should I say the lady's importance rated a first class outfit guarding her...and us...all the way to the plane?"

The brawny figure stiffened. "You did have until that little ambush. Most of my best men were caught in the first trucks. Those who survived helped get you away."

Without warning, a murderous fire erupted from the ridge across the square. Velor made to quickly move off. "I must return to the gateway. It is the only way in at present. The main attack will come shortly. We must be able to resist it or all is lost." He turned in his stride. "It might become quite dangerous close to the entrance, therefore I suggest you remain on this side of the village."

Once in the square, Velor began to channel his entire energy into the defence of the village, or to be precise the defence of these four strangers in his country. Although when it came right down to it, the only one of any real importance, as Senor Castilia had intimated to him a few days ago, was the crippled Inglesa

"They come again!" His Sergeant's voice was scarcely audible above the renewed gunfire.

Positioned behind a pillar, Velor had a clear view of the crouching figures on the parapet as they fanned out on either side of the trucks, the foremost of them almost reaching the first truck before the defenders opened fire, driving their assailants back to their own side of the bridge. Impassively, he watched the fight, his eyes riveted on the obstructing vehicles.

Ever so slowly, the door of the first abandoned truck opened and a soldier, using the protection of the parapet, launched himself into the cabin. Velor caught the action and tapped the shoulder of a soldier beside him. "There is someone in that first truck trying to get it started," he snapped. "I do not want it moved."

For a fleeting moment, the head of the enemy soldier appeared fractionally above the dashboard, Velor's soldier fired.

"Good work, Corporal!" Velor praised, his eyes on the shattered windscreen. "Now let's wait for their next little trick, eh?"

It having been quiet for some time Velor decided to take the chance of crossing the square to find out how the work on demolishing the wall was progressing, to find both Tom and Dane stripped to the waist toiling in the boiling heat helping in the wall's destruction, overseen by the effusive Sergeant Rodrigo.

"Now I understand how you mean to get us out of here, Captain." Dane leaned on his shovel to catch his breath. "But what a drop! Allowing for all the stones from the wall thrown down there to act as a ramp, it will still leave a good six feet for the car to drop."

"Aye, there is every chance of it hitting one of those trees, if it does not break an axle or something first." Tom spat and drew a hand across his mouth.

"It must be done. It is the only way out of here with the woman," Velor responded stoically. "I shall press more of the villagers into assisting you. You must hurry, we cannot hold off these Regulars much longer." Velor swung on his heel as his loyal Sergeant called out after him that it would be done.

"I hope so Sergeant," Velor said under his breath, heading once again across the square to the house nearest the gateway.

Once there, Velor climbed to the first floor, pushing open the door of the tiny bedroom, now a shambles with broken furniture and broken glass littering the floor. "How are things here?" he asked of the four defenders.

"So far the mattress is our only casualty, Sir," the man nearest the window answered with a grin, plucking at the straw mattress shielding the window.

"Should the battle last until after dark, soldier, you may have to use that same straw to feed your night 'mares'." Velor laughed, happy that his men were in such high spirits. "Keep up the good work, and your heads low. Si?"

At the next house, Velor encountered a very different scene, here of the four defenders two were dead, the third, wounded lay on the floor, an elderly woman administering what little help she could to the wounded man.

Velor bent down beside the dying man, a clerk until a few days ago and uttered a few words of comfort, then rose to face the sole survivor.

"Your first fight soldier?" he asked sympathetically.

The man nodded and tried to keep himself from shaking by clasping his rifle tighter. "Yes, Sir."

"I shall try and send you a couple of reinforcements." Velor swung on his heel for the door, thinking as he ran down the stairs why, if this mission had been so important, had they not given him more seasoned soldiers instead of this bunch of amateurs. And why he had not been better informed of enemy movements? Angrily, he kicked out at a stool. And, because of that damned ambush, most of his best men had been killed.

Now that he was cooped up here, he was involving the lives of innocent villagers, and when the Anglos pulled out...if they could pull out, what would be the fate of these denizens?

Velor reached the street and followed the line of buildings back to the gateway, hoping that by now all company Sergeants would have a tally of their strength, if not, heads would roll. What heads were left that was.

"Twenty nine? This is our total strength?" Velor flicked at the single sheet of torn paper in his hand. "We have three dead and five wounded?"

A professional, the Lieutenant, who stood so casually before him, had enlisted at the same time as himself when both had been nothing more that scrawny teenagers, and, although they had never met until five years ago, they were now quite inseparable. Now the Lieutenant was his closest friend, as well as his good right hand man. Good old Jimaneaux, Velor thought, completely unruffled as usual.

"What would you say the chances are of us getting the Anglos out, and us remaining alive, Juan?" he asked addressing his friend by his Christian name, which he did when they were alone.

The man twisted his lip in a way he was prone to do when worried. "We lack the guns, or we could enlist the help of the villagers." Juan's answer was deliberately slow, as he thought out what the other man had asked. "We also lost one of our machine guns in the ambush." He looked past Velor, mentally calculating. "There is enough ammunition for the one we have left if the Regulars decide not to intensify their attacks."

Velor nodded. It was much as he expected.

The sound of gunfire interrupted any further discussion. Velor took off for the gateway, Juan for the houses fronting the gorge on either side of the bridge, no words necessary between them.

"They're at it again by the sound of it," Tom gasped, throwing rocks down the incline.

Still feeling the effects of his beating, he stopped to rest. "Do you think they can hold them off, 'till we are finished here?"

The big American wiped sweat from his eyes, and gestured dejectedly at their progress. "Not if this is anything to go by."

"I'm whacked." Tom held his back. "I need a drink, or something to eat, or you can use me for axle grease. Talk of the devil!" he nodded at Miriam and Bev coming up behind Dane.

"For pity's sake Tom, put your shirt on, do you want to get burned?" Miriam scolded him, as she drew up her wheelchair.

"Sorry boss, I was too busy building a new highway. I forgot myself." Tom touched his forelock in mock submission.

"You both must be worn out." Bev eyed Dane's naked torso admiringly.

"I know time is not in our favour, but you two must be simply starving," Miriam said decisively. "The women have prepared something for you back at the house. I think you should both hurry."

"Sounds good to me ladies. After you, if you will," Tom bowed, reaching for his shirt and jerkin. Conscious of his own blistered sun blotched body, not to mention a distinct lack of muscle tone in comparison to that of his American cousin.

They found the interior of the small whitewashed house refreshingly cool after the heat of the afternoon sun.

Aware that time was of the essence both men sat down hurriedly, Tom almost tripping over the small holdall given to him back at Corona, containing a spare pair of socks, razor, comb and pullover of sorts. In there, too, should be his original pair of trousers he'd bought especially for this once of a lifetime experience, which it surely was. One, he was not too keen on repeating.

"Salad, Tom?" Bev nudged his elbow, drawing his attention to the young woman patiently standing over him, bowl in hand.

Tom made a face of apology.

"She looks a might unhappy at our being here," Dane remarked chewing quickly. "Perhaps we are devouring all her victuals?"

"It's not that at all Dane." Miriam stabbed at a slice of tomato. "She is worried about her husband, he left this morning to work in a neighbouring village. She also has a baby upstairs. The girl asked me what is likely to happen to them after we leave and the Regulars take the village."

Dane stopped chewing. He stared into his plate. "It has become a goddamned nightmare Limey lady," he said bitterly.

Tom felt the chilly silence that followed the man's remark, now wishing he was back at the wall, as he was not looking forward to what was about to happen here,

Laying down her fork, Miriam glared across at the American. "It has not all been a God-dammed picnic for me either, young man. Do you really believe I do not feel for these people? How my presence …all our presence here, has put them in danger!"

Dropping her eyes to her glass on the table, Miriam slowly ran a finger round its rim. "It does not make it any easier that I cannot lift…" she hesitated, a sardonic smile playing on her lips. "I was about to say finger, perhaps I should say leg to help myself or them, but perhaps you have forgotten that I am doing this for their benefit." She tossed her head in the direction of the door to indicate the villagers. "But what I lack downstairs I make up for in the attic, otherwise, Fenando Castilia would not have placed so much importance on my leaving the country with such vital information."

"I thought that mongrel Segovia had all the information?" Bev asked incredulously, putting down her glass of water.

"The micro-film, but not what I carry in my head dear, which is why he is still chasing us."

A look of apprehension crossed Dane's face. "Okay lady, so what you are doing is for the good of the country...or so you say. I may not have lived here as long as you, but this I do know, these people do not give a damn who governs them, just so long as they are left to live their lives in their own way.

"These people have seen dictators, these so called saviours come and go. The only reason they are out there helping us right now, is to get us out of their village just as fast as they can. They could do very well without this kind of so called help from us. Or to be quite frank...you, lady." Dane pushed his chair back angrily. "Anyhow, it is time," he flashed a look at Tom, "we were back at work, we have lost enough time as it is."

"I think time is running out as you English would say," the lean man, whom Tom had now nicknamed Slim, said, cocking his head at the latest outburst of fire, on the way back to their work on the ramp. "Captain Velor has told me there now has been sufficient time for the Regulars to have made their way to the other bridge down the gorge, and could at this very moment be approaching our village from this side." The man gestured to the orange groves below. "The villagers are helping to build the ramp as fast as they can. They wish us to be out of here as quickly as possible."

Dane threw a look at Tom that said, I told you so.

The three men threaded a way through the fifty or so villagers working on widening a gate, and building a ramp that their car could drive down.

At the wall, Tom thrust his hands in to his pockets and studied the rocks below. "I'm glad I'm not the poor sod that has to drive down that," he declared, whistling his incredulity, and asking of Slim, "I suppose it is the same driver who brought the women here?"

"No, Senor it is not. That man is wounded. Captain Velor say one of you must do it. He cannot spare one of his own men. There is now much fighting at the gateway."

The Scot and the American looked at one another.

"You can drive, I take it Mac?" Dane asked hopefully.

"I've had one lesson, albeit an extended one." Tom grimaced at the memory of Miriam's tuition.

"Well, it looks as if good ole Dane has gotten himself the job." Angrily, Dane threw a stone at the wall. "Well let's have a look see from down there, then man." With a sigh, he crossed to the wall and leaned over.

"You must hurry Senor, the fighting…she is getting much louder," Slim called out to the two men who had began to scramble down through the extended gate to the rocks below.

"It's a bigger drop from down here than it looks from the top." Tom screwed up his eyes at the overhang above him. "It would take tons of soil to finish the ramp, and I don't think we have much time as it is." Tom ran a little way back up the ramp dodging the shovelfuls of dirt being thrown down by the furiously working villagers. "Not that I know much about driving, big man, or in this case, diving," he called down to his friend, "but it appears to me should you go down the ramp too slowly, you've every chance of the car landing on its nose. Maybe even finish up with the back wheels caught in the rocks."

Pulling his ear, Dane continued to study the drop. He knew he should be running the car and getting them the hell out of here, but he needed to know what lay ahead. Or in this case below, if he was to succeed at all.

Tom called down again from where he stood on the ramp. "If you happen to go too fast …" the Scot looked away not wanting to see the American's expression when he said it, "I suggest you wear a rubber helmet, for when you land you're sure to bounce and bounce. You could even finish up wearing your balls for earmuffs."

"Okay! Okay! I get the message damn it!" Dane cried up angrily, scrambling back up the ramp to the Scot's side.

"Just warning you," Tom said, a little ashamed at his relief that it was not he who would be doing the driving.

They reached the top of the ramp just as Bev and Miriam arrived back at the gate.

"We'll wait here until the car reaches the bottom, then you two men can help lift the wheelchair down to it." Bev suggested pulling back the chair to let a villager wheel past a barrow full of soil. "We'll wait here for the driver."

"Just coming, Sheila," Dane replied, putting a brave face on it.

Bev's jaw dropped. In an instant, she had rounded the chair, searching for a sign that would tell her, Dane was only joking, and asking in a voice choking with nerves and apprehension. "You don't mean you, Dane!"

"'Pears to be I'm the only fella for the job." Dane found a spot on the wall to fix his eyes on.

Sergeant Rodrigo came back to stand with them now that his work of supervision was done.

"Come!" He touched Dane on the sleeve. "No more talk. We must hurry!"

"Well, that settles it." Dane hunched his shoulders as if suddenly cold. "Let's get it over with."

Bev gave out something akin to a sob and raised herself on tiptoe, and kissed the American gently on the cheek. "Be careful sport," she tried to keep the fear out of her voice. "We don't want to carry the baggage all by ourselves." She watched him go. "See you down there. Okay!" her voice breaking as she stood there.

"Yeah, see you down there," Dane called out over his shoulder.

Now that their work on the ramp had been prematurely curtailed, the villagers began to hurry back to their homes, or gather by the church wall to await the outcome of Dane's attempt to drive the car down the ramp and into the orange grove below in order to escape by that way, a few throwing hostile glances at the foreigners as they passed.

"I'm going down into the grove." Tom told the two women, "just in case anything goes wrong."

So saying, Tom started down the man made ramp and on to the well worn steps which had led to the gate before it had been knocked down and widened to let the car through, but which due to lack of time had not been filled in, thus leaving a six or seven foot drop to the path below.

Once at the bottom, Tom walked to the trees, and turned to look back up at the wall. He shivered, and not from the cold. Then, above the sound of the renewed gunfire, he heard the gentle throb of an engine, and the shape of the black sedan slid into view, the ashen face of Dane at the wheel.

Slowly and carefully, Dane guided his charge down the ramp of earth-covered steps. Then, judging the time right, gunned it over the gap between the last of the steps and the rocks below. For a moment, the car hung there in mid air, its wheels spinning as if held by some invisible hand, then just as suddenly it dropped with a thud on to the path below.

"Good ole Dane!" Tom let out a yell of triumph, bunching his fists. His smile disappearing as the same giant hand once more took hold of the car and swung it off the path, slamming it in to the base of a tree, where, it finally came to rest with an expiring hiss of escaping steam.

Unable to control his temper at their bad luck, Tom kicked out at the ground and ran to the car, and was still a little way off when the front door jerked open and the big American clambered out unscathed.

"Shit!" Dane exploded at Tom, swinging an angry foot at the car. "I thought I had it dead to rights, then it took on a mind of its own, and…" Exasperated, he brought his fist down on the roof.

"Och, never mind, big man, you did yer best. At least, you're not hurt." Tom commiserated. Though he thought, now that the car was useless what were they going to do now, to get out of here?

"Dane! Dane! Are you all right?" Bev shouted from the wall above, her voice shrill above the gunfire.

"Sure. I'm okay, which is more that I can say for this hunk of Junk." Dane called back, taking another kick at their stricken transport.

"Well, as they say Dane, that's the ba' burst. We better get ourselves back up there. Though I don't know what we are supposed to do now." Tom stuck his hands in his pockets and headed back for the ramp.

Miriam ran an exploratory eye over the American after he had emerged from the ramp, her recent confrontation with the man all but forgotten. "You are all right, young man?" she asked him, genuinely concerned.

"Yes ma'am. But I botched up the whole damned thing. I thought I had it cracked." Dane held out his hands to demonstrate what had happened, when Velor came striding across the square.

"It is no good. You failed Senor." The soldier drew to a halt, his voice low, accusing.

Stung by the man's tone, Dane glared down at the smaller man. "What else did you expect? The ramp was about a mile short. Could your driver have done any better?"

"Most probably. This, however, is not the question, which is now, Senor, how do we get you all out of here?"

"Captain! Captain Velor!" As one, they swung to where the slim man stood by the wall pointing to the valley below. "Look my Captain, Private Delago has returned!"

Grabbing Miriam's chair, Tom hurried after the others to the wall, where beyond the orange groves on the far side of the valley, a car, barely visible through the dust it was throwing up behind it, sped in their direction.

Velor grinned. "Shortly after we arrived here, I sent one of my men off in the hope he might find another vehicle, though in truth I expected him to return with a mule or two. But not with that!" he announced proudly.

"Well done wee man!" Tom laughed, now a little more optimistic that they might just make it out of here after all. He was about to turn to share his optimism with the lady in the chair when the sound of an explosion filled the air and the speeding car, now engulfed in smoke began to veer from side to side.

Horror-stricken, Tom opened his mouth to swear a right big Govan sized oath, the curse of which was still on his lips when the car burst into flames.

Perhaps it was only his imagination that had made him believe he had heard the driver's screams all the way across the valley as he leaped from the vehicle, his hair and clothes alight. But it was no figment of his imagination when he saw the burning man throw himself to the ground writhing and screaming in agony. An agony shared by every onlooker, who, like himself, silently willed the burning man to die, who, at last, after what seemed to be an eternity, mercifully lay still.

Wordlessly, Tom turned the wheelchair round, to ask Velor what had happened, when the short stunned silence which had followed the driver's death was broken by a high pitched wailing from those who remained on the wall, who now almost as one, panic stricken, turned to flee for the safety of their homes.

Tom swung sharply back. Through the long spiral of black smoke, rising to meet the evening sky from the burning car, a long line of trucks appeared.

Velor stepped back from the wall. Slowly, taking the remains of a cheroot from his mouth, he looked at Tom, then, to the woman in the wheelchair, who with equal sagacity returned the look. There was no need for words. The enemy had rounded the gorge. There was no way out.

Chapter 10

Spilling out from the truck, the crouching men, fanned out in a wide arc at the foot of the escarpment the action, transforming the recent passive onlookers to panic. Now, they scattered in all directions, some clutching up children from the square as they fled to their homes, wanting nothing to do with this fight.

"Get your men behind the wall there," Velor snapped at Sergeant Rodrigo. "Do not have them wasting ammunition for nothing. I shall be back as soon as possible."

Velor swung round heading for the ramp and his Lieutenant, who already had the situation under control, bellowing out orders and roundly cursing those hapless enough to be within earshot, and in his opinion 'slow as a wet week' at obeying his commands.

"I've taken the liberty of having a cart wheeled to block the hole in the ramp we made to let the car through," Lieutenant Jimanaux informed his superior, snapping a quick salute for the benefit of the other ranks. "Thanks to our earlier endeavours it is now our most vulnerable point."

As he spoke, he and Velor were hurrying to the ramp to scrutinise the tipping of the cart on to its side to block the gap.

"How many do you think there are down there, Juan?" Velor asked, crouching down behind the wall.

"A hundred, a hundred and fifty? It is their armourment that worries me most," Juan answered at Velor's side.

Acquiescing, the Captain rose sharply. "Take command here, Juan." He shot a quick glance around. "Now for our little trick with our one and only machine gun." And, in one swift movement, the soldier was off, crossing the square to the bridge across the gorge, the sound of the first attack on the ramp at his back.

"You three!" He barked at the men manning the machine gun behind the wagon and household articles forming the barrier to the entrance to the village. "Snap to it! Bring that damned weapon with you," he bellowed at them.

Struggling after their trotting commander, the trio set the machine gun up on the farthest environs of the village wall.

"One quick burst when you see something, then follow me!" Velor ordered again.

It was not a difficult order to follow, the fire from the attackers grew fiercer even as they waited. Nearby, a man slumped forward and the Lean Man ran to his side.

"He's dead, Sergeant!" Velor roared at him. "See to your front! Amateur," he murmured, and swung to his machine gunner. "Now!" he commanded, slapping him on the shoulder.

In response, the soldier let off a short sharp burst at the diminutive figures climbing the wall, then the gun crew were off, after their galloping Captain, along the wall to the space made by the ramp.

"Here! Set the gun here! Faster you morons!" Velor pointed agitatedly to the cart blocking the extended gate-come-ramp. "Wait a little," he cautioned the machine gunner.

Crouched behind the cart, he watched the attackers wind their way through the vines, the flatland of the plain behind them. "Let your comrades keep them busy with their rifles a little longer."

Velor cast an eye along the line of soldiers manning the wall then back to his adversaries climbing the slope towards them, judging the distance. "Now! Let them have it now!" he bellowed in the young gunner's ear.

The first burst caught the climbers unawares. The second ripped the low foliage and branches apart, stitching a path from right to left, catching the climbing men as they turned to flee. Then all was quiet.

"Right! You three back to the entrance. By the sound of it, there is more work for you there. Remember, sparingly with ammo!" Velor shouted after them.

Juan slid down, his back resting against the wall as he lit the cigarette cupped in his hands.

"Do you think it will work?" he did not wait for Velor to answer. "Firing from three different positions may fool them into thinking we have three machine guns, but only for a little while. Sooner or later, they will wise up to the fact that only one gun is firing at any one time."

Velor sank down beside his second in command taking the proffered cigarette. "Twenty nine against, say, two hundred, including those on the other side of the bridge."

Juan took back the cigarette. "We have less now, my friend. Had we explosives we could have blown up the bridge and concentrated our entire efforts on defending this side of the village."

Velor took what was left of Juan's cigarette. "They will come again when it is really dark. I do not think we can hope to stop them again, Juan."

"What about the villagers? Will they help?" Juan asked.

Velor nipped out what was left of the cigarette between two fingers.

"Some will. Others do not see the point of dying for someone they do not know. Let us face facts old friend, we are in a very dicey position. We have less than two-dozen…and a few amateur villagers armed with…what shotguns? And who knows what else to combat two hundred Soldados, some of our country's finest? We should know. Until recently, we were responsible for their training," he laughed sardonically.

"Perhaps you should think of setting up a second perimeter, around the church maybe?" Juan suggested.

"Perhaps you are right, Sergeant…as usual," Velor answered tongue in cheek. He rose. "I shall see what can be done."

"We may have to use your church, Father." Velor spoke softly to the priest, drawing him aside from attending the wounded.

"In what way, my son," the man of God asked suspiciously.

Velor's tone was conciliatory as he replied. "As a means of defence, Father. We cannot hope to hold the wall."

"May I remind you this is God's House? A place of peace not of war," the priest rounded on the soldier angrily.

"Then tell them out there." Velor jerked a thumb in the direction of the firing.

"Them or you? I do not know who is worse. All I know, this was a peaceful God fearing village until your arrival."

For a moment, Velor's eyes left the priest to a woman, snatching a child out of the arms of the Escoces, a look of sheer hatred on her face. Clearly embarrassed, the Escoces turned to help with the others.

The soldier faced the priest again. "I know Father, I am a God fearing man myself, but right now, I am more a Soldado fearing man for what they might do to your beloved villagers should they get beyond the wall."

Undaunted, the priest countered. "Even if you succeed in stopping them Captain, what then? Who will defend them when you are gone?" There was a note of triumph in the priest's voice at the look of vulnerability in the soldier's eyes, encouraging him to go on, drive home his point. "Oh yes, Captain I know you and your men are not here by design; far from it. Now your main aim is to get your foreigners out of here as quickly as possible."

Velor stared uneasily around him at the dead and the dying, attempting to erase from his mind the reason for it all. "You are right, Father, that is my aim. However, it is also my aim to prevent as much bloodshed as possible, including that of your villagers, which is why I ask your permission to use the church. What better place to defy the forces of evil?"

"Evil as well as good is in all of us my son. Who is to judge? I cannot prevent you for what you will surely do in the end. You are a soldier, and this building to you is of strategic value only."

The priest rubbed his blood soaked hands on a cloth. "Now if you will excuse me, Captain, I have work to do."

Angrily, Velor watched him go. He was right of course, that was what made it so damned humiliating, the soldier in him already calculating the defence of the place.

Several problems instantly sprang to mind, evacuating the wall meant withdrawing from the portal leading to the bridge, including the houses on either side as he could not leave men isolated there, which in turn left the enemy to cross the bridge unopposed.

Also, if the Plesher woman had not have been crippled then he would have taken the risk of hiding her and her friends somewhere in the village, with their chance of slipping away when the time was ripe. The irony was that it was that lady's infirmity that had created the situation in the first place.

Seated at the table that same lady gazed across the remains of her meal at her sleeping companions: at Bev slumped over the table, her head cradled in her arms; at Dane, his chair tipped back against the far wall. Her attention momentarily arrested by the sound of Anna's baby crying from the room above. To Tom, dear Tom.

Miriam's gaze rested on the young man. What had she done to him? She squeezed her eyes closed, conjuring up on how they had first met. How he'd man handled her and the wheelchair over all those hills. How she'd come to endure his sense of humour and awful puns. She rubbed her chair arm. Was he still perturbed by the prospect of losing his job? Or his house? Or was he now more concerned over different priorities such as trying to stay alive?

Again, she cursed her infirmity.

Slowly. the object of her concern came to life. For a moment, he sat there staring ahead, perplexed as to why he should be concerned by old Mrs Smart's anger at his not taking his turn at washing the stairs. Had he not paid Sarah MacKinlay six weeks in advance for doing them, until his return? And why did he have this gnawing feeling of being unsure as to whether he had turned the tap off before leaving? Nor was he likely to find the answers printed on Mrs Plesher's forehead.

"You're awake Tom, I see." The lady said affectionately. "Dreaming, were you?"

Blinking rapidly, Tom gazed sleepily around the room, his bleary eyes finally resting on the oil lamp, the significance of its flickering light shattering his dormancy.

"It's dark!" he exclaimed sitting up with a jerk. "Velor told Dane and me to wait here until he sent for us all. He said those soldier guys will probably attack after dark, and we have to go to the church.

Tom stood up, his chair scraping the stone floor as he tried to focus on his watch through the dim light and the haze of sleep. "I'd better see what is going on outside."

"Be careful Tom." Miriam caught him by the arm on his way past her to the door. "Please do not go too near the wall."

Staid by her concern, Tom patted her arm. "Don't worry wee wumman, you know me, the born coward." He forced a smile letting go of her hand, stopping at the door to give her a reassuring smile. "I'll nip out before they catch our light outside." Then he was gone into the darkness.

Ten minutes later, Tom lay on his back at the end of the ramp immediately above the steps cut in the rocks, a grenade clutched in either hand and wondering how he had come to be there. Silently, he went over the instructions the soldier had given him on how to throw a grenade. Then, offering up a prayer, threw the grenades in quick succession.

Shaking, though pleased with himself, Tom got to his feet, as Velor, Jimaneaux and his Sergeant trotted towards him.

"What's going on here?" Velor asked in English, glancing at the Scot.

Velor threw a quick glance over Tom's shoulder at the smoke and flames billowing up into the night sky. Stepping past him, he crouched down behind the wall, his eyes on the burning car below. "You have done well my friend," he commented drily, shouting back to Jimaneaux, "Lieutenant I believe we can now move our machine gun over to the bridge. This side is far too well lit up for our friends to attack, thanks to the Escoces here." He returned to stand by his second in command. "Lieutenant, be prepared to repel an attack from the other side of the village. I think our friend here may have given us some time…also an idea." He gave Tom a brief smile which quickly faded as he swung to his Sergeant. "I have work for you to do Sergeant Rodrigo. Find six men and follow me." He shook a finger at Tom. "You have done enough my young friend, now see that you remain indoors where I can find you."

Well pleased with himself, Tom headed back to Anna's house, his mind already reeling with the impact of what he had done and how this was something else to be telling Big Dougie about when he got back home. If he believed him, that was.

Then there was Bev. What would she think of his exploits? Anxious to find out, he quickened his stride. Though now that the realisation of what he had done was beginning to hit him, he felt a sickening feeling in the pit of his stomach. "Well, Aunt Betty you will never know how close you came to havin' Granny's hoose. A pretty face and ye go daft, Ding," he scolded himself. And I hate tae think whit ye would have done for twins.

"What's all the rumpus?" The American's voice floated to him across the square.

Tom strained his eyes for a glimpse of Bev. She was not there. Disappointed, he replied. "It's your car going up in flames. Now, the buggers can't come at us up the ramp without being seen."

"How the hell did that happen?" Dane drew up in front of Tom.

Tom shrugged. "Where are the women? I thought the sound of the explosions would have had them out here to find out what's going on."

"I said I'd find out. Now you can tell them." Dane started to move past. "I am going to see if I can be of assistance. I am going out of my tiny mind sitting around doing ziltch."

Tom pivoted round to follow, until remembering what Velor had said. "Okay I'll tell the lassies all about it."

"Yeah, you do that, Mac," came the answer out of the darkness.

Urging on his soldiers, with the task of hurling as much household combustibles over the wall as possible, Velor swung angrily on the priest. "I do not care what they say Father," he shouted above the sound of the renewed gunfire, "furniture can be replaced. Lives cannot."

Somewhere to his right, a grenade exploded.

"Should they get any closer, Father, we'll find those grenades coming down on us like rain. They are close enough as it is."

For a moment, the man of peace and the man of war stood glaring at one another. Finally, the soldier looked away, directing his attention and his anger at his command. "Move it! Move it you lot! I want a fire tonight, not tomorrow afternoon!" he bellowed, seizing a chair from one of his men and hurling it over the wall.

Jimaneaux appeared out of the darkness. "They are getting a little too close for comfort back there," he gasped. "Can you spare five men, my friend?"

"Any idea of their numbers, Juan?" Velor asked. The priest momentarily forgotten.

"Too many."

The Captain took an anxious look around him, mentally calculating the size of his own force deployed on throwing the furniture over the wall in order to create a barrier which when the time was right he intended to set alight, to assimilate the burning car.

"You three break off and follow the Lieutenant!" he barked out at three Privates running past, at the same time as he caught sight of the tall American throwing a small kitchen table over the wall, suddenly jerk round clutching his arm.

"You are hurt my friend?" Velor weaved through the assiduous soldiers to Dane's side.

"I think it has gone straight through," Dane answered shakily, holding his arm tightly.

"Take yourself over to the Father, my friend, ask the good priest to attend to it." Velor rose from the young man's side to scan the battle around him, leaving the American to follow his advice.

A little later standing with his Lieutenant at the corner of the church, Velor conceded that this would be the ideal place to oversee the forthcoming battle.

The entrance to the bridge lay to his immediate left, the ramp directly across the square, passed the spot where the American had been hit, to the further extremities of the village.

"I think it is now time for our little firework display, Juan, would you not say?"

"Grenades should set the trucks on the bridge alight."

"No Juan. I should like to keep that for a last resort. First, we shall set the furniture alight beneath the wall. Our former comrades are now getting too close for comfort. Leave a token force to defend the bridge and the ramp. Let us concentrate the remainder of our force on the wall, over there." Velor pointed to a fixed position on the wall. "That is where you must set up your machine gun. We will hit them hard upon their next attack. When they reach the barricade we will set it on fire."

"We may not have much time to wait, already our ex-comrades in arms have been sneaking forward to dismantle it. How do you propose setting it ablaze?" Juan asked, his martial eyes roaming over his men crouched behind the wall.

"Curtains? Bed linen?" Velor shrugged. "It is already in hand."

Juan smiled stonily. "And you also expect me to recruit men from those very same houses you have ransacked?" The irony in his voice not lost to his Captain.

"Houses or lives, Juan. Houses or lives," Velor sighed, moving off into the night.

"That is it!" Dane exploded at the seated company. "Why should I get my head blown off? It's not my goddamned country." His outburst aimed both verbally and visually at the woman seated in the wheelchair. "As far as I understand, while I am trying to defend their shit of a village," Dane choked, "these same folk are getting the hell out of it as fast as their legs will take them. I saw close on a dozen getting their asses over the goddamned wall!"

Dane swung on the Scot, his anger reaching boiling point. He was scared and this was his only way of hiding it from the others. "And that was an asshole thing for you to do, Mac, trying to get your ass shot off for these wops!"

"And which foolhardy escapade would this be, Tom?" Miriam expertly wheeled her chair round to face him, intentionally ignoring Dane's tirade.

Embarrassed, but secretly pleased, at being forced to divulge his act of heroism, Tom shrugged.

"Come on MacTavish, out with it," Bev coaxed, leaning forward on the table, her eyes sparkling with amusement.

"It was nothing really."

"So much the reluctant hero," Dane spat out, still in high dudgeon at the lack of response to his indignation. "He went over the wall and set fire to that old car I was driving. Now, there is no way anyone can come up the ramp without being seen."

"You did that?" Bev's eyes shone with admiration. "Well I'll be rooted!" She clapped a hand over her mouth relieved that neither Brit had understood her Strine, as Dane shot her a look of disdain at her unladylike language.

"That was a foolhardy thing to do Tom," Miriam scolded him with a raised eyebrow and a tut of her lips. "You could have got your jerkin all torn and dirty again."

Tom reached for an apple, labouring to hide his pleasure at the women's responses. "Anything Bogey can do..." he mimicked.

"Well I am out of here! This is too much!" Dane threw his one good arm in the air in exacerbation as he left.

Tom jerked a thumb at the vibrating door. "What's up with our American cousin?" He asked pulling a face.

Pouring out a cup of coffee, Miriam slid it across the table to Bev. "He has just found out that as a casualty, he is no longer a bystander. Therefore, if he wishes to play in the game, he must also expect to accept the rules, which right now has come somewhat as a shock to him." She took a sip of coffee and eyed the boy and girl in turn, awaiting their comments.

Tom pushed back his chair. "I think I'll go and find him and, try and keep the big man out of trouble."

"Same applies to you wee man," Miriam commanded him firmly.

"You know me wee wumman, a born coward. Yellow as custard and twice as thick."

As the first wave of attackers reached the barricade, Velor gave the command to set it on fire. Through the smoke and flames the enemy came, few hesitating to throw the obstacles aside, scrambling and slithering up the rocks to the village above.

"Grenades!" Velor bellowed. "At them now!" And as one the defenders rose to hurl their deadly missiles at the foe beneath.

"We'll get them in the open when they turn to run," Velor grimaced, racing to the wall, scarcely bothering to duck.

"If they run," Juan commented at his superior's side.

"If they don't, it will be our turn next for grenades." Velor shot a hasty glance over the parapet. "The barricade has caught. They will be lit up like fairy lights when they make a dash back to their lines."

Juan busied himself reloading his pistol. "If I were them, I'd take my chances and hide in the rocks below."

"And play catch the grenade?" Velor retorted sarcastically, peering through a spy hole in the wall. "Well Lieutenant Jimaneaux, they do not appear to be in agreement with your theory." He drew aside to let his subordinate have a look. "Machine gun now!" he bellowed over Juan's shoulder. "They're pulling back. Now catch them in the open!" The machine gun spat out fire after the retreating soldiers silhouetted in the blazing barricade.

Velor rose stiffly. "That should hold them for a time."

The priest caught up with the commanding officer mid way between the ramp and the machine gun post, asking in a way which might have suggested that the soldier was playing a game instead of fighting for the survival of his men and the village. "Captain Velor, I should like a word with you if it is not too inconvenient."

Velor spun round, biting back an angry retort at the supercilious manner of the man. Then, realising this was neither the time nor place, contented himself instead with a hint of sarcasm. "Well Father, what may I do for you? Though I should appreciate your being as brief as possible, as I have a village to defend."

Unperturbed, the priest drew him aside. "Do you believe reinforcements will arrive in time? If at all? Or will the village fall?"

Unprepared for these unexpected questions, Velor stared into the man's face for a moment before replying. "The soldier who was caught returning with the car...the one that was burned... was the one I sent by horseback when first we arrived here. His orders were to advise Corona of our position, and also all the neighbouring villages of our predicament. As you are aware the man did return, but whether he succeeded in informing Corona or not, I do not know." Velor fumbled in his breast pocket for a cheroot. "Why ask this now, father?" His eyes still on the man's face as he asked the question and anxious to be on his way.

"You sent only one man?" the priest asked scathingly.

"The village had only one horse."

The priest nodded and, for a moment, was amused by the soldier's wit.

"Perhaps there still is a way; a way in which you can save your men and your foreigners...and me, my flock." The priest nodded slowly, for in his mind he had a plan which might just succeed, but only perhaps.

The two villagers and the priest preceded them down the narrow winding steps from the church above, the flickering light from the lanterns magnifying the shadows on the dripping walls.

"Now I know what a screw nail feels like," Tom whispered, afraid of awakening the dead in this eerie crypt.

Behind him, Dane grunted, not quite appreciating the joke. "Where in the name of hell are they taking us?"

"Hell? Maybe even worse, The Gorbals." Tom blew out his cheeks. "It's too cold for hell though, must be The Gorbals."

Suddenly, their descent came to an abrupt halt in a small low vaulted room, where Velor and the priest, in company with two lantern bearing villagers awaited their arrival.

Reaching the last step, the American shuddered, rubbing his injured arm. "Would you please mind explaining what all this is about?"

"Most certainly my friend," the priest replied in English. "We are concerned, as you yourselves must be, that reinforcements may not arrive in time to save us...especially the Senore."

The priest halted for affect. "We...that is Captain Velor and I, agree that the soldier sent earlier may have been unsuccessful in convincing or informing those outside, of our situation. Therefore, the suggestion is that you two may lend more credence to the matter, if you were in a position to do so. Hence our bringing you here."

Again the priest hesitated, his attention centered on one of the villagers setting down his lantern on the stone floor, where for the first time, Tom and Dane became aware of the upturned stone slab and the void beneath.

"I see your curiosity is aroused." The priest managed a lopsided smile. "This is an old crypt. Originally, in more troubled times," the man twisted his face in a gesture of apology. "or should I say in times as troubled as these, this was an escape route used by both inhabitants and priests alike. I myself have never ventured further than this point, as has neither of my good friends here. However, I am assured that tunnel, or passage, call it what you will, emerges about three quarters way down the rocks."

"Our hope is that by your leaving now, you can escape through the enemy lines while it is still dark," Velor continued.

"Hold on there man," Dane held up his one good hand. "If these two gentlemen have never been down there before, how in the name of all that's holy do they know there is a way through there? It could be all caved in for all we know."

"We don't," Velor conceded. "That's a chance you will have to take."

"We?" Tom interjected. "Why we?"

Velor's response was venomous. "It is for your Mrs Plesher you are doing this. We have done our part in defending her this far!"

"It's your bloody countrymen who are doing the killing!" Tom shot back. "We're just tourists come to see the sights." Tom stabbed a finger at the gaping hole. "And this is not one of them."

"There is nothing to be afraid of my friend," the priest intervened in attempt to cool the situation. "No ghosts or bodies in this crypt."

"Well let's keep it that way. I'd hate to start a new craze. Anyhow, we have only your word for it." Embarrassed at hearing the fear in his own voice, Tom swung round to Dane, clearing his throat and attempting to appear light hearted. "As Bogey would say, I don't think much of this 'crypt' do you?"

"Can it Mac." Dane's icy stare shifted from Tom back to Velor. "If we do succeed in getting through the lines, what then?"

Velor took the American's question as a sign of acceptance and, anxious to get back to his command, he quickly replied, "These two men will guide you to the village from where my Private acquired the automobile. From there, you will learn whether he was successful in contacting Castilia in Corona. If not, you must assess the situation for yourselves. Convince the local villagers who are against Biezitos to come to our aid. I believe they will be more inclined to trust you than they would their own as there is no reason for you to lie."

"Convince them to come to our aid!" Tom exclaimed. "Boy, I even have trouble trying to convince folk to buy a raffle ticket." Tom contracted before the look of derision from both men.

Impatiently, the priest ushered Tom and Dane towards the hole, where, lantern in hand the first of the villager's, had began to lower himself into the dark recesses.

"You will be pleased to follow them." The man of the cloth requested politely stepping aside.

"We will not be pleased," Tom muttered, shuffling across to the upturned flagstone, the Captain wishing them all good luck as they disappeared into the dark cavern.

Chapter11

"Tom, where on earth have you been? Look at the colour of your jerkin!" Miriam chided, swinging her chair round to face him. "Let me see if I can clean it up a bit."

Exasperated by what he took to be an irrelevance at this stage of the game, Tom did as he was bid in order to avoid an unwelcome confrontation with the woman, for right now all he wanted to do was to quietly lie down in a corner of his adopted home. Where in earth would have been more appropriate?

"Have you seen Dane anywhere?" Bev asked anxiously.

Tom nodded, handing Miriam his jerkin. "We…" He started again. "He and two other men are on their way to the nearest village for help."

"How do you know this? I think Dane has shot through, and you're covering for him." Bev rounded the table to face him, demanding he tell the truth. "You know how angry he was when he left. He's probably got himself out of here as he said he would."

"Yes, Bev, he is out of here but not in the way you mean," Tom countered. "As I said before, Dane is trying to get through for help."

"But how?" Bev made a clawing motion with her hands.

"I can't say, Bev, Velor told me in no uncertain terms that I must not divulge their escape route. He does not want anyone in the village to find out and start a panic."

Tom sagged against the wall, remembering only to clearly the look of contempt on the Captain's face when he saw him re-emerge from the church. He had told the man how he had become separated in the maze of passageways, but he did not think the good Captain had believed him.

Tom gave a shudder at the recollection of following Dane and his guide only to find himself lost when his own guide's lantern had gone out and he had not known which passage to follow. Panicking in the dark, and hearing nothing except the echo of his own voice, he had decided his only course of action was to retrace his steps before he found himself wondering around that black labyrinth until he died of starvation, or worse.

Bev turned her back on the Scot and reached for a chair by the table to steady herself. She was not convinced Dane had gone for help, though she would like to think so. But, what really hurt was that he had run out on them, especially her. She had never taken him for a coward. Perhaps, his being wounded had changed him.

Tom put his hand gently on her shoulder. "I'm telling you the truth, lassie. Dane is a hero. I got separated from him and the others and had to turn back."

Bev shrugged off his hand and threw herself down in a chair in a corner of the room, drawing her knees up to her chin.

At a loss, the Scot turned to the elder woman for help. "I don't know why she doesnae believe me, Mrs Plesher? What I told her was the truth," he explained in a hush, one eye on the despondent girl. "You believe me, don't you wee wumman?"

"Yes Tom, of course I do. But, then again, I'm not the one who is in love, am I?"

Tom drew his head back unable to believe what the woman had said and sat down heavily. "In love? Who in the name o' the wee man is in love?"

"She is," Miriam replied softly, nodding towards the dejected figure across the room. "Which is why it is so impossible for her to accept that Dane could have run out on her."

"But he hasn't." Tom beat his fist on the table.

"You and I know that. But you must admit, Dane was pretty angry when he left here."

Miriam gave him a half smile. "Honestly, Tom, I do not know which is the harder to understand: Bev in love, or you conversing in your native tongue."

"Have the men stand down," Velor ordered his Lieutenant. Putting a hand to his brow, he stared into the morning sun. "Let them have a bite to eat. Should the villagers and the American fail, it could well be their last."

"You think the Regulars will come when the sun is at their backs." This was more a conclusion than a question from Juan.

"Wouldn't you?"

The Lieutenant peered through the loophole in the wall at the smoking barrier. "What is left of the barrier will not hold them now."

"I know, Juan. I think we should set up the machine gun in the centre of the wall. Give it the widest angle of fire.

"What about the ramp? Surely, they will hit us from there. And now that it is daylight the smoke from the car is of very little use."

Velor sagged wearily against the wall as if all this planning was an irrelevance. "I think they will hit us from everywhere."

Shrugging off his despondency, Velor rose stiffly to his feet, and smoothing down his tunic winked down at his friend. "However, we have been in worse situation than this Juan, have we not?"

"Name one?" Lieutenant Jimaneaux threw after his departing Captain, who was now quickly striding across the square.

Tom watched as Bev prepared a meal in the kitchen, while Anna attended to the child. It had never failed to amaze him how their young host had provided them with so many meals. Had he been in her place they would all have died of starvation by this time.

Anna came out of the kitchen, carrying her baby. Tom made a face at the child and tickled it under the chin and it gurgled with joy. The mother forced a laugh and cuddled the baby to her. She looked up, and Tom caught the fear in her eyes that her laughter could not hide. Not knowing what else to do, he gave her arm a gentle squeeze and a look that was meant to say not to worry, though also ashamed that he was in part to blame for her predicament.

For a moment, their eyes met, then, nodding her appreciation, and holding her baby close, Anna headed for the stairs.

Suddenly, there was a short sharp knock on the door, and Velor strode purposely into the room.

"I must apologise for this intrusion," he began quickly, "but I have not much time as I believe the main attack will come quite soon. It maybe we cannot hold them, if not the priest will come for you. He knows of a place you all may hide until help arrives."

Under the crypt most likely, Tom thought. Aloud, he said. "We'll get Mrs Plesher to tell Anna."

"No, this you cannot do." Velor said angrily. "I cannot make an exception."

"You mean Anna and the wee wean cannot come with us!" Incredulously, Tom stared at the soldier. "But, there is plenty of room down there!" He saw the glower in the soldier's eyes and wished he had kept quiet.

"Where do I draw the line, Senor?" Velor seethed at the Scot. "Do you suggest I save only the women and children? Leave the wounded? And when the Regulars take the village, will they not be suspicious that there are no women and children to be found? And would this not certainly initiate a search, which would most likely result in their being found? You foreigners we may get away with hiding, but no more."

"Captain Velor is right Tom," Miriam sprang to the soldier's defence. "It is most likely that the Regulars already know of our presence here, so the fewer there are to hide wherever that may be, the better our chances, for should I be taken, all of this…" She waved a hand in a wide arc, "will have been for nothing. Remember Tom, these soldiers who oppose us were once the Captain's former comrades. I do not wish to fail him, or many like him who have chosen to leave their regiments to fight for what they believe is right. No Tom, I am much too valuable a personage right now to be taken. This hiding place must be for us only."

Velor nodded, grateful that the discourse was at an end. "As I said before my friends, the priest will come for you when it is time. Good luck to you all, and may God go with you."

"And you, Captain," Mirian said softly.

Velor turned at the door. "Senor Tom, may I speak with you outside?"

On the doorstep, Velor cast a quick glance across the square. "When the breakthrough comes, help the priest take the two women to the church, he will take you to the crypt by the vestry door. Somehow I do not think anyone will take much notice of you all by that time. It may be a little difficult getting the Senora down those winding stairs. However, as she says she must not be taken. Now it is up to you."

It was only the weight of the pistol that made Tom realise what he was holding in his hand as Velor went on. "You may need this if they get too close."

"I don't think I could shoot anyone." Tom shook his head. Suddenly, the American pictures were nothing like this. Bogey could keep his part. "Besides, I don't really know what this revolution is all about."

Velor brushed aside the weapon Tom was trying to force back on him, glaring contemptuously, and mindful of the man's cowardly return from the crypt. "A person's politics need not concern you when he is pointing a gun at you," he said, with as much loathing as he could heap upon his words. "What do you think will happen to your women do you think, especially the young one who concerns you so much eh?" With this, Velor strode off across the square.

The commanding officer threw a quick look to his right, where the wall ended at the gable end of the houses built directly on top of the rocks. This was the least vulnerable point of their positions, now commanded by the ardent Sergeant Rodrigo. The top storeys of which a flanking fire could be directed upon those scrambling up the rocks to attack the wall. The wall itself veering in a long arc culminated several streets away at the gap created by the ramp, now reinforced by an upended wagon cart and the remaining household articles.

Velor touched the arm of the machine gunner. "From here, you will have the widest field of fire, but do not do so until I give the command." He lifted his eyes to the mid-day sun. "Somehow, I do not think you will have very long to wait."

The gunner nodded. His commanding officer peered through the loophole at the still smouldering barricade. "I was not wrong, soldier! Here they come! Hold your fire men!" he shouted to left and right.

Almost immediately, an explosion from an enemy grenade lifted a soldier off his feet. The fragments of a second caught another in the back. Wild-eyed, the man ran in Velor's direction, his screams high above the noise of battle as first he ran this way then another, oblivious to everything but the pain in his back, until mercifully a burst of fire from below put him out of his agony.

Velor turned his attention back to the foe leaping and running through the smoking barricade, clearly worried by the numbers gathering in the rocks below and who were now in a position to lob grenades up over the wall at them. "Wait for it!" he shouted, his eyes riveted on the first line of climbing soldiers. "Now!" And the enemy line went down as one, with the second line immediately behind, pouring over their fallen comrades.

Velor placed a steadying hand on the trembling machine gunner's shoulder, his eyes still fixed upon the advancing line. The Captain waited, calculating the right time. "S...t...e...a...d...y..." he murmured. "Now fire!"

It appeared as if both gunner and weapon exploded simultaneously in relief. The weapon spraying a wide arc of destruction from left to right, scything down the second line.

Again, grenades landed on the cobbled walkway, the red-hot shrapnel raining down upon the defenders, and throwing a man against the whitewashed church wall.

As if from nowhere the priest appeared amongst the carnage to help a wounded man back to the sanctuary of his church. For a brief moment, his eyes caught those of Velor's who quickly looked away, he having more important business to attend to than deliberate the rationale of it all. Suddenly, conscious of a new sound, that of the enemy co-ordinating their attack by the increase in gunfire emanating from the direction of the bridge, Velor shouted to Rodrigo to take over, and sprinted across the square, reaching the archway to the entrance to the village, as the trucks on the bridge he believed to be immobile slowly began to move toward him, shielding enemy soldiers on either side, who poured in a deadly fire upon the defenders.

Breaking into a run, Velor leaped on to the makeshift barricade, then regardless of the lack of cover, tossed a grenade on to the canvas top of the first vehicle setting it alight. His second, aimed at the bonnet of the truck behind, the explosion practically lifting the vehicle into the air.

"That should put paid to their little game for awhile," he shouted, ducking down behind the barricade beside a wounded defender hunched against the archway wall.

Regaining his breath, Velor gestured to the wounded man. "You better have that seen to. Replace someone from one of the houses on either side of here, and tell him to report to the Sergeant here, as quickly as possible."

The Captain watched the wounded soldier hobble off, then turned to the three remaining defenders. "I'll send you replacements...if I can, probably some of the villagers." He rose cautiously to his feet and took another look at the bridge. "However I believe you'll not be bothered by that lot for quite some time, the way those two trucks are burning."

Across the square, a villager ran towards Velor and, at the sight of the commanding officer, threw away his weapon and veered away. Disgusted, Velor watched him disappear down an alleyway. For him, the fight was over.

Now, Velor made directly to where his Lieutenant was loosening of shots by the ramp, passing in sight of Tom standing in the house doorway, pistol dangling from his hand.

Rounding a corner and out of sight of the Scot, Velor ran past an old man sitting close to the ramp his back against the wall, his legs outstretched in a posture of complete indifference to all that was going on all around him, a wine bottle by his side, a small cheroot dangling from his toothless mouth.

Velor threw himself down beside his Lieutenant. "I'm glad someone is enjoying himself." He jerked a thumb in the old man's direction.

"Do not let the old man fool you Captain, he will become the most important man in the village should our friends the Regulars overrun the ramp," Jimanaeux said laughing at his Captain's puzzled expression. "In addition to that bottle of wine, he has also one of kerosene. Whoof!" Juan threw an imaginary bottle at the ramp. "Hence the cheroot."

Velor clicked his teeth. "Then let us hope he is sober enough when the time comes, and does not get them mixed up, or he will be the most important man in every part of the village…and at once."

Juan stared at Velor, his eyes wide in amusement, then unable to control himself burst into laughter, accompanied by his commanding officer.

Lieutenant Jimaneaux wiped sweat from his eyes. "Almost an hour gone. Why do they wait? They had us like fish in a barrel, had they pressed home that last attack."

Velor took a gulp at his canteen. "Perhaps we have hit them harder than we realized," he said, drawing the back of his hand across his mouth. "Either that or they are content to wait for reinforcements. Who knows?"

"I should say the latter," his friend suggested, taking the proffered canteen.

"How are we off for ammo?"

Juan squinted along the half moon wall at the resting soldiers drinking or dousing themselves with water in an effort to keep cool in the fierce afternoon sun. "We have only half our men left, and our remaining defences now rest entirely upon the village comrades. As for ammo? The machine gun has two more belts. Each soldier has twenty rounds left…this includes the rifles the villagers are using. Grenades? Probably a dozen all told. That is about it."

Velor rested the back of his head against the wall. With his eyes closed, he gave the appearance of having fallen asleep, though Juan knew from past experience that his friend was already busy calculating the position. "I had thought should we be unable to sustain another attack we'd retreat to the church. However, is there much point when we most certainly will not have the ammunition to hold them back?" Velor asked the question without opening his eyes, and was therefore blind to Juan's shrug.

"What is the alternative? The longer we hold them, the better the chances are of reinforcements arriving."

Juan's answer prompted an eye open. "Do you really believe this?

"Perhaps we need not worry ourselves, the priest may refuse to let us use his house."

"His house, or His House, Juan?"

Juan smiled. "Knowing what little I do know of this man, I should say both."

Velor struggled wearily to his feet using the higher barricade of the ramp as a shield. "Then I must go and ask him," he said, looking down at his friend.

Velor's gaze shifted to the church. "Tell the men when I give the command, either through you or Sergeant Rodrigo, they must all retreat to the church on the double." Velor swung back to his friend again. "It will be your responsibility to see that all the foreigners reach the safety of the church. Take them to the priest. He will hide them in the crypt."

"You are of the opinion this man will comply with your wishes?"

"With my wishes? No. But, if necessary, with my command, yes."

"We cannot hope to hold off another attack, Father. Therefore I must ask your permission to carry out our final defence from here."

As if he had not heard, the priest continued to rewind the bloodstained bandage on the wounded soldier's leg. "This is a house of God, Captain," he answered, without looking up. "Would you now turn it into a charnel house as well?"

Succeeding in controlling his uneasiness before this frustrating priest, Velor ran an eye over the small place of worship now crammed with dead and dying . "If God is truly on our side, will He not protect us? More so in HIS own HOUSE?"

The priest rose wearily and gestured to a woman to help a soldier, crying out for water, before turning to face Velor. Unable to hide his anger he seethed at the man. "This is an argument used by many Christian countries, Captain. Tell me, over the ages, how much killing and barbarity has been wrought in the name of our MAKER do you think?"

Velor stuck a hand in his belt, the soldier in him coming to the fore. "We have little enough time, Father. I have no time to philosophy. What is your decision?"

"Does it make any difference, Captain? You have already made yours. Or is it my blessing you seek?" The priest smiled sourly. "Or perhaps absolution?"

Now solely the soldier and, angered by the man's self righteousness, Velor drew the priest's eyes to his own, his stare obdurate. "You will help the foreigners hide in the crypt, especially the crippled lady, as she is the most important one."

The priest shrugged assent.

Velor nodded to where a group of women knelt in prayer. "You must have those women removed from here, it is for their own safety, Father," he explained at the man's look of dissention.

"For their safety?" the priest repeated sarcastically. "How safe will they be outside, do you think?"

Velor swung on his heel, and carefully threaded his way through the dead and the dying, sadly aware that over half were villagers, and as he reached the door called out over his shoulder, "That is your decision, Father. When all hell breaks loose, do not come to me for absolution."

The enemy came again at three in the afternoon. It began with sniping from the rocks below, followed by a hail of grenades, reinforced by a barrage of fire from behind the burnt out barricade.

"I believe this is it, Saul," Jimaneaux shouted above the din.

Velor threw him a defiant look. "Not yet, Lieutenant. And it is still Captain to you," he winked.

"I think it is time to withdraw to the church and set the ramp barricade on fire? What do you think, Captain?" Juan emphasised the last word in mock sarcasm.

Velor scanned around him at the bodies of the villagers and his own men, some lying grotesquely where they had fallen, others in their final death throes.

"I think you are right, Juan. Remain here while I find Rodrigo. You must see to the foreigners as arranged."

Velor made to rise, when a new sound reached him from the direction of the bridge, his first reaction was that the enemy had forced their way into the village from that side. Then, the sound came again, only louder, this time it was the high excited cheering of jubilant men that filled the air. Velor gripped his pistol tighter. "Theirs or ours?" he asked of his second in command.

"Only one way to find out." Juan reloaded his own weapon. "You or me?"

"Me of course, you ox! I am still in command."

Grinning, Juan watched him disappear.

Velor trotted through the archway, his apprehension of what he would find evaporating at the sight of the blue armbands of the soldiers fighting on the opposite side of the bridge. Joyfully, he slapped the back of the man he'd encountered earlier running away from the fray. "See, my friend, it pays never to give up," he beamed down at him.

"We have won?" the man beamed back.

"Get both your women to the bridge, we are moving the burned trucks out of the way. Find something the old one can sit on. I want her in one of the trucks. She would make too easy a target in one of the open topped cars." Velor gestured impatiently to Tom and had disappeared across the square before the Scot had time to ask him about Dane.

"What's up sport?" Bev asked from the doorway of the house.

"Seems the cavalry have arrived. I only hope it's not General Custer in command. You get yourself and wee wumman ready while I go and get her something soft to sit on for the journey. And don't you dare say my head will do." When there was no reaction to his joke, Tom went on. "Velor does not want her in a car, he thinks she will be safer in one of the trucks. I hope Dane's with them," he added as an afterthought as he moved off.

"Nice try MacTavish, but the Yank's probably miles away by this time." Bev banged the door shut.

Ten minutes later, the Scot laboured under the awkwardness of a flapping mattress which he had found, lying a little bit away from the ramp. Reaching the archway he started to flap his way across the bridge, passing the relieving forces on the way, the tail of the mattress beating a tattoo against the back of his knees, forcing his legs to dip and buckle.

"Hi there, Mac!"

Instantly recognising the accent, Tom's heart skipped a beat as he searched for the speaker. "Dane, is that you?" he called out, trying desperately to see through the swirling smoke of the burned out trucks.

"Who else old buddy?"

A truck passed close to the side of the bridge and Dane jumped on to the parapet out of the way.

"So you made it Yank! I knew you would!" Tom yelled back, happy that they would all be together again. "If you were to fall into the Clyde, you'd come out…"

The rest of the saying died on Tom's lips as Dane, a hand clutched to his chest, swayed drunkenly on the parapet ledge.

"Tom!" Dane yelled, his eyes wide in horrified disbelief. Then, he was gone, into the rushing waters of the ravine below.

Tom let go of the mattress and rushed forward. "Dane!" he yelled and felt his feet go from under him as he fell, skidding on the slippery surface of the bridge, his hands and clothes covered in the oily ashy mess from the wreckage of the trucks, and as he tried to scramble to his feet found that his right leg would not move, and twisted sharply round to look into the bronzed face of a soldier lying there gripping him by the ankle.

A flash of understanding crossed Tom's face. "Okay, you can let me go now pal."

The face swore at him and pushed his head down, the whine of bullets chipping at the parapet inches above his head.

"Bugger this for a gemme o' sodgers," Tom yelped, covering his head with his hands and burying himself in the debris strewn road. "I thought this was supposed tae be clear o' yon Regular guys?

Angry at the failure of their rescuers to secure the bridge of this deadly fire, Tom visualised Dane's body swirling in the river far below. Poor Dane, he thought, having made it all this way back for this to happen. Shaking, Tom knew what had happened to Dane could just as easily happen to him, and with this he buried himself deeper in to the ash covered road.

The trucks swinging round the bend gave Tom his last chance to look at the village. Behind him, Miriam Plesher sat propped up on her mattress, Bev by her side, a hand steadying the empty wheelchair.

From here, the village gave little appearance of the destruction wrought upon it in so short a time. Only the smouldering wrecks of the trucks, standing on this side of the bridge, gave any immediate hint that anything out of the ordinary had happened in this remote mountain village.

Tom thought of Anna and their emotional farewell, and hoped she would find her husband safe and sound where ever he may be. He thought again of Dane, and that somehow the Yank might still be alive, though another glance at the ravine and its awesome depth as they sped past told him of the improbability of his friend having survived.

He had not told either woman what had happened to the big American. He would, when time was right.

He sighed and sought out the church, of the priest who had striven so hard to save his flock from the futility, if not outright stupidity of it all. Would he ever be able to reconcile his parishioners with each other again?

Tom leaned his head against the canvas side of the truck. What had their coming to that small village done to that peaceful community? Had they not in fact succeeded in setting neighbour against neighbour, with some refusing to help defend their village whilst their neighbours died doing just that?

He clutched the tailgate against the swaying of the truck and caught the name of the village on a rusted metal signpost as they flashed past. "Riaz," he said slowly, pronouncing the name as a child would when learning to read. Again, he whispered the name of the village where he felt he had spent half his life. The name of which he was never likely to forget,

No, he was never ever likely to forget Riaz.

Chapter 12

Velor walked from the open topped car to the truck parked at the roadside. Another half hour and it would completely dark. Rounding the third truck, he came upon the English lady seated in her wheelchair by the roadside, a blanket draped around her shoulders to ward off the sharp wind blowing off the mountains.

"Good evening Senora," he greeted the woman, touching his forehead in salute. "I hope the journey has not overtaxed you too much?"

"I believe I can cope, Captain Velor. Perhaps not with the same efficiency as yourself, but one must try."

Velor inclined his head at the compliment. "As you English would say, one must try one's best." The gleam of his smile contrasted sharply against the deep tan of his skin.

He looked away across the valley to the hills beyond, now barely discernible in the fading light, back to the next truck in line, his soldier's eye recording the troops gathered around the bonnet, eating and conversing in subdued tones, now and again one would steal a glance in his direction to look away just as quickly. He knew the subject of their conversation only too well. Those gathered there were of his unit, the survivors of the ambush and the fight in the village.

It had not been an easy choice to leave the wounded with young Lieutenant Cassa who had headed the reinforcements, though these men by the bonnet did not see it that way. Neither would he have done at that age. To have brought the wounded with them would have put the entire convoy at risk, for many had been in urgent need of medical attention. At least, with Cassa, they had a chance of getting back to Corona.

A soldier left the group and walked over to Miriam and handed her a steaming mug of coffee.

"Will the plane still be there, Captain?" she asked, after thanking the soldier.

"I should hope so," Velor said, watching the man return to his truck. "The deciding factor is whether or not we can reach the rendezvous in time. This road we are on is much longer than the one we followed before the ambush. To have continued on that road, we would have run the risk of encountering other hostile units further north."

Velor patted his tunic for a cheroot. "I am sending a truck on ahead in the hope it will pick up some gasoline for us, as I intend having as few stops as possible."

"Very wise, Captain."

"You are not too uncomfortable in the truck?"

"No. I am all right. I have my mattress."

"It is for your own safety Senora," Velor apologised. "I do not wish to deny you the comfort of the automobilc…"

Miriam interrupted him with a gesture of understanding. "No need to apologise or explain, Captain, you must do your duty as you see fit Ah Tom!" she said as the Scot rounded the corner. "Come help me back into the truck."

"Thank you Tom."

Tom drew the blankets up around Miriam's chin, gently tucking the sides in around her.

"Sorry wee wumman, I thought you were fast asleep," he whispered, sitting back down beside the sleeping girl in the swaying truck.

"I think I was…for a little while." Miriam peered passed the four sleeping soldiers into the darkness. "Where are we Tom? Do you know?"

"I havenae a clue. I only hope it's no' that far from the plane, for my backside is killing me. You'd think I'd been sitting on it all of my life."

"Tell me about it," Miriam chuckled in the dim light of the speeding truck.

"Sorry. I wasnae thinking," Tom groaned at his faux pas.

"I think Bev is asleep. A strange girl, Tom. In my experience, I found it quite difficult to understand colonials."

"Does that go for us lot as well?"

"Good gracious no, Tom, Scots are quite civilized." She thought for a moment. "In their own way, that is."

"Oh well, I can put my haggis away then. Have you ever been attacked by a rabid haggis, wee wumman?"

"No, and I should not like to find out. I don't know what would have the most disastrous affect, a haggis biting you, or you biting a haggis?"

"Getting witty in our old age, are we?" Tom tut-tutted.

"It helps as you well know, dear boy." She laid her head back on to the mattress, her face lost to Tom in the darkness. "It is just one more thing in which I am in your debt." The softness of her voice hinting at the gratitude she felt towards him.

Tom leaned back, wrapping himself in his own blanket, pleased by what the old woman had said, and also by the closeness of the girl. And, for the first time in a long while, and despite the discomfort of the truck, he was quite content.

He closed his eyes and thought about what the soldiers had told him. Everything going according to plan, they should be at the airstrip by morning, providing of course the plane was still there and, so far, there was no reason to think otherwise. So, everything being hunky dory, they could expect to be back in the good ole U.S. of A. by this time tomorrow night.

The sleeping girl's shoulder slid on to his and his heart skipped a beat. He put a tentative arm around her, strangely disturbed at the prospect of never seeing her again after this was all over.

Of course, he'd have to tell her the truth about what had happened to Dane before he got on the plane. He'd get Captain Velor to verify his story, then she'd have to believe him.

Bev made a strange little sound in her sleep and he held his breath, not wanting to awaken her. She was beautiful. At least, he thought so. And, after tomorrow, he'd not have the chance to hold her again. He hoped she'd not waken, as he wanted this to go on forever. Or he decided until he got hungry...or needed the toilet. You're pure dead romantic, so you are Ding, he told himself. And, once again, the bells rang back in auld Glesca Toon on Hogmanay, with the thought of the delectable Sonya.

Velor's car's headlights shone eerily in the approaching dawn, the mountains wraith-like on either side. His eyes stung with the lack of sleep. He closed them, calculating how far it would be to the stretch of flatland chosen for the makeshift landing strip. It would be nice to close his eyes and drift into a peaceful sleep even for only a little while, but he knew he should be thinking of an alternative plan should the plane no longer be there. He yawned and, once more, let his mind drift, this time to what Sergeant Rodrigo had told him about his cousin in Port Lecera, who, if he was to be believed, knew everyone and everything that went on in that costal town, not least of all the tramp steamers plying their way north to the United States.

Velor grinned at the vision of his Sergeant, that paragon of virtue, explaining, even apologising for, his cousin's shady business dealings by saying that his sole reason for mentioning this at all was that in the event of anything going wrong, he was sure his cousin would find a way of getting the foreigners back to America, should it prove necessary for them to head in that direction.

Reluctantly, Velor opened his eyes and yawned at his driver. "Are you tired, Private? It is almost dawn."

"No, Sir." The driver stiffened, ill at ease in the presence of his commanding officer.

"Good. I was hoping to halt," Velor consulted his watch. "Say...in another half hour. That should bring us close enough to the airstrip."

"Yes, Sir," the driver acknowledged, easing himself in his seat. "I should say those trucks back there will almost all be out of gasoline," he ventured.

Velor nodded.

Velor sat squarely on the headrest of the seat of the open top car, his feet firmly planted on the passenger seat. Pivoting to his right, he scanned the open field a few hundred metres away through his field glasses. Adjusting the glasses, he focused on the twin-engine aeroplane standing like a giant bird of prey at the far end of the barren field.

"Take it slowly Private, I do not want us running into anything," he said quietly, sliding back down into his seat.

Again, he swept the open landscape searching for any likely place for an ambush, resting his glasses for a moment on the uncut maize field culminating into scrubland some way to his right.

"If there is any trouble, it'll come from that direction." He pointed to the maize. "One could hide an army in there." He rose again and signalled the convoy to halt. "We'll keep going driver, I don't want anyone who may be watching, thinking that we are in any way suspicious. But, should I give the word, let's get the hell out of here, and fast." His driver's response was to grip the wheel tighter.

Following his orders, the truck immediately following Velor ground to a halt, and Tom, standing at the tailgate, let out a yell of jubilation. "It's still here! The plane still here!"

"Gee that's great okker. Let's have a looksee," Bev cried excitedly, clawing her way to Tom's side, and before anyone could stop her, she was down off the truck and running towards the plane.

"Bev!" Tom yelled scrambling down off the truck, "I think you should wait!"

Tom cursed, and ran after her but, after a while, gave up gasping for breath, and swore again at the slim figure running towards the waiting plane.

Two hundred meters in front of the running girl, Velor's car crawled cautiously forward.

"Captain, Sir, I don't know if you've seen them or not?" The question came from the driver bent over the steering wheel studying the ruts in the ground.

"See what, Private?" Velor's eyes darted from the plane to the maize field.

"Wheel marks Sir," he explained, "on either side of the car. Seems to be a lot of them, and all heading towards the plane."

Velor saw the marks, and out of the corner of his mouth, said very quietly, "turn this thing round, Private, but not too quickly. Let's head back n...i...c...e and slow to the convoy."

Expertly, the driver did as he was ordered, so that, to all outward appearances, the manoeuvre signalled that everything was to their complete satisfaction at having found the plane intact.

They were about half way back to the convoy, and silently congratulating themselves on their successful deceit, when the peaceful scene suddenly erupted in an explosion of gunfire.

"Go man. Go!" Velor yelled at the driver as a hail of bullets stitched the side of the car and, to Velor's relief, saw the convoy also start to turn with him, but not before one of the trucks disappeared in a sheet of flame and belching smoke.

Throwing himself into the back seat, Velor grabbed his driver's rifle and, loosened off a few quick shots at a line of soldiers converging from either side of the maize field. Now, between the line of fire and the last of the three trucks, Velor's car received the full blast of the ensuing onslaught, a following burst of fire shattering the windscreen and showering both soldiers in broken glass.

"Put your foot down and let's get out of here, Private," Velor bawled over his shoulder, snapping off shots at the pursuing soldiers.

"Look Sir, ahead!" the driver yelled.

Velor twisted round. "In the name of all that's holy, what are they doing there?" He exploded angrily at the sight of Tom and Bev running furiously after the fleeing trucks.

For one brief moment, it was in the soldier's mind to leave them where they were and avoid the risk of slowing down, for in terms of the military, these two were expendable. Fortunately for both fugitives, to Velor, no one was expendable, a fact that had endeared him to the hearts of his own men, which is why they had found it so hard to understand why he had left their wounded behind in Riaz.

"Slow down driver, we've two passengers to pick up," he said angrily. And, as the car screeched up alongside them, shouted out, "Quick you two get in!" The soldier's tone further frightening the terrified girl who had hesitated momentarily, but not the Scot, who unceremoniously pushed her inside and threw himself over her in the back seat, and despite her muffled protests, covered her head with his arms.

A bullet thudded into the back door, and the driver rocketed the car across the open field the open back door swinging wildly, with bullets ricocheting off the boot, until they too had left the makeshift landing strip and were roaring back on to the road in a cloud of dust.

They caught up with the rearmost truck a few kilometres up the road and, from its back, gaunt faces stared over them at the road behind. Suddenly, one gestured. Velor swung round, saw the dust cloud and swung back in his seat.

"We'll have company soon. I wonder where they hid their trucks?" he hissed.

He had barely time to reflect, when without warning, a ball of fire leapt in to the air and the truck that had been hit on the airstrip finally exploded swerving across the road, its burning canopy tearing branches from an overhanging tree.

"What the hell is happening?" Velor's driver yelled, braking sharply to his left.

Gripping the dashboard, Velor braced himself as the car broadsided to a halt and, in a moment, was out and running up the road to what was left of the burning truck.

Red hot pain seared Velor's lungs as he raced to reach the first of the wounded lying clutching their wounds in the middle of the road or trying desperately to smother their burning clothes, when a second explosion erupted, throwing jagged bits of metal in all directions.

Blown off his feet, Velor was vaguely aware of a hand hoisting him none to gently to his feet, and a voice saying in his ringing ears, with the smallest hint at humour. "A little closer Captain and you would have gone higher than your rank."

Velor shook his aching head and put his hand on Jimaneaux shoulder. "What a mess Juan!" He shifted his weight on to his other foot and stared at the disintegrating truck completely blocking the road in front of them. "At least, the first truck got clear with the Inglesa," he added shakily. "I hope the driver has the sense to keep going, as we have no way of getting through that mess."

Juan waved a hand at the smoke and mangled wreckage. "So, what do we do now, Captain, and where do we go from here? We can't get through that." He pointed again to the blocked road. "Although we could if we had time."

Velor opened his mouth to reply, when a shrill voice called out from behind. "Captain! Captain! Down the road, Sir. There is a truck coming, and fast. It will be here in a few minutes!"

Juan helped his friend to turn round.

"Keep your weapons ready. Fire if it gets within range," Velor called out to those in the remaining truck. Then, to Juan, "Quick! Get that truck turned round, and get those poor sods into it!" He pointed at the wounded from the burning truck. In the next second adding, "We passed a dirt road a little way back, get our truck to it. I'll try and stop that one coming up the road before it gets that far."

Velor hobbled back down the road to his car. He had entirely forgotten about his passengers. "You two out! Get yourselves into that truck as quick as you can!"

Stunned by the acerbity of the command, Tom and Bev stared at Velor's pointing finger, then, as one, fled for the waiting truck.

"Machine gunners!" Velor bellowed to the soldiers who had managed to haul their weapon and munitions out of the one remaining truck, "follow me!" He threw himself back into his car, and the driver swung it round as the machine gunners clambered with their weapon into the back.

"Open it up driver," Velor shouted. "You two be ready to get out when I give the word," he hurled at the two men in the back.

They were past the dirt road in a flash, the oncoming enemy truck momentarily hidden in a 'S' bend further down the road.

"Halt here driver. Now, you two, up that embankment there, and cover us till we get back! Understand?" he barked at his machine gunners.

"Yes Sir!" both men echoed, jumping free of the already accelerating car.

"Now it's all up to us, Private."

"Yes Sir," the driver answered, his eyes riveted on the road ahead, his hands tightly gripping the steering wheel.

"Well Private if you do your duty correctly, it could soon be Sergeant," Velor offered grimly. "So let it rip!"

His faced etched in determination, the driver thrust the accelerator to the floor and the car surged forward.

"Be ready to jump when I give the word," Velor said, with as much composure as he could muster and, just before they accelerated out of the last bend, let out a shout of "Now! And threw himself out of the car a fraction before his driver.

The hard chippings of the road came up at Velor with unexpected speed, and he winced at the sharp pain in his right knee, bouncing once or twice before landing in a ditch, his head buried in rotting vegetation.

Spitting out grass, he struggled to his knees in time to witness their car career into the oncoming enemy truck and imbed itself on its bumper with a sickening scream of torn metal. The first of his grenades which he had primed in the car threw both vehicles into the air. The second explosion pulverising what was left of the wreckage.

Gingerly, Velor got himself out of the ditch and hobbled over to his driver. "Are you all right, Sergeant?" He emphasised the rank, rubbing his injured knee.

The driver rose shakily. "Yes Sir. Thank you, Sir."

"For what? Your new rank? Or me asking after your welfare?"

The driver dabbed blood from his forehead. "Both, Sir. And you, Sir?"

"Okay. Now lets get the hell out of here."

As he spoke, an enemy machine gun opened up to be quickly answered by their own gun from the embankment. Velor turned awkwardly around.

Enemy soldiers, having splayed out on either side of their burning truck, were running up the road towards them. A few shots zipped into the metalled road around them and Velor and his new Sergeant started quickly back for the dirt road.

"I think we are almost there, Captain." The driver blew out breath and put out a hand to help his hobbling senior and had it quickly brushed aside. "I also think our gunners have decided to head back for the truck."

Hobbling and skipping alternatively, Velor reached the dirt road and the revving truck.

"Must have been a successful idea of yours Captain that has you hopping with joy...eh?" Jinaneaux guffawed, helping his commanding officer into the cabin.

"I still have one good leg to kick your arse, Lieutenant," Velor growled.

Still amused by his commanding officer's discomfiture, Jimaneaux gave a last quick glance that all were aboard and swung himself up beside the Captain. "Put your foot down driver, I don't think it will be long before we have company," he commanded.

Velor glanced at his friend. "I suppose you do know where this road leads, Lieutenant?" he asked drily.

"Nope. Not a clue. Except that this map shows a lake some way down this road." Juan consulted the map on his knee. "At a guess, I'd say ten, fifteen kilometres."

An overhanging branch scraped off the cabin roof. The driver cursed.

"How many do we have back there?" Velor jerked a thumb over his shoulder.

"Four Privates, a machine gun crew, two drivers and two foreigners. Plus ourselves, of course. We also have three injured from the truck explosion." Juan answered nondescript.

At a change of gear to negotiate a sharp bend, they caught the reflection of sunlight on water.

"Sweet Jesus it's a dead end!" the driver exclaimed, adding, "Sir" as he remembered who his passengers were.

There, less than a kilometre away, the road appeared to terminate at a rotting wooden pier, to which an equally derelict fishing boat lay moored. A little way further back, a few ramshackle shacks stood clustered together, a solitary wisp of smoke spiralling from one into a cloudless sky the only sign of life.

"Welcome to the dead centre of our country," Juan grunted at the desolate scene. His comment lost in the trucks sudden lurch into a sharp decline in the road.

"Easy driver, I was not ready for that." Velor winced, rubbing his knee.

"Sorry Sir. The dip took me by surprise," the driver apologised. "I was looking at the boat."

"Aim for the pier, then turn around as fast as you can," the injured officer commanded, flexing his leg.

The truck skidded to a halt and Velor hobbled down from the cabin as quickly as he could. "Get them out, Juan, and follow me…and be quick." He indicated to the cloud of dust on the skyline behind them.

Velor limped across the rotting pier, as the truck turned around, and was well aware of the figure leaning out of the wheelhouse of the tiny fishing boat, a look of quiet amusement on the wrinkled weather beaten face. From behind the old man's extended elbow the face of a girl not yet in her teens appeared, her expression upon seeing the soldiers' one of surprise and fear.

Stumbling over a protruding plank, Velor yelled up at the old man, "Can we come aboard? Can you get us out of here?"

The wrinkled face slowly lifted, his eyes screwed up against the sun. Then the eyes were on the soldier again. "Depends where you want to go?" the voice boomed, its depth taking Velor by surprise.

Velor slipped and clutched at a broken piece of railing. He saw the enemy convoy speeding down the hill towards the pier and swung round to face the old man again. "Up, down the lake? Anywhere away from here," he asked hurriedly.

The old man turned lazily to watch the men struggle with their wounded across the pier. "It's downstream to the coast. Up?" he jerked a thumb. "Goes nowhere in particular."

"Down then!" Velor hurled at him, and was under the wheelhouse in an instant staring up at the wrinkled face. "Pay later?"

The old eyes twinkled. "That figures. Best get those folks aboard as fast as you can, unless you want your friends to join you?" The grey head nodded towards the road.

"Come on!" Velor roared at the company, knowing within himself that they could not get away before the enemy reached the pier.

Jimaneaux helped Bev aboard, pushing Tom up behind her, with the soldiers clambering up over the side as best they could.

The young girl dressed in faded blue overalls, a long tailed shirt tied around her slim waist exposing a band of smooth tanned skin, dark eyes flashing with a mixture of fear and excitement hurriedly, slipped past them to cast off the lines from the rusting bollard.

Suddenly, there was a bang, followed by the sound of screeching metal reverberating around the surrounding hills and, for a moment, all stood rooted to the spot.

"It is Chi…Private Sanchez!" a soldier shouted from the roof of the wheelhouse. "He has driven his truck straight at the convoy. He has caught them in the dip!"

Beside himself with excitement, the soldier provided a running commentary to those below.

"Chi is running for the pier, Captain. Our truck is blocking the entire road. They are firing at him. Oh! No!" The soldier shook his head.

There was no need for anyone to ask what had happened. Even should they have failed to hear the gunfire, the look on the soldier's face told its own story.

"Come on, we cannot stand here all day. They'll soon get around that truck," Velor called out huskily, moved by his driver's unselfishness, and remembering how the man had tried to help him earlier.

Velor swung himself on board. "Let's get moving…pronto…if you are ready?" he added a little more quietly to the old man.

Chapter 13

Velor swung into the wheelhouse beside the old fisherman, barely taking time to introduce himself before asking. "We are trying to make the coast. How far down can you take us?" he asked, looking first at the old man, who said he was known to his friends as Papa, then out at the enemy trucks disappearing back up the hillside.

"All the way, if that is your intention," the voice boomed back at him.

Velor consulted his road map. "According to this, the lake is about a hundred kilometres long."

"One hundred and seven to be exact. Which leaves you precisely sixty three to go." The old man ducked down peering out of the window to port, his eyes obviously fixed on something important.

"What lies upstream?"

The other chuckled at the phrase, and winked at the little girl perched on a ledge by the window. "Upstream lies a shanty town, much like the one we just left, only smaller. It used to be a thriving community at one time. Back when I was around your age soldier, about a half century and several revolutions ago."

The reference was not lost on Velor. However, he had too much on his mind right now to ask the old man why he was helping them. And, despite the blue sashes they wore, which he was sure meant nothing to the old man, did he in fact know who he was helping?

"That's how the place died," the old man went on. "Too many fishermen, too many fish and not enough folk to buy them," he emphasised to a twist of the wheel.

The lurching boat brought Velor back to the present. He indicated to the hillside. "Can those trucks head us off anywhere?"

"Can do, if they know these parts. They will have to go back the way they came. That road back there is the only road. Then, they hit the main road and follow it…say eighty kilometres. Take another dirt road down to Vioga. The lake's pretty narrow there, so they could pepper this old sardine can as we slip through."

"No way we could be there before them?" Velor asked, anxiously scanning the skyline.

"Nope."

"So we couldn't outrun them?"

"Son, a paddling duck could outrun this old tub. Besides, we'll have to heave–to at Hormos Island to refuel. How much timber do you think this old girl can carry?"

"Timber!" Velor exploded.

"Timber," the old man repeated. "Where in the name of Saint Christopher would I get the Pesos for Deisel, even if I had the engine?"

Velor drew a hand through his hair in exasperation and crossed to the starboard window of the tiny wheelhouse. "What about this side of the lake?"

"Could do, except the road there goes clear over those mountains before it creeps down to the coast again. Got any transport I don't know about?"

The point taken, Velor sighed. "We'll do our best to help you refuel and man the boat. Feel free to call upon my men."

"Could do right now," Papa boomed as the soldier stepped out of the door. "Little Eva here usually takes the wheel while I do the stoking. Maybe your men could turn a hand? Eva will show you the way below."

The little girl dropped down from her perch and swung out into the companionway. "Please Senor." She smiled shyly at the squat Captain. "If you will follow me."

Velor hunched his shoulders in a sign of resignation and moved to follow the girl, his eyes on the opposite shoreline and the thick jungle creeping down to the waters' edge. A wisp of smoke curled up past the brown mountains into a cloudless sky, substantiating Papa's story that a road or some form of dwelling did exist on that side of the lake.

"Certainly, my little Senorita, lead the way." The soldier smiled down at the youngster, beginning to appreciate the humour of the situation. "Timber, indeed old man, timber indeed,"he chuckled.

At the same time as Velor was consulting with the old fisherman, Tom found Bev hunched in a corner near the gunnels. "From the frying pan into…well the 'sanpan' is near enough in this case, Bev," Tom joked, squatting down beside her. "Doesn't smell too much like a fishing boat to me and that's fishy for a start."

Bev stared up at him, her face drawn. "Oh Tom," she muttered, slumping forward, her hand clawing at his jerkin for support.

Tom would have held her there all day if he had not been so

embarrassed by the soldiers looking on. "It's all right now Bev, you're safe," he said, gently pushing her away.

It was then he saw the blood on his hand. "Bev!" he choked, "You're hurt!"

Shocked, he held her in his arms, unable to think what to do, incognizant to the soldiers who had come to gently prize the girl out of his arms.

Tom heard the voice but could not comprehend how it came to be there.

"She will be all right, Senor Tom," the voice said again. "Come, I think she would like…" Juan struggled for the right words, "that she find you there when she wakes up. Si?"

Silently, Tom followed the soldiers carrying Bev, meeting Velor and Eva as they alighted from the wheelhouse.

"The Inglesa has been hit," Juan informed his Captain tentatively.

"Jesus, as if we had not enough wounded to contend with. Is it bad?"

Juan shrugged, his eyes on the soldiers gently manoeuvring the girl down the hatchway. "Bad enough without the necessary equipment, and the right know how."

"You have the latter, Juan. Get young Eva to help you. We'll manage to stoke this old tub by ourselves." Velor looked around him as if searching for an instant remedy to his problems. "Let's hope this is all we have to cope with…at least for the time being."

Located next door to the engine room, the tiny cabin where Bev lay on the open bunk was stiflingly hot. Tom wiped the sweat from his eyes and asked in a voice as if afraid to awaken the unconscious girl, "Is she going to be all right?"

Tenderly, Juan examined the wound. He drew back a piece of the girl's shirt and a trickle of blood seeped out of the indentation. Tom looked away.

"I think I can fix," Juan assured him. "First we strip her, Si?"

Tom's jaw dropped as if the soldier had suggested something indecent. "Not me pal. You can if you like…seeing as you're the doctor so to speak." Tom fumbled for the door handle in his haste to escape.

He had always wondered what glories the young Aussie hid under those clothes, but this was not the way he wanted to find out. "You can get the wee lassie there, to help you," he said more firmly, now that he had the door open. "You can let me know when you are through. Be careful, mind," he said, taking a step into the passageway.

Reno Navas, 'Weasel' to friend and foe alike, sat back in the rusting metal chair under the dirty red and blue striped awning of his favourite quayside haunt, watchful of all that went on around him from behind the double sheet of, 'The Truth'.

Now and again, those bulbous eyes, protruding from a skeletal face, would flick across the brouhaha of the narrow strip of cobbles in the direction of two ancient tramp steamers berthed in oily waters of the harbour, to sweep the entire periphery of the waterfront, before retracting once more to the columns of his paper shield.

At this precise moment, those same protruding eyes had fallen on two men deep in conversation standing a few metres away from where he sat, one of whom was the Mexican Captain, who only two short days ago had provided him with as many Pesos as he was likely to earn in half a year. The other, he instantly recognised as that of Hugo Rodrigo. Propping his paper against the sugar bowl, Weasel took a sip of strong black coffee, alternating it with a cooling glass of water, his eyes never straying from the two men.

His curiosity aroused Weasel contemplated why Hugo should speak so openly to the foreign Captain. Perhaps, after all, there was nothing to it. Then again? He reached for his glass, stifling a sudden urge of apprehension that swept through his frail body.

It was well known the length and breadth of Port Lecera that Hugo Rodrigo had a hand in more pies than the proverbial four and twenty. So, what was he up to now? Was he after his, Reno Navas', little piece of pie as well?

Nor would he put it past that Mexican wop of a Captain to double-cross him. Rodrigo had only to show him the colour of his Pesos of which the bastard had plenty and his own lucrative, though illegal, little game was over.

Weasel put down his coffee cup and, when he lifted his head again, a third man had joined the other two. He could not see his face but was sure it was not anyone he knew…yet the figure was vaguely familiar.

He was still searching the recesses of his mind when all three turned in his direction, the lean faced newcomer, now clearly visible to him. "Yes!" Weasel snapped his fingers in excitement. "Cousin Rodrigo!" But, why here in Port Lecera? If his memory served him right, and it usually did, this cousin lived in the far south, almost as far away as the Capital itself. Then, what was he doing here, and in such troubled times? It was unlikely to be a social visit, not in the midst of a revolution.

Not that the revolution as yet had any great affect on such a remote part of the country as this, for his fellow citizens would, as they had in the past, merely sit it out and cheer the victors whoever they me be.

No previous President had ever shown the slightest interest in such a backwater as Port Lecera and vice versa. And, Bieztos was no exception. No, it had to be something of great importance to risk life and limb to travel as far away from home as this, especially under the present circumstances. And this cousin, this tall lean man, was he not some sort of radical?

Containing his excitement, Weasel slowly and carefully folded his newspaper, rose and threw a few coins on to the table and nonchalantly set off after the three men.

Reaching the corner of a busy chandlers, the three men took their leave. The foreign Captain disappearing into the crowd, while the cousins turned up a side street away from the quay.

Weasel followed the cousins, melting into the dark recesses of a doorway as both men climbed into a large black limousine parked by the kerbside, while he looked around angrily for the ever elusive taxi. Then, as one appeared a little way up the street, broke into a run.

"Well, Weasel, and what mischief are you up to today?" the driver asked, flicking cigarette ash out of the open window.

"None of your business Enrico, just follow that car," Weasel gasped, pointing to the limousine.

"Hugo Rodrigo's?" the driver asked in surprise, squinting up at his would be passenger. "Save your Pesos Weasel, he always heads home at this time of day. Take my word for it."

One eye on the departing car, Weasel flung open the rear door. "Just do as I ask, Enrico. Follow that car!"

Enrico looked through his rear mirror at his sweating passenger. "Let me see the colour of your money, Reno Navas," he demanded pointedly, rubbing his thumb and forefinger together.

Weasel swore and pulled out a fistful of notes from his pocket, and leaned forward to peer out of the windscreen. "Come on man or we'll lose them!" he growled in the driver's ear, thrusting the notes into the man's shirt pocket.

Calmly, Enrico started up the cab and slid expertly out from behind a donkey cart. "Your loss not mine," he muttered over his shoulder.

"I told you man, did I not say he would head for home?" Enrico gestured at the long black limousine gliding between two stone pillars leading up a gravel path to a large white two-storied house.

"Do you wish me to wait, o master?" Enrico chuckled.

Throwing him a virulent look, Weasel got out of the cab. "Thanks but no, I'll make my own way back."

"Suit yourself, my affluent friend," Enrico cackled, gunning his vehicle forward. "It's only five kilometres back to town."

For a few seconds, Weasel watched the car disappear, cogitating whether he had done the right thing or not, before taking a few steps up the street to halt adjacent to a large white house, all the while trying to convince himself that there was still something to be gained by investigating further. Then, deciding that there may well be, he crossed the empty street.

Weasel slid round the gate. By keeping to the lawn's verge, and using the bushes as a screen, he reached the side of the house undetected. Somewhere inside, a door opened and the sound of voices, one a woman, drifted through an open window. For a moment, Weasel hesitated, unsure what to do, then cautiously crept along the path until he came to the open window. Now, scarcely daring to breathe, he flattened himself against the wall and offered up a prayer in to the cloudless sky that his imagination was not running wild, and that there was indeed something here for him to discover, other that one cousin merely paying another a visit.

Now that he had come this far, he may as well take his courage in both hands and steel a look inside. Crouching down, Weasel snapped a look through the window and almost fell backwards at what he had seen. His knees trembling he leaned weakly against the wall and closed his eyes. There were five people in the room, the two Rodrigos and two men he did not know, plus an elderly lady seated in a wheelchair. He drew a hand across his brow and opened his eyes blinking in the midday sun, his mind reeling in comprehension at what he had just seen.

Slowly, very slowly, Weasel's expression turned from one of abject fear to one of sheer joy.

Captain Sal Cortez blew cigarette ash off his pile of papers on his desk, and waved impatiently at his Sergeant. "Find out what he wants and send him on his way if you think it unimportant."

"I have already tried, Sir, but he insists on talking to you personally and no one else."

"Very well," Sal surrendered, leaning back in his chair from the paper strewn desk. "But it better be good or else." He drew a finger across his throat.

Sal inhaled deeply on his cigarette and threw a hand at the solitary chair as Weasel austerely came into the room. "Five minutes, my friend, no more. Do I make myself clear?"

Weasel smiled amicably at the officer behind the desk and sat down.

On prior occasions, he would have taken the seat while extolling the man's altruism at taking the time to listen to someone such as himself. But that was before today, for although in the past he had supplied Captain Sal Cortez with some useful little tit bits, never before had he been privy to such crucial, if not profitable information. Instead, he continued to smile at the man whilst making himself comfortable.

"The Inglisa," he started, studying the officer's impassive face.

Sal drew deeply on his cigarette. "The one mentioned on the radio? The one whom the President fears has been kidnapped? The wife of the late British Ambassador, Weasel?" he asked irksomely, his voice rising. "You have heard someone say they have knowledge of her, here in this great metropolis of ours? Is that it, my friend? This is why you are using up my valuable time?" he asked sarcastically.

Feeling his confidence ebb away before this unexpected acrimony, Weasel swallowed hard. "Not quite my Captain. I did not hear of this woman, I saw her, with my own eyes!"

Sal shot forward in his chair steepling his fingers, "You have seen her? And where? How do you know it is she?"

Recapturing a little of his composure, Reno stared directly at his interrogator. "She is crippled, yes?" The officer answered Weasel's question with a nod. "Then it was she. She was sitting in the back of a car with the door open," Weasel lied. "I saw the rug draped over her legs. She spoke in English, then in our own language…this is why it is she, Captain."

Weasel halted anticipating a question, when none was forthcoming, he continued, a little less sure of himself despite this 'great' information he was giving this son-of-a-bitch, Captain. "It was not until I was passed the car that I realised who she must be, by that time the car had gone."

"What make of automobile was it, Weasel?"

Weasel frowned stammering. " Ido not know…only…" he started hopefully, "it was a big black car."

"A big black car?" Sal repeated sarcastically. "Was it a local car or not Weasel? What would you say?" he asked, hiding his impatience behind a growing excitement. "You should know this at least my friend. You, who know all that goes on in our little town. Eh?"

Weasel focused his eyes a little above his inquisitor. "Outsider…definitely an outsider," he nodded as much to convince himself as the Captain.

Sal unclasped his hands and sat back in his chair. "Not much to go on Weasel, is there? For a moment, I thought you had something there. A real good piece of valuable information," he enticed. "There is a substantial reward for her safe return, you know."

Sensing he had gained the man's interest, Weasel's confidence returned. "Come on Captain Cortez, we both know those bullshit broadcasts about the Inglesa kidnapping are nothing more than just that, bullshit," he smiled mischievously.

Sal all but choked on his cigarette at this unexpected outburst. It was the first time this cretin had ever dared speak to him in this way. Usually the tone was servile, the manner quailing. Therefore, to hear Weasel speak to him in this manner, could only mean that he did know something about this business.

Sal swore under his breath at this disgusting little creature, now knowing how he had come to be known by this nickname. Regaining his composure, he swivelled around in his chair. "What makes you so sure it was bullshit?" he hissed.

Undeterred by the Captain's tone, Weasel grinned crookedly.

"The lady I saw today was as free to leave that car as I could have been, even allowing for those useless legs. Neither did I hear her call out for help, and there were plenty of passers- by. So I reckon there must be some other reason…a very important reason, for our beloved President Bieztos wishing her safe return. And if so, a very profitable one to whoever is fortunate enough to find her."

"I shall see what can be done Weasel. On your way out, give my Sergeant the details of where you saw the car." Sal stubbed out his cigarette, the action signifying the discussion was at an end. "Keep your eyes and ears open," he enjoined. "Should we find the lady, the reward is all yours."

Perplexed at his sudden dismissal, Weasel rose and crossed the room to halt by the door. "If I should see her again, or hear something, I will let you know immediately, Captain Cortez."

Sal looked up from his pile of paper, a wry smile on his face. "I am sure you will Weasel. I am sure you will."

Outside, Weasel took the steps down to the pavement one at a time, his brain temporary addled by Sal Cortez's inexplicable attitude towards him and drew a hand threw his hair, neither seeing or hearing the mid afternoon traffic rushing passed.

If he had aroused the man's interest in his story of the crippled lady, why then this summary dismissal, as if suddenly losing all interest in the whole affair? Was it merely pretence on the good Captain's behalf in leading him to believe he did not put much stock in what he had told him? Which was why he, Weasel, had concocted the story of the car in the first place. For, had he told the truth, Cortez's men would have been out at Hugo Rodrigo's house in an instant, and bang would have gone his reward.

He reached the bottom step and turned right along the boulevard. When next they met, he would whet the greedy Captain's appetite a little further, then he would know for certain if Sal Cortez was taking him seriously or not.

Although he had no idea why Bieztos was so anxious to find her, he had already deduced that the lady's intention was to leave the country by ship, and that ship was the Ortago, Captained by his very own Mexican smuggling friend whom he'd seen earlier that day talking to both Rodrigo cousins' on the quayside. But his timing must be just right, for the Ortago was due to sail for Mexico in four days time. So his next meeting with the delightful Captain Cortex must be to discuss the financial terms of what he was sure would end in a mutual business transaction. Or he did not know his Captain of militia very well.

Slowly, carefully, Segovia removed his sunglasses, his action calculated to intensify the fear of the quivering officer. "You apologise for the mistake, Lieutenant. You believed that the person in the fishing boat that left here yesterday was the crippled Englisa? The one whom I have traversed half this God forsaken corner of the country to apprehend!" Segovia stormed, throwing a hand at the ramshackle shacks by the lakeside. "Now, I hear you say you have made a mistake." Segovia thrust his face close to that of the trembling man.

Disgusted, Segovia turned away. It had taken him quite some time to acquire that the Englisa and her friends, who, aided by some renegade soldiers, had made their escape to Corona, only to learn later of their departure for the north, which in turn had forced him to detour around that rebel held city.

He watched a carrion crow rise from a clump of trees nearby, following its flight down the lakeside until obscured by an outcrop of rock.

Three days ago, he had had the satisfaction of leaving a burning village behind. There had also been the incident with that insolent priest. The one who had equated him to a barbaric Roman centurion. Well, now he knew what it was like to follow his, Master. Segovia allowed himself a tiny smile. Now, other villages would know what was in store for them should they choose to support the wrong side, as had the village of Riaz.

It was from this village his adversaries had left for the airfield and, after a narrow escape from there, had again headed north. Yesterday, through this moron here, he'd learned of the convoy's forced separation, with one solitary truck making for this lake.

Still seething with anger, Segovia turned on his victim again. "Can you or your men not differentiate between an able bodied female and a crippled one, Lieutenant? Or are they all imbeciles like their commanding officer?"

Blushing under the insult, the young man opened his mouth to defend himself, then thinking better of it averted his eyes to let the inevitable tirade continue.

"Correct me if I am wrong, but I am led to understand only one truck took this road to the lake, where its occupants…one a woman; not crippled," Segovia lingered on the words, "boarded a fishing boat, manned by an old man and his grand- daughter, and proceeded down this lake? Are my facts correct?" Segovia fixed the junior officer an icy stare. "Then, why, in the name of all that is holy, did you issue a dispatch suggesting I come here?"

The younger man confronted his protagonist, only too well aware of the man's power. He moistened his lips knowing what he was about to say would lay his career on the line. "Earlier, the road north was blocked by one of the rebel trucks," he began nervously. "By the time, we had cleared it the rebels had disappeared. However, we followed the truck left behind to this point. When we failed to prevent them boarding the fishing vessel, our convoy returned to the main road, and should by now be on its way to Vioga…that is a small village some distance down the lake." The young man hastened to explain at his Colonel's impatience. "Once there, it is hoped, due to the narrow channel which the vessel must pass through, our soldiers will be in a position to prevent its passage."

"Very commendable, Lieutenant, but even should they succeed in doing so, how will this benefit me?" Segovia's voice rose, his eyes blazing. "Why not advise me to follow the convoy instead to this God forsaken place?" He waved a hand at the desolate surroundings.

"If you will bear with me for a few moments more, Sir?" the young man pleaded, beads of sweat dripping into his eyes.

Segovia folded his sunglasses and slid them in to his tunic pocket, gratified by the others discomfiture, and nodded that he should continue.

"In the opposite direction," he swallowed, "at the head of the lake," he went on, pointing over Segovia' shoulder, "there is also a small village, though as here it has no telephone, but fortunately for us, it does possess three or four motor launches, or so I am led to believe. With these, we can easily overhaul the fishing boat; that is to say if it has not already been intercepted by our troops at the narrows. Also, I am certain when it is apprehended, those on board will be able to inform us in which direction, or where the crippled lady is headed." Having played his trump card, the Lieutenant drew himself up stiffly, awaiting his senior's reaction.

"What is your name, Lieutenant?" Segovia asked coldly.

He had failed; the Chief of State Security was not pleased by his actions. Already, he saw himself back in a Private's uniform. "Mahora, Sir. Lieutenant Rolando Mahora," he choked.

"Perhaps then, Lieutenant Mahora, I may have misjudged you a little. Perhaps, if there are motor launches in the village as you say, and perhaps if they do get them here on time. Perhaps we may yet apprehend some of the traitorous party."

Ronaldo wiped his brow, his relief quickly fading as Segovia's voice rose in crescendo. "Then again, we may not! Perhaps your bringing me here has already precipitated the escape of the crippled Inglisa! In which case, Lieutenant Ronaldo Mahora, you may wish you had never been born!"

With this, Colonel Roberto Segovia spun on his heel.

Lieutenant Jimaneaux said that Bev had slept since he had extracted the bullet; that was over six hours ago. Tom held his breath and let himself in to the tiny cabin. The sleeping figure lay on her side a thin grey sheet drawn up to her chin, the face pale beneath the deep tan. He sat on the edge of the bed and grasped the bunk above to keep himself from shaking. The sight of the girl reminded him so much of what had happened to her friend Gillian.

God! How long ago was that? What was happening to all of them? To him? It was days since he'd last thought of home or had one of his imaginary conversations with Big Dougie. Could it be that he had subconsciously given up the thought of ever seeing his friend again? Or knowing that what had happened to Gilly and Dane could just as easily happen to him? Despite the fact that he was a foreign holiday-maker, who had the misfortune to stumble in to their little revolution, he could never now be classed or treated merely as a spectator.

The significance of losing his job and his home no longer held the same significance as it had in those early days. Those early days? He closed his eyes. Those early days were in fact only days, not years as they now felt.

"Tom?" The whispered word caught him unawares.

"You're awake." He forced a smile. "I thought we'd have to re christen you Bev Van Winkle."

The girl smiled weakly up at him.

"How do you feel?" Immediately, Tom thought how inadequate the question was. He tried again but failed.

"My shoulder throbs a bit."

"Good pet, as long as your heart does as well."

She gave him one of her puzzled looks, but was too weary to ask for an explanation. Instead, she asked, "Where are we Tom?"

"Certainly not going down the Clyde." Tom rose and looked out of the solitary porthole at the setting sun. "We're still on the lake."

"That's nice. For a moment, I thought we were on the main highway."

Tom felt better at having heard her joke. "Good to see you've still got your Aussie sense of humour. Don't you realise this old tub has enough cracks in it without you adding to it?"

Bev gave a wince and Tom hoped it was at his joke and not her shoulder. He took her hand and sank back down on the edge of the bed. "The soldier who took the bullet out said it's a clean wound, as they say in the pictures."

"Hurts a bit more than the pictures though."

"Aye. I suppose so. There, they get a cheque to dull the pain."

Tom looked away, annoyed by his ineptitude to say something more appropriate. To compound everything else, was he also losing his sense of humour? If he was, he knew of one person who would not mourn his lose, and thought affectionately of 'wee wumman', hoping she was safe, wherever she may be.

"Penny for your thoughts, fella."

"Mmm?" Tom stared at the girl as if not understanding the question. "Sorry, Bev. You were saying?"

"Penny for them," she repeated.

"Och, they're not worth tuppence, to coin a phrase."

"I think I feel a relapse coming on." Bev pretended to be in pain.

Tom had never seen her look so helpless, so desirable as she was now. He would have kissed her, but was unsure what reaction it would evoke.

He got up. "I can take the hint," he said straightening the bedclothes. "I'll come back later. If that's all right with you?"

Bev sank down beneath her cover. "Sure sport. Call anytime, you'll find me around here somewhere."

"How long to Hormos Island?" Velor asked the old man, absently watching Tom come on deck from Bev's cabin.

The other considered the question for a moment. "Another hour or so." The old man sucked on his briar pipe, clenched between his teeth. "We'll heave-to, and take on wood in the morning."

Velor struck a match, its brief flame lighting up the tiny wheelhouse. "Then, they're certain to be waiting for us coming through the narrows," he said, inhaling his cigarette.

Papa moved the wheel slightly to starboard and spat tobacco juice neatly out of the window without removing his pipe. "That's for sure." He leaned forward tapping the compass. "We'll make a run for it tomorrow night."

"You do not have to do this, old man. You could just let this revolution pass you by. It will make no difference away up here." He almost added at your time of life but thought how insulting this would sound to a man like old Papa.

"How much excitement do you think this old man gets around here, soldier?" Papa threw over his shoulder.

"I was thinking more of the youngster," Saul corrected.

The old man gave a half turn taking the pipe from his mouth. "Should anything happen to this old bag of bones, maybe you could see your way…"

Saul held the old man's look. "Consider it done."

Papa turned to the wheel again. "Unfortunately for her, I'm all she's got right now."

"How much more timber do you think we will need, Papa?" Velor asked anxiously.

The old man calculated how much had come on board since they'd started cutting and hauling the wood earlier that morning. "Another two loads should see us through."

Velor nodded. He swung down from the wheelhouse and met his Lieutenant on the way up. "We are a bit low on food, Saul. This old tub only carries enough for the old man and the girl." Juan stepped back from the ladder to make way for his friend.

"What supplies did we manage to bring on board with us, Juan?"

"Mostly ammo. A few tins of meat." Juan scratched the back of his neck.

Velor spread his hands out on the rail and ran an eye over the line of men passing logs from hand to hand. He swung his attention to the bow of the boat where the two machine gunners were hard at work, raising the height of the bulwarks to create a timber barricade. "Hope that works."

Juan followed his Captain's gaze. "For all our sakes, Saul. For all our sakes," he breathed.

"Does all that noise disturb you, Bev?" Tom jerked his head in the direction of the hammering from above.

"A little." The girl's voice sounded weak.

Alarmed by the change in Bev's appearance, but not wishing to show too much concern, Tom searched for something cheerful to say. Also, he must ask Lieutenant Jimaneaux if he would take another look at her wound.

"You've never told me anything about your folks, Bev," he said sitting down on the edge of the bed.

The girl propped herself up on the pillow. "My father owns a carpet store on Pitts Street...in Sydney," she explained, her voice a little stronger.

"A carpet shop! No doubt he's making his pile," Tom chuckled.

Tom fell silent unable to decide what to do next. Perhaps, he should leave. Let the girl rest. Then again, perhaps it was some nourishment she needed. Should he go scrounging for food for her? If there was any around, he'd probably find it where the rest of the wounded were held.

"What about you Tom? What does your folks do to keep the wolf from the door?" the girl asked, her eyes closed.

"I don't have any folks. Well, not parents," Tom answered, still thinking of how many wolves he'd seen in Govan recently; well, at least not the four legged kind.

Bev gave a little cough. She opened her eyes and looked at him sadly. "On your own, are you? Or do you live with relatives?"

"Relatively speaking...I lived with my Granny for a while. She passed away a wee while ago."

"Oh I am sorry Tom, did you lose your mum and dad at an early age?"

This was getting a bit too serious Tom decided, glad that the girl had closed her eyes again. At this stage, his life story was all she needed to cheer her up.

"I don't remember much about my mum. Sometime, I'll tell you about my father." He took a step away. "In the meantime, what would you like to eat? Soup, if I can find some? Would you like that?"

"Don't talk to me as if I were a child," Bev scolded him, hiding her pleasure at this unexpected attention. "But I sure could down some if you can find any."

"As good as done, my little possum."

"Stick to your Bogey impressions sport, your Strine's a bit off."

"That's what makes me walk so funny."

"Strine, not spine, you clown. Now, go and fetch me that soup."

"Yes m'lady. Straight away m'lady." Tom touched his forelock in mock servility, bowing himself out of the door.

"It's one of the Privates." Juan held out the I.D. disc to Velor. "He never recovered from the burns."

Velor flicked his cigarette butt over the side of the boat. "He won't be the last if our plan fails."

"Captain Velor! Captain, Sir."

Spinning round, Saul ran to the stern, Juan by his side.

"There!" the man emphasised, pointing astern.

"Jesus!" Juan exclaimed at the sight of three motor launches rapidly closing in on them.

"Let's have you lot now!" Velor howled at the soldiers who had been resting on deck. "Jump to it lads. Let's see if you can emulate our esteemed marines?" Juan cried, hauling the slower ones to their feet none too gently.

"Can you see them, Papa?" Velor shouted up to the old man.

"Better than you soldier," the voice boomed back. "What do you expect me to do?"

"The boats look a bit dilapidated. Can we at least try to outrun them?" Even as the words left the Lieutenant's lips, he was aware of the stupidity of the question.

Papa shook his head in despair at the soldier's question. "I recognise these boats, they have come from the head of the lake. As they have already overhauled us, how do you expect me to outrun them? So, if you have a mind to go faster, you better start swimming."

Beside Tom, Velor stood eyes fixed on the approaching launches. "You had better get yourself below."

To Tom, the words were said without emotion, as if the soldier still regarded him as a coward for returning from the crypt that day. But, right now, he had other things on his mind. Overawed, he stood transfixed, his eyes riveted on the speeding craft. "I cannae even swim," he blurted out, grasping the rail tighter.

"Much too late now," Juan chuckled, amused by the look on the Scot's face.

Velor swung angrily on Tom. "Go Escoces. I have much more important matters to attend to. Go. Look after your Senorita."

I wish she was, Tom thought, turning away from the barricade, offended by the man's attitude towards him.

Bev, he knew, only tolerated him because there was no one else to turn to at the moment, not as she needed someone to lean on. For he was no 'he' man, as Dane had been, and well the Aussie knew it.

Suddenly, the air was filled by the sound of gunfire. Broken glass from the shattered wheelhouse above landed at his feet and he dived headlong down the companionway, landing in full view of Bev struggling out of her bunk.

"What's up Tom?"

"My arse mainly," he mumbled, rising as quickly as he could from his undignified position. "Get back to bed, Bev. You don't want that wound opening up again."

Despite her protestations, he drew her gently to the edge of the bunk and swung her feet back into bed.

"What is going on up there? I'm sure I can hear gunfire." Bev exclaimed, her head tilted towards the cabin roof, listening.

"Just a little fishing, that's all." Tom tucked the blanket around her and tried to sound normal, though his hands were trembling.

He was about to step back when another burst of gunfire raked the boat, shattering the skylight glass with a roar.

"Shit!" Tom yelled and threw himself over the girl.

"Said the king and a thousand backsides strained," came Bev's muffled voice from beneath Tom's protective embrace.

Tom drew back and stared down at the girl, his eyes wide in surprise. "I've never heard that one before."

"You've never been to Aus, sport."

The gunfire having ceased, Tom retreated to the end of the bunk, again mystified by the girl's change of persona. One minute on the edge of panic, the next calm as the lake they had been sailing on. He gave up. He never would understand women.

"Senorita!" the small voice meekly called out from the open door, two large brown eyes focused intently on the woman.

"You poor little mite, come to Bev." Bev held out her arms to the frightened girl.

"Wish you'd say that to me," Tom muttered.

"Ignore him, Eva," Bev smiled reassuringly at the uncomprehending child. "Come sit by me." She patted the bed beside her. Then, fixing a stony eye on Tom, commanded of him. "Go and make yourself useful up top, MacTavish."

"Some say that's an impossibility." Tom swung himself on to his feet. "See you around…I hope."

"Here they come again!" Velor called out.

For the past five minutes, two motor launches had circled the plodding fishing vessel, raking it with gunfire from their prow mounted machine gun, whilst a larger craft similarly armed and crammed with soldiers, hovered at a respectable distance.

Kneeling amongst the splattered glass on deck of the wheelhouse, Velor cautiously raised his head to window level and bellowed down at his men crouched behind the makeshift barriers. "Here they come again. Fire! Now!"

As one, the four Privates opened fire on the nearest craft, except for Jimaneaux and his machine gun crew who held their fire as ordered.

"Why not us too, Lieutenant?" the machine gunner cried in exasperation, peering nervously through a slit in the makeshift barricade.

"You'll get your chance soldier, and when you do, make sure you do not miss." Juan returned calmly. "Rifles are our best bet at this range."

Juan flung a look down the length of the boat where the four Privates were returning the fire from the circling launches darting in and out like hounds worrying a wounded fox.

With a cry, one of the soldiers staggered to his feet, his hands clasped tightly to his face, stumbling blindly about, until a second burst of fire caught him in the back.

"Sweet Jesus, we're all going to die" the machine gunner sobbed, clutching his weapon tighter.

Vicelike, Jimaneaux's hand gripped the trembling man's shoulder.

"Steady, soldier, steady. The Captain knows what he's doing," he hissed.

By the bow of the boat, one of the men burned from the explosion on the truck attempted to reload a rifle, while his wounded companion dragged an ammunition box behind him. Juan ran towards them, and a line of bullets threw splinters in all directions inches above his crouched body. A spurt of blood from a wounded man splattered his shirt as he ran past.

Snatching up the wounded soldier's rifle, Juan snapped off a few quick shots through the slits in the barricade at one of the smaller launches speeding towards them.

All at once, the craft veered to starboard and, through the spray, Juan saw the helmsman topple overboard. Now out of control, the craft drew closer. Juan fired again and this time found the fuel tank, and the launch erupted in sheet of flame.

"One down, two to go!" someone shouted jubilantly from further along the deck.

At the same time as the launch exploded, Velor threw himself flat from the hail of bullets shattering the compass and every other instrument in the wheelhouse.

Above Velor, Papa, one hand on the wheel, steered blindly, the other hand wiping blood from his face. "They mean business my friend." He grinned down at Velor, as if enjoying the game.

Velor dragged himself along the wheelhouse to the opposite wall, glass crackling under him like ice. "I know old man, there is not a lot I can do about it. I must wait for the right time to use our machine gun. But, for now, the launches are content to keep their distance." Velor shouted to make himself heard above the gunfire, heightened now and again as the larger launch joined in. "We cannot take them both on should they try to board us. That big one is jammed packed with Regulars."

The Captain twisted onto his knees and risked a quick look out of the window. Then, in the next instant, was on his feet, yelling down at Juan, "Lieutenant Jimanaux, open fire!" He pointed angrily at the remaining small launch about to cut across their bow.

It was the first time the launch had come within range of their lighter machine gun, and Juan was not about to miss the opportunity. Giving the order to fire, they hit their target with the first burst. "Swing it round!" Juan called out hoarsely to his crew. "Hit them as they make the turn!"

With the gun almost hard against the makeshift barricade, the crew followed the craft, scoring hit after hit, until it was out of range.

So tense were they that they were unaware of the larger craft having drawn closer, until bullets ripped through the gaps in the rough planking. One burst caught the machine gunner in the chest, throwing the weapon skywards from his lifeless hands.

"Damn! They got my machine gunner, and got away into the bargain." Velor slid back down on to the deck. "Any ideas old man?"

"One." Papa gave a puckish grin. "Who's stoking my boat?"

Velor drew up his knees, reloading his rifle. "The Escoces, the last time I saw him."

"Get him and one of your men up here, and quick."

Velor raised an eyebrow. "The Escoces won't fight, and they're not many of us left. Got an idea, have you?"

"You got one soldier?" Papa threw back testily.

"Nope."

"Then get their arses up here."

Velor met Tom on the companionway, the Scot's face pale at the sight of the dead gunner.

"The old man wants you up top." He jerked a thumb over his shoulder.

Tom nodded, and ran his tongue over his dry lips. "I've stoked the boiler." He pushed passed. "It won't need any more for a while."

"Good. I'll send another man down. That old character seems to have an idea on how to get us out of this. Or so he says."

Velor left Tom and ran down the few steps to the deck, crouching down beside Juan and the dead gunners mate.

Still disgusted at what he saw as his failure, Juan hissed at his Captain. "We missed."

"Not all together Lieutenant, you managed a few hits."

Juan was not to be consoled. "Maybe, but now that they know we have a machine gun, they won't venture so close again."

Velor took a look through the gap in the barricade at the two launches standing off. "At a guess, I'd say it's all up to the old man now."

A few minutes later, busily drawing the tarpaulin over the dead gunner, Velor did not notice the black smoke pouring from the boat's funnel, until a sudden down draft blew it swirling along the deck, blacking out the wheelhouse from view. Suddenly, the ancient craft veered sharply to port, bow waves crashing over the makeshift barricade and sending the deck awash.

"Does the old fool mean to drown us? Is that his way out?" The gunner's mate cried indignantly, cradling his new charge, seawater swirling around his feet.

"Perhaps he thinks he can save us by turning this old tub into a submarine, soldier," Jimaneaux chuckled at the man's alarm.

While he had spoken, the fishing boat had turned round on itself in a tight turn, the sharp ping of bullets ricocheting off the half hidden funnel.

"Port side with that gun, Captain Velor, if you mean to have them." Old Miguel boomed down at him through the smoke haze.

Velor ran to where the replacement gunner and Juan lay crouched behind the barricade, slapping the gunner on the shoulder. "Bring your new toy, and follow the Lieutenant and me. Let's do as the old man says."

Running and slipping on the swaying deck, the three men set up the gun a little way aft on the port side, Velor only privy to old Miguel's intentions.

"Take a peek Lieutenant. See what our friends are up to," Velor said, feeding in the ammunition belt and holding it level for the gunner.

The smaller of the two craft was now heading in the opposite direction to them, having followed in their original wake before Miguel had made his turn.

A fusillade of bullets hit the barricade and superstructure from the small launch as it sped past, its deck slanted towards them in the act of coming about. Suddenly, the speeding craft halted abruptly, its engine spluttering and coughing before it finally gave up, caught it would seem in the grip of some unseen hand.

"Now!" Papa's voice boomed through the smoke. "Now! You'll never get another chance!"

As one, the entire company opened fire on the disabled craft caught up in the fishing boat's nets, Papa steering towards it as quickly as possible.

"Get the bastard before his big brother arrives!" Velor bawled, remembering the fate of his gunner.

In desperation, Velor's men poured round after round into the rocking launch, their targets going overboard either hit or seeking to escape. Then, a flash as the fuel tank went up. Even so, they continued to rake the boat, ignoring the shrieks of terror hurled across the ever decreasing distance between the two craft.

Juan swung round to look behind him. "Here comes big brother!" he shouted, wiping sweat from his brow. "And coming straight for us! Do you think they mean to board us Captain?"

"Wait and all shall be revealed Lieutenant of little faith," Velor chuckled, his eyes on the chasing launch.

As he spoke, Papa swung his craft hard to port, putting the smaller launch between himself and its larger companion, which had reduced speed to pick up survivors, its machine gun and soldiery blasting the fishing boat with murderous fire.

"Can you reach it from here?" Velor shouted at the gunner and Juan, shoving a grenade into each of their hands. "We'll have to be quick before they have the same idea."

"No trouble," Juan laughed grimly.

In one quick movement, Juan was on his feet, tossing his grenade with all his might, Velor and the gunner doing likewise, then throwing themselves flat amid a hail of bullets.

"Let's try again for luck!" Velor passed them another supply, and once again they rose and lobbed their grenades.

A thunderous roar followed this second volley, tossing men into the air of the tightly packed craft, pieces of metal and timber showering down on the fishing boat.

From the stern, they watched the carnage they had wrought. Desperately, survivors thrashed about in the oil stained water, some, their clothes alight, clinging to what little wreckage remained.

"Good God in heaven, what have we done?" Juan whispered as the fishing boat drew steadily away, leaving behind the screams of burned and drowning men. "Some of those men I recognised from our own regiment, Saul."

"Would you rather it was us Juan?" Velor replied softly, turning his back upon the scene.

"Of course not...but what a way to die."

Tom found Bev propped up in bed, a protective arm around the little girl. Startled by his sudden appearance, and afraid of what it might mean, she shot out, "What the hell is going on up there? Those explosions! Are we sinking?"

"No." Tom said happily. "At least, not yet."

Assured by Tom's smile, Eva slid off the bunk, pointing a finger upwards. "Abueo," she called out, making for the door.

"He's all right." Tom put his hands on the little girl's shoulders, holding her back a little as she attempted to brush past him in the confines on the tiny cabin. "Okay." He nodded smiling down own at her.

"Si Senor," she smiled back, shrugging off his hold and disappearing through the door.

"Is everything okay? Tom. I thought for a minute we'd capsized." Bev was not completely convinced by Tom's reassurances, and she drew herself up into a more comfortable position.

"Sure is. Myself and a soldier let the fishing nets go at the old man's orders. He made so much smoke, even I could not see what was happening. Then he turned back on himself, so that the launch that was following us got caught up in our nets."

"Is that what the explosion was?" Bev asked, her face lighting up.

"No, that was the big launch going up later. The smaller launch was left drifting helplessly while we salt and peppered it. The 'net' result, you might say was, we sank it as well."

"Good lord, not puns as well," Bev moaned, hiding her relief.

"Oh, I thought that was quite punny, myself." Tom sniffed in pretence of being piqued at the response to his humour.

"It's all very well for you Tom Bell, you know what's going on up there. Lying down here is not so easy," Bev admonished.

"Sorry lassie, point taken."

Tom was glad she had not witnessed what he had seen, and would not have to try to erase the memory of the burning men, as he undoubtedly would. He still felt sick, never having seen anything like it before in his young life.

Tom took the girl's hand in his. She looked down at the blanket. "I was worried about you, MacTavish. You're all I've got now," she whispered.

Unsure how to react to this unexpected show of emotion, embarrassed, Tom reverted to his native sense of humour. "No wonder you were worried then," he chuckled. "No wonder you were worried."

Chapter 14

"How long 'till we reach the narrows?" Velor asked, shivering slightly in the evening breeze.

An arrow flight of birds headed towards the shore; he followed them with his eyes.

Miguel spat tobacco juice out of the shattered wheelhouse window letting the wheel run free through his fingers before correcting it. "We'll heave-to in a couple of hours, so we will reach there in mid darkness. Or what there is of it at this time of year."

Velor crossed to the opposite side of the wheelhouse, following the birds' progress over the trees which seemed to vie with one another to reach the shore. "Thanks old man," he said, his eyes still on the birds.

"For what? Making an old man happy?" Miguel spat again, replacing the pipe in his mouth. "We are not out of it yet. How many men have you left?"

"Besides Jimaneaux and myself, four plus three wounded including those burned on the highway."

"Not a lot for what you have in mind. What about the Escoces? You will need all the help you can get."

"He won't help... at least not fight," Velor said contemptuously, his back to the window.

"At least, he is stoking the boat, or I'd have him fed to the fish by this time," Miguel snarled. He saw Velor stifle a yawn. "You better get your head down for an hour. "

Velor stifled another yawn. "I've other things on my mind right now, but I guess I can manage a minute or two." He leaned wearily on the door-jamb. "After I do the rounds, I'll make sure Eva and the girl are all right before I turn in. How about you?"

"No need to worry about me, soldier." Miguel gave a low laugh. "I can do this in my sleep."

"That's it fed. Fed up as I am." Tom blew out a long breath, dropping down on to the bunk.

"You've finished stoking the boat?"

"As much as she will take at present."

"When do we reach these narrows they keep on about?" Bev

tidied the blankets around her.

"Oh, some time during the night, or early morning. They won't let us non-combatants in on their secret."

Bev eyed him wryly.

"I won't kill, Bev. Or have you forgotten I only came here for a holiday?"

He didn't like the way she was looking at him. It was bad enough knowing that most on board saw him as a cowardly 'anus crevice', without her thinking likewise. Besides, he had difficulty in explaining it to himself. Although in his imagination, he could see himself receiving admiring looks from lassies and Big Dougie back home when he related his adventures…with a little exaggerated bravado thrown in for good measure of course, which he was certain would ensure a few more free rounds. The truth was that he did not relish the possibility of living with the fact of having actually taken someone's life.

"It's a different ball game now sport. It's pretty far removed from a holiday or student exchange. Or had you forgotten about Gillian?" she asked tersely.

"Of course not," Tom squirmed, feeling that their recent propinquity was falling apart. "But I won't go home a murderer; not if I can help it."

"Not even to help yourself? Or me?" Bev looked at him squarely.

"Dinnae be daft lassie." He rose abruptly, wanting to get away before matters got worse. "Get some rest. I'll take a look in later and see you're all right."

"No need to rush. I'll be here. And if there's trouble, I can always get little Eva to defend me."

Wincing at the innuendo, Tom closed the door behind him.

An hour later, Bev made her way to the foot of the companionway, having decided that should the boat go down, the safest place to be was up top. Also, it was nice not to be cooped up in the stifling heat of the cabin, though it was nothing in comparison to the boiler room in which Tom had sweated buckets stoking up.

Reaching the hatch, Bev drank in the cool night air, gazing across the moonlight lake to the dense jungle beyond. Perhaps she had been a bit too cruel on the Scot; after all, it was his decision.

"Are you fit enough to be up, Bev?" the voice called up to her.

Turning awkwardly on the companionway, Bev stared down at the anxious upturned face of the man who was still in her thoughts. "Yeah…sure," she stammered, blushing at the recollection of their last encounter. "I came up for a breath of fresh air. I suppose you could do with some yourself. It must have been like an oven in that boiler room."

Tom climbed up to her. "Are you strong enough to be up and about? You should be lying down 'till closer to the time."

Suddenly, any disparaging thoughts Bev may have held towards Tom melted as he sat there on the top step of the companionway, the same worried expression on his face. "You make it sound as though I was pregnant. It's only a scratch as they say in the Bogey pictures." She tried to make light of it.

Tom gave an embarrassed grin. "I'm glad to hear it. I didn't fancy having to carry you ashore when the time comes."

"Are you insinuating I'm heavy, Tom Bell?" the girl asked in mock offense.

"Well, I heard the Captain say to give you a wide berth, if that means anything."

"'Nough said," Bev croaked. "Are we friends again?"

"Depends on what you mean by friends? See, me and Big Dougie are what you might call friends. There's nothing he woudnae do for me and there's nothing I wouldnae do for him; that's how we get on so well together, doing nothing for each other." The joke was so old, Tom thought, it should have received a birthday card from the King, but at least it had helped to ease the tension.

Bev let out a gurgle of laughter, wincing at the stab of pain in her shoulder. "So, all you do is hang around with your friend?"

"Now and again. I used to play darts with him until he complained about getting headaches and pleaded with me to get a set of darts instead!"

"Well, I've heard it all now!" she choked. "Come to think of it, I've never heard any of it."

Tom shrugged, happy at the reconciliation. "Not much to tell. What would you like to know?"

"What about sheilas?"

"Sheila's what?" Tom asked, pretending to be perplexed.

"You know…women," Bev laughed.

"Oh!" Tom frowned. "I went with a loose woman once. Stopped

though, her left leg kept falling off."

Bev smiled down at him. "Have I not heard that somewhere before?"

"Aye, maybe you're right. My jokes are like a plate of beans, they have a tendency to repeat themselves." Tom scratched his jaw, feeling a little foolish.

Bev made herself comfortable against the wall, brushing aside the Scot's embarrassment. "You told me about your mum, Tom, what about your dad? You must have had one?"

"Oh yes, he used to visit mum quite a lot. In fact, he has been known to stay with us on occasions. Sometimes years on end."

"You know what I mean Tom Bell. I wasn't implying..."

"That I was illiterate?" Tom suggested with a grin.

She blushed and looked down at the step, scraping it with a finger. "No, I did not mean that.,,and the word is illegitimate, as you well know. Anyway, you were telling me about your dad."

"No. Correction, you were asking me about him."

"Well, anyway tell me about him."

The Scot settled back staring up at the star lit sky. "He had a hard life...well, he would have with me around. Though, come to think of it, so had I. In fact, I was nine before I realised my name was not Hey You."

He heard her chuckle and was glad he had come to this land after all, even if it had to end in a way neither would have wished. Yet, her being here made it all worthwhile. The misery of climbing the hills, the hunger, the danger. Yes, if things did go well it would be something to tell Dougie about.

"Go on then," he heard her say.

"He had a bad accident. He was sitting upstairs on the bus going to work one night...my dad had more jobs than a dog has fleas," Tom explained. "That's why he was nicknamed Lightning...never known to strike in the same place twice." Tom chuckled. "My dad told me what happened. Hughie Woods, the conductor, had shouted up from below the stairs...that's the lower deck to you...are there any seats up there? To receive the usual reply of 'Aye, what do you think we're all sitting on?"

Unaware of the old joke, Bev asked anxiously, "What's so funny about your dad's accident?"

"You wouldnae understand," Tom explained. "As I was saying

before I rudely interrupted myself. My dad was sitting upstairs on the bus when the driver forgot he wasnae driving a single decker, and the conductor was too thick to warn him...well everyone knows Wood's a bad conductor." He shot his enthralled listener a quick glance to see if his pun had registered. It hadn't. "And, he tried to go under a bridge. Instead, he went through it."

"Oh how gastly Tom!" Bev exclaimed horrified.

"It sure was, seeing as it was only Monday and my dad a bought a weekly ticket," Tom sighed.

"Honestly!" Bev cried in exasperation. "Sometimes, I really cannot understand you."

"Is it my accent?"

"No it's not your accent, it's your intent...to make a right Gallah out of me!"

"It was only a joke, Bev," Tom apologised, stifling his laughter at the look on the girl's face.

"Go on then," Bev stormed, trying to keep the gaiety out of her voice, and suddenly realising what the wily Scot was trying to do, now that each passing minute was bringing them closer to the narrows.

"It was Granny who told me how this had affected my dad in later life," Tom went on. "We went to see him in hospital after the accident. He was quite cheery. He said he had to have a wee operation on his head. Although my mum said he should have had one years ago. Anyway, I digress. He said they were going to insert a plate in his head. He laughed, saying that if the operation was so wee, he might get away with a saucer.

"Mum cried at this, and dad told her to cheer up, it might have been worse, it could have been a tea cup. Saying how awkward that could be for him to comb his hair and put his bunnit...I mean, cap on.

"Anyway that's how it all started. The operation to insert the steel plate was a success, and all went well for a time, until he missed coming home at nights. At first this would be once every three or four weeks. Then, as time went by, it became once a week, then twice, until we hardly saw him at all. Mum was demented, she was sure he was keeping another woman. Especially since his wages were fourpence a week short."

Tom waited for the expected protest. When none was

forthcoming, he went on, thinking poor lassie she's taking in every word. Well, as long as it's keeping her mind off what's to come.

"It took the best part of a year to realise what was happening."

"Was your dad seeing someone else, Tom?"

"No, Bev. The police picked him up four nights in a row heading towards Inverness. This was not too serious. It would have been had it been Edinburgh, then we would have been worried. However, Inverness was the clue."

"How come Tom? What was the attraction in Inverness for Pete's sake? And, where in the world is Inverness?" Bev's voice rose in exasperation.

"Not in the world, Bev, in Scotland, Inverness is in the north of Scotland, that's what solved the mystery. It was the steel plate in his head that was doing it. It kept pulling him towards the magnetic pole."

"And you're driving me up it, Tom Bell, you stupid little Scot," Bev cringed, holding her face in her hands. "What a lot of bull shit! I suppose you'll be telling me next he died from a bolt of lightning?"

"Dinnae be so daft," Tom mocked. "He got a conductor with the operation…Hughie Woods. He used to go with him to Inverness as well, 'till his wife found out."

"I can not take any more of this." Bev buried her face in her hands unable to control herself. "Serves me right for asking about your past. But seriously, Tom, where is your dad now? And please do not say half way to Inverness, or you will need a steel plate as well."

"He's dead," Tom said sadly. "The steel plate killed him in the end. Or so my Granny would have me believe. She said he never should have gone diving off Dunoon pier. Straight doon he went, head first. By the time, they got the lifeboat out to him, the ferry had moored itself to his ankles. Died of water on the brain, so they say."

Tom's voice broke, unable to remain serious as he imagined the scene he had just conjured up, and the peals of laughter from the girl. "Well." Tom stood up and stretched himself. "I suppose it was either that or rusting away with all those iron tablets he had to take."

Bev came softly towards him. Reaching up, she cupped his face in her hands and gave him a long lingering kiss before drawing slowly away. "Thank you Tom Bell, you're a good fella, even though your humour is a bit off." Then, she was gone.

Tom stood looking after her, the feel of her kiss still on his lips. The warmth of her body so close to his. Had he imagined it? Or was she trying to tell him something? Or, merely grateful that his humour had taken her in to his own world and, for a few brief moments, away from the harsh reality of the present?

He tried to make himself believe that there had been more to the kiss than that. Though the little grey cells deep within his thick Scot's skull told him differently, as he knew that had Dane still been alive she would not have given him a second glance. Or had she done so, most likely it would have been to scorn him for just the very thing she had just thanked him for.

Yet, hope springs eternal or so they say, therefore still relishing the kiss he refused to think otherwise.

Velor signalled to the company for silence. Gently pulling back the branch of a tree, he strained through the darkness to the lake below.

At first there was nothing to be seen until a dark shape by the shoreline caught his eye. The moon slipping out from behind a cloud did the rest, silhouetting the silent waiting men crouched behind every boulder and tree stump along the route the little craft had to take on its way through the narrows. And, should it succeed on reaching this far, there was still the long line of rowing boats strung together from shore to shore to break through.

"They're there all right," Velor whispered, not turning round. "Waiting for old Papa to enter the narrows."

"The old man will make it." Jimaneaux was full of confidence for the old sea dog.

"Did I say otherwise, Lieutenant?" Velor's voice was stiff, betraying the tension he felt now that the crucial part of his plan was near. He turned to face the tiny company. "We must be quick as well as silent. The Lieutenant and I will lead the way. You two bring up the rear." Velor motioned to the driver and a Private.

He had to do it. He had no other choice. At least, this way, the wounded by remaining on board stood a chance of getting through to the end of the lake, which is why he had to leave the newly promoted machine gunner and one unwounded soldier acting as gunner's mate on board with the old man and the girl.

This much he would say for the old man, he was stubborn. He recalled the look on the weather-beaten face when he had suggested to him it might be better to weigh anchor on approaching the narrows and let the Regulars come on board. He could then explain to them how his boat had been commandeered by Rebels who had forced him to take them this far down the lake. This way there was a chance for him to save his boat as well as himself and little Eva.

"And, if I do?" Miguel had asked contemptuously, "What will happen to your wounded, Captain?" Velor had looked away then, unable to look the old man in the eyes. "Little Eva will be quite safe. If we are to die, then better both together, eh?" The craggy face had broken into a grin. "Would you spoil an old man's fun, Captain?"

His thoughts over, Velor motioned to Tom and Bev. "Come this way, and be careful where you tread. You, Mister Escoces, help the lady, she is wounded."

Tom bunched his fists at the obvious insult to his masculinity, aware that the girl had heard.

They followed the two soldiers through the woods, their intermittent stumbling in the darkness rewarded by low curses from the stalwart Captain, stopping only when they had reached a road leading down to the village where a long line of unguarded trucks stood nose to tail. Here, Velor held up a hand. "We must be doubly careful," he said in English for the benefit of the two civilians, and commanding of his men in their own tongue, "You, my driver, have the task of slitting the tyres of all the vehicles except the one we intend to use. Ensure the one you pick has either a push button start, or there are keys left in the ignition. Take your companion with you. There must be no slip-ups. You understand?"

Velor was pinning his hopes on a chance remark some time ago by Sergeant Rodrigo whom he remembered saying had a cousin in Port Lecera, that this was where the zealous soldier might have taken the Inglesa. If not, there was nothing left to do but try and get these two foreigners out of the country from there.

As his two men slipped into the darkness, Velor spoke to the man and woman. "You must remain here. When you hear the sound of the truck, run for your lives. You are capable of running, Senorita?" he asked concerned. Bev nodded. "Good," Velor sounded relieved. "The Lieutenant and I, however, have a little matter to attend to."

"What about the old man and the wee girl?" Tom gestured towards the lake, gripping the Captain by the arm. "Will they get through?"

"This is no time to concern yourself Senor Escoces, that is soldiers work. Now, do as I say and wait here."

Silently, both soldiers dissolved into the night, working their way to an advantage point from which they could view the narrows.

"How long?" Juan asked, settling down behind a bush.

"Half an hour…maybe less."

Juan half rose. "I think you are wrong, look…there," he gestured to beyond the village.

At first, Velor heard or saw nothing, then as if in tandem to the beating of his heart came the distant throb of an engine. Slowly, at first, rising in tempo as the tired old vessel struggled to lift itself, heaving into view, no more than fifty metres out from the shore.

Suddenly, the entire shoreline erupted in a crescendo of gunfire, raking the tiny craft from stem to stern.

"God what have I done!" Velor gasped at the intensity of the gunfire.

"Perhaps, we should help at little," Juan suggested, rising and examining his weapon.

Now, the sound of their own machine gun on board added itself to the uproar. The deck ablaze, their makeshift barricade splintered and buckled under the sheer weight of the firepower directed against it.

The boat was directly beneath the two soldiers now, the flames lighting up the wheelhouse where old Miguel lay at an angle under his steering gear, guiding his vessel with the aid of a mirror towards the boom of rowing boats.

"More steam!" he bellowed at the open door. "Come on, little Eva, keep stoking." His voice trembled at the thought of the young girl heaving the logs in that oven of a place directly beneath his feet. "Dear God," he prayed, "let her at least be spared from my folly."

As old Miguel prayed, an even heavier burst of fire hit the already disintegrating wheelhouse, slivers of glass and wood finally finding their mark. Stung, clutching his lacerated arm the old man let the boat run wild. "I curse all you Regulars. Let your next shit be a porcupine!" he bellowed with rage at the roof.

Suddenly aware of his charge, his wound forgotten, Miguel rose to his knees, grabbing the wheel and cursing wildly at the sight of the rowing boats filled with soldiers coming towards him.

"Standby for boarders old man," he whispered to himself, as a bullet grazed his cheek, and he dived for the safety of the wheelhouse deck, though instantly encouraged by the sound of their own machine gun opening up. "Give it to them lads!" he shouted above the tumult, and steadying the wheel with his one good hand.

Miguel rose and took another quick look, his voice booming with delight at the sight of the rapidly emptying rowing boats bobbing about in the frothy white swell of their wake. "So far, so good. Well done my men," he chortled in reference to his makeshift crew. "Now, all we need is a battle flag for this old tub."

It was then he saw the rock overhang for the first time. "God in heaven! They can drop grenades down our funnel from there as we pass below them!" he hissed, flopping down to his shelter once more, a worried frown replacing his recent grin.

Putting the danger of the rock behind him for a moment, the old man concentrated on building up speed in preparation of ramming the boom of rowing boats. He blew down the tube and heard the small, frightened voice of his little grand- daughter on the other end. "Are you all right, Eva, my child?" he asked gently, in a voice appearing to lack all urgency.

"Yes Grand Papa. Are we going to sink? If so, can I come up beside you?"

"No, my little one, we are not going to sink. In a little while we shall be safely through the narrows. But, I shall need all the speed I can get out of the old girl. Can you ask your friend there beside you to give me all you've got. Eh?"

"Yes Grand Papa. Paul is stoking the fire by himself. He says pretty girls should not spoil their hands. But he is hurt Grand Papa. Can you tell him to let me help?" The tiny voice pleaded from below.

"Your friend the soldier is quite right little one. Do as he says. Your job is of equal importance. You must watch the dials for me. Ask your friend to stoke until they approach the red."

"But you told me that was dangerous Grand Papa! That is what you taught me must never happen," the small voice called back anxiously.

"Yes, little one. But not tonight. Tonight, we must get this old lady to fly. And, this she will only do when she reaches the red.

Can you do this for me?"

"Yes, this I and Paul can do for you," Eva answered, her voice a little calmer.

"Good, little one. Now, I must prepare the lady to fly."

Miguel replaced the tube, happy at having thought up something to take the little girl's mind off what was taking place around her. So, what if the dials did reach the danger level? With the old girl looking more like a fishing net than a fishing boat, what more harm could befall them?

In attempting to prevent the tiny craft from splitting the boom, the enemy fire from the shore had reached a new intensity, illuminating the entire shoreline as the vessel struggled past. Through his mirror, Miguel alternated his attention from the boom to the rock overhang, more afraid for the soldiers on board being exposed directly to the fire which would inevitably follow when nearing the rock, than for his own safety.

The severity of the crash when it came took him totally unawares, throwing him across the wheelhouse deck, his one good hand saving him from crashing into the opposite wall, as his craft pitched and tossed in the unseen swell. Then, as suddenly as it had all started, they were through the boom and heading directly towards the overhang.

"We must do something," Juan shouted in his Captain ear. "That overhang will make them sitting ducks!"

Velor knew any attempt for them to fire upon the rock would give away their own position and with it the possibility of being cut off and getting back to the waiting truck. Yet, it was inconceivable that they should do nothing, after all the old man was playing his part.

"We must get up the hillside behind them if we are to do anything constructive," Velor shot back. "Come on, let's go!"

With as much speed as they could muster the two men stumbled and cursed their way through the dark woods, drawing up a few metres above the saucer shaped overhang where its defenders poured a deadly fire into the approaching craft, leaving them little to do except lob grenades on to its unprotected deck when it passed directly beneath them.

Velor shot his Lieutenant a quick glance. "Grenades first, then as much firepower as we can muster?"

In quick response, Juan lobbed the first grenade, Velor's an instant later, the twin explosions hurtling the unsuspected machine gunners into the water below. Instantly followed by a devastating fire from both men, that caught the remaining defenders by surprise.

"The boat's had it Juan," Velor expertly injected another clip into his weapon. "There's no returning fire."

"Someone's still alive, their making smoke, Saul."

Steadily the little boat came on, black smoke from its funnel mingling with that from the blazing deck.

In between bursts Velor witnessed Regulars breaking cover, running to the shoreline in their determination to halt the stricken vessel. Suddenly, without warning, a machine gun opened up from the doomed craft, scything down the exposed men.

"That will teach the cocky bastards a lesson," Juan shouted, lobbing another grenade at the overhang.

"It's our turn next, Juan," Velor spat, "they've spotted our fire. They'll be making their way up here soon. Let's go!"

"One last volley for the old man," Juan grimaced, as the fishing boat passed out of sight beneath the overhang.

"Come on, Juan, before we are cut off!" Velor shouted anxiously, already heading back in to the woods. "There is nothing more we can do now."

Darting a furtive backward glance at the overhang, Juan glimpsed the blazing outline of the tiny craft emerging from the other side. The old man had made it, all he had to do now was to keep her from burning herself to the keel. "All he had to do!" Juan spat. The splintering of a branch inches above his head reminding him of his own situation.

Chapter 15

The big soldier threw Weasel in to the solitary chair, jerking the briefest of salutes at his commanding officer as he left the room. Sal Cortez glared at the contemptible creature on the other side of his desk, bunching the crumpled paper in his fist.

"It's a different ball game now, my friend," he seethed, thrusting his fist under the nose of the agitated man. "Do you know what this is?

Weasel gave a quick nervous shake of his head, completely off guard by this unexpected onslaught. Did this man not want his information? Or perhaps he did not want to pay for it? "I have information for you. I know where the crippled lady is, or should I say, will be shortly," he stammered, in a vain attempt at pacifying this violent man. "We have only to settle upon the amount. My information was not easily obtained, you understand."

"You listen to me, you swivelling little toad!" Sal lurched across his desk, grabbing Weasel by the lapel. "Your reward is the least of my worries. This is what worries me now! You too, when I tell you who it is from."

Sal threw himself back in his chair, leaving his quarry to contemplate, while he calmed his anger by lighting a cigarette. He inhaled deeply and blew out smoke. "That came from Colonel Segovia," he said, pointing at the crumpled piece of paper lying by the ashtray. "You have heard of Colonel Segovia, Reno Navas?"

Weasel's answer stuck in his throat. He looked dejectedly across the desk, the vision of his reward rapidly fading.

"You led me to believe you knew the English woman's whereabouts. This I told my superiors, hence the interest of the Chief of State Security in our little affair. Do I make myself clear, Weasel? Colonel Segovia is on his way here at this very moment to Port Lecera!" he shouted.

Weasel felt as though his heart would burst through his shirt, so fast was it beating. He had never seen Sal Cortez so angry before, and was now afraid of this man and what he was capable of doing to him. "I am in possession of such knowledge," he stammered, fighting to look the Captain squarely in the face…but…I," he played his last card. "I shall require some finance…"

"What!" Sal roared, rounding his desk.

Weasel leapt to his feet knocking over his chair in the process. "For expenses…you understand," he cringed, backing against the wall, his hands held high to protect himself. "There are those who will tell me nothing without the sight of a few Pesos!"

Weasel pressed himself against the wall as Sal stepped closer. "You would not have us loose the lady now for the sake of a few Pesos?" he squeaked. "Not with Colonel Segovia making his way here. Would you?"

His anger momentarily abating in the knowledge that this insect of a person was right, Sal withdrew to his own side of the desk. "I will arrange to have my Sergeant give you what you require," he said, with as much composure as he could muster.

Weasel let out a long sigh of relief and straightened his collar, his eyes on the floor to hide a glint of triumph at having successfully prised something out of this son of a bitch, only to hear Sal hiss, "But only for expenses Weasel. And, to show our mutual trust for each other, I shall have my Sergeant accompany you…for safety's sake, Weasel, or in the event of any of your so called acquaintances proving a little reluctant to assist you in your inquiries. Eh? My friend."

The stinging rain blown by a cold wind off the sea, found Weasel huddled in the shelter of the doorway. In the dark recesses behind him, the big Sergeant blew his nose for the hundredth time that evening, reminding him that he was not altogether alone in his misery. Wiping rain from his eyes, Weasel darted a quick look at the solitary ship berthed a few metres along the quay, its riding lights twinkling in the inky darkness of the night.

The Sergeant blew his nose again and retreated still further into the doorway of the derelict shop. "For your sake Weasel, I hope you've got this right, or Segovia will have Bolognaise for supper…yours," he said nasally.

Wincing at the thought, Weasel shot another quick glance across the narrow street at the dim doorway opposite where he knew Sal and Segovia also waited.

He was sure he was not mistaken. He'd watched Rodrigo go aboard this same ship these last three days, which meant only one thing, that his intention was to smuggle the Englisa out of the country by ship, and that ship lay only a few metres away from where he now stood shivering.

"It is almost midnight, Weasel," the nasal voice sang out teasingly from behind. "I think your greed has brought you nothing but trouble. Yes?"

Weasel glanced at his watch, reluctantly agreeing with the big man's deduction, his stomach in knots with the long wait and what lay in store for him should he fail.

He could have led them straight to where the Englisa was hiding, but to do so now was tantamount to admitting he had known all along as to her whereabouts.

Out in the bay, an old cargo ship rode at anchor, her anchor lights bobbing and heaving in the swell, intermittently lost from view by the solid sheets of rain hitting her broadside. Weasel shivered again, not only from the cold. What would he not give to be out of here, even out there on that old rust bucket before Segovia decided he had enough and that he, Reno Navas, had failed. As if in answer to his thoughts, the hunched figure of Sal stepped out of the doorway and beckoned him with a flick of his hand.

Chocking back his fear, Weasel nervously turned up his collar and stepped into the street to meet him.

"Colonel Segovia is not a happy man, Weasel," Sal said, his head retreating further inside the upturned collar of his greatcoat. "He asks if you are at all reliable, and if this is not some sort of trick?" The soldier looked over Weasel's shoulder screwing up his eyes against the driving rain to the old cargo ship lying out in the bay and to the lights of the town beyond.

"A trick?" Weasel stammered, his stomach lurching. "What sort of trick could I possibly pull…against such as yourself and the Chief of State Security? And to what purpose?" he pleaded.

"Colonel Segovia is not at all interested in your motives, Weasel," Sal hissed. "Like me, he is anxious to get out of this cold and shitty night." Sal stuck his face menacingly into that of the frightened man. "Perhaps since it is unlikely that the Englisa and her companions will make an appearance, you will be kind enough to explain how you came by this information, and who it was that so unpatriotically took money for that purpose."

Weasel searched around for a means of escape. It was all over, his greed had seen his downfall. Then, as if to lend credence to this thought, Segovia stepped out of the doorway. Crossing to where they stood in the centre of the street, and completely ignoring the informer, he addressed his junior officer. "I think we have wasted enough time here. Bring this man along, Lieutenant, there are one or two questions to which I require an answer. Perhaps, in more comfortable surroundings."

Beside himself with fear, Weasel broke past the Lieutenant to face the man he dreaded so much, his voice pleading. "A few minutes more, Excellency. I am certain my information is correct. I know that this is the ship in which they mean to smuggle the crippled lay aboard. I know this is true!"

Segovia drew back from the whining man as if was diseased. "If you are so convinced, perhaps you should tell it to them," he grated, pointing to the berthed ship.

Weasel's eyes left those of his tormentor to the sleeping ship coming to life, then to the cobbles at his feet, the dull throb of the ship's engines in his ears.

Ignoring the trembling man, Segovia swung on his heel, snapping out an order. "I will have the ship searched. If the lady in question is indeed aboard as our friend here so adamantly believes, then it is possible she did so earlier today, or even yesterday."

Segovia strode purposely towards the solitary ship all the while firing out orders over his shoulder at those trotting obediently behind him. "It will take some time before she has a full head of steam. She intends leaving on the tide. Find the Harbour-Master, I shall want to go on board immediately he brings the necessary papers." He halted abruptly at the foot of the gangplank and lifted his eyes to the Mexican flag flying from the masthead of the awakening ship. "I do not propose to create an international incident by going on board before I am in possession of those papers. Do I make myself clear?"

At least a half dozen heads nodded in unison, before scurrying off to carry out his bidding.

An hour later, inwardly beside himself, Segovia watched helplessly as the gap between ship and shore widened. To those around him, he still had complete control over the situation. So, carefully lighting a cheroot to reinforce the illusion, his eyes on the hull of the ship ploughing its way through the flotsam and jetsam bobbing in the oily harbour, he asked of Sal, "You have that slime in custody, Lieutenant?"

"Yes Colonel," Sal answered, profoundly relieved that the 'great man's' anger at Weasel was not also directed against him.

"Good. Now, when that moron of a Harbour Master condescends to honour us with his presence, we shall take a little trip out to your ship. Perhaps, this time we shall be more successful in finding our mutual friends."

Forty five minutes later, Colonel Roberto Segovia stood in the bow of the Harbour-Master's launch, taking a final look through his binoculars at the passing ship, his frustration by no means abated by the fact that his search had failed to find the foreigners on board.

If they were not there, then where? Had he come all this way to this God forsaken part of the country on a wild goose chase?

He had been on the point of boarding one of the launches back on the lake when word had reached him from this imbecile of a Lieutenant standing beside him that the lady had been sighted in this dump of a town. Whether the other foreigners were with her no one seemed to know. Well, if he and that mongrel they called Weasel were wrong, they'd both pay dearly for it.

Angrily, Segovia clutched the binoculars tighter and again focused on the ship, before sweeping passed a rusting tramp steamer ploughing its ponderous way into the open sea, the Panamanian flag whipping at the masthead in the strong sea breeze, and for the hundredth time cursed the thought of that lady having eluded him.

It was then he saw them, the figure of a man and a woman leaning on the rail, between them a woman seated in a deck chair. There, less than a kilometre or so away sat the root of all his troubles, and he was unable to do a thing about it.

She was smiling now, brushing back a wisp of hair blown by the wind, and gesturing now and again at the sea. Her eyes wandered in his direction as though aware he was watching her, and her smile widened.

It was no use, he was too late. Another few minutes and the ship would be in international waters. He had been duped, led into watching the wrong ship.

Instinctively, he ordered the launch after the steamer. The thought of a final chance of beating this crafty old woman at her own game and ensuring his own survival paramount in his mind.

Seizing the big Sergeant's rifle, Segovia slid back the bolt, and steadied himself against the swell as the distance between the vessels shortened.

He could see more clearly now. He lifted the rifle to his shoulder. The launch rose on a crest and he looked along the sight of his weapon. The deck was empty. They were gone and, with them, his last chance. Dejectedly, Segovia let the rifle fall.

From the steamer's port side, Tom shaded his eyes against the wind, the outline of the coast now barely visible on the horizon. Memories flashed through his mind, of a holiday he would never forget. Of people he had met. Places he had seen. Hills he had climbed, and events…some of which he would store in the recesses of his mind to recall in happier times, when they were not so poignant. Gentle good people, such as Tino, Pablo Carlo and Chico. He took a deep breath and wondered if they had all made it home. Of Anna and her child and the humble folk of Riaz. Of old Miguel and little Eva and the remainder of their 'crew'. Had they reached the end of the lake safely, while Captain Velor and his Lieutenant and the rest of the soldiers had made their escape, and with their help, he and Bev to Port Lecera?

He felt Bev's touch beside him and saw her gaze in the same direction. No doubt her own mind filled with thoughts of her friend Gillian, and her final resting place. And of Dane, the big American. He had still not told either woman about him, that could wait until later.

Sadly, Tom turned his back to the rail and the country he had looked forward to seeing all his life, knowing he would never see it again.

Tom stared out of the window at the skeletal shapes of the idle cranes standing like giant giraffes in the dismal November afternoon. His eyes wandered to the line of sheds on the riverbank, now partly obscured by the rain and the encroaching darkness, the euphoria of being home now long since gone.

He turned from the dirty rain splashed window, and stared blankly at Big Dougie bent over his drawing board, and relived again the disappointment of his own home coming.

He remembered it had rained as he sat on the tram, but by the time he had reached Cathcart Road the sun was out. On any other occasion, it would have been a rather dismal September day, but now as he looked out of the tram's rain splattered window, he derived a feeling of comfort accentuated by the conversation of two elderly women sitting in front of him.

"Aye the price o' meat noo a days. Up again. The only thing that comes doon in this country is rain."

"Yer right there, Nancy. And, if there's another war, it'll get worse."

"Ye can say that again Bella. See yon wee bloke in Germany…whits his name? Chancer o' somethin' or ither…him and his Nuremburg Rally."

"Is that no' the name o' a German bike?"

"Dinna be daft, Bella…as I was sayin'."

Still chuckling, Tom stepped off the tram and crossed over the glistening tramlines to the corner of his own street, puddles in the pavement reflecting the tall grey tenements of his childhood. Where mothers called from the upper storeys to off-springs playing in the street below that it 'was time tae come in.'

A little further on, lassies played skipping ropes in the middle of the street. He drew nearer. A peever slid over chalked squares and hit against his shoe. Without thinking he hopped into the centre square and kicked the polished stone with the outside of his foot.

"Who said you could play?" A small cheeky voice called up at him.

"Maybe he's jist a big lassie himsel'" an equally small child suggested, coming to stand by her pal.

Blushing, Tom stepped out of the chalked lines. He thrust his hand into his pocket and drew out a handful of coppers and threw them on to the pavement, where they were instantly swooped upon by a half dozen raggety bums thrust in the air as they bent to retrieve them, and cries of amazement at there being a 'scrammel' withoot even a weddin' as he walked on.

Tom followed Big Dougie's pen, recalling his reunion with his Aunt Betty, and her joy at his homecoming. She'd sat him down before a plate of mince and tatties, her joy as were her tatties short lived, as she started her tirade.

"Whit in the world possessed you tae go aff tae a country fu' o' foreigners?" she demanded angrily. "Is Troon no good enough for you these days?"

She crashed a cup of tea on to the table and stood back arms akimbo. "Whit dae ye think I felt like when yer pal Dougie came tae my door havin' been sent roon by yon Mister MacKendrick, tae ask where ye wis? Me! Yer auntie! And I didnae know ye were no' even hame!" She clipped Tom with her dishtowel and sat a dish of custard in front of him. "Hu…miliated I was." She ranted on, while he pretended to be completely engrossed in his custard. "Do ye know the trouble I went tae find oot whit boat ye were on? And if that was no' aw, I had tae keep payin' the rent on yer Granny's hoose and take a turn at the stairs! Then wid ye believe it! There was ycr pal back at thc door again, tae tell me if ye were no' back at work by the end o' the week yer job was lost."

Tom reflected on that first night he'd spent at his own fireside, and how the bent rib in the grate had reminded him of how many times in best forgotten occasions, he had longed to see it again, it having become a symbol of home and all the safety that came with it. How to be sitting there would be the ultimate in contentment, having sworn to God that if he made it home, he'd never moan again. Which was like promising Him that should the blinding headaches sustained after a Saturday night's kicking not prove terminal, he'd never drink or swear at a Celtic supporter again.

How many times in the sweltering heat of that torrid land, bitten by every conceivable pestilential species, had his thoughts flown back to Granny's house. How her wee antidotes had helped lift the spirits of Bev and wee wumman.

The house was cold and he missed Granny more than ever. The house had remained the same as before she died, as he had had not the courage to remove anything. To him, it was still Granny's house.

His eyes fell on the newspaper wrappings of his fish supper lying on the table, the grease and vinegar still seeping through the photograph of a little man with a funny Charlie Chaplin moustache who was giving an even funnier salute. If everyone was as funny as that he thought, there would be no revolutions to worry about.

But, why did he feel so miserable, having for so long dreamed of this minute? And why was he not out with Big Dougie, chatting up the lassies and having them all over him like a rash as he told them about his 'heroic' exploits in that faraway country?

His despondency annoyed him, especially since he did not know why. Then, he knew why, as he saw Bev's face in the grate. It was because she was not here to share these moments with him, that was why.

It was on the way back to America on that old rust bucket that he had finally plucked up the courage to tell the women of how Dane had met his fate, which, much to his surprise and relief after a little quizzing and rationalizing, they both appeared to accept.

As they drew nearer to their destination, Bev had become a little kinder, warmer to him, even condescending now and again to laugh at his jokes.

Two days from port, feeling time was running out, he had gently probed Bev about her plans for the future, which he now so desperately wanted to be part of, for, if he did not know it before, he did now, he was falling in love with her.

"You've never been to Scotland, Bev?" he asked, settling down on her cabin couch.

"No. It's one place I've always hoped to visit. Our next door neighbours came from there. They say it always rains. Is that true?"

"Not at all!" Tom replied indignantly in defence of his country. "Sometimes it snows!"

Bev laughed.

"It's a bonnie country Bev, all it needs is a roof on it."

She stood with her back to him combing her hair and she laughed again. His eyes roamed over her slim figure, and he had a sudden urge to sweep her into his arms and tell her that her place was with him back home in Scotland, but he knew, however much he wanted to, he would not.

What had he to offer a girl like this, even if he still had a job to go back to? After all, her folks were 'monied'. Had she not told him about her uncle having a sheep station in the outback which took three days on a horse to ride round? And, to show how unimpressed he was had joked, "Aye, I know the feeling, I bet horses that slow myself."

Bev turned. She leaned back against the washbasin. "Do you ever get a summer in Scotland, Tom?" she asked him in all seriousness.

"Of course!" he exclaimed horrified at such a misconception of his homeland. "Only last year we had two ... Tuesday and Thursday I think it was."

"Really Tom Bell!" she made a fist. "I do not know how anyone could put up with you. You'll be telling me next, you get Indian summers."

Tom scratched his head, knowing his answer would exasperate this bonnie lassie even further. "Not an Indian summer, Bev. A Red Indian summer…you know a patchi' rain every day?"

"If you do not mind, Mister Bell, is it within the realms of possibility that you might now and then condescend to do a little work?" The ostentatiously sarcastic voice of Mr MacKendrick cut into his reverie. Tom's vision of Bev in the shabby cabin of the old tramp steamer quickly faded and he hoisted himself on to his stool, conscious of the silence that had descended upon the room as all awaited his usual retort, and their amazement when he held his tongue; each mystified by this strange new character in their midst.

"Never mind him, Ding. He's just jealous because he never got his name in the paper, as you did. By the way," Dougie tapped his teeth with his pencil. "All right fur the night? I've got two stoaters lined up just burstin' tae hear yer exploits in darkest…whatever it was."

"If you don't mind pal, I think I'll pass on this wan."

Dougie studied his friend in disbelief. "Whit? You can pass? Then you should be playin for the Jags no' watchin them. But whit's the matter? You've never been the same since ye got back. Did ye pick up something oot there ye shouldae have?"

Suddenly, Tom felt tired of it all. Being home was not how he'd imagined it: there was no Bogey finish to this picture where they faded into the sunset and lived happily ever after. He lifted his pencil, but all he saw on the sheet of blank paper, was their final day on board when the ship docked in port, and the U.S. Customs officials had arrived with two representatives from the exiled revolutionaries.

They had sat in the lounge, or what had passed for a lounge on that floating rubbish bin. One of the exiles had bent forward and kissed the back of Miriam's hand.

"You are a heroine of our beloved country," the small man said floridly.

Miriam smiled up at him from her wheelchair, her eyes glowing. "Should my success contribute to the freedom of your country, Senor, then I am well pleased. However," Miriam gestured at Tom and Bev, "I could not have accomplished any of it without the help of my two friends…and in turn their friends, who sadly died."

The official bowed slightly to Tom and Bev and solemnly expressed his commiserations, before turning again to Miriam. "You have succeeded in securing what we most urgently require?"

Miriam nodded. "It is all here." She tapped the arm of her wheelchair.

Letting out a short excited breath, the second official quickly crossed to Miriam's side, where, fumbling in his briefcase, he took out a long thin screwdriver. Then kneeling beside the chair deftly unscrewed a nail from the underside of the armrest and slid back the arm.

"And to think I didnae have the price of a pair of socks!" Tom cried in astonishment at the plethora of shimmering stones.

"Sorry Tom," Miriam pulled a face. "But mum was the word."

"I could think of a different word," Tom said sourly, eyeing the second armrest of stones.

"They belong to my country, Senor, and will help us overthrow that tyrant who calls himself President," the first official explained to Tom, who was not really listening but was still trying to calculate how close he had been to a fortune these last few weeks. And faintly heard Bev in the background ask, "But how Mrs Plesher? We saw Segovia's men rip your chair to shreds."

"Quite right, my dear," Miriam wagged her head. "Of course that was the old chair. As you may remember, Senor Castilia supplied me with a new one." Miriam ran her hand through the stones. "You see these were waiting for me in Corona…in the garden, in a statue of Pan to be precise." She halted at a moan from Tom. "Something wrong Tom?" a worried note in her voice.

Tom rubbed his forehead. "Nothing wee wumman, nothing." Then under his breath, "And that's exactly what I've finished up with…nothing."

"So you see," Miriam continued, "I…we…have brought you all that was required of us Senor, including the information you so urgently awaited."

"All of it Mrs Plesher?" Bev asked, clearly puzzled. "You mean all the information stored in your head. But, what about the microfilm? You had to hand that over to Segovia. I was there, remember?"

Miriam scratched her nose. "Yes I did, didn't I my girl. If I had not, I am afraid it would not have gone well for any of us."

"Then you don't have all the information? Segovia has the micro film?" Tom cut in, as a sharp intake of breath escaped one of the officials.

Unperturbed, Miriam eyes travelled from both officials back to the questioner. "Yes and no, Tom."

"You mean the film you gave Segovia was a fake?" Bev asked, her voice full of admiration.

Enjoying herself now that she had the company's full attention, Miriam shook her head. "Oh no, it was real enough, Bev, Colonel Segovia is no fool. Had I presented him with a fake, as you put it, he would have discovered this in no time at all, then it would have gone badly for us all."

"That I can imagine." Tom rubbed his chin. "I got a wee sample of it myself."

Wheeling herself across the lounge, Miriam lifted Tom's jerkin from the table, and, with a pair of scissors, nimbly picked at the stitches of the torn part. "That is why Senor Castilia took the precaution of having two copies made for me before I set off."

"My good Co-Op jerkin!" Tom exploded. "You mean to say I've been in possession of inside information all this time?"

"Precisely, my dear boy."

"From when?"

"From the night we first met Bev and her party in the hotel."

"Now I remember," Bev gasped. "You asked Gillian," the girl's voice dropped at the sound of her friend's name, "to bring you back a few personal things, and a needle and thread."

"What I don't understand," Tom ran a finger along the arm of the couch, afraid to look at Miriam and the answer to his question, "Why my jerkin? I could have lost it a dozen times over?"

"Your good Co-Op jerkin that cost you so much? I very much doubt it Tom. It was the good old Scots thrift I was relying on," Miriam chuckled.

Both officials, who had been listening intently to the discourse, raised a laugh.

"Well, what if we had got separated...and we did?" Tom looked at her defensively, angry that she had not confided in him, although he already knew the answer. "And we didnae meet again...or I got killed or something? Or just plain walked out on you."

"Somehow, I do not think your hero Bogey would have done the latter." Miriam stared directly at him, challenging him to contradict her.

Tom knew she was right. His resentment faded. "Here's lookin at you babe." His face broke into a grin as he mimicked his hero. The tension broken, everyone laughed.

Dougie drew himself across the desk. "Whit's up with you Ding? If I didnae know ye better passin' up the chance o' two dolls, I'd say you've been brainwashed, if I knew it wasnae a physical impossibility." Dougie stuck his face close to his friend's. "Is it maybe ye think yersel' too good fur the likes o' us seein as ye got yer name in the paper? So that them, up in the big office, will think twice o' sackin' you. It wouldnae look good if that got in tae the papers, eh."

Dougie pulled back, drawing a hand along mid-air to read the imaginary headlines, "Johnston and Son chuck oot local hero. Unable to afford extension to the premises to accommodate local hero's heid." Dougie let his hand drop with a thud, glaring at his friend.

Tom pushed back his stool. How could he make his friend understand how he felt? "I'll just slither through the door sideways." He was angry now, a lot more than he could understand. "And make my way tae the Klugie…that's where all the big knobs hang oot. Unlike some piss artists I could mention!"

Dougie's voice reached him at the door. "Okay Humpty Dumpty. He was a big heid too you know."

Tom drew away from the window. Today's weather, unlike yesterday's rain, was cold and raw. Already winter was in the air. Unconsciously, he scratched at an insect bite o the back of his swollen hand, a reminder of where he had been during the Northern summer. Suddenly, aware of his action, he cursed at having forgotten to put on the cream the doctor had prescribed for him. "God! How I wish I'd never heard of Inca culture," he groaned.

Sliding on to his stool, he drew his work towards him. Bev's face smiled up at him from the white sheet of paper. It will not do Ding, he told himself angrily, she never really had any time for you. It was

Dane she loved. You were merely a fill-in, a stop-gap, someone to lean on until she was safely out of there. So, stop kidding yourself that she had any real feelings for you. Remember at first how she could not stand you? Well then, forget her. Besides, even if she did fancy you, what kind of life could you possibly give her? A single-end complete with black sink and coal bunker.

Tom put his pencil in the sharpener and slowly turned the handle, his thoughts still on the Aussie girl. She, on the other hand was used to showers every morning, and he did not mean the weather kind either. She also had a daddy who owned a carpet shop. Tom sighed. Better come down to earth, he was no catch, especially to someone like her.

"Mornin' soda heid." Dougie came in and slid on to his stool opposite him.

Suddenly, Tom felt better. He was no worse off that before he went traipsing across the world. After all, he still had his best china. "How about the pictures the night, Dougie?" he asked enthusiastically.

"Skint are you?" Dougie asked in mock disdain, inwardly happy at Tom coming round. Still, it would do no harm to let the wee shite squirm for a while. "I don't know if I can fit you in to my busy social diary, pleb, seen' as Moira and me are steppin' oot the gither."

Tom searched back a hundred years to the night of the Hogmanay party. "Whit! Big Moira frae dispatch!" he whistled in disbelief. "You must be hard up."

"Well we can not all be stoatin' aff tae darkest America. By the way, did ye take yer torch?" Dougie nudged his companion sitting next to him.

"Very fun Dougie. And it's darkest Africa, no' America, ye ignoramus.

Dougie shrugged his shoulders. "Please yesel', as long as you knew where it was."

"Well? What about it are we on fur the night?" Tom asked politely.

"If ye say so darling," Dougie replied seductively, above the catcalls of their fellow workers.

"Package for you, Bell." The austere voice of Mr MacKendrick cut into the ribaldry. "I sincerely hope you do not intend using Johnston and Son as your personal mail box, after all Mr Johnston junior has had to contend with since your return?" the irate manger added gruffly, handing him the small package.

Tom took the cigarette sized package, intrigued by the London post mark and slid it into his pocket, aware of a half dozen eyes on him, led by Dougie.

"Are ye no' goin' tae open it, Ding?" Dougie asked, full of curiosity. "Who is it frae?"

Tom returned to his stool. "Somebody," he replied absently, thinking of the postmark. "I'll keep it 'till dinner time."

"Maybe it's a medal frae the King," Dougie suggested, hopefully amid a few cries of agreement from the others.

"Medal? Tom grunted. "You're the only wan that meddles around here Dougie."

"Oh, please yerself."

Tom stole a furtive glance at the clock on the wall above Mr MacKendrick's desk. Twenty minutes to the horn, he thought. I'll give it another five, then head for the toilet, his curiosity having got the better of him.

Ten minutes later, Tom sat on the toilet seat gasping in astonishment at the three stones sparkling up at him from their cotton wool wrapping. Unable to believe his good fortune, he leaned back against the iron cistern, the package in one hand, Miriam's letter in the other.

Dearest Tom, it began. I hope you are in good health and this package reaches you safely. I decided to have it delivered to you and hopefully by a certain Mr MacKedrick in person. If successful you must let me know his reaction.

As you will see the contents of this little missive is in gratitude of your service rendered to me and an equally grateful country. A country sadly still in the grip of the tyrant Biezoto. However, I hope this will soon be eradicated. Also, you might be pleased to know Captain Velor and his Lieutenant are safe and giving a certain Colonel Segova quite the run around.

I have not heard from Bev, since we left the ship. I believe you spent some time with your uncle and aunt in the U.S.A. before travelling home. Bev, I understand left straight away for Sydney.

Well Tom, I shall close now. Please take care where you have these little items assessed as they are extremely valuable, as I should not like you to be swindled by your fellow Glaswegians. Now you can tell Mr MacKendrick , and if you wish Mr Johnston to keep their jobs.

God bless you Tom, I shall always think kindly of you. Keep in touch.

Miriam Plesher.

Tom felt a lump in his throat. He pulled the chain and opened the door.

By the time, he had returned to the main office Mr MacKendrick was in a near state of apoplexy. "Bell!" he fumed, "there is now a telephone call for you! It came to me through the Big office. You can take it over there in the main office. I shall put you through from my office," Mr MacKendrick stormed.

"Somethin' awfy phone..y aboot a' this Ding," One of his pals called out to him as he lifted the receiver.

Tom held a hand over his ear to shut out the guffaws that greeted the pun. "Hello! Hello, is anybody there?" he called into the mouthpiece.

From far down the receiver, a small sing song voice answered him. "Hello Tom, is that you cobber?"

Startled, Tom stared at the phone, his heart beating wildly. Was his hearing playing tricks? "Yes..." he stammered. "Is that you, Bev? Where are you?"

"Sure is sport. I'm in London, Pommie land." The voice grew stronger, louder.

Tom wasn't sure he had heard correctly, so loud was his heart beating. Surely this was in his imagination; wishful thinking. Perhaps, she only wanted to say hello, before saying cheerio, on her way home to Sydney. With his luck, Tom thought, Sydney would be the name of her boyfriend.

"Hello, Tom, are you still there?" the voice asked anxiously from the other end. "No need to hang up on me you miserable Scot, I'm paying for the call."

Tom laughed across at Dougie who mouthed in return. "Poor bugger, now I know why you were acting so daft." Dougie turned to the rest of the office. "By the look on his face lads, it must be a lassie on the other end. Yees no' think so?" A chorus of agreement acknowledged his assertions.

Tom returned to the phone. "I sure am Bev. But I thought you had left for Down Under?"

"So you don't want to see me, you tartan good-for-nothing," came the reply in mock dismay.

"Of course I do!" Tom shouted down the phone amidst an outburst of catcalls from around the office, which brought a fuming Chief Clerk to his office door, his anger drowned out by the sound of the twelve o' clock dinner horn, and Tom yelling, "get on the first train up here and I'll meet you at the station. By the way, did I tell you I love you, you Aussie Sheila?"

"Well! Does that no' beat a'!" Big Dougie shouted to all within earshot. "I suppose this means it's aw' aff between us fur the pictures the night, then Ding?"

Tom let the phone drop back in its cradle, and beamed across at his big friend. "It was only a Bogey picture, and I've seen it afore. They live happily ever after."

Tom shifted to the irascible figure of the Chief Clerk stamping impatiently in his office doorway. "Here's lookin' at you sweetheart," he called out to him, touching his forehead in mock salute.

And, with a last knowing grin at Big Dougie, Tom swung on his heel for the door.

The End

Printed in Great Britain
by Amazon

18755886R00154